For
Arthur & Greta

GROUND ZERO

You're in it like the proverbial needle in a haystack & in other indiscernable ways given our stimulating relationship over the past 20+ years

Love!

11/01

GROUND ZERO

by
Paul Lysymy

FEATURING: **GUIDE FOR THE APOPLEXED**

Pittsburgh, PA

ISBN 1-1-56315-261-4

Paperback Fiction
© Copyright 2000 Paul Lysymy
All rights reserved
First Printing—2000
Library of Congress #99-65325

Request for information should be addressed to:

SterlingHouse Publisher, Inc.
The Sterling Building
440 Friday Road
Pittsburgh, PA 15209
www.sterlinghousepublisher.com

Cover design: Michelle Lenkner - SterlingHouse Publisher
Typesetting: McBeth Typesetting & Page Design

All rights reserved. No part of this publication may be reproduced, stored in a retrieval system, or transmitted in any form or by any means—electronic, mechanical, photocopy, recording or any other, except for brief quotations in printed reviews—without prior permission of the publisher.

This is a work of fiction. Names, characters, incidents, and places, are the product of the author's imagination or are used fictitiously. Any resemblance to actual events or persons, living or dead is entirely coincidental.

Printed in the United States

For Bamiyan, Tania and Petra, on fording the Cyber: *veni, vidi video, vici*

and

Hanna, the non-philosopher's non-philosopher &
persona mucho grata

ACKNOWLEDGEMENTS

A special vote of thanks goes to James Gobets, Sandra McGilloway, J.A.S. (in memoriam), René Samson, Michael Prescod, Raini Brown, K. Srinivasan, Eva Gerlach, Edgar Cairo, Viktor van Bijlert, Erik Hoogcarspel, Tonny Kurpershoek-Scherft, Prof Masao Abe, Jos & Franc Knipscheer, Scot Rollins, Robert Warmenhoven, Duurt Alkema, Klaartje de Vrueh, Johan Schaap, Guido van Schelt, Kevin Salt, and especially Amir Vosteen (for invaluable software services rendered), as well as Cindy and her SterlingHouse staff, without whose indispensable involvement this book would certainly not have looked anything like it does, either in form or content. Each in their own way, singly or at times jointly, they and many others - ungraciously but not ungratefully unacknowledged here - had a hand in helping to scrub down and dress up the original maverick manuscript.

"How lucky you are these days! When I was young there wasn't a good master to be found. At least I couldn't uncover one. But the truth is I was rather simple when young, and made one blunder after another. And the fruitless efforts! I don't suppose I'll ever forget those days, if only because they were so painful. That's why I come out here every day. I want to teach you how to avoid the blunders I made. How lucky you are these days!

"I'm going to tell you about some of my mistakes, and I know you're clever enough – everyone of you – to learn from what I say. If by chance one of you should be led astray by my example, the sin will be unpardonable. That must be avoided at all costs. Indeed it was only after great hesitation that I decided to tell you of my experiences. Remember then, you can learn from me without imitating."

- *Bankei (1622-1693), translated by Lucien Stryk and Takashi Ikemoto*

"The most impressive fact in man's spiritual, intellectual, and poetic experience has always been, for me, the universal prevalence of those astonishing moments of insight which Richard Bucke called 'cosmic consciousness'. There is no really satisfactory name for this type of experience. To call it mystical is to confuse it with visions of another world, or of gods and angels. To call it spiritual or metaphysical is to suggest that it is not also extremely concrete and physical, while the term 'cosmic consciousness' itself has the unpoetic flavor of occultist jargon. But from all historical times and cultures we have reports of this same unmistakable sensation emerging, as a rule, quite suddenly and unexpectedly and from no clearly understood cause."

- *Alan Watts*

EPILOGUE

HAMBURGER ZEITUNG

'Ich binn ein Hamburger'
says charismatic WWW leader with relish
Herman Gnuticks arrives safely
after preempted bus hijacking

(by Gunther Braunzweiger)

Hamburg, July 20, 2000 – After a memorable tour of the Netherlands, and expulsion by the Dutch government as non persona grata, so to speak, it is now our turn to welcome the entire WWW gang of happy-go-lucky 'morphoclast' life-artists to our humble port city. Apparently not fazed in the least by the attempted hijacking just inside the German border around midnight last night, Herman Gnuticks in an exclusive interview with this reporter stated, "We take any contingency in our stride. It's the secret to our success."

Asked whether he bore a grudge against the neo-Nazi skinheads, who plotted against him and his associates, HG replied, "There is a place in the scheme of things not only for rats and cockroaches, but neo-Nazis, too. In fact I prefer them to some journalists I know."

* * * * *

That night major and minor polemicists pro and con – in Frankfurt, Bonn, Berlin, but equally in capitals across Euroland and even farther afield – pored over *Guide for the Apoplexed*, commissioned as they were to submit peppery reviews to electronic and print media forthwith, following all the ruckus *im Niederlanden*.

That same night – not quite by coincidence – hundreds of miles to the south, whitish smoke-rings wheeled skyward from a Vatican City chimney, as cratefuls of HG's heretical works – anonymously delivered to the pontiff's doorstep – were unceremoniously incinerated back into chastened ashes from whence, according to gospel, they'd come. Stunned pilgrims ambling across Saint Peter's Square were agog at the miraculous phenomenon, speaking of epiphanies. The more sober brethren among them speculated on abrupt papal succession. A handful of zealots, however, were convinced Armageddon was at hand. WWW *agents provocateurs,* never far away, airily dismissed the nullity of the apparently weird affair.

And that very night, too, hundreds of miles to the east, in classical Vienna – next stop on WWW's crowded itinerary – Miss Anna Liszt, distant kin of the genius composer, seated in her tranquil, ornamental high-ceilinged study, flicked on the thin halogen beam of her Finnish designer floor lamp that she was still paying off in 24 uneasy installments. Clued in by an anonymous tipster, the assiduous ethnomusicologist set out to crack the numerological code to the notational transposition of *Guide for the Apoplexed* – supposedly – into its concerto counterpart, *Opus Zero*. But her unerring intuition told her that there was also something deep Indo-European about the work and that she should not rule out in advance certain subcultural raga-'n'-roll motifs.

Though the going would no doubt be tough, the delicate but dapper lady sleuth trained the bundle of bright rays onto the pages of the twin booklets before her, intent to stay the course; twin booklets because long ago she'd not only subscribed to Nabokov's injunction to always read pencil-in-hand, libri and libretti alike, but also to his commercially cunning yet no less helpful suggestion "to eliminate the bother of back-and-forth leafings [by] purchasing two copies of the same work which can then be placed in adjacent positions on a comfortable table."

And, as she was wont to do when slightly tense and anxious – especially so in the face of the daunting task ahead – she intoned half audibly:

* * * * *

    Entranced, Ms. Liszt rose slowly, polyphony & polysemy, assonance & dissonance uppermost on her mind, and wandered over to her pink baby grand. Tentatively, she planted a duplet on the ivories, shook her head in disapproval; tried a second, a third, only incrementally more satisfied.
    Just as she was about to jot down a semi-inspired chord on a blank sheet of music paper, a piercing scream shattered her concentration. She dropped her pencil and made a beeline for the kitchen, the source of the disaster, she knew.
    There she found her teenage daughter over by the sink running cold tap water on the fingers of her left hand. A trail of rich-red droplets led from the vegetable still life on the counter to the sink.
    "Liebchen, what happened? You alright?"
    "Oh Mutti! I'm afraid to look. I think I cut off my fingertip!"
    "Oh no! Here, let me see!"

"I was making us some gazpacho. It's so hot out. But the knife slipped while I was dicing onions. Gott o Gott I feel faint…"

In the taxi on their way over to the emergency ward of the nearest hospital, Ms. Liszt, tightly clutching her distraught daughter (kitchen-towel-wrapped finger already blood-soaked), shuddered at an eerie premonition to do with the work she'd just embarked upon. Could there be a link? Was the accident no mere coincidence? She had been warned in advance by reliable sources but had lightly dismissed it as silly superstition.

But now she began to have second thoughts. Perhaps abandon the project altogether?

※ ※ ※

ONE

It was front-page news that first week in July of the year 2000:

COURANDSTAD NEXUS

Bomb threat delays flight
WWW's Herman Gnuticks 'delighted to be back in Holland'

(by F.Fokko Okkels)

Amsterdam/Schiphol, July 6, 2000 - Finally, after several previous postponements, Herman Gnuticks and his entire gang of practical jokers landed at Schiphol international airport last evening. The plane, which was late due to a bomb threat made by a dastardly detractor of the Worldwide Welcome Wagon (WWW) on departure from San Francisco, landed here safely at approximately 18:45 hours – ETA plus 5.

There was overwhelming attendance from the side of the Dutch media during an impromptu press conference hurriedly convened at the Hague's historic downtown Hotel de Botel, recently downgraded from a 3 to a 1-star establishment after having rated failing marks from the Province of South Holland Health Inspector earlier in the year. Management promised improvement and expressed its gratitude to "a sporting Heer Herman" for honoring the reservations made for him and his retinue, "despite a few cosmetic flaws."

"Rats and cockroaches have their place in the scheme of things," the Wiseguy from the West was quoted as having said. "I even prefer them to some people I know," he'd added facetiously – strictly off the record, of course.

Strict security

WWW's highly capable in-house bomb disposal expert and Vietnam vet Colonel Jerry Can, keeping a low profile, strolled nonchalantly among the crowd scrutinizing any and all suspicious types, of whom, it must be said in all honesty, there were few – fewer at any rate than might've been expected given the group's magnetic attraction on the peripheral in society. But with the crank call to the carrier on which they'd flown in freshly in mind, the explosives expert was taking no chances.

Further assistance was provided by right-wing fascism & left-wing ecofascism anti-terrorist squad leader Sockeye Savage – making Arnold S. look quite the wimp – and his band of Chippendale musclemen who kept the somewhat unruly crowd of well-wishers at bay, as dozens of uproarious buffs had come to greet the charismatic leader of the Worldwide Welcome Wagon, in Holland on a brief stopover visit to promote the Dutch translation *(Krijg geen beroerte)* of his latest book titled *Guide for the Apoplexed* – about which more later in our Weekend Supplement exclusive book review!

Paul Lysymy

Jazz

Asked whether it was pure coincidence that the sojourn to the Netherlands, his third in a dozen years, happened to take place precisely during Holland's renowned North Sea Jazz Festival, Jim Dash, WWW's colorful PR chief & official spokesman said, "God does not play dice." Asked further whether that was a opaque reference to the group's leader, who by the way is known to be a fanatical lover of jazz, Jim Dash sped off waving his hands aloft, signaling the end of the news briefing. He was followed single file by a small army of merrymakers, among whom Mental & Environmental Bloc Parents President R. Cane and his wife Sugar; Otis Nyx, otherwise known as Onyx, "the semi-precious jewel in the lotus", presently heading WWW's exclusive Gin-Zen Society, with its unique Rent-A-Rishi scheme; Siddhartha "Sid-the-Kid" Dixit, commanding the Buddha Boys Brigade ("We don't take no xit from nobody"); Lou & Lulu Lupus, famous husband and wife team - running their Lone Wolf Pack, seeking out the solitary seekers in search of salvation; newcomer Kay Dance, former Miss Margarine USA ebony beauty queen, and Quintuple A's (Afro American Arts Anonymous Association's) Prime Mover!; punk rock band members Harpy & the Herpes; and last but not least the team's R&R chief Hugh U. Ewe, who, whenever roll is called, can never resist answering "Present, present, present."

And indeed all were present, in the flesh, so to speak – barring *agents provocateurs* of the Special Sciolism Task Force comprising Theo Dicey, Ann Thrax, Jean Jacques Plateau, Sue Veneer, Artie Ficer and Chick Aynyry off on clandestine missions across Euroland - as lights glared, shutters snapped, camcorders hummed to capture the arrival in town of this unique caravan of comedians, of whom more in later dispatches.   [con't p. 6].

Turning to page 6 of the paper, under BACKGROUND INFORMATION, it said:

[con't from p.1] And no wonder there was such excitement in the air. 'Prof. Gnuticks' had caused quite a stir while on tour throughout the New World to publicize his cause célèbre (and to promote his latest book). In a head-on confrontation with Utah Church Fathers, for example, he had coolly denied charges of messianic tendencies, blasphemy, not to mention illicit sex, gambling practices, tax evasion and worse. Said he by way of prevarication, "God also plays dice", adding in an irreverent reference to the white-mopped genius of science, "The second happiest thought of my life!"

Not insignificantly, he seized that same photo opportunity to appear with his svelte aerobics diva, the aforementioned voluptuary Kay Dance – known lovingly to her fans as KD – to give a sneak preview of her hottest new skills on offer for the '00/'01 season developed especially to sate the appetites of a famished U.S. public keen not to miss out on the latest craze of her making, namely the "Let Enlightenment Strike" lifestyle, the soon-to-be fad everywhere. Such tantalizing delicacies as Mirthful Earth-girding, Cosmic Bungee-plunging, Dualing-to-the-Death, and Terminal Hair-splitting were demonstrated with Verve, Elan, Panache & Brio (KD's four pretty Secondary Movers).

The advanced course on offer in a series of special workshops for the uninitiated, and treating of Herman Gnuticks' mysterious neologist miracle-find known as Nonism – a no-stick, non-fixion mental concept, referred to glibly in a recyclable folder as "a parting thought", "the vanishing step" and even "the last word in life" – also accounted for a powerful undertow exerting such a pull on a growing stream of devout followers groping to end the Kali Yuga now.

The end of history?

All of these colorful characters were present in the crowded lobby of derelict Hotel de Botel, itself amply symbolizing the decrepit structures of an old and creaking earth in desperate need of rejuvenation – an explicit plank in the group's public platform.

Answering a loaded question put earlier by a senior political analyst present at the briefing, as to the possibly preemptive content of Francis Fukuyama's (read: F. Hegel's) bombshell notion that "history is over", an inscrutable Herman Gnuticks parried, and I quote: "What is history but the residue of personality; and what is personality but the residue of experience that comes up and bites you in the butt when you least expect it? Don't forget that we ourselves are the creatures who EMIT TIME!" He spoke the latter two words as if capitalized, and thus highly significant in some – as yet – undefined way. Adding pedantically, "This apart from more principled objections: History, the passage of spatio-temporal events, implies as it must, the non-spatio-temporal. Now there you have the true End of History!" Asked whether that was a fair statement, HG retorted: "Don't forget that God also plays dirty. His dice sometimes are loaded."

Here too, readers may be interested to learn that HG, renaissance man in a postmodern world, keeps abreast of the latest developments in what he likes to refer to as "Tomic Theory" - a snide reference to the revolutionary discoveries of particle physics which formally ended the Greek metaphysical notion of atomism that held sway for so long - the notion that fundamental particles cannot be "cut" any further (a-tom).

Or as he put it in a tantalizing excerpt from another one of his monographs *The Scheisenberg Uncertainty Principle*: "The turning point, as most will be aware, was the infamous "two-slut experiment." The experiment which clearly demonstrated the dual nature of nature, and thus of man. As repeated trials have shown under laboratory conditions, man will definitely behave differently when homing in on one, or two sluts." When someone corrected him by pointing out that it was the 'two-slit' experiment, HG was quick to reply, "Slit, slut, what's the difference?"

And as if that were not enough, he trotted out his own "Big Twang" theory.

It was all these striking facts together which had led to further insights into the true nature of light (and enlightenment!) which led trailblazing theorist HG to often blurb: "Eat more light!," which indeed he did on this occasion, and on which he promised to shed more light during his stay in the Netherlands. Talk about your barable being of lightness, eh folks?

Interviews

The brief two-week stay in the Netherlands by WWW notables will be punctuated not only by several radio and television interviews but also by open forum discussions in Amsterdam - an unprecedented "university roast" hosted by Holland's renowned Dr Anja de Boer, shapely occupant of the Heidegger Chair. Immediately following, WWW's 1st Fourth World Conference will be convened during which a 10-point program is expected to be unfolded enlisting the efforts of the masses in tackling the hard issues challenging the globe's immediate survival. Posters already pasted up all over town announcing the event and mobilizing the public, read: "The Earth, Our Treasure, Milieu-naires Everyone."

In this connection, Emeritus Professor of Ecosophy, that burly, bearded Swede, Rex

Kars, who in a related capacity also heads the Motown anti-automobile lobby, will have significant results to report on sustainable alternative sources of energy which should be of special interest to us here in flat, windy and watery Holland.

It is hoped that WWW's comprehensive 6-continent initiative will signal the decisive turning point in the protracted struggle, which has seen such a drastic decline in living standards in the southern hemisphere and the attendant deterioration of our biosphere.

Asked as to his NGO's chances of success, the reply was, predictably almost, "God only knows. But he's out to lunch just now."

To which yours truly can only sign off by remarking, We're in for a mighty hot summer.

* * * * *

Numerous other in-depth articles appeared on the WWW visit, and in addition there was a spate of spin-off standard news agency reports distributed by INA - Internetherlands News Agency - reprinted by syndicated provincial dailies, clippings of which Jim Dash's deadpan polyglot assistant, "foot-in-mouth fumbler" D. Bacle dutifully kept on file, culled from the stacks of papers and magazines provided by Hotel de Botel's management in a gesture to woo back lost clientele. The news was even picked up by some of the international wire services and dispatched across the globe - to the U.S. in particular, where the WWW gang enjoys quite a loyal following.

* * * * *

Almost exactly two years earlier to the day, in the summer of 1998, on a previous whirlwind transit visit, the WWW gang had *not* made the Dutch headlines, and F.Fokko Okkels had had a slightly less pleasant encounter with the motley gang whose arrival he alone had covered back then. What a difference those couple of years had made. At that time there had been no media madness surrounding the stopover scheduled to publicize Herman Gnuticks' book (R)aping Einstein, a series of essays, including the popular What Buddha Knew, on the state of the modern sciences – the social as well as the physical – and the need to augment their innate empirical bias by the non-empirical; relativity by the non-relative; temporality by the non-temporal; locality by the non-local, et cetera. There had been no INA coverage, no radio or TV interviews, no media circus whatever. Only an overeager Okkels had been baited by a genuine Dutch red herring, dangled before his oversensitive ichthyophilic nose...

GROUND ZERO

✸ ✸ ✸ ✸ ✸

Divulged Holland's number one scandal sheet at the time:

COURANDSTAD NEXUS

'Dutch connection' reveals true identity
Nonism Guru Gnuticks is former saltwater taffy vendor

(by F.Fokko Okkels)

The Hague, July 8, 1998 - In an exclusive scoop, Flavor & Fragrance Fellow Dr. Harm Bontekoe of Dordrecht has divulged the true identity of WWW's Herman Gnuticks (HG), presently honoring our tiny nation with a visit. It seems that after a "fierce falling out" between the two men, Dr. Bontekoe – presently hard at work in his multinational's pioneering labs, in close collaboration with an auxiliary recombinant DNA team doing research on a revolutionary psychochemical inducer to steer the evolution and hopefully hasten the upliftment of mankind by 'growing a 7th sense, perhaps even an 8th' – decided to approach the *Courandstad Nexus* with the shocking revelation that Guru Gnuticks is none other than former saltwater taffy peddler and peripatetic protagonist beachcombing bum Len Jordan, of *Birth In Berkeley* fame – Bontekoe's hugely unsuccessful sortie into novel-land. "It's the same traducer gadfly of old," your reporter was told.

Objection

It seems that the two men met many years ago when Dr. Bontekoe, one of Holland's few potential Nobel laureates, studied organic chemistry at the eponymous campus in California so notorious during the days of sex, drugs and rock 'n roll, flower power and revolution in the streets, back in the Sixties. (It was there, we are told, while ambling along Telegraph Avenue that his 7th sense thesis first occurred to him: "Just think what pleasure it will provide mankind, not to mention the commercial implications which are truly staggering! A whole new field of consumer products to explore and exploit!").

Dr. Bontekoe, who wrote the above-mentioned book chronicling his recollections of those topsy-turvy days, which saw his academic studies dramatically, aborted, apparently did so without HG's explicit permission to feature him as his protagonist.

"He bluntly objected to my publishing effort, calling it 'a heinous invasion of privacy.' But I know better. It does not suit our self-professed savior to be unmasked as a 'simple candy merchant'," rebuffed an undaunted Bontekoe.

Obviously bothered, the good doctor added, "Any idea how he introduces himself these days? Well? I'll tell you then. 'Herman Gnuticks is the name, enlightenment the game.' Now I ask you? Is that beneath contempt or what?"

Jim Dash, WWW's high-profile public relations officer, was inexplicably unavailable for comment this afternoon. "Out on an errand," his fawn-faced footboy D. Bacle informed us. And Sockeye's guttural grunts in response to my probing queries were too "savage" to warrant pressing. Nor was an answer forthcoming to the question as to how such a major breach in security could've taken place without his knowledge. Again, the dictum "A flaw unto himself" is quite apt here, too, as Dr. Bontekoe pointed out, saying somewhat incoherently, "Give him enough rope and he'll string anyone along, the bastard. But no more. I've had it up to here. I'm at the end of my rope."

Meanwhile, out in the parking lot, even the group's UV-tanned touring coach driver and trouble-shooter par excellence, Jill Oppy - literally a Jill-of-all-trades - when asked as to her opinion regarding the painful Bontekoe disclosures, said, "Sorry, but I'm in a terrific rush. Engine trouble. Know where I can score a Phuel Philter for my Incu-Bus, P.D.Q.?"

And, indeed, off she sped, head over heels, wiping her flushed face with a dirty grease rag she pulled from the back pocket of her overalls. A pretty sight indeed.

Interview

Presumably, this thorny issue surrounding WWW's foreman will be resolved soon in an exclusive interview with HG himself. It would seem petty to say the least should the charismatic leader renege on his solemn promise to provide an outline at least of his far-reaching schemes. Restatement here may serve to remind the visiting celebrity that our tiny Nordic nation awaits with bated breath not only the piquant details of his clandestine past but also the putative answers to more substantive issues pertaining to the alleged aim of his present mission.

* * * * *

By Dutch standards, the weather had been rather balmy and sweat stains were already starting to limn tell-tale rorschachs in the armpits of HG's Miles Davis T-shirt. How could anyone have doubted the ulterior motive for his visit? Over 100 top American and European jazz musicians in town, with choice concerts for the picking three nights on end the second weekend in July. Any astute observer might've extrapolated HG's movements from New York, New Orleans, St Louis, Chicago, Newport Beach, to Big Sur, to here. But none had.

None but the intrepid F.Fokko Okkels, that is. This little runt of a reporter, however – his alopecic pate bobbing up and down among the thick crowds as he tried to keep tread with the striding gait of the 6-foot "Professor of La-di-da Deconstruction" – was certainly determined to spoil the better part of HG's morning. But a promise was a promise, and besides, the interview was a key element in the media campaign so meticulously planned by Jim Dash.

So HG dutifully let himself be hounded by Okkels in and out of Compact Disc shops where he had gone in search of young Dutch "transcreations". Highly recommended by cognoscenti, HG was determined not to leave the country without a stack of local CDs to augment his not inconsiderable collection, though Fokko kept trying to divert his attention to lighter, more popular fare, his favorite being treacly accordion music featuring strident snare drums.

They crossed a tree-lined square, the American Embassy to their left, glimpsed the Dutch Parliament on their right, located on De Hofvijver; while a bazaar – second-hand books plus antiques - attracted a multitude of bargain hunters.

HG thought to look for some Dutch classics, stopped to finger a pair of archaic-looking ice skates, admired a polished grandfather clock, but in the end bought nothing. A nearby street organ piped a cheerful but nasal tune, the smell of bees wax mixed with deep-fried fish saturated the air - common elements in the overall assault on the senses of any foreign tourist to Holland. The chestnut-lined square, Korte Voorhout, was pleasantly crowded, the shade cast by impenetrable foliage soothing to the eyes, though HG, who hastened to a nearby cafe for the interview, wore Polaroids.

Okkels, in hot pursuit, had on his thick, red horn-rimmed glasses that made him look pathetically absurd rather than cool as intended. His beige pants reached only to his ankles – revealing his white socks – an image the Dutch appropriately refer to as "hoog water in de polder", or high water in the polder – that typical hick fashion designed to keep one's trouser legs dry in case of flooding in low-lying farming areas. The man also cultivated a nasty habit of rearranging his private parts every few minutes, as though his underwear pinched.

HG had noticed it without saying anything, as also the way the reporter had of shamelessly picking his nose in public - all in all a most distasteful countenance, unfortunately assigned to him as company that day.

An overeager Okkels nearly tore HG's thin linen jacket as he abruptly dragged him by a rumpled sleeve into Houtstraat, a narrow one-way lane. Moving at a trot past another of the many antique shops stuffed to the ceiling with dusty flotsam where HG might well have liked to tarry, Okkels dove into an open doorway from where alien, tinny-sounding chansons emanated.

They stepped across a willless junkie sleeping on the front steps of the "Honolulu" - a coffee shop-cum-bar renowned for its loud "Hawaiiisms" splashed across the walls and ceiling, put there by its avant-garde owner/artist, a jovial 300-pound Polynesian with a diminutive Italian wife whom Okkels had featured in the *Courandstad Nexus* on the occasion of their festive opening some years back.

Once inside, they found a seat away from the silless picture window, feeling like gillless fish in oxygen-starved environs. The hand-written menu card on the table around which they huddled listed a host of goodies in four languages. Carcinogenic clouds of cigarette smoke stimulated one's craving for espresso, cappuccino, rich desserts. Fokko offered none of these – anxious as he was – heaving a sigh at the impending moment of encounter with him they were already referring to in some quarters as "The Platinum One."

"We should be safe here for a while," Okkels reassured himself more than his guest.

To HG, he seemed excessively animated, this unappetizing little reporter who insisted on getting his story.

Out came a hand-held microcassette recorder, a voice-operated Philips, which he placed in the middle of the marble tabletop. He swung the camera strap over his head and placed his battered Nikon next to the tape recorder.

"Watch these for me a sec? Weak bladder. Be right back," Okkels winked at HG, excusing himself. As he rose, he fidgeted some more with his family jewels, turned and headed for the john, trailing a lethal, sour B.O.

When he returned, the third degree began in earnest.

* * * * *

The tabloid's headline screamed:

COURANDSTAD NEXUS

Herm charges: 'Harm did me a lot of harm'
DR. BONTEKOE ACCUSED OF PLAGIARISM, AND MURDER!!!

(by F.Fokko Okkels)

The Hague, July 10, 1998 - In an exclusive interview this morning, Herman Gnuticks, philanthropist tycoon and leader of the Worldwide Welcome Wagon (WWW) accused his one-time companion and close buddy – our very own Dr. Harm Bontekoe – of plagiarism, character assassination and libel. In a press release embargoed till later this evening, WWW's Chief Scribe alleges that it is he who is featured as antagonist in Dr. Bontekoe's – and I quote – "work of friction, or should I say work o' fart." Continues he: "I'm cast in a highly dubious role. Is it ethical, I ask you, to have your personage hijacked without permission? I can prove that Harm based his scandalous novel on my life. And in doing so he behaved quite the unscrupulous double agent for the sole purpose of cannibalizing me and my seminal conceptions developed over some 20 years and intended to usher in a new era. I've got incontrovertible proof."

If this were all, it would be bad enough. But there's more. HG, in addition to plagiarism, accuses Dr. Bontekoe outright of embezzlement, adultery and premeditated murder no less! Charges, moreover, strenuously denied by Holland's foremost Flavor & Fragrance Fellow.

"He'll answer in court," was all that the Debonair Doctor of Osmics was willing to say when contacted on telephone. "I'll sue him for every penny he's worth. And frankly, that's a pile," Dr. Bontekoe assured us.

But Herman Gnuticks was unrepentant. "Harm did me and others a lot of harm. He killed my best friend, cuckolded me, and cost me a couple of grand minimum," the Board President of Crypto-Illiterate Productions (CIP) maintained – CIP, for those who don't know, is the nonprofit foundation which oversees WWW and its many subsidiaries that grosses millions of dollars annually, its funds distributed across myriad small-scale projects, aiming to benefit the world's poor and underprivileged.

[Note: De Courandstad Nexus, as always, will keep its readers abreast of latest developments, as and when these unfold over the next few days. This affair is a can of worms our country has not seen since our Prince Bernhard was defrocked in the Lockheed affair. Not only are preeminent reputations at stake here, but through its pullulating effects, this gathering storm may soak tens of thousands around the globe. We are afraid that, as is so often the case, it will be the little guy who will get burnt in the end.]

* * * * *

TWO

Okkels had done his homework; that, at least, could not be denied. He'd studiously scrutinized Bontekoe's 800-page novel as though it were scripture. Reading between the lines, something he'd become pretty adept at in his line of work, and substituting names and identities, he was able to reconstruct a pretty good picture of what had actually transpired in Berkeley a couple of decades before – or so he thought.

At the time an anonymous face in the crowd, HG (a.k.a. Len Jordan) had been caught up in an unseemly affair involving a dozen or so commune members shacking up together off campus in the late '60s, early '70s. The rowdy bunch, indulging in every form of decadence imaginable, had made life difficult beyond belief for themselves and others. At the end of misadventures galore of sheer epic proportions which occupy the bulk of the book, HG gets mangled in machinations of his own making, and descends into a catatonia so deep that he lost track of many weeks of his life.

From the context, Okkels had understood that when Len Jordan (HG!) finally surfaced, he managed – but just – to escape from the clutches of a madman, a Vietnam vet who subsisted on a remote beach somewhere on the California coast. Meanwhile Bontekoe winds up, literally, bumping off HG's main adversary – the novel's antagonist, a "feral poet" who had been instrumental in pushing HG into a nightmarish LSD abyss. Bontekoe makes it appear as though his victim trips and falls down a flight of stairs, breaking his neck; a neat and clean death which moreover goes unquestioned by local police. A common household accident. One can't be careful enough. Indeed!

When Okkels first read this account, the wicked, evil deeds on the part of all concerned had sent chills down his spine, one used to many a chill over the years of reporting for the Dutch gutter press. But it was addiction to the thrill of such spine-tingling chills that had become the narcotic mainstay of his life, leaving him to crave ever more and stronger fixes of sensationalism.

Okkels had learned to keep his pieces short – much as it pained him, for the material volunteered by HG had been copious. The usual editorial constraints had compelled him to be brief, all too brief, he realized as he ruminated over the wealth of information he'd not included in his article.

An example. HG had been remarkably forthcoming: "Sure, some of the events described by Bontekoe in his scabrous novel did occur, but as newspaper reporter you must be aware that it is not the hard facts, but their interpretation which counts; the slant taken, the insinuation, the views subtly superimposed, the palimpsestial effect. Besides, Bontekoe's constant distortions reek of foul play. And that's why I'm here talking to you now," HG had explained to Fokko. "It needs to be cleared up once and for all. My reputation has been seriously called into question. Besides, it hurts. It is a painful blow to discover that you have been implicated in a subterfuge so deceitful as to defy the imagination!"

"Of course, of course. Please go on," an overeager Okkels said to coax HG into an extended confessional. He was taking notes as fast as he was able. At the crucial moment his microcassette recorder had refused service. No batteries – he was baffled – and no time to get any at such short notice. HG, as always, was on a tight schedule, referring to "this strait-jacket chronocracy of ours", and unwilling to miss his next appointment, of all things with a rival paper!

HG had continued candidly, "Well, it must be pretty obvious. Now that I've made the big time, Bontekoe comes up with his cheap allegations about a sordid past. So I sold saltwater taffy in the streets of Berkeley for a while to pay the bills! BFD! I also worked in a car wash. So what? Is that so bad? What else can be his motivation but to discredit me and my group out of some deep-seated jealousy stemming from a grudge he's borne against me for decades. It is not very pleasant for me to admit, but Bontekoe cuckolded me and as if that were not bad enough, stole many of my possessions when I was down and out and sold them for a profit. It was a pure stroke of luck that I later managed to get some items back from a local pawnshop. He must've thought I was a goner, never to be heard from again. And admittedly, I certainly came close; skirted, yes, even courted death in those days. But I pulled through, no thanks to him."

HG had paused to wipe his brow with a handkerchief he pulled from his pale yellow jacket. The place had been rather stifling, why with the atmospheric heat, and the steam generated by the coffee shop's hissing and puffing machinery.

Okkels had peered over his glasses at HG, before firing off his next pointed question.

"You are perceptive, Fokkels," HG tried to compliment his interviewer.

"Okkels, that's Okkels, Fokko Okkels, if you don't mind," the reporter, noticeably irritated, corrected HG.

"Sorry, right, of course. Okkels. What kind of name is that, anyway? Sounds funny to an American, if you can appreciate that."

"Yes, yes. But both are perfectly good respectable Frisian names, I can assure you."

"I see. Anyway, where was I? Oh yes. Your question as to motive? We both know that Bontekoe's book was a flop, and he probably hopes to benefit from the publicity by dragging me into this controversy. Who knows, could be his flavor and fragrance lab research is not panning out. Something like that. Why not ask him yourself?"

Okkels banged on the table with the palm of his hand. "That's what I suspected all along. I tried to tell my editor when I went after this story."

It's what had clinched it for him, Okkels knew. A clever reporter needed an edge. And what an edge he'd come up with: one that cut wood, and hopefully a lot of flesh to boot.

"Well, I'm grateful for your insight, Okkels. It's best this thing is sorted out once and for all. Turn the tables on old Bontekoe. Clear the air. Besides, your reputation will be enhanced, while the publicity will do me a world of good. And hopefully harm Harm! He'll be sorry he ever crossed swords with us, eh?"

This was music to Okkels' ears. He could kill three birds with one stone. Boost his standing, plug HG and undermine Bontekoe. What more could a newspaperman ask for? A journalism award? That would surely follow in due course!

* * * * *

That night Okkels had felt slightly nauseous when – on the cheap newsprint of a rival paper – he saw the grainy half-tone photograph of Herm and Harm caught in a relaxed pose, arms on each other's shoulders. Whether withdrawing from intimate embrace or about to lapse into one was irrelevant. The treacherous twosome had pulled a fast one on him and it would probably cost him his job. Had he been too gullible? Yes, without a doubt. A veteran like himself, having the wool pulled over his eyes like a rank novice. He'd swallowed hook, line and stinker. How could he have been such a fool? Greed and ambition had made him lower his guard. Everyone knew WWW to be an outfit of pranksters not to be trusted.

The fact that he'd written an insinuating series on Bontekoe some years back, photographed him and his twin daughters, bare-bottomed and all, in that Dordogne nudist camp, must doubtlessly be seen as the reason for this little act of revenge on their part. In addition to the publicity they'd now managed to milk from his paper at his expense, his credibility would be undermined. Okkels would now surely be the laughing stock of all Holland, if not the entire Benelux and beyond. Not only had he failed to cut Bontekoe down to size – for Fokko hated big fish in his little Dutch pond – now he himself had been reduced to the minnow he secretly knew himself to be taken for in certain media quarters.

As he slumped on his couch at home that dreadful summer of 1998 – his pooch Harry yapping for its evening chow – Fokko had groaned in despair, removed his thick horn-rimmed glasses that hurt the bridge of his nose and slid them on the coffee table in front of him. Feeling utterly crushed, he'd rested his puffy red face in the palms of his hands forked at the wrists. He'd felt feverish, sick to his stomach.

The phone rang every few minutes and he could hear his answering machine click on and off. He had many informants (and informers) everywhere on the prowl. Plenty of juicy stories to go after if he so desired. But he did not, and instead felt dejected; dejected to the point of resorting to suicide when in a rare moment of insight the futility of his life hit home full force. The very thought, however, frightened him out of his wits and in a superhuman effort to inflate his punctured ego, he recounted some of his triumphs, not least among which the embassy scam that had caused a major furor a few years back, an incident that had had international repercussions.

It had done much for his standing in the *corps diplomatique* and generated a spate of invitations besides from rival governments of the discredited one – several attachés had been sacked; a couple of senior ambassadors "rotated" to out-of-the-way, C-rated countries in Africa and Latin America; and in one instance, a cabinet crisis in a befriended South Sea island nation had only narrowly been averted; parliamentary questions had been asked and judicial enquiries conducted.

This all to his credit, but at a price. The methods he'd used had involved on duplicity and guile, his ethics highly questionable, and somewhere along the line the nickname 'mestkever' (dung beetle) had cropped up, a tag that had stuck and which had severely stung him, though it never managed to slow him down.

In his zeal to excel, to strive for perfection, he rationalized almost anything. But then he, F.Fokko Okkels, served a larger cause and simply would not be restrained. Why others couldn't understand that, he couldn't understand. People were just too petty if not petulant, envious of even the small degree of success he'd booked in a tinker-toy nation where the main evening news tended to concentrate on a two-cent hike in the price of butter, or the birth of a baby gorilla in the local zoo, while elsewhere in the world wars raged or nuclear power plants melted down.

He'd felt the irresistible tug of perversion and flipped opened the evening paper in which that hideous picture appeared of his two most recent adversaries. He spread the classifieds across his lap. Indolently, feeling more forsaken than usual, he reached for his unlisted cell phone to punch his favorite 0900-number – the so-called sex lines. His spirits were only somewhat buoyed when he listened to yet another tantalizing instalment of "Royal Lust". The husky voices on the other side made deliciously vile allusion to sodomy, necrophilia and a combination of the two, which particularly excited Fokko. His needs were varied and great, not to say insatiable.

But not even this form of therapy – "from impotence to omnipotence", as he thought of it, a variation on the "from-rags-to-riches" theme – produced any results worth mentioning in the down-hearted reporter on this particular occasion, and with a pitiful mutter he sank back into the stiff leather pillows of his immaculate white couch.

Yet perversion seemed the best antidote for what ailed him just then – a near-schizoid state triggered by a hormone-fired adrenalin rush, his favorite endocrine cocktail – and with the full force of his warped imagination he conjured up his two exes and their present lovers, all four of whom heightened his sense of inferiority till he could stand it no more. Driven to utter despair, head turned to the ceiling, he screamed a tortured scream, which sent his pet dog scampering out of the room. And still he couldn't manage to rebound to any sort of life, imagining the most horrendous and blood-curdling reprisal actions, plunging all those oppressing his life to their deaths in a ravine of razor sharp and rusty metal blades, slicing them to ribbons.

His regular diet of fetid journalistic fare had put bread on the table for years. But then man can't live by bread alone, Okkels realized, and something was dreadfully amiss. Was there a link between his lifestyle and his life? And why did others view him as they did? Scanning the vaulted chamber of his mind, he reckoned that no one loved him, that he loved no one. Not even his own flesh and blood, not his parents, not his children – two teenage girls from his first marriage, and a five- and six-year-old from his second. None would ever see him of their own accord, in fact, avoided him like the plague – a sure sign, he knew, which more than anything summarized the bankruptcy of his life, the bottom line tallying to zip.

The charges of incest were never substantiated. It had been their word against his. But it constituted the reason for his familial abandonment nevertheless – a de facto quarantine. During more lucid moments, he was convinced that his beef with Bontekoe stemmed from subconscious projections, finding his own repressed sexual aberrations seemingly substantiated in a Dordogne nudist camp – in a man, moreover, infinitely more successful and accomplished than he could ever hope to be. He'd always been prone to believe the worst in others in order to ameliorate the pain caused by his own shortcomings – the perfect qualifications, moreover, for doing the Nexus Society Page, he'd been told on numerous occasions by certain reproachful columnists writing for more "reputable" papers, supposedly. "Let he without skeletons in the closet cast the first bone," Okkels had written in his own defense with the one hand, forcing shut his closet door tighter than ever with the other.

His recurrent dream of being abducted by himself – Okkels kidnapping Okkels! – gagged and bound, had left him baffled and on the verge of desperation. Yet professional help was out of the question, for he brooked no authority outside himself, knowing as he did the hypocritical nature of man better than anyone. He'd written up enough stories on twisted shrinks to know that collectively, they were an incurably sick lot. No wonder really, following as they did in the footsteps of "Freud the Fraud", a sick soul who turns out to have doctored his findings to accommodate his half-baked theories as recent revelations had plainly shown. No, when it came to that, it was just he and his alter ego to the bitter end, Okkels had pledged.

His mind was clouded, pertinent events hazy and distant. He was not usually prone to such anguished soul-searching, thank God, and the distinct discomfort he felt informed him why. It was an effort he could not sustain for very long and it took close to a hundred guilders worth of 0900-numbers to look for the relief he sought, relief that stubbornly eluded him nevertheless.

Harry, his little pet terrier, seemed to know all this intuitively, and as if to compensate his boss's near-palatable dejection, displayed its uninhibited joy at his presence, the earlier incident all but forgotten. It yapped up a storm, leapt on and off the couch, and with its cold, wet nose nuzzled Okkels' fat face, flushed by the ambient heat. Its dogged affection annoyed the sultry Okkels more than a little, its shrill barking intensifying his blossoming headache into a steady locomotive throb.

"Alright, alright, you'll get your goddam chow! Now shut the fuck up!"

Reluctantly Okkels rose to feed his adamant pet, put on his glasses, and lumbered over towards the kitchen, the dog prancing around and jumping up against its boss for pure joy and in anxious anticipation. Scurrying in and out between Okkels' legs, the frenetic little critter caused him to trip and lunge forward against the built-in oakwood bar, toppling a constellation of tumblers and decanter to the floor in a deafening racket of shattering glass.

"You bastard! You goddam motherfucking bastard!" Okkels shouted, surveying the damage.

The terrified terrier stood frozen on the spot, knowing full well the extent of its guilt.

Okkels turned around, eyes blazing, and in a blind rage kicked the cowering dog a good one in the ribs, sending his pet sailing clear across the leather hassock and against the edge of the wrought-iron-and-glass coffee table. Yelping pitifully, the mortally-wounded animal crawled away under the five-seater couch, a faint and labored yammering, muffled and barely audible, coming from deep within its opulent sepulcher.

Okkels knew he'd never sunk this low before, and despised himself while blaming Bontekoe for his woes. It was all due to that bastard who'd put one over on him. And he swore revenge. He'd dig up the dirt on him, and on HG, if it was the last thing he ever did. And he knew just the man to help him do it.

* * * *

THREE

Odel Wneeg was the thorn in the side of Froukje Vrolijk, the prostitute whose establishment Fokko Okkels used to frequent fairly regularly. Not only for pleasure, but for business as well. Froukje's clientele was good for a truckload of stories, inside pointers of where to look for people's dirty laundry, something for which he'd developed quite a nose; and palate. Froukje's houseboat brothel located in a McDonald's wrapper-strewn Amsterdam canal was as rich a source of information as any self-disrespecting journalist could wish to have.

Alas, the place had become run down since Froukje decided to leave the business and go into counseling, but that's where she would now once more be invaluable to Fokko. For Froukje followed the lead of none other than the incomparable Herman Gnuticks, peddling his neologist Nonism notion.

One of her most faithful students, qua attendance, was Okkels' old drinking (and snorting) buddy Odel Wneeg, former student activist who, ever since he'd relinquished a career in Politics-of-the-Left, had turned sour and resentful. The man's critical knowledge of matters eso-and-exoteric, however, was truly astounding and that now would stand Fokko in good stead.

Odel was secretly in love with Froukje and even though utterly "breastfallen" – as she referred to it half-jokingly – could not bear staying away from her, even though he knew she adored HG. That the relationship between Froukje and HG was a purely platonic one only made matters worse, for he knew that he would never possess her wholly as long as HG's reputation held. And so Odel's obsession in life was to undermine HG's teachings in order to win back his beloved Froukje. Only by driving a wedge between the two could he hope to succeed, and he spent most of his not inconsiderable talents researching the minutest aspects touching on the central doctrine advanced by the WWW group and its leader.

In so doing, Odel represented the perfect intellectual crutch for Fokko Okkels, a shortcut to achieving his avowed aim: the unmasking of the "Masqued Masqueraider" – as HG on occasion had openly referred to himself. Together with Odel Wneeg's help, Okkels stood a fair chance of succeeding, and doing mankind a service in the bargain.

He now dug up a yellowed back issue of his paper's Weekend Supplement boasting a fading photo of Froukje in front of her houseboat (appropriately Christened The New Whorizon) proudly pointing to her professional "shingle" that read: "Come As You Are" – her brothel's motto, painted brashly in bold orange letters over the entrance, below which some disgruntled impotent client had spray-painted "sexperts & laywomen".

Dutch Glory at its best, Okkels reflected, suppressing a vengeful smile. It all came back to him as if it had been only yesterday. But to get the facts straight, he skimmed the interview he'd done with Froukje in which she gave full credit for her change of profession to none other than HG, who'd got to know her through Bontekoe while on one of his overseas jaunts many years previous.

Just how the Bontekoe-connection had been established was the subject of yet another article, which in turn had led to the Dordogne photo series that he now almost regretted. It established a direct link to his present woes, and he was not at all sure whether he would do it all over again given the opportunity, considering the mess he was in.

But that was water under the bridge and the only realistic option open to him now was trudging straight ahead, bear it and grin. He was more determined than ever to see justice done, for his own sake, but now also for Harry's. And Okkels redoubled his efforts. He had all the ammo he needed in the pages before him. What remained was to find a way to prime it, time it, and take aim.

Carefully he sifted through the material on hand. He noted that one of Bontekoe's pet projects was pheromone research, and as it turned out, Froukje and her brothel had collaborated on field tests in connection with sex-enhancing scents. The day of the interview she had admitted with great candor to him that she went along with the Bontekoe experiments due to the measure of respectability it conferred on her establishment. Besides, collaboration with the researcher's renowned scientific institute had been a watershed, publicity on the subject tapping fresh sources of customers from ritzier joints mushrooming all over the metropolis. For in her cutthroat business, any slight advantage could mean the difference between solvency and bankruptcy.

Froukje's "manager", the one with the real business sense, had been the macho clothes horse Luigi Xix (pronounced "khsikhs"), otherwise known as 69 – about which more later, though suffice it to say the man died a tragic, tragic death. One fateful night he slipped with the slick soles of his custom-made Italian shoes on a used condom carelessly discarded on deck of the flat-bottomed houseboat, tumbled overboard and was not found until many days later, floating sea-bound, belly-up and bloated, in the Amstel river, whose impure waters brew a most delicious beer – though don't ask how.

It had been a highly enervating night when, to the warning cries of an alert passer-by, the entire crew of girls – the best collection of whores flesh you ever did see – clad in skimpiest undies, had clambered on deck, anxiously scanning the cold, dark surface of the placid canal waters for any sign of their favorite pimp. No one had dared jump in after 69 in their see-thru freudian slips, for fear of catching their death of pneumonia.

And so Luigi was reported missing, presumed drowned. A team of aqua-lunged navy divers did not turn up anything resembling a body early the next morning (for the accident had occurred in the wee hours of the night, back in the autumn of 1996).

What they did turn up was everything *including* the kitchen sink – belonging to the houseboat across from theirs, renovated not long before. The couple of dozen corroded bicycles, shopping carts, umbrellas, refrigerators – you name it – that were dredged up were par for the course; the whole sordid load hauled off to the nearest landfill high-rise site on the outskirts of town by a fleet of green municipal vehicles dispatched especially for the occasion.

Rubberneckers had lined both sides of the canal in order not to miss any of the big city entertainment.

Fokko had spent a lot of time with Luigi, useful as he'd been as his very own "deep throat" – rear window onto (or rather trap door into) the Amsterdam underworld of crime, which constituted another major slice of Okkels' repertoire of staple copy. During those days, while exchanging information on various and sundry affairs, Okkels had chanced upon a bunch of messages written by Froukje on behest of HG, and using him as a hypothetical adversary. He still vividly recalled most of this "he-mail", because that's exactly what it was, "hateful electronic mail" which he'd surreptitiously downloaded onto his own voracious IPC (impersonal computer), its cold and calculating extrasomatic memory teaming up with Okkels' in his pursuit to defame wherever, whenever and whomsoever possible.

Froukje's very first letter, which constituted a final exam of sorts, was a real eye-opener to Okkels, suggesting as it did that he'd stumbled on to a secret society, a widespread network of collaborators conspiring to achieve a common end. He'd gathered that part of the initiation rites of the group was to react to the work of key individuals – on HG's behest – in an attempt to sway more and more pivotal minds. The idea being that effective action could move mountains; a well-placed charge could topple an otherwise impregnable edifice, the way old chimneystacks are brought down like dominoes.

Not that Okkels quite understood the crux of their coded messages, though ostensibly an open secret, it stubbornly eluded him, despite Odel Wneeg's coaching. But that made him all the more determined to unravel the conspiratorial plot he'd unearthed. What was utterly unmistakable was the forcefulness, and forthrightness of the communications, the singular, unrelenting drive, the forging ahead towards...towards what? Okkels wasn't sure. It was all so intangible as yet, so abstract.

What Okkels was sure about, however, was Froukje's fair mastery of the technique, as amply demonstrated by her poison PC-letter to a small-fry New Age author named R.A. Wilson, a trial case that could lead to bigger game. In his Quantum Psychology this Wilson fellow elucidates his contextual standpoint with reference to a whole shopping list of "isms": "In an attempt to minimize semantic noise (knowing I cannot eliminate it entirely) I offer here a kind of historical glossary, which will not only explain some of the technical jargon (from a variety of fields) used in this book, but will also, I hope, illustrate that my viewpoint does not belong on either side of the traditional (pre-quantum) debates that perpetually divide the academic world."

Wilson then proceeds to summarize existentialism, phenomenological sociology, ethnomethodology, pragmatism, instrumentalism, operationalism, the Copenhagen Interpretation ("copenhagenism"), general semantics (Polish-American engineer A.Korzybski's attempt to reformulate a new non-Aristotelian logic to remove essentialism from speech and thinking), E-primism ('English without the word "is",' an invention of D.David Bourland, Jr., a votary of Korzybski's), and finally transactional psychology.

After having thus qualified his work, Wilson concludes his "Fore-Words": "I also assert a great unity between these traditions and radical Buddhism, but I will allow that to emerge gradually in the course of my argument.

"For now, I have said enough to counteract most of the noise that might otherwise distort the message I hope to convey. This book does not endorse the Abstract Dogmas of either Materialism or Mysticism; it tries to confine itself to the nitty-gritty real-life contexts explored by existentialism, operationalism and the sciences that employ existentialist-operationalist methods."

As Okkels later discovered Mr. Wilson fit neatly into a pattern of popularizers and/or synthesizers of modern physics and psychology, meant to usher in the New Age, along the lines of Fritjof Capra (*The Tao of Physics*) and Gary Zukav (*The Dancing Wu Li Masters*), which HG himself had chosen to elaborate on in his own, inimitable way. Though Okkels could not have known it at the time, it was to be the subtext of HG's later *Guide for the Apoplexed,* the sequel to *What Buddha Knew* and of course *(R)aping Einstein,* a wide-ranging, eclectic work quoting relevant authors at length.

Whether or not the "Wilson letter" Froukje Vrolijk composed had actually been sent, let alone received, was something that could not be ascertained. Nor was it particularly relevant. Though Okkels had taken a couple of uninspired cracks at contacting the addressee in order to get his reaction, he'd drawn a blank and let it pass. Wilson's publisher in Arizona had apparently pulled up stakes, left no forwarding address, and that was the end of it.

In a number of other instances, Okkels had been more successful and could document that similar provocative correspondence had not only been dispatched, but receipt acknowledged, albeit it of a rather disappointing nature. Not every hit was an instant conversion, far from it. First reaction often was of a negative, hostile sort, generating virulent denials and aggressive verbiage. But the Wilson file was illustrative of the scope and content of the WWW quest, and as such exemplary, and thus relevant here.

As Odel Wneeg had to explain to an ignorant Okkels, the Wilson letter was intended to deconstruct the author's work, if not destroy it, taking Derrida's *Of Grammatology* as its model.

"Granma Tology? Who the fuck's Granma Tology?" an incredulous Fokko had posed, managing only to get Odel's dander up – though no doubt Derrida himself would have been elated by this lucid illustration of deconstruction-in-action.

The letter had read:

Dearest Mr. Wilson,

You don't know me, but you saved my life once. Now, many years on, my life is again in need of saving, and I wonder if I can count on you to help me out one more time? But before getting to the point, maybe I should just briefly introduce myself first.

Born in Amsterdam for non-evolutionary reasons 31 years ago, I'm an ex-prostitute named Froukje Vrolijk. Personally, I much prefer the gender-neutral word "prostitute" to the loaded word "whore", which sounds harsh and demeaning, not to say sexist. Why, for example, is it that men are called "womanizers" while women are branded whores? Why not call the female equivalent of a womanizer a "manizer"? It would seem much more sensible in this emancipated day and age, wouldn't you agree?

I hope you don't mind me being candid like this, sir, me not knowing you and all? I tend to forget that we Dutch are fairly liberal, if not libertine, and that we may be considered too direct – forward even – to the liking of many. Not that I figure you for one of them conservative, prudish American types, to the contrary. That's what gives me the confidence to make this desperate appeal to you, you see.

You must forgive me, but I'm easily distracted – nervous as I am writing to a real big shot like yourself, sir. Rereading what I've written so far, it strikes me that I haven't even got past a proper introduction yet. Please bear with me, if you will. Like I was saying then, as a former lady of the night I sometimes used the convenient alias Wanda Little, because who could refuse such a tempting offer, right? "Hi, Wanda Little?" – to which I often received imaginative replies, usually but not always in the affirmative. Like, "Don't mind if I do" or "Not married, I take it?" or "Depends on how much it'll set me back", that sort of thing. But there was also the occasional uppity types, acting quite offended: "Why, aren't we being forward!?" they would say indignantly and walk away in a lather.

Given half a chance, I used to provoke such pussy-whipped men by telling them the updated version of the old fable about the little Dutch boy, Hansel Brinker, who saved Holland from flooding – you know the one. Well, there is the modern-day feminist equivalent of a Dutch lesbo, Gretchen Brinker, who stuck her finger in a dyke! There's also an improvised version of it I made up especially for my astronomer clients, where Gretchen sticks her finger in a black hole and saves the Contracting Universe from collapsing into a Big Crunch. Get it, Mr. Wilson?

Anyway, it was great fun, those early street-walking days. For one thing it taught me that love is not the key, but the lock! And once I learned that lesson it was all downhill. I soon graduated to "doing" conventions that came to town, cause they were right up my alley, so to speak. I handled "soft" scientists, I handled "hard" scientists. Often one led to the other. No, no, wait, don't take me for a crass ass, please. What I meant to say is that my (soft) sociologist contacts would tell their (hard) astrophysicist friends, and so on and so forth. This way I also learned a little about all their respective fields, combining business with pleasure, in a manner of speaking.

Such repartee, Mr. Wilson, such intercourse! And all by word of mouth. But that's me, sir, always trying to improve my position, standing up for my rights, even though I found myself mostly recumbent – and on the wrong side of the tracks to boot. After all, if there is one thing Holland is proud of it, it is its unflinching democratic traditions, where everyone is born free and equal before the law. And I ought to know about the law, Mr. Wilson, cause I was clued in personally by a number of my best customers – both appellate and high court judges – passing through, so to speak, on their way home from court.

Another good thing to come out of these frequent encounters with my international clientele was that I became conversant with the English language, which now stands me in good stead, I hope (that and my wordprocessor, which I virtually use as a prosthesis!). My agent/manager, unfortunately now deceased, who was also a kind of cybernetician/hacker on the side, even programmed/ designed some revolutionary software/hardware which has been of inordinate value to me ever since. He added these unique options to my keyboard which give me instant Humor (F31), Wisdom (Shift F31) and Unmitigated Gall (Ctrl F31).

Alt F31, however, I was never to touch under any circumstances, a proscription I have long since violated, needless to say, along with every other conceivable one, of course!

There was also a whole range of extras like Understatement, Disingenuity, Neologism, Pun, Euphemism, Synecdoche, Simulacrum, Agitprop and even Triple-Entendre, Metaphor Mixmaster, you name it, all the sort of stuff required for any kind of Basic+ correspondence.

In case you're wondering as to my innovative manager's name? It was Luigi Xix (pronounced Khsikhs, of Greco-Italian extraction), but that was too difficult and everybody just called him 69 (from the Roman Numerals L Xix, get it?). This, of course, was quite appropriate, considering his (a)vocation. But I digress (Crtl F32).

By far the best thing that happened to me in those wayward, waylaid days is that I got introduced to your work, Mr. Wilson. You see, a rather strange type, pretty screwed up – especially after I got through with him, if you know what I mean, and maybe you've heard of him – the Polish psychiatrist Professor Isaac Kinki, Izzy Kinki to his friends (and believe me he "iz", or at least "waz") – in one of his frequent absentminded moods left one of your books behind on my dresser. Now, I've never been merely your happy hooker-type exactly, like Xaviera Hollander, my notorious compatriot; much more your "curious courtesan", like Mata Hari, that other, more mysterious Dutch sister-in-sin, wanting to get to the bottom of things (Shift F33, pun intended). And so, before returning your book to Izzy, I read it from cover to cover in one go in the midday dinginess of my brothel houseboat anchored placidly in the murky waters of a downtown Amsterdam canal.

Anyway, to cut a long story short, you opened my eyes, as it were, stimulating my higher faculties, both of which were a nice change in my profession. I mean, by and large, folks try to keep you in the dark as much as possible. That is until, oh happy day, you came into my life, Mr. Wilson, and I've been grateful, not to say indebted, to you ever since (Shift F33, tongue-in-cheek; you get the idea, so I'll knock it off).

To illustrate that I was destined for bigger and better things than what prostitution had to offer (though many of the things prostitution had to offer were pretty big, and couldn't be better), and that I am indeed the serious, reflective type, and not just another dumb buxom Nordic blonde, I can tell you here that I had already become quite active in organizing the girls up and down our canal into a tight-knit group, a labor union of sorts – though labor being one of the things we tried to avoid like the plague, mostly through effective prophylaxis.

What I am trying to say is that I found it very helpful in my situation to publish a monthly "round robin" which I used to photocopy and distribute in my spare time, and which I (in)appropriately titled Our Organ (Ons Orgaan, actually, but it translates well in this case). And I clearly recall several pieces I wrote extolling the virtues of prostitution as an undervalued social service. Just think of all the housewives we saved from being battered by draining their husband's testosterone-fueled aggression, for fun and profit...

In other words, Mr. Wilson, my fondness of people and wanting to help them, coupled with an inclination towards the intellectual rather than, or in tandem with, the more physical aspects of life on the fringe of society, made me jump at the suggestion in your milestone work Quantum Psychology of organizing group sessions for the general upliftment of (wo)mankind. And so that is exactly what I did, sir. And these days I am the proud co-founder/director of a local WWW chapter operating from a Community Center in the Hague (Den Haag). Over time ours has grown into an ambitious syllabus of classes based on your teachings, where we confidently tackled both practice and theory. I say tackled, past tense, for reasons, which will soon become apparent.

So you see, Mr. Wilson, that is how you came to save my life the first time – both what was left of my peace of mind and my immunological system (!), in these days of rampant HIV & AIDS. Will you save me a second time as well? I sure hope so because I am in acute danger of backsliding into infamy. But lest this sound too enigmatic, please let me explain.

As I was saying, your book was very useful with its many practical suggestions for directed exerzices (my Speller balks at this word you seem to insist on writing with a zed, instead of an es? Why is that, sir?).

Paul Lysymy

So far, mostly middle-class housewives and retired or semi-retired gentlemen have joined, and frankly, I'm having a hell of a time massaging their staid, Burgher mentality. Funny, eh, how by that age the mindset congeals into fixed molds which are so hard to crack (makes me want to bang them upside the head sometimes, I swear).

I mean, apparently they are dissatisfied with their lives and come to me 'cause they want to change. But in making the attempt they accuse me of trying to change them. It's sort of a paradox, isn't it, Mr. Wilson?

Why aren't we already always what we should be? And if we are, why do we want to be different from what we are? And if we aren't, why aren't we? Do you understand what I'm saying, sir, cause I sure don't.

Which raises the question of why people simply don't know all there is to know? All these brilliant (wo)men over the centuries who have invested – and still invest – so much of their intellect to elucidate the unintelligible. Life seems such a flawed miracle that way, and that is utterly incomprehensible to me (Alt F31, the forbidden fruit!). Why bother with a miracle if it's going to be flawed? Maybe you could shed some light on this aspect of your own "crusade" – though that also is not the real reason why I'm writing to you.

"Out with it!" I can hear you scream.

So alright already.

What's troubling me then is this one dude, the only truly "creative" one in the group so far, too creative for his own good if you ask me, who seems to relish challenging me (read: you!) at every turn. I've been at the point of chucking him out on several occasions, but that seems petty, and self-destructive to boot, cause the other members of the group will get the impression that I can't handle him and worse yet, that your method may not be flexible or versatile enough to cater to a pluriformic crowd. And in Holland that is a definite no-no. So that is why I thought I'd consult you, Mr. Wilson.

Specifically, this guy Herman Gnuticks, or HG, I'm talking about – a Latter Day Sophist, as he calls himself, or alternatively, the Gardener of Eden – says that logically, ontologically and epistemologically speaking (whatever that is) your arguments are weak. Now, personally I'm not qualified to judge, because to me, philosophy is too complex and I get all tangled up in all that legerdemain, hairsplitting casuistry of theirn. (I only know these terms from a brief stint with a septet of sociopathic metaphysicians long ago, but that is a whole other kettle of cuttle, as you Yankees say! They discussed endlessly how many pinheads can dance on the head of an angel. Boooorring stuff!)

But to give you a handle on this fiendish friend of mine, HG says that he strenuously disagrees with one of your main tenets, Mr. Wilson, namely that there "is" no "deep reality", a theme you take a great deal of care to develop. This is a very serious charge, which you ought to take very seriously, sir, and not just take seriously, but address. I'm serious here!

In plain Dutch (which is what we speak here in Holland, Mr. Wilson, in case you didn't know), HG tells me that you are so preoccupied with science and relativity, that you overlook the simple fact that relativism can only be relativism by virtue of being coupled to its opposite non-relativism (or absolutism, if you prefer), and no matter what else you do, the two cannot simply be divorced, unless you intend to practice auto-mutilation (another typically Hermanesque statement; HG relishes what he calls his "mongrel doggerel"!). In any case, whole schools of philosophers seem to have reconciled themselves to the fact of this inextricable dualism long ago, according to my irascible acquaintance.

GROUND ZERO

Of course science, restricting itself (arbitrarily, HG says) to empiricism, (arbitrarily) ignores the non-empirical (and thus non-empirical intuition, the Supreme Wisdom of the Orient).

Herman Gnuticks: "This is symptomatic of the philistine attitude of 'What you don't see, hear, feel, smell, taste won't hoit you' (sic)." He is kind of the cynical type, Mr. Wilson, our Herm, bordering on the misanthropic (which reminds me, for laughs he once posited a Misanthropic Principle to offset the Anthropic. It states that this universe does not exist because man does not exist and so is not here to observe it. In Cartesian terms - or what HG refers to as "the spirit of conduitism", it would be something like, "I do not think therefore I am not." He also mixes it into a potion of Buddha's Bromide, the converse of Darwin's Dogma, namely: extinction of the fittest (instead of survival of the fittest...). It all depends on how you look at it, HG says.

Talk about reversing all one's polarities, eh, Mr. Wilson?

Anyway, that is why I need your advice, sir. Please provide me with an effective antidote to his deadly poison, on the double, won't you? Cause I'm not sure how much longer I can hang on!

But this is not all, Mr. Wilson, no sirree bob, Robert Anton. There's more, much more. For instance, HG claims that you offer your readers the category of "meaninglessness" in a purely "gratuitous" manner – as merely a throwaway category to be dispensed with as quickly as possible – failing to comprehend, apparently, that the "meaning" which you (over)value, is only possible against a backdrop of "meaninglessness".

"What is one without the other," a diabolical HG posed pedantically. By proposing as many realities as there are individuals, you're falling into the trap of choosing the Many over the One, which is myopic to say the least, since the one is the obverse of the other.

Finally, Herm gloats that mathematicians like Roger Penrose are catching on to this Operating Principle of Duality, by, for example, broadening their axiomatic base in order to depart from the narrow "continuity bias" of the ancient Greeks tacitly adopted by benighted (wo)mankind, and expanding this crippled and crippling concept to include its Siamese "discontinuity" twin. And voila, he (Penrose) comes up with spinors, twistors, cohomology and other gems. Earlier, of course, white-smocked master quantum mechanics had already faced up to "indeterminism" to supplement classical Newtonian "determinism". And look what a revolution that unleashed, eh, Mr. Wilson, sir!?

Then there's Ilya Prigogine who found that order miraculously emerges from chaos (disorder), reversibility from irreversibility, and vice versa.

Finally there's also the locality/non-locality paradigm to contend with, Mr. Wilson, the EPR experiment as reformulated by J.S. Bell, and later conducted by Alan Aspect.

It seems there's no end to it, sir, if you listen to HG, why with the dastardly finite/infinite pair always lurking just around the corner. He says it only stands to reason – Heraclitean reason!

Boy, what a card this guy is; a card in a game of his own choosing.

And that's all very well, but meanwhile I'm getting victimized, Mr. Wilson. Take E-prime, sir, my favorite part of your approach. HG "is" no less critical of E Prime – an understatement since he rips it to shreds, virtually, claiming that it is "archaic hat" and "too little, too late". E-prime doesn't go nearly far enough, according to him – which is not surprising considering what a heterodox radical HG is.

Here he referred me to traditional texts on Mahayana Buddhism where Gautama Buddha himself no less is said to have taught that "enlightenment cannot strike" as long as one thinks in terms of "is" and "is not". In a way the "old codger" – that's what HG calls Gautama, Mr. Wilson – used non-Aristotelian logic even before Aristotle had a chance to think it up, let alone for the likes of Lord Russell and Sir Karl Popper to rail against it two-and-a-half millennia later. How's that for precocity, eh, Mr. Wilson?!

HG (theatrically quoting Buddha from memory): "This world, O Kaccana, generally proceeds on a duality, on the 'it is' and the 'it is not'. But, O Kaccana, whoever perceives in truth and wisdom, how things originate in the world, in his eyes, there is no 'it is not.' ...Whoever, Kaccana, perceives in truth and wisdom how things pass away in this world, in his eyes there is no 'it is' in this world...Everything is' - this is one extreme, O Kaccana. 'Everything is not' is another extreme. The truth is in the middle."

(Parenthetically, Mr. Wilson, HG, in his disconcerting game of one-upmanship, cites historical evidence to the effect that Buddha himself strayed from his own maxim, revealing a subtle but distinct prejudice. Quoting from S. Radhakrishnan's Indian Philosophy (p.526/7), he documents his case: "Buddha announced the golden mean, though his own teaching was not quite true to it. To prefer celibacy to marriage, fasting to feasting, is not to practice the golden mean. The Gita denounces the religious madness of the hermits and the spiritual suicide of saints who prefer darkness to daylight and sorrow to joy. It is possible to attain salvation without resorting to the cult of narrowness and death.")

Leave it to HG to wind up a passage like that by offering me, his captive audience, "satori sushi" in jest, kissing his bunched fingertips and saying, "Exquisite! Out of this world, or should I say otherworldly!"

And while we're on the subject of cuisine, did you know that Buddha used to eat pork?! It's true. At least according to HG, who said to have read it in a reliable reference book. Not only that, but the pork he ate once was spoiled and Buddha nearly croaked!

"Just think," HG told me in one of his more speculative moods, "with a little bad luck Buddha might've gone the way Islam or Judaism went afterwards and saddled us up with strict dietary laws. But luckily he didn't. What would've become of our weekend barbecues otherwise, eh?"

When I reminded him that Buddhism did proscribe the eating of meat altogether, not just pork or beef, HG denied its historic authenticity. "Buddha loved venison stew. Why else do you suppose he hung around Deer Park?"

Whattaya gonna do, sir?

But to get back, HG applies these two pieces of quaint a-logical wisdom to refute you, saying that to deny "deep reality" is only to affirm it, one of his favorite hobby-horses being the formulation (à la Heraclitus): "Everything implies its opposite; affirming is denying."

The other one he abuses to no end (à la Buddha) is that "the world is not real, or unreal, nor neither, nor both, nor different from neither or both." Ditto for the notion of Self/no-Self.

He says it is utterly unforgivable – a second, even more serious charge which you ought to address, Mr. Wilson – that you say that Buddhism claims no-Self (which you do, Mr. Wilson, in several places).

As a movement, Buddhism arose partly in contradistinction to both the "eternalists" and the "nihilists" of the day, HG assures me. And the way out of such artificial dilemmas is to follow the Vedic/Upanishadic exhortation: "Neti neti" [i.e. not this, not that – which by the way you seem to attribute erroneously to the Chinese, HG alleges, when on page 192 of your book you say that they, the Chinese, "have had more experience with this system than anybody else (more than the Hindus, even)...".

It appears that the Ancients of India remain unexcelled, and as the graffito recently discovered on a 5000-year old outhouse wall at a Mohenjo-daro archeological site says: "Their karma ran over our dogma" (but then not in English, naturally, 'cause as you well know, sir, the sun was not to rise on the British empire for many millennia).

So what's left of the English language, HG asked rhetorically, if you eliminate the verb to be (and with it Being and Becoming), as well as all nouns and pronouns for fear of hypostatization – an ever – present danger?

"We'd be reduced to ostensive pointing and grunting, by golly," according to HG.

He constantly undermines our group's activities in this way, Mr. Wilson, cutting the ground from under my feet and leaving me utterly empty-handed, if not empty-headed. Makes me feel like a downright quadriplegic sometimes. And when I ask him why, he taunts me by saying that he is the "primus inter pares exponent of PMB" – Postmodern Militant Buddhism (the title of one of his many publications in this field; uses the pseudonym D. Bunker in this connection).

Not only is he a prolific writer, Mr. Wilson, he's also set up this "21st Zentury CitiZen" correspondence course, whereby he dispenses "enlightenment for the price of a postage stamp".

"I'll zap anybody," he once boasted, "even your precious Mr. Wilson, if you want me to."

He, its Chief Scribe, is always saying (and writing) contentious things like that, sir. Personally I think it's cause he chain drinks coffee. But he denies it. So get this, sir, when I told him he was in denial, he denied that, and retorted I was in affirmation!

No doubt you would like some other examples, Mr. Wilson, which I won't withhold (how could I?):

-he defines (wo)man as "a terminal case of the splits";

-he admonishes me to quit "wallowing in duality" – another favorite phrase;

-he claims to have discovered "0-degree pre-Big Bang background radiation", or alternatively, "interregnum Big Bang silence". Whereas the 3-degree Kelvin microwave radiation discovered by A.A. Penzias and your relative (?) R.W. Wilson is only a pitiful 15 to 20 billion years old, his own 0-degree radiation is infinitely older (according to his worked-up, but as yet unpublished, data).

This on the serious side.

But then there is his warped sense of humor, making things up as he goes along. Makes you wonder where he gets his stuff, sir, don't it? The supersilliest joke goes: "Says one Babylonian king to another, 'Gotta ziggurat, Ham baby?' Says Hammurabi: 'Sorry, man, but I don't smoke.'"

Now I ask you???

And guess how he characterized the U.S. for being the No.1 gluttonous consumer nation in the world – after President Bush's visit to the Rio Earth Summit way back? A Banana Cream Pie Republic.

I shan't even mention the one about his claustrophobic pet turtle – but then I guess I already have, huh?

Another example: "Few know," HG once volunteered, "that the expression 'The buck stops here!' was not coined by President Truman at all, but by an avaricious banker relation of his, who meant it quite literally."

Do you suppose it's true, Mr. Wilson? President Truman a plagiarist? Personally I don't buy it. I think HG was pulling my leg. What do you think? Just like the time he told me that he had once attended a farewell party thrown for a retiring cartoonist friend of his, who concluded his speech with the words, "And so dear friends, this is where I draw the line."

He says he takes his lead from Ken Kesey's Merry Pranksters, you remember, Leary's old sidekick.

Could you please help me, Mr. Wilson, sir? Cause it's one minute to high noon and I'm out-flanked and out-gunned – metaphorically speaking, you understand.

By the way, you don't have to worry. HG knows I'm writing to you. He told me to say hi, and to tell you that he is "accepting your challenge at cosmic dominoes". When I asked him what he meant, he said that your book ends in zero, as follows:

    Universe
    - <u>Universe</u>
    0

("The result of subtracting the universe from itself," as you put it so intriguingly). His own Guide for the Apoplexed (a working draft only at this stage) starts and ends with zero. Zero, Mr. Wilson, as you will see if you read his "nonograph" (as opposed to a monograph) apparently plays a central role in human evolution. But I don't get it. To me, "zero" means nothing. To him it means "The Gateway between the Dual and the Nondual Realm" – stuff like that.

If you get it, would you be so kind as to explain it to me, preferably in terms of Transactional Analysis which you're so fond of, so's I can understand it too? Though come to think of it, what's there to transact when faced with zip? No object, no subject...

HG assures me that though you're fairly well advanced on the road to Taohood, Mr. Wilson, you still lurch dangerously away from the Middle. Your books he sees as a ludicrous and unconvincing bluff. "Don't fall for it, Froukje," he warned me, pointing out that here and there in your disquisitions, you indicate that you are of the opinion that if only the proper language is found, the elusive may be captured.

On page 191 of Quantum Psychology, you write regarding the non-local quantum system, that parapsychologists lack the "operational vocabulary to make their work precise and scientifically crisp."

HG impugns that you still fail to grasp the function of language in matters subtle, Mr. Wilson, not unlike Heidegger, the stepfather of existentialism, or von Neumann, or your precious Korzybski, or even Dr. David Bohm for that matter, all of whom tried to tinker with language to get at the evanescent.

"God," HG assured me once, "is most assuredly not in the details! Nor in the generalities, for that matter!"

As for Wittgenstein, his early insight, HG says, of language as model of "reality", was far inferior to his later insight of language as manifestation thereof – a revelation which so blew his (Wittgenstein's) mind that he didn't publish anything thereafter, HG says meaningfully. Alas, old Ludwig fell short of the ultimate insight (witness his peculiar form of apostasy), as have most western luminaries, according to HG - and thus by implication you, too, Mr. Wilson, and me, of course, riding on your coattails, and basking in your reflected glory.

Surely you can see why this undermines your authority, sir, and, by implication, mine? I suppose having HG snuffed would be too outrageous to contemplate, huh, Mr. Wilson? Though I still know a few underground hit men – 69's Mafioso blood brothers – from the old days when I dabbled in sex, drugs and rock 'n roll. Just give me the go-ahead, and I'll see it done, sir! That's how desperate I am, Mr. Wilson.

But then what can I do, sir, when he maligns you like that, or when he calls you the Pimp of Neopop Psychology, and me its Madame? Isn't he asking for it???

Will you write soon to let me know what to do? I'm truly at wit's end! If I lose my source of income running the string of Wonderful World of Wilson groups, I'd have no choice but to return to my old brothel in the red light district of Amsterdam – that dank and dingy canal houseboat which made me quite seasick on busy convention nights with all hands (and other parts of the anatomy) pumping away – and you wouldn't want that, now would you, Mr. Wilson?

You see, sir, it's easy for HG to talk. He's practically independently wealthy. Dough just keeps on pouring in. All these senior citizens keep bequeathing their money and property to him. But it ain't right, Mr. Wilson, and I won't have any of it, though he offers, saying he wants to be my "saccharine daddy".

What he does, you see, is he implants hypnotic suggestions while on his "altruistic rounds" through retirement homes around the globe. It's like taking candy from babies. The old folks kick the bucket and suddenly he's in their last will and testament, sole heir yet. Surprise, surprise!

And he's so slick and slippery that no one catches on. All except me, that is.

Whattaya think, Mr. Wilson, should I turn him in, or would that be too churlish of me?

One last comment just to give you a bead on this HG rascal. He says you were getting warm with your treatment of solipsism, but tragically stopped short (hint, hint). It seems Bertrand Russell, whom you also admire greatly, felt himself "constitutionally incapable" of accepting it, though intellectually, "qua logician", solipsism is irrefutable, according to that same Russell, who, HG informs me, flip-flopped between contradictory points of view throughout most of his adult life.

It seems he died "dualing to the death", according to HG's diagnosis – whatever that means.

But then if you think about it, the common sense notion of an independent world existing 'out there' must in the final analysis be taken on faith - remaining an assumption, despite all common sense. Our senses are fallible, as is well known, and Russell writes somewhere that 'this physiologist's argument is exposed to the rejoinder…that our knowledge of the existence of the sense organs and nerves is obtained by that very process which the physiologist has been engaged in discrediting, since the existence of the nerves and sense organs is only known through the evidence of the senses themselves."

Here, the Early Sir Bertrand's Idealism lords it over the Later Lord Russell's Realism, while the latter's logical atomism also gets points off from Guru Gnuticks!

But we won't stir up that traditional metaphysical hornet's nest here, now shall we, Mr. Wilson? If it ain't been resolved in 3000 years, it ain't about to be resolved by us, now is it, sir?

HG refers to solipsism as the "cerebral chrysalis" (wo)mankind must pass through on the way to cosmic consciousness. The reason, he explained, is that when the self is cornered into this logically tenable but intuitively untenable position, the light may dawn and the self transmogrify once and for all (extinction of the fittest???).

So instead of denying solipsism (which, as you may recall, is tantamount to affirming it), you must show some gumption and lock yourself inside that hermetically sealed space-capsule cocoon of solipsism until you "perish" or else are "reborn".

This according to the gospel of Herman Gnuticks at least, who asked me to pass the message on to you, sir, which I gladly do.

In this connection, Mr. Wilson, when I mentioned your reference to Russell's proof, you know, where he argues that we have two heads, not just one, HG used it to try to convince me to 'stop counseling dimwits and go back to the houseboat, because you could make a mint charging your customers double for fellatio. Don't forget that two heads are better than one'.

You see what I mean, sir?

You know, Mr Wilson, when HG and I were watching a replay of the '88 European Cup Soccer Championship (the Dutch were victorious, you may recall), there was this fisheye lens shot from a blimp. From that great distance you could see the crowd doing a "wave" – you know, throwing their arms up sequentially so as to create the illusion of a wave going around the stadium. Well, as the shot zoomed in, you could see the smooth, continuous wave break up into individual, discrete persons. Then you could distinguish the ball being kicked around the field, also nice and discrete, like a point particle. Momentarily, if you squinted your eyes, you could even see both particle and wave simultaneously!

But we "know" the ball comprises atoms, which comprise subatomic particles, which comprise (probability) waves, ad infinitum. Particle inside wave inside particle inside wave...

Exercise 1

Sit in rapt attention in lotus, half lotus, armchair or even Lazy Boy position. Wear shirt with buttons, any kind of buttons will do. While mumbling a mantra – any mantra will do – unbutton your shirt, at first slowly, then speeding up as you progress with the exercise until the discrete, individual steps begin to flow into an undulating wavelike motion. Notice the effect without drawing any conclusions.

T-shirts, polo shirts, and certainly any sort of zippered shirt don't get it. The shirt or blouse must be of good quality since due to frequent unbuttoning and rebuttoning, buttons tend to pop off and the subject will spend more time sewing buttons on his/her shirt or blouse, then time meditating – which is counterproductive to our purpose here.

If at first you don't succeed, don't lose heart. On average between one and two and a half million (un)buttonings are required to achieve satori, which by virtue of its very nature is no achievement at all.

(CAUTION: this exercise, too, like everything else in life, can be a detour to enlightenment! Hence no money-back guarantee.)

From what I can gather, Mr. Wilson, HG's purpose in the above exercise is to demonstrate graphically that motion (space/time) as human category of thought inescapably compels us to think in terms of waves or particles. There ain't no other way to picture motion (just try it and see), and this leaves us as (neo)Kantians and others have pointed out, with time, space and causation as insurmountable obstacles to penetrating duality, or the world of appearance. This is also science's claim to fame in sticking exclusively to the empirical. At the same time this is also why non-locality and non-causality, must ultimately remain unintelligible to us. When we drop causality, anything goes, and science flies out the lab window.

Science, which had earlier unsatisfactorily made the ad hoc postulation of wave/particle complementarity, and not to be stymied, is now finding a more cogent model in superstring theory, which incorporates not only relativity and quantum mechanics, continuity and discontinuity, determinism and indeterminism, but also particles and waves. The vibrating superstring produces "energy notes", which we register as subatomic particles.

In this connection HG points out (as have others) that, "We're right back to good ol' Pythagoras and his mystic band of "enumerator bookies", seeing number in everything. And thus in their own way these 'Greek Geeks' have been 'stringing' us along down the 'anals' of history for close to 2500 years. And it's time it stopped!"

HG's only responsibility in life, he says, is to pull us from those gory entrails kicking and screaming, by the scruff of the neck if need be. For it is conmen like them who have tried to pawn off monistic monoliths on us over the centuries, be it in the form of number, energy, experience, vitalism, consciousness, materialism, spiritualism, not to mention gods in a variety of colors and flavors.

Exercise 2

Call any ten surviving Nobel Prize laureates on the telephone and ask them which one of them has ever seen a number, an energy, an experience, a consciousness, a god?

Make a list of all non-observables, which play such a big role in daily life.

(I pass on these authentic, copy-righted Herman Gnuticks exercises without his permission. They are meant for your eyes only, Mr. Wilson, and certainly not to be reproduced anywhere, anyhow.)

But you know, sir, it seems that scientists don't give a hoot about such subtleties. To them it's their precious mathematical formulas and their correspondence to reality that counts, the predictive power they derive. The reason is, HG lectures me, because they're not interested in enlightenment. It's power they're after, eking out a niche in the academic, industrial or publishing (!) worlds.

We're much better off that they remain benighted, HG says, in as much as it keeps them with their noses to the grindstone, unraveling the riddle: In the process they turn up many nourishing facts, like birds do juicy grubs – information, and technology, which cater to our creature comforts.

But in the meantime, little do they realize that the riddle unravels as long as the riddler keeps riddling. And even when trailblazers like Roger Penrose and John D. Barrow point out that unraveling the riddle may mean no more than compressing strings of num-

bers into more elegant, compact strings of yet other numbers, most pay them no mind. The fact that not all strings are in principle compressible, is something that does not occur to them and will keep the researchers researching, and that's what counts.

(Wo)mankind self-servingly strives towards unifying experience, even when it proves ununifiable - as Einstein found to his chagrin. This seems to be a crucial point, Mr. Wilson, this unifying drive, I mean, and thus the bent towards monism, or HG wouldn't have bothered to ask me to tag along to the Royal Library to dig up a translation of Ernst Cassirer's classic book(s) Substance and Function & Einstein's Theory of Relativity.

"I don't want you to take my word for it," HG justified his request for me to join him one Saturday morning.

So I cancelled my hairdressing appointment, keen to help ferret out the recommended reading.

In retrospect it was the best move I ever made, sir. Not only did I learn a great deal about ontology, ontogeny and "ons" in general, but as it turned out, Laurens, my hairdresser, went berserk that very morning. He actually tried to commit suicide in front of all the ladies by dunking his electric straightener into a basin filled with water, luckily succeeding only in short-circuiting a fuze and plunging the entire building into darkness. Several of the women customers were able to overpower him before he could hurt himself with a pair of scissors, I read in our local paper that night. Poor Laurens was inconsolable, and just to be on the safe side was admitted to the psychiatric ward of Amsterdam Medisch Centrum (AMC) for observation.

And so, in retrospect I was mercifully spared what was later described to me as a "horrible, horrible incident". Of course we should've seen it coming, Mr. Wilson, 'cause everyone knew that Phil, Laurens' boyfriend, was cheating on him. Just as we all knew that Laurens was insanely jealous. But you know love blinds, don't you, and poor Laurens refused to see despite ample evidence of Phil's escapades. Nor did anyone have the guts to tell him to his face, sir. Me neither.

But why am I talking about Laurens? I was talking about Ernst Cassirer, remember? I'm sorry. Where was I? Oh yeah.

Renowned neo-Kantian of the Marburg School, Cassirer, writes on page 328 of his book, or rather wrote... 'cause he died over 50 years ago. (Seems that one day a student ran into him while he was walking to class and tapped him on the shoulder to ask a question. The venerable old professor turned around, smiled, and collapsed into the student's arms – dead of cardiac arrest! Takes my breath away, when I hear stories like that, Mr. Wilson. Talk about stranger than fiction, eh? But there I go again.)

To the point. Cassirer had the following to say:

> But although being and non-being, similarity and dissimilarity, unity and plurality, identity and opposition are objectively necessary elements of every assertion, they cannot be represented by any content of perception. For just this is their function, that they go beyond the particularity of sensuous contents in order to establish a connection between them; and while both the sensuous contents participate in this connection in the same sense, the latter can be pointed out directly in neither of the two particular elements as such. The relation between the heterogeneous fields of sense-perception could not be attained, if there were no structure, which remained outside of their special characters and thus outside of their

qualitative opposition...The concept of unity of consciousness here first gains a firm foothold and sure foundation. If we rest in the content of the particular sensation nothing is offered us but a chaos of particular experiences. The perceptions are packed together in us like the heroes in the wooden horse, but nothing is found that refers them to each other and combines them into an identical self. The true concept of the self is connected with the concepts of the one and the many, the like and the unlike, being and non-being, and finds it true realization only in these. When we comprehend the perceptions under these concepts, we combine them into one idea, – whether or not we designate this unity as "soul." The "soul" is thus, as it were, conceived and postulated as the unitary expression of the content and as the systematic arrangement of pure relational concepts.

Heinz Pagels in The Cosmic Code gets the prize for brevity when he says the same thing: "The unity of our experience, like that of science, is conceptual, not sensual." (As a former conventioneer groupie, I love that sort of talk, don't you?)

In his Mysticism and Logic, Russell writes, "That the things which we experience have the common property of being experienced by us is a truism from which obviously nothing of importance can be deducible...The generalisation of the second kind of unity, namely, that derived from scientific laws, would be equally fallacious, though the fallacy is a trifle less elementary."

How wrong can a genius be, eh, Mr. Wilson? Ha ha.

It is this and similar arguments which leads the incomparable Lord Russell, and before him, William James and other Radical Empiricists (neutral monists) to suggest that the entire notion of a universe may be a fallacy. A multiverse is much more likely, though we by dint of our ego&anthropo-centrism will rope it into a universe at all cost anyway.

And so we're back to the aforementioned One/Many antipodal pair. (HG asks, "Is man the trap that catches universes?" It amounts to the same thing to my mind, though he prefers to speak of a "nulliverse" or 'emptiverse', using adapted PMB terminology).

I can sort of understand what he's getting at, Mr. Wilson, if you figure that no one to date has yet seen a "universe" (see ExerciSe 2, above). If anything is a universal abstraction, it would be a universe, eh, Mr. Wilson? It certainly would be what you'd call a "non-observable", right? I mean, we're sort of caught within this "perception bubble" (or Leary tunnel, as you say) on all fronts (which makes me about as claustrophobic as HG's pet turtle, just thinking about it). So we experience what we experience, and to date that's never included anything remotely resembling a universe of any sort or description.

Why is it, Mr. Wilson, that this sobering thought should bring on such a fierce attack of vertigo in me, in addition to suffocating claustrophobia?

There is only one way out of this bind, sir, if I understand our HG correctly, and I wonder what you make of it?

"As always, the way out is the way in, just as the way in is the way out."

There seems little choice, according to Gnuticks the Reprobate, but to wake up. How? Nothing to it: The Vanishing Step, take it by letting go. Put less prosaically, more poetically:

*Grasping, letting go,
Grasping, letting go,*

*Moving like an earthworm
Through the soil.*

Well, I guess I could go on and on, Mr. Wilson - and I guess I have, huh. But I had to give you something to go on so that you could prescribe a cure that will save my life, save me from prostitutional recidivism otherwise known in the trade as backsliding ($100/hr).

May I end by thanking you in advance for your help with my thorny problem? I'm quite at a loss as to how to proceed.

Meanwhile I'm off to have some promotional buttons made, which HG refers to as "Clip-On Icon-O-Clasps". I'll be sure to send you some as soon as they're ready, sir. It's the least I can do after what you've done for me – and what you're about to do...

Thanks so much for your patience, Mr. Wilson, and so long.

Unlibidinously yours,

Fronkje Vrolijk

*C/o WWW,
P.O.Box 63444,
2502 JK The Hague,
Olland (EU)*

* * * * *

FOUR

Rereading this lengthy epistle – one pregnant with substantive content and insubstantial intent, rife with omission and commission also – had redoubled Okkels' determination to get to the bottom of the enigma. What on earth could it mean? Not only was he dying of curiosity, but figured his own readership would be as well, and if only he could find a way to unravel the mystery, strand by strand, his journalistic reputation would be established once and for all. All his suffering would have been worth it, and he might be able to land a cushy job as senior columnist, a goal he'd coveted from day one. He'd show those supercilious bastard colleagues of his, disparaging and berating him at every turn! Perhaps he'd even be offered a professorship at one of Holland's prestigious universities – others, not much better qualified than he, had been appointed.

An ambitious Okkels dreamed away in this manner, until rudely woken by one of the myriad banalities of life, the proverbial thump back down to earth. In this instance it was a phone call from his editor-in-chief, Ms. Rijkje Dijkstra, coming in on his cell phone. Whether he'd mind getting his ass over to the office to explain why he'd single-handedly made the Nexus the laughing stock of the whole of Holland?!

Okkels pondered his options, which were few. It didn't take him long to decide to bare his soul to his boss. All things considered it seemed the best stratagem. Not that he had much of a choice; her penetrating eyes could see right through him, as past experience had proven on numerous occasions.

He had hoped to crack the case and present it in bite-size bits, not only to her, but the world at large. It was not to be, apparently; time had run out on him. In a life jammed with deadlines, this particular one had killed him. And he thought that if he was going to have a fighting chance, he'd better play it aboveboard, on the up-and-up, something he was unaccustomed to, thoroughly disliked in fact. It just wasn't his style. But now he was left no choice, especially in view of Dijkstra's preemptive call.

So, in preparation for the showdown, and to optimize the slim, slim chance he had of saving his skin, F.Fokko Okkels gathered the entire stack of documentation he'd accumulated over the years – manila folders containing mainly computer printouts, piles of photocopies, and a dozen letters of the type presented above but addressed to various VIPs worldwide. Together the complete file made for an impressive case history, and he hoped to god Dijkstra would be lenient with him.

Given an opportunity to explain, Okkels banked on the fact that Ms. Dijkstra might just appreciate the gravity of the affair – an affair characterized by what Odel had termed the Herzogian-complex, after Saul Bellow's brooding hero who also had resorted to lunatic correspondence. The difference being, however, that Herzog was a crushed, neurotic individual, while HG was anything but that.

WWW's cold and calculating rationale was that the world had become a Global Village, à la Marshall McCluhan, and that what they were doing was nothing so very different from maintaining neighborly contact as in the days of the old-fashioned insular world.

The analogy of a peripatetic Socrates buttonholing anyone he ran across in the agora to chew the fat was an emblematic image which particularly appealed to the WWW in-crowd. Why with all manner of high-tech microelectronics virtually ubiquitous, and mass communications at everyone's fingertips, there was nothing so extraordinary about their approach, which paralleled that of the ancient father of philosophy himself, but then transposed to postmodern times. Their handy catch phrase was: "All the evidence is in." What remained was to put it all together, and share out the fruits of their wisdom. Or as HG put it: "Explaining a way, without explaining away."

To Okkels was left the rather tall order of comprehending and then exposing the inner workings of the group before they pulled the wool over the eyes of yet more innocent, unsuspecting people. It was a noble goal that gave meaning to his life.

* * * * *

Newspaper publishing being what it was in Holland, that is, a murderously competitive business, *Courandstad Nexus* shared its accommodations with a number of affiliated papers and magazines in order to cut overhead. The Publishing Group to which they belonged was housed in a drab concrete, steel & glass structure on Wibautstraat, Holland's equivalent to London's Fleet Street, a busy thoroughfare just outside downtown Amsterdam. The *Courandstad Nexus* had been swallowed up not long before in a hostile corporate takeover that despite vociferous objections from trade unions and journalist associations had gone ahead, dangerously streamlining the Dutch print media to the point of jeopardizing press pluriformity.

To the *Nexus,* however, it was a godsend because the paper would surely have folded as a result of severe mismanagement that had led to sprawling debt. The old editor-in-chief was put out to pasture, a new one appointed, the staff trimmed, format modernized and advertising boosted to make the operation cost-effective. It was thus that the *Nexus* rose from its own ashes, with everyone on their best behavior till the paper would once more show a profit. Okkels, too, had made it by the skin of his teeth, and he knew that he could not afford to goof up as he had.

After a lonely 45-minute commute from his home in downtown the Hague where he rented an apartment, Okkels parked and made his way past security without so much as a cursory nod. But then Okkels was everywhere preceded by his reputation as a "klootzak" (a common 8-letter Dutch word literally meaning ball-bag, i.e. scrotum), acquired long before he earned the accolade of "mestkever". The term had a far wider significance than the mere reference to his nasty tic of reaching for his privates in public, referring instead to a generally foul attitude towards one's fellow human beings. For those in the know, Okkels' attitude problem stemmed from a humongous inferiority complex, for which, as is so often the case, he tended to overcompensate royally in other domains.

Being thoroughly ashamed of his humble roots – his family had been sheep farmers just outside Beetsterzwaag up in the North – Okkels, who had early on resolved to escape from their sheepish ways, cultivated an autodidactic bent. Despite heavy claims on him to perpetuate the family homestead, he'd fled rural Holland swearing never to return. And ever since he'd rudely scratched and clawed his way up the social and corporate ladders, or at least tried his level best. The half-dozen rungs or so he'd managed to ascend afforded him sufficient elevation to look down on enough people to feel just that little bit superior required to make life worth living. Alas for Okkels, the big city never held much more in store than the endless series of pathetic near-life experiences he'd left behind. And in an important way this explained his driving compulsion to live vicariously through the celebrities he came in contact with during the course of his work for Courandstad Nexus.

This on the nurture-side of the equation. As far as the nature-side was concerned, Okkels, to his chagrin, could not shed the defects of inferior, inbred genetics that clung to him like skin – literally: blotchy, oversensitive and excessively dry and peeling skin, manifesting, among other things, as dandruff on his shoulders (usually epauletted or padded because too narrow).

His forehead was too large, a fault further emphasized by his bald pate with the friarly nimbus reaching three quarters round, and his eyes too widely placed, giving him a slightly "fishy" look.

His teeth, or what remained of them, were a dentist's nightmare, or heaven, depending on how you looked at it – with cavities spontaneously forming inside what were considered impregnable fillings. This propensity towards dental decay was a modest inheritance from his father's side, and rather than treat his teeth well, he cultivated enamel rot by nonstop stuffing his mouth with the cornucopia of sweets the Dutch are famous for, most notably "drop", that noxious licorice candy sold and consumed by the ton in confectionery-minded Holland.

The oral flora that consequently thrived in the paradise that was his mouth, exuded a stench that even had he brushed regularly – which he didn't – would have taken a gallon of mouthwash a day to neutralize. Consequently few could bear to come within several feet of Okkels as he also suffered from excessive intestinal gas caused by a congenital digestive ailment passed along on his mother's side.

Apart from between-meal snacks to satisfy his unmet social needs and wants, Okkels, who oddly skipped breakfast more often than not, was fond of eating copious lunches and dinners to make up for it. He never cooked for himself, however, and frequently went on binges bordering on bulimia, "eating out of the wall" as the Dutch say ("uit de muur eten"), that is, from the battery of built-in dispensing machines you find in public places like bus terminals and train stations: grease-drenched croquettes and meatballs being his favorites; nor could he pass up any opportunity to down a herring or three, with extra onions of course; or scarf French fries whenever he'd pass a stall, "patatje oorlog" ("fries at war") topping his list – a reference to that odious combination of topping comprising a dollop each of mayonnaise, ketchup and peanut butter sauce (!) lavished on this meal-size carbohydrate-rich snack.

His obsessive overeating in turn left him with a noticeable paunch that pulled his shoulders into a slight slump, giving him at a glimpse, the appearance of a pregnant hyena.

Some simply ignored him for all these shortcomings, others pitied him, while others mercilessly detested him for it, holding Okkels personally responsible for the unpalatable cumulative effects of his physical appearance.

Not being a party to such privileged information, however, the security staff of the newspaper building tacitly fit into the latter category, as they watched their least favorite reporter pass, judging him only on the extent of their personal interaction, or in this case, lack of it.

Carrying his manifold invisible burdens, oppressing him more than usual, Okkels bumped the turnstile with his briefcase, squeezed into a closing elevator, and was hoisted up to the fourth floor, the new home of the Nexus ever since the forced merger that had gobbled them up.

It was the price to be paid for years of dwindling subscriptions in an anemic economic climate that had seen advertising revenue drop with the advent of commercial satellite television. Only the most drastic financial and editorial intervention had ensured viability, and it was under these adverse conditions that Okkels had to fight for survival, and had by and large managed well enough.

There was an as yet unsaturated market for the type of sewer journalism he excelled in, and it was for that reason that his presence was tolerated for as long as it had. Mobilizing public opinion, and herding sheep, it had occurred to him once, shared a remarkable congruity of purpose. And he begrudgingly had to accept that perhaps he'd inherited more from his folks than just exclusively undesirable traits.

The hustle and bustle of several dozen frenetic reporters hard at work at computer terminals distributed throughout the capacious floor felt familiar and comforting to a harried Okkels. Ordinarily this was home away from home, though today he would much rather have preferred to stay away for obvious reasons. Picking his way through the orderly chaos, exchanging a few words here, a few words there, as he interacted with preoccupied colleagues, he wondered how many more times he'd hang his coat on the chewed-up wooden hanger that adequately symbolized his relationship with the newspaper – used, abused and undervalued.

It was not like him to worry, however, and in a momentary upsurge of gumption, he resolved to go down fighting. Having made this courageous decision, he felt better somehow. He cursorily glanced through a stack of mail and the scribbled Post-it messages littering his desk – nothing that couldn't wait. He popped a half-eaten chocolate bar left in his out-tray and went to face the music.

Once in Rijkje's outer office, Ans van As, her personal secretary, gave him a look of mock pity, and buzzed her boss, announcing Okkels' arrival.

"Good luck," she said, rubbing it in just enough to make a noticeably nervous Okkels feel just that much more ill-at-ease.

But Okkels wouldn't dignify her insolence with a reply of any sort and forged ahead. He'd weathered many a storm in his day, and this one too would pass, he reassured himself. Besides, he'd struck out long ago not only with Ans, but every other female colleague in the office, including the coffee lady, and the All Cape Verdian women's cleaning crew, and had nothing to lose, no pretensions to keep up. His reputation in this regard was at low ebb, so to speak. Neither had he been able to keep his sex-tourism trips to Thailand secret for very long from Ans, who'd trumpeted the information around forthwith.

Ms. Dijkstra, his no-nonsense chief, tended to pull rank. She was all too aware of Okkels' lack of social skills and as always tried to keep interaction brief and business-like. Now, too, she got straight to the point.

Peering severely across her rectangular bifocals, she looked up from her cluttered desk. "Sit down!" she commanded.

He agitatedly itched his privates before meticulously closing the door behind him, hoping to avoid what was to transpire from leaking out. For Ans was a notorious gossip and considered it a particular challenge to extract the juiciest tidbits from private exchanges in the inner sanctum for wider dissemination. After all, in her own modest way, she too belonged to the sorority of newspaperwomen, with broadcasting an ingrained trait in need of constant exercising. How she did it, Okkels never knew, but no secret could ever be kept from her for very long.

Electronic bugs? They were a decided possibility, Okkels thought, considering that more often than not she was the primary source of leaks pertaining to him – the main stream, and not some minor tributary only. He still couldn't figure out how she'd come to know about his inflatable Miss Piggy doll stealthily obtained from a German mail-order house. But she did and there you had it.

"I know how it looks," Okkels began, settling himself in one of the modern ocher-colored office chairs with the self-adjusting back, hoping beyond hope to be able to bluff his way out. "But I'm on top of it, believe me."

Rijkje could not suppress an acerbic sneer – an expression, she had always felt, accommodated her facial features readily most of the time. It sort of came with the territory, and she'd have to watch it, but with Okkels in the room she put it to good use.

"Making fools out of us all is your way of 'being on top of things', as you put it?" she asked in her sonorous, smoke-cured voice. She took a drag of her cigarette and exhaled, saying, "O, c'mon Fokko, it's me you're talking to, remember!"

And suddenly, with some alarm, she blurted out, "Don't you *dare* smear that under my desk!!"

For Okkels, nervous in the face of this unpleasant confrontation, had been mining a rich vein deep within his left nasal shaft. Having assayed the mother lode he'd retrieved, he was about to deposit the poop for safekeeping when he was caught in the act.

At moments like that, he disgusted Ms. Dijkstra more than usual and it was all she could do not to toss him out on his ear.

"And what in heaven's name is that god-awful putrid smell?" she had wanted to exclaim, but knowing its source to be Okkels, didn't. Instead she lit up another cigarette, the smell of the ignited sulfur doing its deodorizing job well. That she now had two cigarettes going at the same time did not seem to matter – though it raised the awareness that she ought to cut down. She had chain-smoked as long as she could remember and despite insistence from her GP hadn't had the nerve to get chest X-rays made, fearing the worst.

"Oh, sorry, sorry," Okkels apologized, reaching down and wiping his finger on his socks, the same finger he then used to push back the bridge of his thick glasses that had slipped down his nose. It was a common diversionary tactic he used whenever he became too self-conscious – one of an arsenal of tics he'd been blessed with at no extra charge.

"No, look, really, I suckered them into it. They're supposed to be such altruistic do-gooders, but see what a stunt I let them pull. They've more or less gone and compromised themselves. And we're the ones they appear to have bamboozled. We hold the moral high ground here, don't you see!"

Rijkje's mocking smile turned into a blank stare. "Are you serious?" she asked in utter disbelief. "You, F.Fokko Okkels, are talking moral high ground? To me? With your reputation? Oh please, give me a break, will ya?"

It was all she could do to refrain from referring to him by his nickname of "the dung beetle", a term she thought more than befitting for her society page contributor.

She angrily rubbed the life out of the half-smoked cigarette she hadn't wanted in the first place. The ashtray was filled to overflowing and a stale tobacco odor impregnated her crammed office, books, papers, everything. The air-conditioning system didn't help matters, especially since it had a tendency to malfunction at peak summer temperatures, as happened to be the case. Talk about your sick-building syndrome.

"Whattaya mean?" Fokko acted wronged innocence, something he was not very good at. "I've got a faithful readership! I'm good for my fair share of circulation."

"The two are not to be confused," was Rijkje's biting reply. "Your contribution to circulation figures and your warped sense of morality. On average your moral high ground is well below sea level, like most of Holland. Besides, it's an open question whether we're gonna come out of this unscathed."

She flung an envelope at Okkels, which might've taken out an eye but for the fact that he wore glasses. "Bontekoe is threatening to sue us for libel. Seems he never even talked to you about this Herman Gnuticks fellow. Is that true? 'Cause if it is, consider yourself fired, Fokko."

"Relax, will ya," Okkels tried to sooth his irate boss. "Of course he'd deny it. But I've got a witness. Odel Wneeg will back me on this one, don't you worry."

Ms. Dijkstra gave him a penetrating look, tantamount to demanding further clarification.

"Okay, so technically I didn't get it from the horse's mouth. But Bontekoe blabbed to Odel, who passed on the news to me. It's how I get most of my info. It may not be first-hand, but it's not quite second-hand either, knowing Odel the way I do. It's sorta in-between."

"Oh, that's just peachy," Ms. Dijkstra said, throwing up her hands in exasperation. "A new concept in information-gathering, folks, something between first and second-hand. First-hand-and-a-half, shall we say? Must you flaunt every single rule of our goddamn Code of Conduct, Fokko?" Okkels was sorely trying her patience. But she'd nail him this time; go for the two-pronged attack.

"What about the Gnuticks interview?" she demanded.

"What about it?"

"I'm sure our legal department would like to have something tangible should this thing go to court."

"Court?" Okkels swallowed hard. "I don't know how to tell you this, Rijkje, but I must've forgotten to put fresh batteries in my tape recorder. There was no time to run out to get any once the interview was under way, so I'm afraid I ended up taking notes. I got 'em here somewhere..."

"What?! Never mind the damn notes. What good are they? They're not gonna stand up in court. You could've fabricated them for all anyone knows."

"I thought for sure I'd checked before going to the interview," Okkels defended himself meekly. He couldn't figure it, he really couldn't. He was always so careful, but he'd been overwrought about meeting HG close up and it must have slipped his mind. He always kept his recharger going at home and routinely switched batteries. But then he was only human, and to err was human. It was only that he was much too human, erred much too often, and usually when he could least afford it.

He made one last desperate gambit. "Not to worry, Rijkje, dear. The letter's pure bluff, and he knows it," Okkels said, though he was severely shaken by Bontekoe's move. He'd frankly not expected it. Bontekoe had been clever, very clever. He knew that Odel would snap up any disinformation pertaining to HG, hating him as he did, and Bontekoe also knew of the Wneeg-Okkels link through his acquaintance with Froukje. Okkels' caution would be short-lived, Bontekoe must've reasoned, knowing of Fokko's mistrust of him, for he'd not be able to resist spilling the beans on HG if he thought there was something to be gained by it. And that there was – a scoop the size of Keukenhof Gardens.

And so it had transpired. When HG had reacted in earnest to the Bontekoe charges, Okkels had thought no more of it. The Bontekoe disclosures must've been authentic, and he'd decided to print the story. He'd misled Dijkstra because he'd been misled by Odel whose mind buckled under jealousy from unrequited love for Froukje Vrolijk. Odel had callously been deceived by Bontekoe, undoubtedly trying to get even for the fast one Okkels had pulled on him years back – those compromising nude photographs of him and his little girls splashed all over the inside *Nexus* pages and insinuating unsavory incest.

Okkels now was trying to salvage what he could through a calculated exercise in damage control. As calmly as he could he slipped the envelope Ms. Dijkstra had so viciously flung at him under his chief editor's ashtray-cum-paperweight without having read it.

"I've got a gut feeling about this thing, Rijkje. Give 'em enough rope to hang themselves, and we'll be in a position to report the execution. Whammo! Front page photo of Gnuticks and Bontekoe dangling in the wind. I'm telling you."

"Convince me," Rijkje said in her most defiant tone, conveying to Okkels that she meant business.

He took the hint, lugged his briefcase onto his lap, snapped it open and extracted several thick folders and a dog-eared copy of *Birth in Berkeley*. "I've got it all documented. Sure, I admit that I haven't figured it all out as yet, but it's a question of time. And when I do, it'll be hot news, believe you me. Would I steer you wrong?"

He might've chosen his words more carefully, because Ms. Dijkstra had plenty on Fokko, and he'd better watch his step. Everyone on the staff was on permanent probation, he no less than the rest, more so perhaps. Rijkje was only the first tier of management keeping an eye on the staff's functioning. Above her there were several supervisory committees, apart from the Executive Board – which meant Waterreus. There wasn't all that much leeway to screw up, and this Gnuticks/Bontekoe case had the potential to make or break not only him, but the Nexus as well. And on the face of it, to the impartial outsider, things looked grim as they presently stood. Okkels'd gone and shouted accusations and counter-accusations from the rooftops, only to have the controversy backfire on him, on them.

Okkels thought a minute. Rijkje was leafing through the first of the files placed before her. She had decades of experience and Okkels could virtually see the neural computer in her head doing its assimilating cybernetics.

"How long've you been on this?" she asked, preoccupied. "This is not your run-of-the-mill stuff. Not quite up your alley either."

Okkels felt a surge of renewed confidence. "It's too big to discuss here, now," he said, gesturing, catching as he turned, Ans' sly glance through the plate-glass window, and, he surmised, an expression of disappointment on her face. Could it be she sensed the turning of the tables in his favor? It was uncanny. Bugs, no question about it. The place was bugged alright.

"Why don't we discuss it over dinner?" he proposed boldly.

"I don't think so, Fokko," came the instant reply. "It'd give me indigestion, I'm sure. This'll have to do, I'm afraid."

She was a hard-hearted woman, and none of Okkels' tactics were likely to work on her. "Let's have the essentials."

Okkels took a deep breath. The essentials. Good luck. If he'd been able to do that, he'd have felt better himself. As yet the crux of the affair eluded him, nor did he have a good clue as to how to force a break in the case.

"It's not that easy," he stalled. "But it's big. Real big."

"You're telling me," Rijkje retorted. "Big enough to sink this entire ship, with everyone on board, you, me, them," she said, with a sweeping gesture of her wizened arm, and clearly indicating the hard-working staff visible through the picture window in her office. "Tell me what you know, and let's see if we can't figure it out together, shall we?"

It sounded rather patronizing and Okkels looked for signs of ridicule on Rijkje's face. He'd never known her to be straight with him, yet she was equally incapable of being disingenuous. But when in doubt, let it slide, was his motto, and so he said, "It'll take time. There's all these files, letters, background reading, Bontekoe's fat tome..." He looked for sympathy in Ms. Dijkstra's eyes but found none.

She was tapping her pen on the desk. He was sorely trying her patience, again.

Okkels looked forlorn. "You can't expect clarity in 25 words or less."

"So take 250," Rijkje challenged, putting down the pen and adjusting the strap of her petite wristwatch.

"Not even 2,500 words would do."

"Then it's not an issue for *Courandstad Nexus*!" his chief editor barked, leaning forward.

Only slightly fazed, Okkels ventured, "Not as it stands, no. But I was trying to tell you, it's only just breaking now. Consider it an investment. The pay-off is down the line."

"Look, this is getting me nowhere fast. I need some goddam answers. Waterreus is on my back, and you know I don't like people on my back."

This was an ominous allusion to the President of the Board of the overarching Holland Publishing Group, an imposing man, both of physical stature and hierarchical standing, a man with a lion's mane of white hair who made you tremble just to be near.

"I've got to feed him solid facts or he'll chew my ass," Rijkje said in her characteristic hard-nosed style. She fumbled with a fresh pack of cigarettes, keeping her eyes on her uncooperative charge. In the lull that followed she lit up.

Okkels, easily sidetracked, couldn't help but imagine Waterreus snacking on Rijkje's ass, and he could feel the faintest revulsion, for Rijkje wasn't exactly his cup of tea, nor anyone else's as far as he could see – too much skin and bone, with the rest sinew. He himself preferred lots of succulent pink Miss Piggy flesh himself.

It was time to play his ace in the whole.

"I've arranged an exclusive interview with this HG fellow. I'll give him to you, raw. You can grill him if you like. I'm sure all will be revealed then. How's that?"

"Very generous of you, Fokko." Her tone was unmistakably saturated with irony, a rebuke Okkels-the-pachyderm conveniently chose to ignore.

"If you still feel that the story is a dead-end, I'll drop it," Okkels said, looking hopeful, as hopeful as he could manage under the circumstances, which wasn't very. He knew that Rijkje was immune to any form of contagion – anyway, he'd never been able to infect her.

Still, to his relief he could see that her curiosity was getting the better of her, and when quite abruptly she said, "Okay. Now get the hell out of here. I got work to do," he took it as an extraordinary victory and it was all he could do to suppress his elation.

He'd live to write another day. And with any luck, with Rijkje's acumen, HG would crack under her third-degree, and he, Okkels, would be vindicated, his job at the *Nexus* safe.

It was a stiff penalty, relinquishing the interview, but well worth it, considering.

Not altogether dissatisfied with his performance, Okkels repacked his briefcase and exited the office, catching Ans' blank stare as he passed. There'd be no thrills for her at his expense this day, he thought, as he reached for his crotch, raising himself erect as he scratched an itch, inadvertently letting a noxious cloud of gas escape – audibly so.

What he failed to see, however, was Ans clasp her nose betwixt thumb and index finger – a form of nonverbal communication at the passing of a "mestkever" – meant for no one in particular.

* * * * *

The affair had worked out well for Okkels, in part because the affair had worked out well for Rijkje Dijkstra, in part because the affair had worked out well for Waterreus. The *Courandstad Nexus* had published a rip-roaring interview with Herman Gnuticks, peppered and salted with a generous sprinkling of typical HG hyperbole that pickled the fancy of the Dutch reading public and boosted the paper's newsstand circulation by several percentage points, which pleased Waterreus, which pleased Dijkstra, which elated Okkels.

Ms. Dijkstra had more than lived up to her reputation as the Doyen of Dutch Journalism by engaging the Chief Scribe of the Worldwide Welcome Wagon in spellbinding repartee recorded virtually as photo-ready copy, word for word, and which behooved rereading to catch all the pregnant meaning.

Okkels was cleared of any charges of transgression of journalistic ethics, as HG, on behalf of Bontekoe and himself, had disclosed their good-natured risibility of purpose, which never was allowed to turn nasty, that is, too nasty, justifying his methods as "A little friction makes me human; a rub between the cosmic plates", and leaving it at that. HG'd strung Okkels along, only because Okkels, strung along by Odel Wneeg, had tried to string Bontekoe and himself along in turn. All had gained, none had lost, and the public was entertained, if not informed – nay, edified – in the process.

"There is not only a place in the scheme of things for rats and cockroaches, but dung beetles. And dung," according to HG. It was all a question of recyclability to avoid ecocide, which was what ultimately mattered, apparently.

"You're lucky Okkels forgot his batteries or your interview would've been on the record," Ms. Dijkstra chided HG on meeting him in a mutually convenient neutral venue the next day.

"Which reminds me," HG had said, pulling a couple of penlights from his pocket. "Borrowed these while Okkels went to the john before the interview. So trusting of him."

"Good God!" Ms. Dijkstra uttered in astonishment, her mouth dropping to the slack-jawed, doubly-unhinged position.

"Two can play at Odel's game."

Only slightly recovered from the shock, she muttered, "Game? Game? What game?"

"You really don't know, do you?"

"Know what?"

"I guess Okkels must've kept you in the dark," HG said, adding more pensively, "or perhaps he's not figured it out himself. Which is not at all unlikely in view of his IQ."

"My head's spinning, Mr. Gnuticks. Would you please elaborate?"

"Alright then, here goes. Okkels calls Harm, you know, Harm Bontekoe, with some outrageous story Odel Wneeg foisted on him. But ol' Harm, always thinking on his feet, is clever enough to realize right away what's up and that WWW could use the publicity, even if it appeared negative on the face of it. It can always be corrected later on, yielding yet more freebie publicity. Standard practice, in other words. But apart from such pragmatic considerations, Harm's got a bone to pick with Okkels from long ago. You know about that, don't you? The distasteful photographs..."

"Yes, yes, vaguely, it was before my time. Most unfortunate, I agree. Sounds like vintage Okkels. And I'm sorry. But you mean to tell me that Dr. Bontekoe did not level those charges against you? Odel fabricated them?"

"Looks that way. He's got it in for me. It's a long, sordid story but it seems Odel's in love with Froukje Vrolijk and will do anything to discredit me and my outfit. Thinks I'm brainwashing her or something. Like some Charles Manson, Jim Jones, David Koresh."

"So...lemme see..."

But Ms. Dijkstra was straining, and HG helped her out. "So Odel feeds Okkels disinformation about Bontekoe. Okkels' favorite jumbo can o' worms. He tastes headlines and naturally dives right in. Seeks corroboration from me. Meanwhile, Bontekoe had, of course, already alerted me through Jim Dash, my PR man, as to what was brewing. Me, I just went along for the ride. I figured the thing's gotta work itself out. There'll be a lesson in it for Okkels down the road, too, if and when he wakes up. Hope you understand, Ms. Dijkstra, but Fokko's been on Harm's case a long time."

"No, I understand, really. You may not believe this, but I'm actually very grateful to you. Okkels needs correction badly. Maybe this'll teach him that lesson you're talking about. It's long overdue. Lord knows I haven't been able to bring him to heel, and not for lack of trying, believe you me," a disheartened Ms. Dijkstra confessed with a sigh. Then suddenly, as the true significance of the revelation dawned, she sat up erect. "But, but, does that mean that you won't be pressing charges against the Nexus?" she asked, visibly less oppressed.

"Why should I? You're doing me an invaluable service. Book sales are way up since day before yesterday, thanks to Fokko. I only hope he's not too crushed, poor guy?"

"Oh, I sincerely hope he *is*!"

* * * * *

It had been touch-and-go, but once the initial hurdles had been cleared and the preliminaries over, the interview-proper went off well. Ms. Dijkstra covered much ground and not only had one of the topics been HG's passive knowledge of the Dutch language, but his sincere appreciation of Dutch literature, and its fair appraisal. Over the years - 20 to be exact - he'd let himself be guided by Bontekoe's recommendations after mastering the basics, grammar and vocabulary. His high school French and university general elective German had made the task considerably less harrowing than it might've otherwise been. And although he spoke with an American accent thicker than a double-chocolate malt, comprehension of the language of the Lowlands was not much of a problem, barring a few subtleties, which were serious, enough when the context was deceptively misleading. This especially applied to questions of idiom, proverbs, and prepositions which could, and did, throw him off badly on occasion. But that quaint sort of blundering only lent a certain piquant spice to any encounter, for listener and speaker alike! It even induced HG to suggest that "a contemporary Tower of Babel would be a novel attraction to any cultural amusement park."

There could be no doubt that HG had run a catch-up race, but he had made a noble effort to read a smattering of modern works as well as some of the classics – van Kooten, de Winter, Nooteboom, Mulish, 't Hart, Reve, Hermans, through Vondel, Multatuli and Couperus, through Erasmus and Spinoza, the biggies of Dutch literary tradition.

He'd especially lauded the work of Carry van Bruggen, who unlike the aforementioned Dutch authors was perhaps the least known, and yet the most significant. "More so even than Spinoza!" a genuinely excited HG had exclaimed to a not easily impressed Ms. Dijkstra, who had nurtured a special fondness for the author of *Prometheus* (1919). This work comprised matchless treatment of the antagonistic relationship between society and the citizen, or the collective and the individual.

Rijkje Dijkstra, before turning to a career in journalism, had done her master's on Van Bruggen – who herself had been a valued columnist for a prominent Dutch newspaper in her day - and she had relished a thorough-going exchange of views on this, her favorite subject – one so dear to her (otherwise callused) heart. For life had not always been kind to Ms. Dijkstra, though she bore her scars with great fortitude.

"Had HG seriously meant what he'd said?" a nonplussed Rijkje Dijkstra asked, on broaching the central theme of *Prometheus*? And the answer had been an unequivocal and resounding: "Yes!"

Asked to elaborate, HG launched into what are by now hallowed words of praise, mostly deserved, though there had been criticisms as well, also mostly deserved.

"Such iconoclasm, such sobriety, such courage! Relentlessly equating the sacred with the good with the merely useful! Reducing to a pile of rubble all those staunch, upstanding pillars of society, of the church! Making mince meat of Bossuet, Bishopric of Condom!" HG had raved, and Ms. Dijkstra had felt a spark of his passion jump the gap that separated them. And again – more like a jolt – when he quoted Van Bruggen quoting Spinoza who had already known, and exposed, the hidden agenda of society, of the church, when he revealed it to be nothing other than "to make the people obedient, not wise."

It was for this reason the church always insisted on the notion of free will, since moral responsibility requires, utterly demands it, for without it there was no one to pin sin on. A purely omnipotent god could not expect anything very lofty from mere impotent pawns, after all. And so a measure of free will was an indispensable element of Christian dogma – or as HG referred to it: godma.

And on, and on. Ms. Van Bruggen had been a literary omnivore. But that, impressive enough in itself, was not so much unique on a continent where rigorous educational standards covering all the classics was fairly commonplace – especially in her seminal period, the first half of the 20th century. Though not a professional philosopher, her ontological and epistemological credentials were impeccable, HG attested. Her starting point in matters analytical was the only one feasible: contrast. ("The only reality is contrast" and "Distinction is all.") Without contrast, there is nothing that can be said, and discourse ceases. Only when the principle of contrast is firmly established does one have the wherewithal to proceed.

Though by and large, Aristotle said many a foolish, misleading thing in his day that was to frustrate scientific progress for centuries to come, he had been astute enough on the subject of opposites. Hadn't he recorded in his *Topica*: "...for opposites are always simultaneous by nature...so that the one is not even more intelligible than the other", observing further, "that it is perhaps not possible to define some things in any other way...for in all such cases the essential being is the same as a certain relation to something, so that it is impossible to understand the one term without the other, and accordingly in the definition of the one the other too must be embraced", and finally urging us that "One ought to learn up all such points as these and use them as occasion may seem to require."

Well, now, occasion did indeed seem to require!

In this connection Van Bruggen had written:

> *If we see no contrast we cannot distinguish. Anyone who has ever given a series of lectures on books and people of different eras will have experienced that it is indispensable in treating of a subsequent era to constantly refer back to the features of a previous era – to place that previous era as it were alongside that being discussed – in order to highlight the contrastive effect; without it the average listener would accept all he heard as 'natural' and 'self-evident' thanks to his adaptive ability, which is both good and bad for people at the same time. It is the precondition of our lives and brake on our development. It makes that we can no longer distinguish ourselves within ourselves. Because, after all, we only notice things through their contrast with other things. That is why we learn through contrast.*

What was equally impressive was Ms. Van Bruggen's assimilation of relevant facts into a comprehensive theory of Historical Process, culminating in a modern age she tended to think of as being characterized by an irreversible state of enlightenment – by which she meant the full realization of the futility of choosing between Prometheus (man's benefactor), and Jupiter (man's oppressor). *Tertium non datur* or "no third choice" was possible, according to her, and here she resigned herself to Shaw's "contented pessimism" or Galsworthy's "a smiling certainty".

It is of the latter's *Inn of Tranquility* that she wrote:

There we are not served the cloying drinks of 'optimism' and 'idealism', which anaesthetize and dull the conscience of the fool into a cowardly complacency – nor the pithy potions that exhilarate the myopic into an undifferentiating frenzy – nor are the indigestible dishes served of 'scientifically proven facts', 'incontrovertible' and 'incontestable truths'. And whosoever wants to linger there must be packed at all times in order to travel onward into haze-enshrouded, unknown regions, at the first call.

Amen!

Ms. Van Bruggen's dialectics spanned the many tortuous centuries from the Middle Ages to the present, ineluctably moving in cycles from well-nigh individual-less members of tightly-knit, repressive societies, through intermediate stages of rebellion and revolution, through retrograde phases, to eventual liberation, and a modern form of (illusory) near-sovereign individuality, embedded within the liberal democratic nation-state. Though Francis Fukuyama never mentions Ms. Van Bruggen, hers would certainly have been an eye-opening contribution to his celebrated theme of "the end of history", the terminus of the historical process itself – not really surprising considering that she, like Fukuyama, was a neo-Hegelian at heart.

And not only had she anticipated Fukuyama by a mile, she had also laid the groundwork for the later analyses of people like Camille Paglia, who similarly zigzagged between selective antipodes (male/female, art/nature), mutually exclusive categories, to arrive at an integrated view of historical process as it relates to art, as opposed to Fukuyama's politics.

Writes Ms. Van Bruggen:

Dissolving the (social) distinction between 'mankind' and 'nature' restores all natural forms of expressions: (sensual) love first and foremost and as such woman. Where love is a sin, woman is despised and feared as seduction. 'The arms of woman are the nets of the devil', the medieval church fathers taught; in the Renaissance, together with love, justice is done, as we know, to women as well.

It is a theme she returns to over and over again.

But Van Bruggen's first love was and remained literature, and for that reason appealed to HG more than either Fukuyama or Paglia did – with Rijkje Dijkstra's hearty concurrence. And on that score Van Bruggen mined a mother lode of literary works for their symbolic content, ranging from Pierre Corneille to Pico della Mirandola, Thomas Morus to Anatole France, Rousseau to Shelley, Vicomte de Bonald to Bossuet, Galsworthy to Lessing, Vondel to Shaw, Milton to Machiavelli, Sheridan to de la Rochefoucauld, Petrarca to Bayle, Carlyle to Taine, Hugo to Ibsen, Comte to Scott, Hobbes to Bergson, Cervantes to Shakespeare, and on and on and on!

"But," Ms. Dijkstra had wondered aloud after the mutual admiration for Van Bruggen had been established, "where do we go from here? What's there left to say after Carry?"

And that's where WWW's central theme came into play, one that HG had come to render explicit. And Ms. Dijkstra had listened, transfixed by HG's explications which though articulate were not at all easy to grasp, because in essence "ungraspable". She thought she could follow the erudite transitions from Alexis de Tocqueville (with his constant hammering on the twin principles of liberty and equality – "the natural consequence of the Second Law of Thermodynamics in the field of politics," according to HG, in as much as any and all concentrations of energy, and thus power, are broken up and dispersed) – to Einstein's special and general theories of relativity (and thus radical relativism, with its implications for later Structuralism, Deconstruction and Postmodernity in general).

It had been a long, long road the West had traveled to rid itself of ingrained notions of cultural superiority and progress - the idea that history indeed was an inexorable march of the White Man, onward and upward, in development, complexity, intelligence. Science, philosophy, literature and art were saturated through and through with the subtle and sometimes not-so-subtle bias that western man occupied a privileged position in the world and that non-western societies should be judged by his standards. Not that this Eurocentric male viewpoint was unnatural, to the contrary, in view of the unprecedented and earthshaking achievements in the sciences racked up since the darkling Middle Ages, culminating in the myriad boons of the Industrial Revolution. But that had not made the tacit assumptions any less of a self-deceiving distortion.

In the arts, for example, as the American philosopher and art critic Arthur C. Danto had pointed out early on, the deleterious notion of progress usurped from philosophy had equally been misapplied and had consequently thwarted creativity. Instead of forever straining at the bit, people could now relax and compose, paint, sculpt what truly appealed to their discerning sense of esthetics rather than embark on forced marches imposed by sterile conception of where one ought to go next, though that terrain, too, lay open, for those so inclined, needless to say. There were simply no holds barred. The veritable regime of terror posed by modernity, with its stringent dictates, had at long last been toppled, allowing the breathing space that would automatically reinvigorate the arts, as indeed it had philosophy.

Sure, there was always the danger of retrograde trends afoot in the world. Powermongers everywhere would always find an apparently sterling cause to abuse for their own dim, unarticulated purposes, always instantly recognizable in their absolutist disguise. Non-arguments always reared their ugly head with an appeal to one-sidedness, like the universalist view on human rights, for example. But what could it possibly mean in a vacuum, isolated, and out of context? In the frigid bosom of outer space one couldn't tell a human right from Eve.

Though appearing noble, human rights enshrined in formal documents soon tend to degenerate into global arm-twisting and brow-beating, which could lead to death and destruction in the name of humanity as surely as any religious or nationalist cause ever did. And after wars and crusades big and small, who needed more of the same?

"No," HG recommended, "begin by placing human responsibility first, not last, and human rights last, not first: then balance them against animal rights, *and* plant rights *and* mineral rights for that matter, and down the road – way down the road – rights would perhaps balance rights. Not that wrongs will ever be banished, mind you – merely kept in check. Only star-struck idealists, by pushing for more end up settling for less. And there's been too many idealists already. The dawn of a brand-new era, is upon us, is always upon us," he'd aphorized on the spot.

But Ms. Van Bruggen had not lived to see it – that brand-new era – and a perceptive HG had pointed out why not: blindness, caused by flawed arguments, beginning on page 1 of the Introduction, and culminating in the very last chapter of her otherwise stunning work. Freely translating from that as yet untranslated classic *Prometheus,* HG had pointed out that its author had ruled out a separate will, without at the same time ruling out its opposite. And according to her own constant reminder (badgering, some would say), the one meant nothing without the other.

Sternly, she had written: "That the actual realization of 'Unity' inescapably implies the renunciation of the illusion of the free personal will, is self-evident.

Whether that Unity is denoted as World-idea or World-will or World-energy or World-process or even 'God' in the Spinozan sense, its recognition instantly precludes a will of one's own..."

In view of her anti-establishment, anti-ecclesiastical crusade, hers was perhaps a forgivable but no less flawed argument. It had been a long and tiresome struggle, escaping from the jaws of an oppressive Absolute, into the world of Relativism, and Van Bruggen had been a guiding light, concluding Prometheus with the inspiring words: "The readiness is all," indicating an openness and flexibility few could muster, and this so very, very early on. Van Bruggen had gone a long way, but like so many before (and after) her, she'd stopped short, tantalizingly short.

Over 500 pages on, after a rigorously argued central theme leading to the brink of enlightenment, Van Bruggen concluded: "...skepticism is presently dropped with the realization that this all is vain pretension and self-deception and that no one is exempt from taking sides, even though reason teaches him the absurdity of taking sides. The bare functionality and utter relativity is seen of the dichotomy between Justice and Injustice, Light and Darkness, and nevertheless it is accepted, because it must be accepted."

Indefatigably she went on, reiterating that in a slow evolutionary process man comes around to seeing the inevitability of having to take sides in life:

> Should we struggle for Prometheus-Satan against Jupiter-Iahveh? No, let us storm no heavens, no citadels, no Bastilles, because Prometheus may not win, we may not win with Prometheus. Corruption burgeons in triumph, tyranny in power, self-affirmation in the dogmatic 'yes'...
> And so then that truth, which history, as we have shown from the outset, so clearly and incessantly demonstrates, but which mankind could not see, before its eyes literally were opened, (that truth) has found its expression. And what Plato recommended, what Ibsen asserts...what Voltaire offers as solution...that now too is the reply of the converted skeptic, who has relinquished the fiction, the pretension of not taking sides, and feels compelled to choose, because irresistibly wanting to choose...Thus man accepts and fulfills his own folly, which he knows to be folly, as his fair share.
> And as such the last word in the Prometheus problem appears to have been said...and yet it is not enough...he must be

'Prometheus', knowing that he must first be 'Orestes' and thereafter 'Jupiter' shall be, because of his inextricable fate, and that moreover it serves no purpose, that all together it is but a moment in the self-unfolding of the Absolute, which has itself as purpose, nothing but one single revolution of a wheel, that has no other purpose than to turn eternally. All his 'ideals' (are) fuel for an unquenchable fire that has no other purpose than to burn, weight in a scale that shall never tip and of which he knows that it shall never tip. 'Jupiter' is in the one scale and 'Prometheus' in the other, for all eternity - divine self-unfoldment mirrored in their struggle, the Absolute aimlessness...

All this had been quoted *in extenso* in HG's essay on *What Buddha Knew*, a copy of which had been gifted to Ms. Dijkstra, and which she had carefully read before the interview, an interview which burst all natural bounds in her zeal to get to the bottom of HG's message. To her chagrin, however, HG had first seen fit to undermine the central thesis of Ms. Van Bruggen's *Prometheus* by pointing out her implicit bias against free will and in favor of determinism. This was painfully apparent from statements such as, "Not human purpose but universal necessity is at work here as elsewhere." And "...that human beings are nothing but creative instruments, and that they are often destined to fulfill a task, which they themselves do not realize and for the consequences of which they (like Melachton) instantly recoil."

"Conduitism" was the self-explanatory term HG had coined to reflect that widespread – Cartesian – attitude, otherwise known as "immanence". To HG it was as repugnant as any of the forms of transcendentalism that plague (wo)mankind, to this very day.

It is mainly on her own that Van Bruggen struggled to free herself from the yoke of tradition and to look afresh upon the world, and for that she deserved great credit, HG had eulogized, and Ms. Dijkstra had nearly wept. All that Existentialist and later Postmodern hype ("meta-twaddle" according to one British critic) had been spared her. Van Bruggen, contrary to her own urging had opted for determinism rather than free will, an otherwise unforgivable mistake for someone of her logical rigor. It demonstrated better than anything that despite her great alacrity, she was a captive of Aristotelian two-valued "either/or" logic, and oblivious to the liberating realization that multi-valued "neither/nor" logic is required as antidote against dogma – dogma of any sort, but especially dogma with bite.

"Ultimately, she too followed the countless multitudes down the ages straight across the most treacherous precipice of all into that vast yawning chasm where classical western two-valued logic will mercilessly beckon the heedless like so many hypnotized lemmings. Yet the remedy is so simple, it's child's play," HG had summarized. "The enlightened view (the no-view view) – not itself a view – demands the enlightened choice (the no-choice choice) – not itself a choice. Stated simply, the solution Ms. Van Bruggen sought reads: 'not free will or determinism, nor neither, nor both, nor different from neither or both.'"

And here HG had referred Ms. Dijkstra to T.R.V. Murti's impassioned defense of the no-view view as not itself being a view; as also his cogent insight, an urgent plea almost, that it does not lead to Nihilism: "As we have pointed out before, the 'no-doctrine-about-the-real'...is confounded with the 'no-reality' doctrine."

Murti goes on to caution: "This may appear to men accustomed to assess things with the norm of the empirical as non-existent; but it is not non-existent in itself. The objection assumes that the spatio-temporal world perceived by the senses is real, and that that alone is real." Murti reminds the reader that this issue already plagued the Ancients long ago, and he quotes from Sanskrit texts to this effect.

"Difficult as it may seem to grasp, sufficient practice finally can lead to a shattering moment of insight which once and for all wipes away all confusion in this regard. Practice, in other words, does make perfect. No more agonizing whether the world is real or not: the world is not real or unreal, nor neither, nor both, nor different from neither or both. There is no Relative or Absolute (non-Relative), nor neither, nor both, nor different from neither or both. Ditto for the notion of Self, or no-Self that had plagued mankind from the very dawn of history – and being in fact the constitutive element of the very notion of time, and thus of history!" HG had held forth, concluding with a smile, "Hope you're not Zen-O-Phobic, Ms. Dijkstra, 'cause 'Only when one is left *no* leg to stand on, can one stand with both feet squarely on the ground!' as one of Onyx's Gin-Zen Rent-A-Rishi's once put it."

It was a chain of reasoning HG was to invoke whenever the need arose, and judging by its application, the need arose often. His approach was honed to cut through extraneous machinations of mind and had an astounding power of persuasion, as Ms. Dijkstra discovered, when towards the end of her stimulating encounter with HG she began to experience bright flashes of energy discharging in her head that relieved an unnatural tension in her brain, building till she could stand it no more and radiating to all her extremities.

Momentarily, she thought she would suffer a seizure, but after peaking, the tingling sensation gradually diminished to a tolerable flux, trailing into a sweet afterglow. In all her long years in the business she'd never known such a thing and looked with wonderment upon the man who had apparently induced this phenomenon in her. She could never be accused of being an intellectual weakling, a daydreamer capable of being easily swayed by one of superior alloy. And she'd come away cleansed, invigorated, enthralled as she'd been carried to the brink of what could only be described as "psychophysical orgasm". And at her age at that!

Whereas her mentor, Carry van Bruggen, had led her to insights into a mechanism that dissatisfactorily dissolved its constituent elements into an indistinct homogeneity, an abstract Unity, HG pointed the way beyond, beyond this vague and nebulous monolith of a suspectly cerebral Ideal, to a fresh and bright new world that has been the siren song of philosophy and religion throughout the ages. Nothing less! For in the final analysis that was the sober culmination of (wo)man's quest, which by its very nature was no quest at all.

And that now had been brought within reach, suddenly, unexpectedly.

*****

FIVE

This was the state of affairs on the recent arrival of the WWW troupe described in the opening *Courandstad Nexus* article written by F.Fokko Okkels.

Meanwhile, HG's WWW had made a lasting impact on the Dutch scene through a network of cells distributed throughout the land. Petty criticasters referred to it as "an irreversible metastasis, a cancer infecting the very fiber and body politic of the nation", but that was mostly sour grapes, 'cause few, if any, wielded such influence as HG did. He made waves in the placid little Dutch pond, not just ripples, which was unforgivable. Not that they didn't like waves, it's just that they preferred to make them, not see them or rather feel them being made by some upstart outsider.

And now HG's work, under the adapted Dutch title *Krijg geen beroerte* lay fresh and crisp in all major book shops in Holland, as he made his way from sales point to sales point in Jill Oppy's Succu-Bus, kept on standby while her Incu-Bus had its phuel philter replaced.

Surrounded by stacks of his new book and life-size cardboard cutouts of himself, HG, at prearranged venues throughout the Netherlands, gave his autograph to those who so desired. It was part of a well-oiled promotional book tour organized by his own people in collaboration with his Dutch publishers. His entire gang was involved in one capacity or another, each fulfilling a special duty in focusing public attention on the literary efforts of their leader. It was a formula that always drew vast crowds without fail; a tried-and-tested approach that was not only fun for customers, but for the WWW participants themselves who visibly delighted in their work.

It was standard practice for WWW's rock band, for example, to begin their warm-up act by playing catchy and precise amplified rhythms atop a flatbed truck, starting a few blocks away and drawing throngs (like some modern-day Pied Piper) towards the bookstore singled out for the occasion. In Holland this approach fit smoothly into established practice, since Dutch commerce had long ago discovered the advantages of employing street fairs of various sorts and description to drum up business. Especially with the North Sea Jazz Festival in full swing, the residents of Holland's major cities were primed for a good time – the Hague's populace moreover boosted by a horde of jazz fans in town for the duration, hailing from as far afield as Italy, Russia and, of course, the US of A. It was a truly international affair, and it was an astute publicity team that insured that there were always English, French, Spanish and German-language editions of all the many HG publications on hand as well.

Thus it was that a festive procession headed by WWW's rock musicians and their scantily but outrageously clad lead vocalist – Harpy (& the Herpes) – snaked through a major Hague shopping street on route to one of Holland's best known book stores, part of a successful nationwide chain, Weijers BV.

Meanwhile, HG arrived in a stretch limo, preceded by Sockeye Savage and the rest of the gang, clearing a path as they went – this to the rousing cries of fans vying for HG's attention and that of his entourage. Kay Dance and her girls in particular drew shouts and cat-calls as they gyrated to a kind of *a cappella* hum they'd polished into the group's signature tune.

As the throng pushed and shoved and made its way to the book stand where HG was to accommodate the autograph-seekers, the store's worried manager, a fastidious, somewhat gaunt man sporting a moustache and bow tie, led the way, desperately appealing for calm. That sales would boom was self-evident to him, but whether his store would survive the mayhem was quite another question, as here and there carefully stacked displays were toppled by the unmanageable throng keen to get a closer look. That he had lived to see the day that megastar status generally reserved for rock musicians would be bestowed on scribents was something that he could still not quite fathom, and he wasn't at all sure that he applauded the development. Several of the cardboard cutouts of HG, looking extraordinarily life-like, were gingerly carted off by souvenir-hunters, unchallenged by any of the security people the store had on hand for the occasion. But that was the least of his worries. Dire visions surfaced of scuffed covers, torn title pages, and dog-ears, not to mention soaring pilferage rates – why with all those damn foreigners in town.

Nervous and distrustful, the manager eyed a crowd he did not recognize as his customary clientele.

But his concerns were unjustified. Sales were brisk, brisk indeed. Never in Weijers' long history did so many books change hands in such a short time - against legal tender! And not only HG's latest, but also numerous of his older (as yet untranslated) titles. There was a 'reading frenzy' in the air that stimulated the appetites of the hungry multitudes, and which for the moment anyway led to book sales like never before. It was as if literacy had been rediscovered, and people realized afresh what cultivation of the mind meant. Of course, WWW's innovative video clips broadcast on local TV channels, virtual saturation coverage over a 2-week period preceding the visit, had made a considerable impact, on youthful readers especially; many also had followed the newspaper and magazine interviews, part of the media blitz planned by Jim Dash and his people, and HG's many juicy anecdotes had obviously excited sensibilities across a wide spectrum.

Those who contended that the novel was dead, were wrong, dead wrong.

HG had harvested great appreciation with his tale of how he'd come to eventually link up with his Dutch publishers after a nearly disastrous first encounter. It seems that when years ago he'd first called the gay couple who also ran their own retail outlet, a centuries-old renowned bookshop in Amsterdam, they had been rather curt. Though HG had been calling long-distance, the response had been a chary, "I'm counting my money right now, please call back another time."

HG, a difficult man to catch off guard, had had a paroxysmal fit of laughter and somehow this had caught the publisher's attention. Barely managing to compose himself, HG assured him that with a little luck they'd make a lot more money, much more than they were counting just then.

The teeming crowd in the bookstore was now proving his point. And his Dutch publishers' time and effort were being amply rewarded; would be even more amply rewarded as second and third printing runs were more than likely. It was only unfortunate that HG could be in only one place at a time, and even so could only place one autograph at a time. Though he worked like a dog, diligently pushing his pen as fast as he was able, the turnover rate could never exceed a book or so a minute, at the most. Why, with any sort of dedication in legible script, sales were necessarily restricted. Not that everyone insisted on a personal autograph for numerous books were sold without; some also with substitute signatures by anyone of the gang that potential buyers could corner.

Even Froukje Vrolijk, on hand for the Weijers stint, was joining in the act, placing her own signature on behalf of HG – with express customer approval, of course. It was a timely promotional venture for Froukje, and her association with the Worldwide Welcome Wagon promised to pay off handsomely. Her own upcoming work of nonfiction was nearly ready; the date of release they were shooting for: the gift-giving holiday season at year's end, Santa Claus ("sinterklaas") and Christmas ("Kerst"). With a little luck she might even be nominated for the Noel Prize for Literature, a biennial end-of-the-year affair sponsored by Holland's powerful Association of Bookstallers & Kiosketeers.

The Dutch Feminists Movement, with whom Froukje had closely collaborated on the exposé, had commissioned her to focus much needed attention on the victims of white slavery in Holland. And Froukje, with her vast experience in matters meretricious (she'd unofficially been crowned Queen Meretrix I), had undertaken to have these unfortunate women who flooded into Amsterdam's Red Light district from all over Eastern Europe, tell their own tales of woe, first-hand. Hence the book's ambiguous title: *In the Witness' Box*.

Where this work would be unique, its proud publishers had promised, was in its stratified socio-demographic analysis, focusing equally on prostitute and client. Concerned community leaders, including pertinent politicians (Justice, Home Affairs, Housing, Public Health) who had been given abstracts in advance, already shuddered in anticipation of the potential fallout, likely to result from the cogent two-track top-down, bottoms-up approach championed by Froukje, and said to shed new light on these traditional ills, souring relations between the sexes from the dawn of history.

And indeed a not insignificant percentage of autograph-hunters were avid Vrolijk-fans that most inauspicious of days.

Inauspicious, for it was while madness was at its peak that Sockeye Savage's raw voice could be heard to thunder across the bookstore din: "Hit the deck! He's got a gun!"

This was instantly followed by two firecracker crisp shots. But miraculously, Sockeye, saved HG in the nick of time, crashing to the floor and scrambling to safety behind a pile of boxes filled with virginal copies of *Guide for the Apoplexed*, now serving a serendipity purpose as safety shield.

Hysterical screams shredded the air and people fled the shop in blind panic; a wild stampede ensued in every direction, customers pouring out into the streets from all available exits. Hardly a display was left standing as bodies tumbled over each other trying to get out of harm's way. It was a miracle that no one was hurt, barring some minor cuts and bruises.

As quickly as the trouble had begun, it was over. And there, on the floor lay the lanky figure of a man dressed in black, face pushed into the wall-to-wall coir carpet – strewn with books, bags and footwear – hands already cuffed behind his back.

Three of Savage's men roughly hoisted the culprit to his feet and swung him around to face his intended victim, HG, who had struggled back to his feet.

"Odel! You?!" Froukje Vrolijk gasped.

But Odel Wneeg was unable, unwilling to speak, the look of agony plain to see on his face, one eye badly swollen. Without further ado, he was escorted out of the bookstore past the rubbernecking crowd.

Wailing sirens could already be heard in the distance and within minutes a Hague police VW Rabbit sped off, carrying Odel to his temporary new home at HQ a few blocks away.

In the ensuing silence, Sockeye fingered the cardboard cutout that had flanked HG before the shooting. Two neat bullet holes ventilated HG's image, one in the chest, one in the head.

"Nine millimeter," was all Jerry Can said to his colleague, in his matter-of-fact voice, eliciting a wan smile from HG.

"In one ear and out the other," added Sockeye, pointing out that the opposite cutout - between which HG had stood - made a near-identical twin.

* * * * *

COURANDSTAD NEXUS

Herman Gnuticks barely escapes assassination attempt; Acute slant to obtuse triangle

(by F.Fokko Okkels)

The Hague, July 8, 2000 - Two shots intended to rob WWW's Herman Gnuticks of his life yesterday just barely missed their target. Only swift action on the part of his personal bodyguard averted a tragedy that would have plunged the entire group into deep crisis. They were Wild West scenes indeed – unknown in our country – which transpired in one of the Hague's most reputable book shops.

During what had been an otherwise highly successful public relations event, abrupt gunshots sowed panic among an unsuspecting crowd of fans, there to lay their hands on a copy of HG's latest book. Said the noticeably upset store manager: "I thought such things only happened in second-rate novels, which we scrupulously banish from our shelves as a matter of strictest company policy!"

Though it is too early to tell, it looks as though the motive for the shooting is nothing but a common *crime-passionel*.

Witnesses have identified the would-be assassin as one O.W., long-time acquaintance of F.V., herself a close associate of WWW's Herman Gnuticks, and present during the incident.

HG, unwilling to comment on the spectacular affair, stated in his characteristically droll manner, "I've heard of a warm welcome, but this is ridiculous. First that infamous Dallas book depository, now a bookstore in the Hague. What is it with such places?"

F.V., famous "encounter counselor" and former Amsterdam lady of the night, wished to say only that she was shocked to the core. "I knew O.W. was in love with me but never dreamt he'd go this far." She said she felt very bad about having posed such a threat to HG's safety while on book tour in the Netherlands. "I hope he'll be able to forgive me for being so irresistible," she added remorsefully. "I solemnly pledge to do what I can to be more repulsive from here on out."

In a first reaction, handcuffed from the back of the police car that spirited him away, an unrepentant O.W. is reported to have said that his only regret was that his bomb threat had failed to keep HG off Dutch soil in the first place!

And so another little piece of the puzzle falls into place, folks.

Though O.W. will be held incommunicado for thrice 24 hours – as routine police procedure demands – before being arraigned, eager readers of *Courandstad Nexus* can rest assured that they will get the assailant's full story at the earliest opportunity, or my name ain't F.Fokko Okkels.

* * * * *

SIX

It was a brand-new, and needless to say, controversial concept in Dutch TV talk shows. Everyone, including host, guests and audience, buck naked! Even camera crew, producer, director, stark to the bone! Though lights were suitably dimmed and the set tastefully designed, nothing could hide the bare facts of life.

The idea behind the new format was as simple as it was effective, as the name of the show revealed, *The Naked Truth*. Its intention was to delve deeper into the very soul and psyche of the guests interviewed, with a considerable measure of frank and free audience participation welcomed, expected, demanded even. Society, it was felt by the broadcasting company, needed to be stripped, literally and figuratively, of its myriad taboos, deceits and subterfuges. A no-holds barred approach right before the eyes of the nation, a pure, wholesome product, unadulterated, fresh and refreshing.

The new formula had yielded such exciting results during trial pilots that the broadcasting company had managed to stretch the relatively progressive Dutch censorship laws to breaking point – the main proviso being that the program be aired well after prime time so as not to unnecessarily shock youthful viewers. High expectations had panned out and ratings sky-rocketed, revealing in the bargain not only that people watched the show in their hundreds of thousands, but that a sizable percentage did so themselves stripped to the core.

And not only had the show won wide critical acclaim throughout Holland, but from the Flemish-speaking Belgian viewers as well. It was even rumored that there was a possibility of late-night screening on daring French and German networks – with customary subtitling and/or dubbing of course.

Still it was a somewhat daunting prospect to have your "nose powdered", so to speak, and pancake applied where one would normally never imagine to, in an attempt to ward off studio-light glare. Usual coiffeur duties were augmented by pubic hair dressing, with optional application of labial lipstick for the fashion-conscious fairer sex. Numerous comparable adaptations had to be innovated, but that was a small price to pay for the exciting results.

In the end, HG, handsomely made up, strode confidently on stage after the extravagantly flattering introduction by the show's flamboyant host, Freek Vreeken, an average physical specimen himself, but with a panel-side manner that made him one of Holland's premier TV personalities. He had been married and divorced no less than six times, lastly only a few months back, yet he was still considered quite a catch by most Dutch females (and some males as well), and regularly got bags and bags of fan mail.

Minutes earlier there had been the predictable ooo-ing and aaah-ing as Freek had come on stage in his typical audacious swagger, flirtatiously winking at a string of nubile young things in the front row, who screeched and squealed, squirming in their seats.

After graciously welcoming HG and praising his robust physique, Vreeken seated his guest and offered him the drink of his choice, and a snack, meanwhile engaging in some noncommittal small-talk before the fireworks began in earnest.

"How's the missus?" asked Freek.

"Just fine, thanks."

"And the kid?"

"Eric? Heavily into drugs."

"You don't say! Cocaine, crack, XTC?"

"Oh, no-no-no, nothing like that. "He's in wholesale pharmaceuticals. An aspiring medicine man."

"I see. That kind of drugs, eh?"

"Sorry if I gave you a scare."

"Only goes to show, I guess, that language is alive and kicking."

"Certainly is. Right in the teeth."

As was normal procedure, the audience then got first shot at the guest, by way of getting acquainted, breaking the ice, and it was a bespectacled young man with a jovial smile set on a pair of jowls the size of a small donkey who had the courage to raise himself upright, overcoming his natural modesty.

"What do you think of our small country, Mr. Gnuticks? Any first impressions?" he asked, his penis dangling insolently as he spoke, affirming the latest broadcasting adage since the appearance of the show that "a bird in the bush is worth ten on the air."

"I like it, I like it. Holland, I mean. Really, I'm not kidding," HG stressed when he met an expression of disbelief from his host. It's not my first visit, as some of you may know, so I'm already a bit accustomed to your Dutch ways. Besides, Holland has enjoyed a wonderful reputation for its tolerance and hospitality throughout the ages, as is commonly known. Just think of all the skeptics, heretics and anarchists who found refuge here over the centuries: René Descartes, Pierre Bayle, John Locke to mention but a few. Such a den of iniquity your country was, and is! It's a wonder you've managed to survive. But you have, have thrived, I dare say. And I see it reflected here today in this very show,

The Naked Truth, which is representative of your nation's openness, its receptivity to new ideas and lifestyles."

This was only warm-up talk, and HG, not quite ready to wax too seriously at this early stage, turned from his host back to the questioner and while shifting uncomfortably in his chair, crossing his legs, in a mock effort to cover his thingamajig, quipped, "Openness and transparency is all good and well. But why this table must have a glass top, I really don't understand!"

After the expected laughter, he continued, "No, but talk about first impressions, your Dutch names are a howl sometimes. I've been hounded by a journalist named F.Fokko Okkels, familiar to you all I'm sure, and now I'm the guest of a Freak."

"That's pronounced 'frake', not 'freak'!" the TV host corrected HG. "Short for Frederick."

"Of course, I beg your pardon, but since I was asked, it does take some getting used to, you know."

"And vice versa," Vreeken retaliated. "I'm reminded of the time my second wife and I were having a drink in a San Francisco waterfront bar on our honeymoon to America many years ago. Or was it my third wife? I forget. Anyway, her gin fizz was quite flat, and Lena, or was it Rosy, I don't remember, no, Lena, yes, Lena complained to the bartender, 'There's no prik in my drink!' To which the guy replied, 'Oh, we can soon fix that, lady,' and he pretended to unzip!"

Loud laughter, and a spattering of applause from the audience, Vreeken in an aside informing HG that "prik" in Dutch means carbonation, and not what its English homonym might suggest.

"Any other questions?" Freek invited.

"How did you first get interested in philosophy, Herman?" an elderly woman asked. "My granddaughter and I would be very interested to know," she said, gesturing to the frail teenager seated next to her. "Janneke is thinking of reading philosophy at Leiden University next year. We're so proud of her," the woman beamed. "She'll be the first, since we're mostly a family of cheese merchants, you see."

"Why yes. It would be quite a switch. And it's a funny thing you should mention that, 'cause my own folks were plum farmers," HG replied, "and they weren't too pleased, frankly, when I changed my major from hands-on engineering to hands-off philosophy. But as it turned out I had practically zero aptitude for things like tensile strength and torque, and quite a bit of impedance to the current fad in electronics, if you know what I mean. So what happened is that to chalk up general elective units in college, I took a History of Philosophy class, just for the hell of it. And it opened new vistas of opportunity for me. Or I wouldn't have been here today, now would I?"

HG paused, swigged his OJ, gobbled down an olive. He continued, "I remember the very first week we had an oral quiz and I was called on to answer a question about the battle of wits between the British Empiricists and the Continental Rationalists. 'Who was the prophet of Königsberg?' our prof had asked. 'Anyone? You, Mr. ...ah...Gnuticks. Won't you tell us?' I racked my brain for a moment and highly embarrassed at failing so early on in the semester, answered: 'I can't.' 'Absolutely correct,' the prof said to my surprise. 'I. Kant, Immanuel Kant, was indeed referred to as the prophet of Königsberg. A-plus, Mr. Gnuticks. Well done.'"

Chuckles, followed by a ripple of polite laughter.

Undaunted, HG proceeded, "Well now, that initial success at unwittingly bluffing my way through is what in part made me decide to try to continue my lucky streak. And it's stood me in good stead ever since, I mean bluffing my way through, not philosophy per se, which I'm not much good at. It was later that I switched from the History of Philosophy to the Philosophy of History. All this was in the '60s you understand, and nowadays of course, in this post-historic age, the philosophy of history is itself history..."

When the outburst of mirthful derision subsided, HG added, "For what is history but an appendage we each drag along, like a snake does the skin it sloughs off?"

"While we're on the subject," Freek interrupted, "could you explain in layman's terms your view on Radical Relativity, which I believe is related to this whole contentious issue of postmodernity?"

HG's forehead furrowed as he considered an appropriate avenue of approach.

"Imagine, if you would, the sturdy foundation on which a skyscraper is to be built. Though we all know that such skyscrapers can and have been built, and those that have by and large still stand, we also know that their foundations are embedded in the earth's crust, which is part of a system of shifting tectonic plates floating on a molten metallic core. The earth itself, of course, is flying in orbit round the sun, which is part of a galaxy moving in space, which is part of an ever-expanding universe. Dizzying enough for you," HG asked, attuned to his host's body language – a white-knuckled Freek clamping on to the table top for dear life.

"As any planetary show will inform you, we're hurtling through space at a terrific speed, yet in daily life you notice nothing of this violent motion. The ground under our feet feels as rock-solid as the skyscraper's foundation seems to be. Ours is a platform in space from which to operate, from whence we relate to everything around. And remember if you will that to relate is to know and to know is to relate. There simply is no other way."

HG took another sip to lubricate his throat. "Einstein was one of the first to rigorously enforce the strictures of relativity in physics. The other sciences have since followed suit. We've come a long way from old Ptolemy who said that the earth was the center of the universe, with its absolutist bias. Fifteen hundred years later, Copernicus upset the apple cart when he claimed that the earth rotated round the sun, rudely pushing us from center stage, and seemingly condemning us to subordinate cosmic status, with all its dire consequences for the theology of the day. In fact, it's hardly been a decade since the Vatican rehabilitated Galileo, as you may recall. To the relief of the popes, however, it was modern astronomy that reinstated us to a dubious primacy by showing that both Ptolemy and Copernicus were right, but only in a way. In an expanding four-dimensional universe, which moreover may have had a finite beginning in time, and thus required a god, the stars are moving away from each observer, no matter where he, she or it happens to be. No outpost is remote enough or it is at the heart of where the action is! A sobering thought, implying as it does that all knowledge claims ultimately refer back to the individual knower. It is here that philosophy and science nicely corroborate each other."

"So where does postmodernity come in?" Freek queried, a bit dazed by the tour de force undertaken by his studio guest so early on. You could hear a pin drop and he wasn't sure whether his audience was enraptured or just plain overwhelmed.

Freek saw it as his job to keep HG honest and to that end didn't mind using heavy-handed tactics.

"Same difference, really," HG obliged. "Radical Relativity equals postmodernity when applied in the social sciences, anthropology, linguistics, the arts, you name it. There is just no solid, that is to say, absolute, place or standard of reference to be found anywhere with which to conduct any sort of inquiry, because all frames of reference are relative. Mind you, not Zero Ground, but Ground Zero. For the longest time man assumed that his particular vantage point was somehow privileged, and all conclusions were tacitly derived with reference to prevailing standards, which in practice generally meant Caucasian, Christian, white upper-class male. Non-western cultures were tacitly assumed to be somehow second-rate, justifying racism and colonialism, neo-colonialism and cultural imperialism. And it is only in the last hundred years or so that people have begun to wriggle free of such ingrained and crippling prejudices. It's all part of that more general shift towards the cult of individuality we see worldwide."

"Ah yes, the *Nexus* interview. The collective versus the individual. Now we're on the same wavelength. So that's what all the fuss is about?" Freek asked.

"*My Life in a Nutshell; autobiography of a worm*, I can heartily recommend that illuminating volume in the *Popular Illustrated WWW Educational Series*. It reveals all. Unfortunately it has not yet been translated into Dutch."

"Oh, but we can soon remedy that," Freek said, looking straight into the camera and pontificating: "A word to the wise publisher who may be watching!"

And to the audience: "So when you get home tonight, throw away your copies of Foucault, Lacan, Barthes, Levi-Strauss, Lyotard, Ellul and their cronies..."

"I wouldn't go as far as to do that," HG interrupted, "It would be a perferct waste of money." Timing being his secret, he paused just long enough, then added nonchalantly, "A garage sale on the other hand, to recoup some of your losses..."

An awkward backdrafting guffaw could be heard, like that of a tormented mule, and HG peered into the audience against the bright lights to identify his discerning fan. He flashed him the 'thumbs-up' sign, then went on, "How, I often wonder, are future generations to denote their own brand of modernity, Freek?"

"I give up? How?" the TV host batted back the question.

"I don't know, really, without reverting to some sort of mathematical system of subscripts that will cover the next few hundred thousand years or so. I haven't found an elegant solution yet, nor to my knowledge has anyone else. It would seem unreasonable to saddle up future generations with our present idle pretensions regarding postmodern, post-historic societies. And one can stretch the prefixes post-, postneo- and neopostneo- just so far, if you get my drift. Perhaps you ought to hold a contest, invite suggestions. What we need to insure is a contemporary modernity for everyone, now and in the centuries ahead. A modernity in every pot, so to speak."

"Preposterous!" Freek exclaimed. "Or," bethinking himself, "should I say, postposterous!"

"Well, if not for us, do it for neo-posterity's sake," HG joined in the fun.

"Enough already! I accept your challenge. We'll get to work on it right away. Seems quite the fashionable postmodern thing to do, come to think of it!"

"There you go!" HG complimented his host's good sportsmanship.

Freek then yelled unceremoniously to his producer off stage, "Got that, Wim? Let's get cracking on it, team. Why not start by passing out cards to these folks, gauge their opinion?"

It was the sort of spontaneity Freek had become known and loved for, and he harvested a deserved round of applause which he graciously accepted by rising and wiggling his willy at his fans. He bowed to the thunderous applause that followed, shouting from underneath his armpit as his face dipped from view, "Bravo! Bravo!!"

When he retook his seat, his cheeks a bit flushed from the exertion, HG hinted, "I hope to hear the outcome of your little poll."

"Of course, of course. Besides," Freek said, genuinely excited about the idea, "it's quite an optimistic thought, implying as it does a certain longevity for planet Earth. It suggests an open-ended future instead of the dismal *fin de siecle* doom and gloom of the last decade. Gosh! How lovely it was to peer across the rim of the new millennium earlier this year, eh?"

"You said it," HG concurred.

"So what's down the road?"

"More Radical Relativity, I'm afraid. As a matter of fact the plural name of your country, the Netherlands, reflects this very well – one Netherland each for every man, woman and child, yet a fully integrated, firmly united Netherlands of which you can properly be proud."

"Along the lines of Pierre Nora's 'Les Frances', you mean?

"Pierre who?"

"Hahaha, very funny!"

"May I just lodge a disclaimer here, Freek, for the benefit of all those critics who're bound to assail me for even broaching postmodernity, widely considered to be such a vile and reprehensible trend? Just for the record let me say that I do not now, nor have I ever subscribed to it. Attempting to comprehend a notion, after all, is not the same thing as advocating it. And the mere fact that I refer to postmodernity from time to time should not be taken as an endorsement in any way, shape or form. I hope that's loud and clear?"

"Certainly is."

"Perhaps I may just add that by his own standards, the postmodernist is rather a fictitious species. 'Why?' I hear you ask. Well, because postmodernity rejects even the most evanescent essence of in-dividuality," he said, deliberately chopping the word individuality in two.

"Instead, postmodernists like to refer to an elusive sort of 'di-viduality', or rather 'multi-viduality'. What I've referred to as 'multuality', if you like, another one of those neopostneologisms of mine signifying the fluid state of awareness of that constantly shifting network of interrelationships giving rise to one's self-reflective sense of identity, bobbing and weaving, flitting and fleeting on the knife-edge of existence...phew!"

Demonstratively he took a deep breath. "No postmodernist worth his salt will stoop to tag such an undefinable being, for to define is to freeze, and to freeze is to kill this rarest of species so susceptible to hypothermia."

"So what you're saying is that the postmodernist who claims to be a postmodernist is by definition no postmodernist at all?"

"You got it."

"Boy, that's a relief," Freek exclaimed, theatrically wiping his brow. "You can sleep peacefully tonight, folks. No postmodernist under your bed. Hopefully none in the closet either! And don't forget, you heard it first on *The Naked Truth*. From none other than Sir...Herman...Gnuticks!"

Loud applause.

"No, but seriously, we'd do well here to recognize a variation of the old trap of having to choose between a self and no-self. This time we are offered many selves, which is just as short-sighted. Because then we are stuck with a disconnected manifold that bears no satisfactory relation to a central self."

"Why not?" Freek querried.

"Cause what you'd get is a central self of subordinate status – a precariously integrated self, having fleeting existence – assuring us of a compounded condition it could not, by definition, be witness to."

"Still, there's no preempting critics, HG, as you ought to know better than anyone. They're gonna make mince meat out of you anyway. Can't deny them their due. Once a bloodsucker always a bloodsucker."

And to the camera, "Hi Leo. No, I'm not talking about you, honest."

HG smiled at the obvious reference to Freek's most notorious nemesis, Leo de Leeuw, the man whose singular source of glee in life it was to berate the amiable TV host after every performance. The name had cropped up several times during the preliminaries and HG had duly registered the mood of vendetta that pervaded the air when it did.

"Talking about leeches," HG said, "you know the fable of the bunny and the snake, don't you?"

"The bunny and the snake? No. How's it go?"

"Well, this bunny meets a snake and asks the snake to please tell it what it looks like 'cause it has no clear image of itself, and it would so like to figure out who it is. The snake obliges, grazing the bunny with its tongue. 'You are warm and soft. You have long ears, and a cute little cottontail. I know! You're a bunny!' the snake surmised. 'But won't you tell me who I am,' the snake asked in return. And the bunny, eager to return the favor, begins to feel the snake with its paws. 'You're cold and slimy. You have no ears. Your tongue is forked. I know, I know! You're a critic!'"

Uproarious laughter, and even some stamping of feet, which prompted Freek to intervene.

"I'm afraid you'll pay dearly for that one, HG m'boy. No snake…ah, critic will take that lying down."

"I'm afraid you're right. But then there's a place in the scheme of things for critics, too, don't you think?"

Pleased at having posed a question that had got them off on the right foot, the old lady with the sagging tits and wrinkled tummy sat down to a flurry of appreciative applause, her granddaughter whispering something to her and lovingly stroking her shoulder.

"Next?" the host invited generously as if HG were on offer.

"Oh," HG interjected, "before moving on, I had wanted to dissuade that young lady over there from majoring in philosophy, unless she doesn't mind starving for a living. Better learn a trade, sweetheart, like bricklaying or something," he said caustically, signaling the other questioner already standing, to go ahead.

When the laughter had subsided, a bespectacled and rather solemn-looking young man, hands clasped behind his back, asked, "What I wanted to know, sir, is what your hobbies are, if any?"

"Well, I love to curl up and write a good book," HG said jokingly. "No, but seriously, picture frames. Collecting picture frames is one my favorite hobbies."

"How odd," Freek Vreeken butted in. "Pictures, yes. But picture frames?"

"No, no, not at all. I find picture frames much more enthralling than the pictures they usually contain, don't you? In fact, some of the picture frames I have stumbled across are so fascinating that I'm tempted to frame them."

Hilarious, almost giddy laughter.

An earnest, deadpan HG: "And what could be more delicious than to kick back in the privacy of one's own picture-frame gallery, listening to a nice factory-fresh blank CD going full blast, while sipping a glass of tap water. Room-temperature, of course."

"Well, folks, HG's obviously enjoying pulling our leg here," Freek concluded, beaming broadly.

"Only a little. I don't have to reiterate, do I, that I aim to shatter illusion, not spin it, and this hobby of mine fits right in with that."

"I guess I read you wrong there, HG. You obviously intend your anecdote to be of heuristic value. Won't you explain?"

"Imagery, of course, any imagery, is a way of providing positive content to cogitation, whereas the root insight into the true nature of being is best achieved, and communicated, by most effectively applying that insight; by nurturing the unconditioned, resisting the temptation to co-determine content. Hence attention for the picture frames rather than the picture. Compare it to Malevich's framed blackness, if you like, but then going a step further. The crucial vanishing step. The vanishing step one takes by letting go."

"I realize, of course, that Malevich was exploring fresh ground, but this does put things in a new light. Or should I say dark?"

"What you must resist, as I had to at first, is to take the frames and assemble them into a new art composition, which can then be framed. Cause that'd be meta-art. Old Plato'd have a cow."

"How's that?"

"Well, he considered art as twice removed from 'real' life, a cheap imitation. Meta-art would be thrice removed from his notion of True Reality, whatever that is..."

"Right! Time for a break!" Freek said, jumping to his feet and performing an outrageous hip-shaking jiggle.

And as he did so, the studio was plunged into total darkness, while WWW's rock band, Harpy & the Herpes, burst into a deafening number. On came flashing colored lights in syncopation with the loud music. The exhibitionistic band members had the disadvantage of having their ample tools concealed behind their instruments, though not Harpy herself, whose lithe body-painted frame displayed its uncanny talents – just her and her hand-held mike.

For the next part of the show, a change of pace to perk up the program and pique viewer interest, the studio's special ultra violet tanning lights and the pleasantly gurgling artificial waterfall were switched on, after everyone had donned protective goggles distributed during the break. *The Naked Truth* not only pretended to foster mental, but physical health as well. People would leave, if nothing else, with their minimum daily dose of vitamin D.

Addressing the audience, Freek Vreeken said, "I don't have to remind anyone of the scenes of pandemonium at Weijers bookshop in the Hague the other day, do I?" And peering through his designer goggles sparkling in the bright lights, he said to HG: "Some people have all the luck. Miraculous escape from an assassin's bullet, unprecedented publicity, and unrivalled book sales. Whatever happens, you seem to come out ahead! Tell me, how do you do it?" The talk show host spoke with genuine admiration in his voice, and, for those listening closely, a touch of envy. He himself dabbled in the art of word-processing, having several popular titles to his name.

He awaited HG's reply with interest, while the camera panned away.

"Just lucky, I guess?" was the cursory reply.

"But it does seem rather bizarre to me, I mean the assassination attempt. At least we're not used to that kind of furore here in tranquil old Holland. I must say, you enlivened our little country considerably since your arrival. Got any more tricks up your sleeve?"

"One or two," HG smiled.

"Won't you let our audience in on them?"

"That would spoil the fun, now wouldn't it?"

"I suppose. I've read *Guide for the Apoplexed,* of course," Freek said, more pensively now, showing a copy of the Dutch translation to the camera for the audience at home, its shiny dust jacket shimmering in the blinding studio lights. Though I don't pretend to fully understand what you're trying to say, attempted murder seems farthest from its central theme, namely enlightenment. How do you reconcile the two?"

"I don't. They reconcile themselves."

"Yes, but, what I mean is, to my mind, manslaughter and enlightenment jar somehow."

The TV host harvested a round of approving murmurs from his captivated audience, clearly hyper-responsive to the dialogue by now.

"I think that may be because you confuse enlightenment with paradise. And in doing so, good with evil, in fact, opening the entire lacquered Pandora's box of antipodes. Or as I once wrote, 'Happiness infused in murder...'"

"Beg your pardon?" the host queried, grateful that finally his show began to live up to its literary pretensions.

HG concentrated a moment, accepting the open invitation. He then quoted from memory:

"Hosanna! Have you heard? How could you?
Happiness infused in murder!
Colic in our throats!
Could you stab another? Another could!

"Hallelujah! Have you heard? How could you?
Heaven is on Earth!
Holocaust is in the rosebud!
Sweet honey lies in hell!
Could you heal another? Another could!"

"Ah yes. Back to man's dual nature, I guess. Still I don't really understand the crux of what you write, Heer Gnuticks. I get the distinct feeling that there's something that escapes me. Could you elaborate?"

"It's important to remember what I said earlier, that I'm not spinning illusion, rather attempt to shatter it. And that's never simple given that most people are caught in their own web of illusion and there is no cut-and-dried formula to extricate them. My approach in *Guide* has been designed to explore a course that will have widest possible applicability. And since our philosophers and scientists are the ones who have most consistently and persistently tackled the issue, I decided to build on their achievements."

"Hence the copious references and quotations?"

"Right. A bit of name-dropping, granted, but with a difference. One must acknowledge the works of the past and move beyond, though strictly speaking, there is no beyond, of course, nor, for that matter, a past. I've tried to make it all as accessible as possible since what generally tends to happen is that the scholarly, academic types abuse the achievements of others to entrench themselves in positions of power – notably in the universities, of course – where they beat people over the head with the established names in an attempt to 'out-associate' each other, as Alan Watts used to say. I repudiate that sort of thing. What I've attempted to do in Guide is put things in some sort of perspective for those who would like useful references they can turn to should they so desire, that's all. I only hope it won't get in the way, cause in the final analysis the written word, by leading, misleads. So also *Guide*."

"That is a problem, isn't it?"

"You bet. And as far as that goes I'm guilty as charged. However, as extenuating circumstance I admit to having sought to entertain in the bargain. That's not to say it will appeal to everyone. And in order to satisfy diverse tastes I also try alternative approaches these days."

"Such as?"

"I'm working on a computer novel for our website just now. Exploring philosofictional possibilities, a brand-new genre with some scope, as market surveys have borne out. Some people prefer it to academic study, we've found."

"What's your latest work about, if I may ask?"

HG, deviously, "It's about a best-selling author on tour to promote his latest book. During an autograph session, he is shot at. Gets invited to tell his story on a TV talk show…"

"Touchez, touchez." Turning to the audience: "I guess we'll just have to be patient, eh?"

Some polite titters.

"You have quite a reputation as a comedian, HG."

"Oh, I don't know about that."

"No, no, don't deny it. What's that one-line novel I've heard so much about?"

"Oh you mean the do-it-yourself, fully compressed, all-purpose novel?"

"Exactly!"

"The entire alphabet plus handy punctuation kit."

"That's the one. And whattabout your one-page novel?"

"Where my protagonist crosses a one-way street in the opening scene and gets killed by a joyrider going the wrong way?"

"That's the one."

"Ah. But the pregnant description of the impact!"

"I also heard rumors about an ulitmate whodunnit?"

"That's just a parody. In the final episode entitled *The Butler Did It Not*, Colombo catches himself off guard with one of his nonchalant trick questions and spills the beans. Turns out he's the culprit all along."

"Ahuh! Right! But on a more serious note. Let's take your *Scheisenberg Uncertainty Principle*…I have your recyclable folder here somewhere, let's see…Yes, here it is. This obviously is a pun on Werner Heisenberg, one of the great German physicists who helped develop the quantum theory. His Heisenberg Uncertainty Principle is what you might call the cornerstone of that theory, and as I understand it, of quantum cosmology as well. And in a typical Herman Gnuticks spoof you lampoon the poor man with your Heisenberg-Scheisenberg pun. Isn't that just a little below the belt?"

"Do you really think so?"

"I'm asking. I'm only asking. It's my job, don't forget."

Laughter.

"Let me point out off the bat, if I may, that Herr Heisenberg had been dead and buried – or perhaps cremated, I'm not sure which – for a dozen years or more when I wrote SUP."

"SUP?"

"That's how I abbreviate the Scheisenberg Uncertainty Principle. It's such a mouthful otherwise."

"Aha. And HUP would stand for the Heisenberg Uncertainty Principle?"

"You got it. Secondly, you may recall the more principled reason for my SUP hypothesis. It is an argument by analogy drawn from physics and applied to psychology. After all, if men like Heisenberg, Schrödinger and Niels Bohr are right, and the subatomic world is ultimately indeterminate, a world where only statistical probability applies and where individual cases cannot be predicted, but only averages over aggregates pertain, then one might come to wonder what that means to the emergence of our very own thoughts?"

The TV host looked quizzically at HG.

"Consider for example how thoughts arise seemingly 'spontaneously', often 'randomly' and out of 'nowhere', just like subatomic particles do. Especially just before falling asleep, or on waking, or when we're ill or drugged, when we have less of a feeling of being 'in charge'. At such moments we can feel startled by the emergence of our thoughts, more so than when we are rested, healthy and energetic and in the thick of our daily doings – when the weft and warp of the phantom self arises naturally through the ongoing process of differentiation and integration. At moments of reduced concentration our thoughts may also appear shot full of holes, like Swiss cheese, being somehow both continuous and discontinuous – subject to free association, ultimately an unpredictable, creative process."

Freek seemed to mull this over a minute.

HG continued, "Of course there is a second aspect to this whole issue having to do with that attendant sense of self that I referred to, and which is naively thought of by the multitudes as the subject having those thoughts."

A pensive Freek nodded, signaling HG to go on. "Postmodernity revisited. Remind me to get back to that later," Freek said more to himself than his guest.

"Experiment has discredited the old notion of the Cartesian theater, a single site in the brain that is the seat of consciousness. This plays havoc with the notion of a single self, suggesting sooner a multiplicity of Selves, ideally arriving at consensus through an inner dialogue; though that dialogue equally capable of being stymied and leading to confusion and indecision through the emergence of potentially conflicting or incompatible 'discourses'. This scenario has indeed lent some credence to the doctrine of postmodernity with its multiplicity of views existing side by side. Recognize here the plurality versus unity argument all over again, Freek, the One versus the Many. Needless to say, my own position is to reject the autologic of strictly limited either/or choice, though I don't need to reiterate it here."

"Glad to hear it, HG. Though clever as you are you've managed to reiterate it nonetheless, haven't you."

"Have I? Never mind that. Let's get practical, shall we?"

"By all means. Let's."

"I'd like the people in the audience to try a little hands-on psychology experiment," HG said. "Have you ever considered that the more you try to get a grip on your self, the self supposedly having these thoughts, the more that self eludes you. Try it. No one has yet succeeded. It is of course simply impossible, getting a grip on your self. Nor is it surprising really since it takes a fresh self for each self that tries to get a grip on the Self."

He paused a second to let this sink in, noticing that some persons were squirming in their seats, jittery from the exertion, giggling at the furtive, failed attempt.

"And still there's no denying that each of us has this sense of self," Freek asserted. "What do you make of it, I mean, should you be asked to hazard a guess."

"As long as you promise not to take me literally."

"I promise."

"Well, I did once propound the 'tie-twister' model of self," HG said with a smirk on his face.

"I might've known. Okay, let's have it."

"Actually it may not be so far-fetched after all," HG recommended the speculative model of self he was about to unveil. "Consider it to be the counterpart of the superstring in subatomic physics. With duality as theoretical ground, the tie-twister adequately represents duality's most salient feature, a polar whole."

"A polar hole?"

"No-no-no-no. A polar whole, not a polar hole."

"Oh, I see, very funny. So what about this polar whole?"

"Well, a tie-twister is a pretty innocuous little object in its linear form. But bend the ends around and twist them together, and presto, you can use it to tie up something, get a grip on it. Like a garbage bag."

"Are you saying that the self is like a garbage bag?"

"Those are your words, Freek, not mine. Though there's something to recommend that view – present company excluded, of course."

"Of course!"

"But what I was getting at is that neurophysiologists have found all these micro-circuits in the brain. And what, after all, is a micro-circuit but a tie-twister turning in on itself? Instead of twisting flexible ends together, we use matching pairs of concepts to get a grip on things. I suggest that for every micro-circuit there is a contributing strand of self in the form of activated conceptualization. In some respects it is vaguely reminiscent of the simile in ancient Indian philosophy where thought patterns are likened to run-off after a rainstorm. Where does it flow other than through channels that have been scored by torrents from earlier downpours?"

HG paused, rolled his eyes upwards, oblivious to the jungle of light fixtures overhead, and recited:

"Thunder in the Lightening of Words
Gave birth inside my brain
To stir up all the worlds, detached,
Until its meaning came,
Till Man & God & Brain dispatched
That Man & God are naught
But eddies on the Brain
From currents in the Blood..."

"Say," Freek interrupted, "do you have a history of 'art attacks' or what?"

"Congenital, I'm afraid," HG replied, smiling. "This one's left over from my materialist days."

Freek was obviously quite pleased at cleverly having reversed the roles for a change. It was HG who was usually on the receiving end when it came to collecting royalties on quotables.

He was slightly jealous that way, thinking of a thin volume of one-liners from HG's hand passed to his staff during preliminaries for the show, of which two samples now sprung to mind: "All odes lead to Om", from a piece on comparative psychology East and West; and the rhetorical flourish: "If humility makes you humble, does futility make you fumble?" in the context of comparative ethics East and West. Or had it been on the power of negative thinking? Freek couldn't quite recall.

The controversial cover of the booklet (a purple-and-green woodcut print on vellum of a circumcised Adolf Hitler wearing a skullcap, attentively reading the Old Testament) had stuck in his mind, not only because it had triggered an avalanche of vehement reaction from conservative quarters worldwide; nor that it had introduced a new concept – that of the self-hating German; but because that shocking cover had made an undeniably important statement on the role of juxtaposition in the arts. And juxtaposition, after all, was HG's favorite in a stable of hobby horses.

To Freek's chagrin, however, his own moment of innovative glory passed without shafts of lightning or bolts of thunder, and HG swept on, accustomed as he was to swift and uncompromising repartee.

"Of course, it's not really anything new, as you may know, my tie-twister model. Just think of the snake biting its own tail, a common mythological conception to account for the origin of the universe. Who knows, it may even have played a role in the invention of the wheel some 6000 years ago; the circle in general, and the closely related conception of infinity, as Gore Vidal suggests in his novel *Creation*; or the very conception of conception, as I suggested in my favorable review of that book for a local paper decades back!

"There's also the documented case in more modern times where it proved of practical help in the field of chemistry when Kekulé dozing off in front of his fireplace dreamt of a chain of carbon atoms turning in on itself. When he awoke he had hit on the ring structure of benzene! But, let me hasten to add, wholly superfluously perhaps, that I'm not endorsing any 'correspondence theory of reality'! What's more, as you are no doubt aware, analogies – being analogies – tend to be skewed. They break down sooner or later, and that can lead to a nervous breakdown – for the entertainer of the analogy that is. Because don't forget that to entertain an analogy based on an analogy of an entertainer entertaining an analogy of an entertainer entertaining an analogy takes an entertainer of that analogy entertaining the analogy of an entertainer...of an analogy..."

"Cut!!! You've made your point. Would I be far wrong to conclude then that the self is a many-splendored chimerical sort of thing?"

"Let me answer that in the following way. Special *Muppet Show* guest Peter Sellers once said when asked by Kermit the Frog that he used to have a self, but that he had it surgically removed. Of course he was putting one over on both the materialists and the mentalists of the day, because it is as absurd to think that you have a self, as to think that you do not."

"I happened to catch that particular show. One of the best, in my opinion. Remember the massage he gave Link? Fabulous stuff, simply fabulous," Freek eulogized one of the all-time greats of comedy.

"But Kermit's point, as representing the naive view, was well taken. Who or what is this Self we know more intimately than anyone or anything else in life? Like most people, I, too, wrestled with that one for a long time. Later I came to referee such matches for others, as the Buddha Boys will demonstrate a little later on. It's also where the *Scheisenberg Uncertainty Principle* came from, out of that enervating experience. It's a pretty frustrating realization, or it can be at least when it occurs to you that as science has discovered, matter on a subatomic level eludes certain determination. If we are made up of matter, as science assumes, we ourselves must also on a subatomic level elude certain determination, as must any aspect of us, like our own Selves, our thoughts. Or, for that matter, the Heisenberg Uncertainty Principle itself, qua thought."

"You mean to say that if ultimately, at base, everything is indeterminate, so is the very formulation that says that everything is indeterminate?"

HG was on a bit of a roll now. "You got it. But it gets more interesting. Recall Gödel's theorem, which says that a system, if complete, is inconsistent; and if consistent must be incomplete? In principle it holds for all human systems of thought, of which mathematics is only one example, though a notable one of course. And so if Gödel's theorem is complete, it is inconsistent, and if it were consistent, it would be incomplete, and in need of completion, where after inconsistent. In any case, it stands to reason: for a system to be complete it would by definition need to include all opposites, and therefore be inconsistent as well as consistent – Heraclitus knew that 2500 years ago. Gödel provided us with the rigorous mathematical proof, nothing less, but nothing more either."

"Didn't the famous British mathematician Roger Penrose have something to say about this in his memorable *The Emperor's New Mind*?"

"Yes. It was in connection with the ongoing AI, artificial insemination...I mean, artificial intelligence argument – sorry, I couldn't resist."

Freek waved him on. "Don't expect any 'immoral support' from me. You're on your own."

He was getting the hang of it, to HG's delight.

"You're incorrigible, Freek! I love it. Keep it up." Then, a bit distracted, "Where was I? Oh, yes, Penrose. He makes the point that computers, which are basically algorithm processors, that is, structured and bound by the rules of mathematics, must obey Gödel's theorem. But since the realization of the truth of Gödel's theorem is in itself non-algorithmical – so Penrose claims – computers cannot in principle ever come to be aware of the truth of Gödel's theorem, though they obey it."

"That sounds like a clever argument to me," Freek said, sounding somewhat unsure of himself.

"It does sound clever, but like so much in science and philosophy, it's more a question of begging the question: *petitio principii*, not to say *ignoratio elenchi*."

"How's that?"

"Well, if you *presuppose* as Penrose does that realization of the truth of Gödel's theorem is non-algorithmic, and if you also already assume that computers cannot be conscious, then it does indeed follow that an algorithmically programmed computer can in principle never be conscious and thus aware of the truth of Gödel's theorem. But that is the whole point you want to prove, isn't it, and not *presuppose*?"

"Yes, yes, perhaps. So where does that leave us?"

"In a Hilversum studio?"

Laughter.

"Actually it is a common ailment, an inherent weakness of our rational, logical bent of mind."

"You mean that we assume what we want to prove?"

Acknowledging Freek with a slight nod of the head, HG said, "Take Darwin's theory of evolution. It is quite in vogue today, though in modified form, the rough edges having been polished away by the tide of thought that's gone into it. But still, the idea of the survival of the fittest is a household concept which itself has apparently survived by withstanding the tooth of time. In a post-Darwinian sense, of course."

"You mean Darwin-minus-progress?" Freek commented succinctly, continuing in the same breath, "Which reminds me of something Bertrand Russell once wrote on what he referred to as 'evolutionism'. Something to the effect that it is a widely held view that organic life developed gradually from the protozoon to the philosopher, and that this is an undeniable advance. To which Russell adds with characteristic British understatement that unfortunately we are given this assurance by the philosopher, and *not* the protozoon!"

"Yes, compared to the majority of stuffy philosophers, Russell certainly is fun to read. Though I'm not sure he gives Darwin a fair hearing. There's some evidence that the man himself was not blinded by the notion of evolutionary progress like most of his contemporaries. Neither, as was prevalent in certain other circles, did he cotton to doomsday scenarios of Niwradian devolutionary regress and unnatural selection."

"Niwradian?"

"Darwin - Niwrad..."

"Always balancing the scales, aren't we, HG?"

"What can I say? I'm a fine-tuning stickler. And while we're on the subject, there's another, more deeply ingrained bias at work here."

"Namely?"

"That in all the sciences observation, experimentation and theorization are reserved as the exclusive domain of a particular slice of humanity, and so tend to contribute to a subtle, self-fulfilling prophecy?"

"What do you mean?"

"Well, aspiring scientists must hold certain credentials of age, mental and physical health, IQ, a predisposition towards rationality, high ethical standards of honesty, to mention but a few of the fairly arbitrary selection of human traits. Members of this elite, a secular priesthood of sorts, reinforce and perpetuate this stringent set of predilections at the expense of others."

"You don't take Darwin seriously then?"

"Seriously enough to gauge the man's merit and find him lacking on several counts. Ask yourself, for instance, what it means for a species to have survived because it is fittest? Isn't it rather a circular argument? Because how do you define fittest other than in terms of survival, while to account for survival you refer to a species' fitness? It's tantamount to equating survival and fitness, blurring any distinction between them, and as a consequence formulating an utterly redundant statement. It contributes nothing new and might as well be culled as excessive baggage."

"I see what you mean."

"What he ends up saying is that what is is because what is is best suited to be. And doesn't it also express an explicit prejudice to the effect that what survives is fitter than what does not? Doesn't it show blatant favoritism towards existence rather than non-existence? The opposite would hold equally untrue."

"You mean survival of the unfittest?"

"It's got as much going for it. Besides, this preoccupation with existence tends to discount the efficacy of the non-existent. And it is easy to demonstrate its absurdity. Take for example the notion of the adaptation of species to 'empty niches' left by the extinction of rivals. If anything, it stresses the significance of absence as much as of presence. Because then what is is because of what is not. Recall in this connection, if you will, the Taoist saying that we treasure doors and windows for what is *not* there, as much as for what is."

"But you're not going to deny, are you, that there is a deep-seated drive towards life, towards living, and that any creature cornered will fight for survival?"

"Surely, Freek, you must know by now that I neither affirm nor deny? Ever. But ask yourself what sort of evidence we have for what is no more than our anthropocentric projection?"

"Anthropocentric projection? Wouldn't you fight for your life if attacked?"

"What if I did? Would that prove that I did so to try to survive? Not really. It would simply be out of orneriness. I wouldn't give anyone the pleasure of killing me. Just as I wouldn't give anyone the pleasure of pulling or pushing me in a direction I didn't want to go. That wouldn't so much mean that I resisted going in that direction as that I didn't want to be compelled to do so. Same with defending, or appearing to defend your life."

"You're saying it's only action-reaction?"

"I'm just offering a less loaded explanation which resists reinforcing prejudicial views. And to provide some additional food for thought – though actually, in your condition, you're better off on a strict diet, Freek m'friend. What to make of self-sacrifice? Martyrdom? Suicide? Euthanasia? Pacifism? Celibacy? Homosexuality, for that matter? None of these are particularly survival-oriented, are they?"

"Guess not."

"Plus, if you think about it, much of Darwin also turns out to be due to his male chauvinist viricentrism..."

"Say what?"

"Viricentrism: preoccupation with the aggressive male perspective on things, including economic and political power, and that whole circus of procreative acrobatics. Fairness demands it be counterbalanced by an equal measure of gynaecocentrism, wouldn't you agree?"

"Ahummm."

"But Darwinism presents us with other shortcomings, faults galore in fact. What of the unchallenged survival of otherwise 'inadequate' species? Or the demise of supposed 'fit' species through dumb bad luck such as natural disasters? Potentially all these possibilities account for a hugely heterogeneous mix of species with variable rates of survival. On closer consideration it's not much of an argument, only vaguely descriptive, not prescriptive at all."

"You mean rationalization after the fact?"

"I do. In any case Darwin gets himself into hot water on another score."

"Pray tell."

"He runs into bogeyman Heisenberg by accounting for creatures' adaptive capacity in terms of genetic mutation, which is either chemically or radioactively induced and thus in the final analysis quantum mechanical in nature. And thus indeterminate, putting it quite safely beyond our reach."

"Really, HG! Isn't that pretty reductionist of you?"

"I tend to think of it as oxydationist myself, Freek. But seriously, if you stop to analyze many of our most common concepts, you run into this problem. For example, quantum as well as non-quantum indeterminacy, are interpreted as accounting for contingency in, among other things, evolution. But how do you tell the difference between contingency and providence? One man's contingency is another's predestination. The more unlikely an event, the more it smacks of interventionism, and it's only a question of arbitrary preference as to which one chooses – itself, again, an instance of indeterminacy...or fate, whichever you prefer. Determinism held sway for centuries, now the pendulum has swung back to indeterminism. Doesn't that tell you anything?"

"It's starting to. But let's take it one step at a time, shall we? Would I be correct in ascertaining that Darwin's true contribution remains the idea of adaptation to local change, period?"

"That appears to wash. Change is a neutral, relative, radically relative term. Remember Einstein?"

"We won't soon forget Einstein, will we?" Freek said to the audience, who was following the dialogue like a tennis match, with Freek serving, and HG volleying.

"The days of the absolute were numbered by the time Darwin came along. His greatest contribution was to debunk the prevailing idea that things had always been as we find them. In that respect his notion of evolution signaled a revolution."

Nodding agreement, Freek pursued his somewhat parabolic questioning, it being a bit retrograde, "You know, it just occurred to me, HG, if everything is changing all the time, then a person noticing this supposed change is himself also changing, right? How then can a person who knows only change in himself and in everything around him know the absence of change?"

"Well, change being a relative term, it only makes sense in comparison to something that changes in an identical matter, so that respective changes cancel and appear as stasis, or a state of rest – like bodies in motion. In the case of humanity, we share a great deal of such 'common sense' which permits us a basis, a platform of relativity in space on which to build our storehouse of knowledge."

"Back to the platform in space, eh? Ground Zero?"

"Just a helpful metaphor for the man in the street. On the other hand, remember that the only thing that does not change, is the notion that everything is always changing."

"Again nicely balancing the old scales, eh? I suppose by analogy, the vexing question as to why there is something rather than nothing, should be rethought, according to you. There isn't something rather than nothing, but something and nothing. In other words, no something without nothing, no nothing without something."

"The question then becomes," HG hinted, "with so much something around, where to look for the nothing..."

"And I don't suppose you're going to tell us?"

"I would if I could. But telling, would be telling something, not nothing, don't you see?"

"In that case, shall we move on?"

"You're the boss."

"To the Anthropic Principle?" Freek said, peeking at his notes.

"Now there's a tautological gem."

"The world exists because I exist and am here to observe it, Freek chimed in. "If the world was not just so constituted that it could support living observers, like you and I, there would be no one here to even ask why it existed."

"I see you've boned up for our meeting," HG appraised, pushing onward. "Let's take another example, shall we? We are told by scientists that the speed of light is constant for all observers – being roughly 300,000 km/sec. It is this constancy of the speed of light, by the way, that is an indispensable ingredient in Einstein's theory of relativity. But note carefully that the constancy of the speed of light insures that everything is relative, except the speed of light itself, which is independent of the speed of the observer measuring it! Curious, don't you think? Or not?"

"Since you're offering me a choice, I'll opt for the 'or not.'"

"Why?"

"If I were to wager a guess, I'd say that the one implies the other. Because if everything is relative then relativity itself must be relative to something, requiring light in this case to play the role of the non-relative." Surprised at his own facility with the fresh material, Freek said, "Hey, folks, that was easy!"

"I'd watch out if I were you, Freek. You're starting to sound like me."

"Is that so bad?"

"You tell me."

"I'll tell you afterwards."

"As you wish. I'll press on, then."

"By all means."

"There must be something very special about light, then," HG said provocatively. "What do you suppose it could be?"

"I haven't a clue. Other than that primitive peoples everywhere worshipped the sun. The earliest religions crystallized around it, let's not forget. And no wonder really considering its overwhelming power; the influence on our lives of the sun; and later of fire, light bulbs, et cetera."

"Right. But has it ever occurred to you that light is both medium *and* message? Or put differently, messenger magically turning into message."

"How?"

"Because our brains work electrically, and thus magnetically; also electromagnetically, and probably quantum mechanically as well, according to certain luminaries."

"That's all good and well, but can we test your hypothesis?"

"Which one is that?"

"About light being both medium and message?"

"No, because no matter what experiment you devise, the toolmaker is intimately linked to the tool. It probably also accounts for the dilemma we face in conducting the two-slit experiment."

"How's that?"

"The thing must wriggle out of our grasp somehow, since the distinction between 'grasper' and 'graspee' is a tenuous one. The experimenter is forced to take cognizance of the error of his ways. The light photon paradox, acting as both particle and wave, signifies the introduction of the disjunctive elements of discontinuity and indeterminacy, don't you see, the point of transformation where self turns into other."

"And the other way around?"

"And the other way around. It's what turns the trick."

"Damn frustrating business, I must confess."

"True. Especially if you consider that it is the constancy of the speed of light that insures a universe where cause always precedes effect, and common sense, or the so-called Boolean logic we employ, holds us in its iron grip. The same logic, by the way, that insures that we live in a universe where cause always precedes effect."

"Oh, please!"

"And what of the notion that when looking up at the night sky what you see, or what you think you see, is the firmament as it was millions of light years ago.

Because of the huge distances and the finite speed of the signals carrying the message, you're seeing something that is not 'really' there at all. It's only an emblematic image in your 'mind', whatever that is. But even at ground level, you only see the mediating signals, namely reflected or emitted light rays, and thus never the 'real thing' supposedly doing the reflecting or emitting, which even if it were 'out there' would not be *what* it appears, or *where*."

"Pretty please?" Freek folded his hands as if in prayer. "Pretty, pretty please?"

But to no avail. Heedlessly, HG went on. "If you like that, you'll love the following," he smiled, a bit maliciously.

"Something tells me that I won't!" Freek sputtered.

But HG, ignoring the futile plea, continued at a clip: "It is a traditional philosophical truism that all human experience can be reduced to the Subject/Object dualism – at least it was until Nietzsche came along, and later Heidegger and others. But their *ad hoc* assertion to simply forget about part of this dualism and adopt monism instead is not convincing. Their saying so does not make it so. To the contrary! Nor do they in fact escape the dilemma in the end, as they would have us believe. They remain as inextricably entangled and confused as the next guy. And indeed their private lives were a mess."

"You're not going to bring their private lives into this, are you HG?"

"Me? Wouldn't dream of it. No, let's keep it strictly dispassionate, shall we?"

"Glad to hear it. My show has a reputation to uphold, you know. The mere fact that Nietzsche went stark raving mad towards the end of his life should not be held against him. It could happen to anyone, you, me..."

"God forbid," HG scoffed.

"Don't say that unless you mean it!" Freek scolded his irreverent guest. "Why needlessly offend the sensibilities of my atheist viewers, of whom I have legion!"

"It's just an expression, for god's sake."

"Herman, Herman, Herman. Never mind. I take it that you disagree with the unilateral abolition of dualism in favor of monism à la Nietzsche, Heidegger, Sartre?"

"I don't mean to single out philosophers. Scientists have not fared much better despite breath-taking advances in various fields. To date they're as badly divided on the issue, even though most try to sweep it under the carpet. There's no straight-forward stance that can be taken on whether the world is objectively real or not. Isn't that rather strange? It may seem perfect common sense to assume that there is a world 'out there', but it is purely an article of faith and we are simply not entitled to make any such hard-and-fast claim. Experts remain divided, though the subjectivist view makes no sense to most scientists, even though their own objectivist view cannot be proven! And this is a highly telling weakness of science," HG concluded.

"What is?"

"Well, that scientists tend to take on faith something of such fundamental importance, while insisting on the most stringent empirical verification for everything else. But then this is not really surprising if you consider that empiricism itself presupposes there to be 'a world out there'. As a matter of fact it is more or less synonymous with empiricism – the conducting of experiments, the testing of hypotheses, these are the hallmarks of modern science. And this is its generally *un*acknowledged Achilles heel, disguised instead by votaries as its strength."

"I'd never really thought about it in quite those terms," Freek confessed, scratching his head. "Tends to put a lot of what we know on the skids, does it?"

"Yes and no," HG answered. "If you see science as a socially-structured activity which moreover provides people with a livelihood, and hence a vested interest, it does not make much difference one way or the other. This, of course, is the myopic pragmatist view."

"I take it you don't approve?"

"Oh, I don't mind one way or the other. But to paraphrase the advice Woody Allen once gave his preteen niece in one of his movies, 'Don't listen to what scientists say; look at what they do.' In other words, it's not really their interpretation of the facts that is significant. Or to paraphrase Heinz Pagels: the interpretation of empirical data is itself not an empirical enterprise. This rule of thumb highlights the crucial role metaphysics plays in any empirical endeavor, something most hard-nosed researchers would much rather prefer to forget, inasmuch as they are aware of it in the first place."

Here Freek interrupted HG.

"This is not turning into an anti-science or anti-intellectual declaration, is it?"

"Not at all. In fact I'm glad you're giving me the opportunity to deny that charge so often leveled against me by oversensitive, misguided people. Science has its use, but that does not mean that one must uncritically swallow all that it dishes up. The way I see it, scientists will continue doing what they do, if for no other reason than that it pays the bills. The honest ones will admit it up front.

"Like the team leader researching the anomalies of proton/neutron spin I read about who said that he'd rather have something unexpected turn up rather than nothing, cause it kept him in a job. No pretension there. After all, despite the impression raised of being on the brink of knowing all, frontiers are merely being shifted back. There's no question of getting ahold of any 'ultimate reality' that will crack the mystery, though it continues to function as the proverbial carrot dangling in front of the benighted scientist's nose. At most we gain a certain facility in dealing with the physical world. You see, scientists, owing to a tried-and-tested methodology, are fairly trustworthy scouts, delivering the goods more effectively than others wandering off in the dense jungle of possibilities. And mankind obediently follows the beaten path which has proven successful, though in an ultimate sense one path is basically no different than another. Only more useful is all. But if you see science as a 'truth-seeking' activity – a substitute for defunct religions – then you're in deep epistemological manure, because ultimately there is no solid ground on which to take your stand, and truth turns out to be relative. Radically Relative."

And here, on HG's instigation, egging them on while imitating his host's hip-shaking wiggle, the audience chanted "Ground Zero! Ground Zero! Ground Zero! Ground Zero!"

Freek raised his hands in mock surrender and shouted: "Time out! Time out!" And when the noise subsided somewhat, proposed: "Whattaya say we listen to another hit song from the band?" The TV host was visibly fatigued at this stage, groggy from the fifteen rounds of sparring with HG. Going the full distance with a heavy-weight – or just a heavy? – had him reeling on the ropes, plum tuckered out and keenly looking forward to a week's vacation on the French Riviera to catch up on some reading in connection with his next guest, a decidedly unprofound lyrical poetess, a woman who meant what she said, and said what she meant – a lovely change from the excruciating form of mental isometrics that had nearly given him a hernia of the brain!

Five minutes later, with the studio temperature raised by at least five degrees, after a 100-decibel electrified interlude, Freek resumed his interview:

"Now, where were we? Oh yes. Right. I'm suddenly so disoriented that I can't think what to ask you."

"That would seem to me a good time to conclude the show."

"Yes. No! What I mean is that your philosophy, if that's what it is, is very disconcerting. Shouldn't philosophy help one gain a degree of clarity about major issues in life, rather than stymie one's thinking?"

"Well, yes, that used to be the idea. But look what that kind of philosophy has led to, system-building.

"Yes, yes. No doubt you'll tell me next that all the old ideologies have been discredited."

"Well, you know Freek, all the old ideologies have been thoroughly discredited," HG said glibly. "Don't you find that?"

"Thank you very much. But are we to stop building systems altogether? Surely, as you say, we need some sort of platform in space from which to operate? Ground Zero! Are you advocating a destructive rather than a constructive life, if I can put it that way?"

"I'm not advocating anything of the sort. Hence Ground Zero: it's neither positive nor negative, if you've noticed. Just beware, and be aware, of what it is you're doing, that's all. Don't fool yourself, cause that's a pretty foolish thing to do."

"HG, as we say in Holland, you are as slippery as an eel in a pail of snot!"

"Why thank you, Freek, I take that as a compliment, though I really wish you hadn't said that."

"Said what?"

"The slippery bit."

"Why not?"

"I'm reminded of a story I haven't told for years and years."

"Well, let's have it!"

"It's about my old soccer-playing days, you see, way back, when I scored the winning goal."

"You played soccer? A red-blooded American?" Freek asked, in mock astonishment.

"Yes, love it, more than baseball, or American football. Anyway, once when we had played an amateur competition match, sponsored by our local real estate company – Leadbetter Realty, if I remember correctly – it was written up in the *Valley Spreadsheet*. As I said, I happened to have scored a goal that day, something rather unusual for me..."

Laughter.

"...and the next day the paper said about yours truly that: 'His dick was too slippery for the goalie to handle.'"

Uproarious laughter.

"Supposedly it was a printer's devil, but I suspect the typist of having done it on purpose, substituting 'dick' for 'kick'. It is a rather inviting thing to do, isn't it? And I might've done the same, given half a chance."

"As indeed I would," Freek said with a mischievous smirk on his face – a dead giveaway to his guest, really, who nevertheless was caught with his pants down, so to speak – when his interlocutor continued slyly, "Cause as I always say

HG, 'Speak softly and carry a big dick!' Uhhh, I mean, stick, stick, carry a big stick!"

This brought the house crashing down. Not only did Freek catch his guest utterly off-guard, but the meekly volleyed 'So why don't you? Speak softly, I mean?' was totally drowned out by the deafening foot-stomping of the audience.

Naturally the TV host milked his success for all it was worth, jumping up and prancing around the stage for close to a minute, while a bemused HG watched the exhibitionistic display of this Dutch phenomenon in hushed amazement. The cloggy put Jerry Springer to shame, he had to admit. And yet there was something clean and healthy, wholesome and innocent, about Freek that made it all acceptable somehow – unlike Jerry's Okkels-like mysophilia, come to think of it.

After all, HG had been given the thumbs up for appearance on *The Naked Truth* by none other than WWW's Triple L, Lesbian Liberation Leaders, whose withering, nay shriveling, gaze he ordinarily dreaded so. After having closely scrutinized Freek's credentials the inseparable duo, Ms. Ann Dry and Ms. O. Gyny, authors of a reference work on feminism that included a chapter on Holland (*Dutch Dykes behind Dutch Dykes*), had lavished unprecedented praise on Mr. Vreeken and his impressive track record of upbeat and edifying campaigns – inside as well as outside the studio.

The otherwise stern, not to say austere, ladies had lauded Freek's singular quest to expose insiduous societal prejudice and discrimination, especially as regards women. A notable passage – quoted at length herewith – had read:

> Over the years his show's great candor and openness has demonstrably contributed to the nation's physical and mental hygiene balancing, among other things, the scales of male-female relations. A steep decline in ailments and aberrations, for example, AIDS and teenage pregnancy, has been recorded. A spate of doctoral theses on the subject has since borne this out, among which from our very own in-house 'Masters & Johnson', that winning May & December physician-psychologist partnership, the proleptical Pro Phil Laktik and that no less proactive Pro Ms. Cuity (nicknamed Madame B. Ovary by some wit, who shall remain nameless). All this, of course, under the aegis and sanguine matronage of Ms. M.T. Ness herself, presiding over the WWW's conscientious Board of Governors. And indeed, there is broad consensus on Freek's screwpulous insistence at all times that groupies use the best protection money can buy during frequent backstage orgies. Proof pos-

itive of the efficacy of this salubrious policy is the fact that in all his long years at the top not a single paternity suit could ever be pinned on him or any of his crew. No, in that regard Holland is indeed the pilot nation it rightfully claims to be, a guiding light in the long night of history from which we are only now emerging.

When eventually an exuberant Freek, professional that he was, stopped horsing around and settled down, catching his breath, he seamlessly segued into the show's finale.

"So whattaya say we call it a 1:1 draw? A point for you, a point for me?"

Spontaneous applause. A nod from HG.

"Maybe that is as good a place as any to end. 'Cause I'm afraid our time's up, folks," their host spoke over the applause which was continuous by now, on instigation of one of the stage-hands who egged on the audience.

And as the credits began to roll, the television screens at home showed a freeze-frame of Freek and HG caught in animated discussion. The interview had run long, way long, though much remained to be discussed. Alas that would have to wait for a return visit, an invitation graciously accepted by HG off-camera.

Meanwhile Kay Dance and her girls – those Sibilant Sisters – came on stark naked and gyrating provocatively, humming their *a cappella* signature tune. Their excruciatingly close harmony encore spontaneously harvested a standing ovation from some of the more virile men seated in the audience:

> The miramar of love comes roaming,
> Deep from in the heart, abiding where,
> When all the time that love seems lost,
> Love is so, and so, and so.

The rippling, well-oiled musculature of "Sid-the-Kid" Dixit and his Buddha Boys Brigade in the background glistened beneath the bright studio lights. They acted as male chorus line for the occasion, shackled and handcuffed as for a bizarre S&M affair. Though for lack of air-time the people at home were denied these cheap parting shots, the studio audience enjoyed what was billed as WWW's famous "auto-wrestling match": each member of the Brigade engaged in a fierce Greco-Roman struggle with himself till they dropped to their knees. And after hilarious, protracted antics that sent the audience into a complete tizzy they ended up pinning themselves on the floor in a graphic demonstration of their leader's skeptical message, abundantly symbolizing the crucial Home Stretch on the Road to Liberation.

Houdini-like they finally broke their self-imposed shackles, sprang to their feet and pranced off stage to jubilant shouts of cheer. The second they returned, to the insistent slow-clapping of the audience, confetti came raining down from the catwalk in dazzling cascades. Next, overhead nets containing hundreds of colorful balloons were released, inundating the audience who leapt to their feet. Young and old alike clutched as many of the festive prizes as they could lay their hands on, while, to further drive home their sobering message, the Buddha Boys mingled with the audience, puncturing as many of the balloons as they could.

At first, of course, people did not quite understand and tried to shield their artificially inflated possessions, taking the unwelcome assault as rather a spoil-sport sort of thing to do; some even put up fierce resistance, which threatened to escalate and get out of hand. But as soon as the purpose of the exercise became apparent, opposition turned into keen cooperation – and the show ended with a bang, or rather a whole bunch of bangs – as not a single balloon was left in tact.

* * * * *

Concluded Leo de Leeuw in the final paragraph of his vitriolic column the next day, "Never! Never, never, never in my entire life have I heard such pitiful palaver and dreadful drivel as was aired in the Herman Gnuticks interview – or should I say 'interphooey'. Freek Vreeken, *The Naked Lie's* dishonorable host, ought to be compelled on pains of severest penalty to broadcast the staunchest of warnings before-hand cautioning impressionable minds that his odious brand of psychological onanism is extremely harmful to the viewer's mental health. Perhaps wholly superfluously, let me vent my heart-felt 'yuch, yuchie-yuch, yuch yuch!!'"

* * * * *

SEVEN

Anybody who was anybody attended the reception hosted by HG's Dutch publishers, Sjef and Gerrit (G&S Press), who also happened to be Harm Bontekoe's publishers, that being less of a coincidence than it might seem.

Harm had been a scholar (and author) of some repute within the Netherlands, and on his recommendation HG was taken on board. Harm's epic novel *Birth in Berkeley*, which HG had eventually helped him bring out in America, had fallen flat. And its later Dutch translation published by G&S Press didn't fare much better for that matter. He'd understood after long agonizing that he'd gone overboard on his first major work of fiction, and had thereafter stuck to essays and short stories – apart from popularizing his professional commercial work on flavors & fragrances, coupled to his recombinant DNA research on developing 'a seventh sense, perhaps even an eighth', conducted in collaboration with a team from a prominent Dutch university.

But it had pained him that *Birth in Berkeley* had been a flop, and by way of self-castigation he routinely performed a little ritual to appease the publishing gods, as he explained to HG while strolling across a freshly mowed lawn behind the mansion where the reception was being held on the outskirts of Laren – in Holland's affluent and rustic heartland.

"Sorry I was late, but I stopped off at Vinkeveenseplassen on the way over."

"Say what?" HG asked, in eternal wonderment at the Dutch accent.

"Vinkeveense..., yeah well, these lakes, kind of a recreational area, angling, sailing, windsurfing, that sort of thing. Once a year or so I go there to do penance."

"You, Harm, religious?"

"Hardly. But still, I can't resist. It's a sobering experience."

"What is?"

"Casting my thesaurus upon the waters."

"Your what?"

"I never told you?"

"No, of course not. Something like that I'd remember, believe you me."

"It goes back to before your Full Court Press helped me publish *Birth in Berkeley*. I had first canvassed the market for myself, not wanting to bother you and all. You'd hardly set yourself up in business, remember? This was way before the success of your Crypto-Illiterate Productions, before you became the spin doctor you are today – that mandarin among tangerines. You had no standing in the publishing biz and practically no clout to speak of. Frankly I didn't want to sell myself short; wanted to optimize my chances. But when there were no takers, I sorta had to settle for your ludicrous Tidigitation Press. No wonder my book flopped."

"Thanks a lot!"

"Yeah, well, can you blame me?"

"Sure I can. But go on."

"I'd sent a bunch of queries to U.S. publishers and literary agents but it took forever to get past their sentry secretaries. I was beginning to feel pretty ice-O-lated here on these frigid Nordic shores, littorally speaking you understand."

"Hey, I thought I had copyright on that sort of stuff!" HG objected vehemently.

"The hell you do. Eat your heart out, fellah! You wanna hear the story or don't you?"

"Not really," HG replied coolly.

But Harm was undaunted. Besides, he enjoyed reminiscing, as his 800-page novel had made abundantly clear.

"I sent my manuscript to a half dozen agents or so – a real racket, I tell you, set me back many hundreds of dollars in reading fees alone, but what the heck. Finally, after many, many months, one of them wrote back that though he saw potential – even compared my work favorably to several prominent contemporary writers – he didn't have the time to do the vast editorial pruning required. A verbal jungle, he said. Too much underbrush, he complained. Way overdone. 'The resonance of language, not of experience,' he wrote. Even quoted Shakespeare, Othello, if I'm not mistaken: 'mere prattle without practice.' I was flattered, sort of, yet crushed, cause his parting advice to me was to throw my thesaurus into the Zuiderzee and start over."

"Good call! How astute of him."

"You mean his recommendation to start from scratch?"

"No, an American agent knowing about the Zuiderzee. Most wouldn't know where to find Holland in the atlas, let alone any topographical detail."

"Yeah. I was impressed, too, and sorry he didn't invest in me," Harm said, ruminating a bit, then snapping out of it – so much water under the bridge.

"So what'd you do? Follow his advice?"

"Religiously, at least once a year or so. Bought me a stack of cheap paperbacks at a bargain basement sale once, paid four guilders each I think - couple of bucks U.S. Well worth it. And whenever I have the urge, I stop off at the nearest body of water and ceremoniously hurl *Roget* to the fish. I usually take advantage of the opportunity to feed the ducks, take some action photographs of windsurfers, you know, with Nel and the girls along. Make a picnic out of it, take sandwiches and cold beer. But thesaurus-tossing remains one of the regular features in my life. Sure I didn't tell you about it? Must've. That I proposed it to the Netherlands Olympic Committee for inclusion as a new event?"

"You clown! You vandal! Such sacrilege!" HG feigned anger, slapping his friend about the cheeks and chin, Harm meekly defending himself though he had a good 4-inch reach on HG, and at least 30 pounds.

Nel, Harm's wife who stood alongside her husband, joined in the fray, teasingly jabbing him in the ribs.

"Precies wat ik ook altijd gezegd heb. Nou, of niet soms? Een pure geldverspilling, nog afgezien van het slechte voorbeeld dat je aan de meiden geeft."

Nel didn't speak much English, unlike Harm, but HG got her drift. She basically agreed with him, found it a bad example for the girls and a waste of money to boot.

She nursed a wine glass containing orange juice, from which she took an occasional sip. She was not a beautiful woman to look at. Her face was a bit coarse and she didn't wear make-up to make up for it either. Never had. She was the daughter of a sugar beet farmer, staid and stolid, but Harm loved her for it.

She and HG now exchanged looks of solidarity.

Instinctively she looked away, over towards the pool behind a hedge of sculpted box, where her twin daughters frolicked in the shallow end. All was well, but still she didn't feel at ease. They weren't her kind of folks, these pampered people. Too much ostentation, too. Always looking whether others were looking. She much preferred the simple life, away from the crowd, puttering about the house – sewing, polishing the silver, baking cakes, roasting chickens. But for Harm's career she met her social obligations. It'd been difficult for her, the transition from rural to urban life. But she managed. Sturdy stock, like Belgian draught horses - plowing, plowing on, ever and anon.

"*Birth in Berkeley* was a bit overdone, you gotta give that to the man," HG laughed, cultivating the lull in the conversation.

"He was pretty sharp, I admit. I'm only sorry he didn't make the effort to work with me. In hardly a page of comment this West-Coast agent, I forget his name, had fathomed my 'POV problem' - didn't care for my 'omniscient narrator'. Plus, he assessed forthrightly, 'non-native speaker trying to outdo the natives.'"

"It can be a problem, though it didn't slow up Nabokov."

"Thanks a lot." Harm acted insulted by the comparison.

"What can I say. Stick to what you know best."

"You mean osmics?"

"Don't turn your nose up at osmics, Mr. Flavors and Fragrance Man. It's nothing to sneeze at, you know," HG quipped.

"Boy, that really stinks!" And here a playful Harm raspberried HG, who took the mild reprimand in his stride.

A passing waiter took their empty glasses and offered fresh, exotic-looking cordials, perspiring beads of condensation that trickled in rivulets down their cold, bulging glass bellies.

Publishers Sjef and Gerrit, excessively powdered and perfumed as usual, picked their way through the happy assembly. They'd spotted their guest of honor being monopolized by the Bontekoes and dragged him off to meet a VIP who'd apparently just arrived.

The vast garden was abuzz with chitchat, a pleasant drone of voices that practically drowned out the live chamber music coming from the patio, barring a crescendo or two – snow-covered musical mountaintops rising from the storm-tossed sea of din. Huge marble and aluminum abstracts glinted in the bright afternoon sun. The formal garden borders were alive with a riot of color punctuated by towering fox gloves, giant nicotiana, holly hock; lumbering bumble bees laboriously airlifting cargoes of nectar back to the home front; the shrubbery beyond pruned in geometrical patterns – hearts, clubs and spades – best recognizable from the second-floor balcony of the opulent mansion belonging to the affluent gay couple, who were avid bridge-players. The ivy-covered brick facade undulated in a slight breeze that made the hot afternoon barely tolerable.

The overflowing crowd wandered at will throughout the property as "tout" literary Holland flocked to one of the most prestigious residences in 't Gooi, the Beverly Hills of the Low Lands. Hilversum, too, Holland's Hollywood, dutifully gave *acte de presence* and F.Fokko Okkels was having a field day rubbing elbows with TV and movie stars, all but the most publicity-hungry generally trying to avoid him like the plague. But Fokko had been invited on explicit urging of HG, who felt he owed him, after the pranks he and Harm had pulled on the tabloid reporter over the years, sensing that he still bore a bit of a grudge against them.

Okkels overworked his microcassette recorder – this time with freshly recharged penlights – as he took advantage of the opportunity of interviewing whomever he could, which meant all those who couldn't escape in time, at times leading to some pretty embarrassing situations.

But his big break came when one of Holland's hottest romantic young couples arrived, rumored to be on the verge of getting hitched. Every tabloid hound in the country would've given his right paw to be the one to scoop the exact date of the social event of the decade – but none had managed the trick so far; hence a salivating Fokko lingering in eager anticipation by the mansion's portico. He was determined to be the first to spot Dries en Wilma they second they'd come around the bend of the splendiferous flower-border-lined driveway.

He sped over to them, but found the otherwise inseparable couple entangled in a lovers' spat just as they emerged from their shiny red Rolls. Okkels beat a hasty retreat when an irate Wilma shooed him in his zeal to insert himself between her and Dries, whose dander was also up. He'd never seen them like this; no one ever had.

The couple's rage was momentarily diverted to their mutual foe, but the minute Okkels had turned his back – not believing his luck at their misfortune – the pair resumed their tiff. Recriminations flew back and forth, staccato gestures, a flurry of obscenities, followed by a less than graceful exit.

The couple never did make it to the front door, Wilma speeding off in the chauffeur-driven limousine, while Dries imposed on an old friend of his who was just leaving, for a ride home.

Okkels was already busy drafting the story, heading indoors to find a fax: "Love nest in tatters / sordid one-night stand torpedoes match of the decade / who is the mystery woman in Dries' life? Will Wilma wait?"

But before he could complete his mission, one of the staff intercepted him.

"You're Mr. Okkels, aren't you, sir?"

"Yes I am."

"Please come quickly, it's your dog, sir."

"Something happen to Linda?"

"Yes. Well, no, not exactly," the man said, leading the way to the patio.

"Oh my god," Okkels exclaimed when he saw a huge mastiff unabashedly copulating with Linda in broad daylight. His Rottweiler bitch was apparently in heat, and had he known he certainly would never have brought her along.

Party guests tried to ignore the painful scene as best they could, though furtive glances were cast in the direction of the unusual form of entertainment on offer.

Okkels tried to intervene but nearly got his hand amputated in the mastiff's maw, not about to be denied its due.

Without hesitating the intrepid reporter reached for a nearby garden hose hanging on a reel at the side of the house, turned on the tap and trained the nozzle at the fierce canine swain. He gave the animal a thorough soaking, which seemed to cool it off considerably and after a bit more wriggling, the dogs parted, Linda, Okkels' playful young Rottweiler clearly relieved at being liberated from the strange ordeal.

Joke Op 't Land (Dutch for Johanna and pronounced Yokah), somewhat tarnished and fading star of stage and screen, came rushing over, corralling her pet and severely reprimanding him in public.

"Naughty boy, Janus. Naughty, naughty, naughty!"

And to Okkels: "I'm so sorry, please forgive me, Fokko."

"It's quite alright, it wasn't your fault. It's in the nature of the beast," he joked, trying to make light of the situation.

Joke and he had known each for many years; ran into each other fairly regularly at the many (incestuous) occasions Hilversum offered its own — always and forever the same old faces.

"Besides, Janus obviously has good taste," Okkels added, tacky as usual.

"Oh, you!" Joke was stumped for a reply. People might've overheard, though the curious onlookers had already dispersed, the spectacle more or less over.

Both dog owners walked their pets to their respective cars in the parking lot out front and locked the animals inside — careful to leave the windows open wide enough for fresh air to enter on this sweltering day, but not so wide as to allow the dogs to jump out.

On the way back inside, Okkels took advantage of the opportunity of interviewing Joke about rumors that were circulating of her being asked to star in an upcoming television series based on a stage play she'd done the year before on the life of Keetje Tippel — yet another in the line of (in)famous Dutch prostitutes. And in this instance, too, as in the case of Xaviera Hollander and Mata Hari, there were overtones of "hometown girl makes good," in as much as the heroine in question rose to the occasion by overcoming poverty and ignorance against overwhelming odds. A truly heart-warming story of downward mobility that embodied all the sterling personality traits of the stalwart Dutch female in the face of austerity and hardship.

"Yes, well, I do hope to get the part, though no decision has yet been taken," Joke was saying coyly, high heels clicking on the flagstone entrance, the freshly white-washed hall of the house just beyond — the massive oakwood doors invitingly swung open to welcome the hordes of guests.

"But enough about me, Fokko, how've you been lately?"

This was her big chance and she put on a convincing act, making Okkels believe that there was more to her deepening interest in him than wresting a promise of getting her puss in the Courandstad Nexus the following day – and nudging out her arch rival Chantal van Onderen, that cunning vixen bitch she'd already spotted prowling about.

Though Joke didn't let on, she felt very insecure about getting the part in the TV series. Others were in the running, she'd been told by her agent – in an oblique reference to Chantal – and a little extra publicity at this stage might just turn the trick, he'd hinted. Times were tough and she wasn't getting any younger – the deprecating term "Hoar of Hilversum" already having been heard in some circles, he'd shuddered, and so had Joke.

"You *will* do everything in your power to get maximum exposure, won't you, Joke dear?" her agent had insinuated, and Joke took that to mean prostituting herself to Okkels if need be. It was well worth it considering what was at stake here. Not that her virtue was unblemished. To the contrary. It was no major sacrifice to her since she took special pride in personally testing the quality of mattresses procured by residents of 't Gooi, wed or unwed, young or old, crepit or decrepit. It was all part of her meticulous career planning – and quite in line with the coveted part she wanted to land so desperately. Practice after all did make imperfect.

A stately oak in the middle of the vast garden cast a welcome island of shade to which sun-toasted reception-goers repaired whenever the wilting midday heat became too much for them. Others emerged from the cool living room, located behind the spacious patio, to fill up vacant places.

Catering staff dressed in modish grenadine shorts and sleeveless shirts mingled with their ample *hors d'oeuvre* platters and silver serving trays holding festive tall drinks.

Gerrit en Sjef were busily recounting the trite anecdote of their initial encounter with HG.

Their target was a University of Amsterdam professor of philosophy and her business-tycoon husband who'd done a stint long back as State Secretary of Economic Affairs in a center-right Cabinet.

She, Anja de Boer, and a handful of other privileged scholars represented academe, who after all had early on expressed a keen interest in HG's work. More than that, they'd been among the first to press the publishers to consider taking on HG, but that had only served to dampen Gerrit & Sjef's sense of enterprise. By and large academic interest in an author meant the kiss of death: a sure-fire guarantee of a disappointing launch, followed by an anemic trickle of orders, and terminating in excellent prospects of slumping sales charts, red figures, and tax write-offs. But they had finally gone ahead with the venture when it turned out that HG didn't confine himself to dry specialized treatment of his subject. Rather, he injected his work with juicy anecdotal material that somehow struck a healthy balance between format and content. Besides, WWW's high-profile book tours virtually guaranteed perpetual public interest.

And it was typical, just then, too, of HG's broad appeal that one of the waiters neglected his catering duties to draw HG out about some conjecture or other that had intrigued him for some time, and about which he wanted "a third opinion", while the professor and her husband laughed politely at Sjef's rehashed – and refried – tale of their first encounter dished up for the occasion.

"It was nearly 6 p.m. when HG rang us long-distance that first time, and Gerrit and I were just closing up. It was a Friday evening, I remember very well. We'd had such a hectic week, truly hectic, and we were simply dying to take off for the yacht," Sjef regaled his guests.

"Yes," Gerrit chimed in, in his high-pitched, strident voice, "we were readying the cash register for Monday morning when HG called, and I recall quite losing track of counting the 100 guilder banknotes…"

"It's oh-so irritating…" Sjef added, intensely reliving the nonevent.

"Of course we have our staff, but we both still insist on taking an active part in all aspects of the business, and I don't have to tell you that the stately facade on Herengracht is our pride and joy. Everyone knows that."

Indeed, everyone did and it did not need repeating. But repeated it was.

"I was sooo annoyed when in the middle of counting our money HG telephoned that I snapped, I tell you. I just snapped," Sjef emphasized. "I quite lost my head a moment. Don't forget, we get dozens of calls from aspiring writers, most of whom will never amount to anything. And then this *American* on the line, rude and outspoken, with that hideous accent!"

He grabbed HG by the wrist, chuckling adorably; which was answered by a forbearing smile.

"I was simply boiling, I tell you, when he kept insisting we take on translation of a work we'd never even heard of, by an author we didn't know from Adam."

"It was several years ago, don't forget, before HG's star had begun to rise. And philosophy is not exactly our genre. Nor do we do many translations ordinarily, apart from the staple romances," Gerrit supplemented his lifetime companion, by way of apology more than anything. "Too risky. Much too risky."

The philosophy professor nodded understandingly, her husband distracted by the many beautiful people dotting the lawn, instinctively straightening his tie. A titivating Kay Dance strutted her stuff; Sockeye in baggy trunks poolside surrounded by admirers, his magnificent torso gleaming in the sun; and while HG's rather wiry and frenetic interpretress Polly Glot was caught in a 5-way conversation with a publishers delegation from the former East Bloc who had just purchased the translation rights to *Guide*, her male stenographer Dick Tate took detailed notes; look-a-like decoy, the Brit Sir O. Gate, mimicking HG's idiosyncrasies to a T, was having some fun at his boss' expense, entertaining astonished guests who really could not tell the two apart.

Meanwhile none other than Ms. Picture Perfect, Chantal van Onderen, the unrivaled diva of Dutch cinema on whom Ir. De Boer had had a terrible Humbert Humbert-like crush ever since her preteen screen debut, was approaching HG's party from the opposite direction. He himself was just placing his autograph on a paper cocktail napkin the waiter produced when Chantal made a splashy entrance in the vaunted, airy way she had about her. She was hot stuff, and what's more, she knew she was hot stuff.

"Say cheese!" a jack-in-the-box Okkels ordered, popping up out of nowhere and snapping a picture from the most advantageous angle to catch HG and Chantal – allowing ample space for the others to be conveniently cropped and relegated to the darkroom floor back at the office.

"Oh my, don't let me interrupt," Chantal chirped, knowing full well she was interrupting, but knowing equally that HG's vicinity was where the action was, publicity-wise. She had an eye, and nose, for the toadies of the tabloid press and always managed to get herself into a few papers or magazines every week of the year. They knew she sold copy, and she knew they knew.

Okkels failed to see the murderous expression on Joke's face, inconspicuously watching him from a distance, as he lavished his attention on Chantal. He didn't realize the strain Joke was under of late; and she could use Chantal's unblemished young talent like a hole in the head.

When Gerrit had done the honors introducing everyone, Sjef picked up where he'd left off, the bystanders – all artificial smiles, faces pricked up – mustered what interest they could.

"Yes, it's true, I did tell HG that I was counting my money and that he should call back at a more convenient time. Horrendous in retrospect, of course. Simply horrendous, I admit. Must've made us look quite the money-grubbing Babbitts, eh HG?"

"Embarrassing, sooo embarrassing! You have forgiven us, haven't you?" Gerrit cooed, putting his arm around HG's waist and swaying in tandem.

"Well, not really," HG kidded, obtrusively patting his publisher's broad buttocks.

"Oh, you! You're such a tease!" Sjef effervesced. "Isn't he a terrible tease?"

"Look, there's Sjaak and Elly, please excuse us, won't you?" Gerrit said excitedly, dragging his companion away by the arm. "Now, come along Sjef, we mustn't neglect any of our dear guests."

"You can have HG all to yourselves for awhile, Anja honey," Sjef managed to get out, craning as Gerrit pulled him along. "But only if you promise to give him back," he giggled, winking meaningfully at HG, who winked back amiably.

The twosome, dressed in finest Italian summer suits and matching creme-colored wide-rimmed felt hats, traipsed across the lawn straight into the open arms of a whiskered gentleman they apparently knew well, intercepted short of Sjaak and Elly who had to patiently wait their turn.

"Just one more," Okkels ordered, trying to entice his prey into a special performance. "For tomorrow's front page!"

No sooner had the shutter snapped or Chantal in her ebullient way was off like a jittery butterfly, Okkels in hot pursuit, quite oblivious to the envy this generated in Joke's ample bosom, half hidden behind a rhododendron bush.

Relative peace descended on the threesome who remained. Professor Dr. Anja de Boer took elegant drags on her slim cigarillo, a sight to behold, her aristocratic features well proportioned, eyes sparkling, a faint flush on her cheeks from the afternoon heat.

Her mind was as sharp as a surgeon's scalpel, with which she was wont to sanitize her environs of the putrid flesh of metaphysical cancers. She had a reputation to uphold, and uphold it she did. HG had once overheard her say to an obstreperous, slightly inebriated philosophaster who had cornered her into a suffocatingly intimate *Verklammerung* at a reception held in her honor that reflection on the questions mattered, and not so much the answers he cared to provide. That had momentarily tongue-tied the fellow, though not for very long. And to shut him up once and for all, she'd added, "For questions are the human equivalent of dogs sniffing each other, and frankly my dear I don't much care to be sniffed by you just now," shunting him onto a remote siding from whence there was no way back onto the main track without severe loss of face.

Awe-struck, HG had witnessed this painful little incident that had left the man no option but to retreat, tail between the legs and muttering the expletive Anja de Boer was most sensitive to: "Spiderwoman".

This was a snide reference to a term of deprecation early on inflicted on new-world adherents of Reconstructive Post-structuralist Deconstructionism where the notion of arachnoid web-weaving played such a central role. Their detractors had eagerly seized on discoveries of an anthropological nature to cast the movement in a light of primitivism when it turned out that the mythological conception of the origin of the universe prevalent among certain South American Indian tribes was based on precisely such arachnidan visions. In the folk tales of these "backward" tribes the Supreme Being was believed to be a spider with the world as its web, which turned out to be a rather sophisticated intuition that went a long way in matching the symbolism of mainstream Postmodernity, while at the same time vitiating its very novelty in a crushing manner.

As these things go, after a vituperative series of exchanges splashed across the pages of professional journals that somehow also made the popular dailies, Dr. de Boer was promptly branded "Spiderwoman" by a surly old goat of a neo-classicist literatus with an axe to grind. And Anja had been haunted by the term ever since. But as ever she thrived in adversity, demonstrating her true mettle by making short shrift of, in this case, too, that pseudo-obsequious creep out to inflate his own ego at her expense.

HG had appreciated Anja's sense of self-assurance, her decisiveness in dealing with adversaries of whatever caliber or disposition, though he'd known it to be a cover, one he took no pleasure in blowing; blowing sky-high when he did.

He was aware that at such times her abrasiveness was symptomatic of the power game she was accustomed to playing in order to maintain her prominent position within the university hierarchy and the wider concentric circles of the intelligentsia beyond, nationally as well as internationally. Not that he begrudged her her status, to the contrary; it served a purpose, and he'd rather she warmed the Heidegger Chair, than anyone else.

To be sure, they disagreed on Heidegger, as on most issues philosophical, but that was a healthy sign though regrettably one of their earliest encounters had degenerated into a bit of a row over esoteric detail. Afterwards, to clear the air, HG had composed a ditty on the spot, lionizing Anja's positive contributions in neutralizing her hero's more negative propositions, the refrain of which went, twice repeated: "Heidegger-degger-degger, Heidegger-degger-degger, Heidegger-degger-degger-do."

It was this same tendency of riding the banality-profundity axis to the hilt that on another occasion had led to HG posing the rhetorical question on a related issue: "Is it true what I've heard tell, that it was really Mrs. Jean-Francois Lyotard who wore the pants in the family, and not her husband?" To which he'd added, "Just like Mrs. Levi-Strauss!" Stumped, Anja was.

And then there was the anecdote about his son, which HG relished recounting for a nonplussed Anja de Boer. It seemed that a precocious Eric, at age 11, had taken after his father in matters prosodic by reacting to a bedtime story about the Standard Model (HG loved the edifying approach to parenting), by spontaneously writing down a poem which could go on *ad infinitum,* or, depending on the *gravity* of the situation, contract. Little Eric aptly called it "The Expanding You Know Verse", and it went like this:

        You Know   (etc)   You Know
                                    You Know
        You Know   You Know
        You Know
                                    You Know
        You Know   You Know
        You Know
        You Know (etc)   You Know

In this connection, HG also related his son's pubertal preference for light cones while his little pals still snacked on snow cones.

It was HG's unconventional, non-academic style that both intrigued Anja de Boer and put her off. But as HG was fond of pointing out, it had been Heidegger among others who had stressed the corporate nature of the university system, that bastion whose hegemony over the life of the mind was strictly enforced through an insidious regime of strong-armed power politics of the body, that bore all the hallmarks of totalitarianism, something Heidegger knew all about, having enjoyed the Fuhrer's personal patronage. And it was that in turn that put HG off.

Consequently his uncompromising, oft provocative approach precluded close involvement in academic treatment of issues, though he tried to keep abreast of developments. He absorbed the useful without raising it to gospel, like the aforementioned Lyotard's supplement to scientific knowing - and thus breaking science's self-anointed tyrannical autarchy in this regard. According to the Frenchman other forms of knowing included knowing how to act, live, listen, et cetera, all of which could potentially lead to "good" statements of a denotative, prescriptive or evaluative nature.

There are, after all, a zillion little bits of information that get us through the day which are generally never acknowledged as knowledge because they are so unassumingly common, ranging from picking one's nose, to tying one's shoe laces, making the bed, or love, to driving a car, pitching a tent or cooking a sumptuous dinner.

"Get out of the rain or you'll get wet!" being as accurate a prediction based on tried-and-tested homespun experiment as anything any trained test-tube jock ever made.

"Get out of the street kid or you'll get run over", being another, with some considerable survival value that must've saved the life of many an urchin.

There is more under the sun than scientific knowledge alone, bad news for the scientist, perhaps, but good news for the rest of (wo)mankind, according to a contentious HG, who in passing pleaded for the blessings a "Nescientific Revolution" could bestow.

But by and large WWW's leader tended to confine himself to concise verbal sorties directed against any and all deviation from the purely nondogmatic stance – in whatever field – using an equally simple as effective arsenal of arguments fashioned along the lines of Sextus Empiricus' tropes, or Nagarjuna's for that matter – a close Asian contemporary ($\pm$ 150 AD).

"Give the skeptic the benefit of the doubt", he was fond of saying to the partial-at-heart, "without at the same time subscribing to skepticism."

Speculative metaphysics was a wonderful field, where he, like most, enjoyed dallying, but from which one needed to know when and how to extricate oneself – a perennial problem, and the challenge par excellence for the discriminating individual.

Though men like Heidegger and Wittgenstein had pioneered the road back from medieval scholasticism and modern rationalism to context-bound socially-structured relevance ("games" of all manner and description), they had remained hopelessly hamstrung and unable to clear the final hurdle. Both men had been documented (crypto) theists to the very end, and had they not been, as an indefatigable HG had repeatedly pointed out, they would most assuredly have been confirmed atheists – due to that irresistible pull of the mental pendulum that still held them in its sway.

Evidence, hard evidence, of enlightenment, true and penetrating insight into the ultimate nature of (non)being, namely rejection of either extreme, was utterly absent – not only in Heidegger and Wittgenstein, of course, but most thinkers, no matter how original or revolutionary they might appear.

Though castigating these trailblazers for making valiant attempts at reaching full enlightenment would have been chary of HG, he nevertheless needed to distance himself unambiguously from the error of their ways in order to make a fresh start – a fresh start that was more than mere patricide of course.

In more reflective moods, he'd equally point out the invaluable contributions these men had made, having no qualms adapting the brunt of his polemics to the requirements of the day. And when he did, he likened any of the premature answers to the most sophisticated equation of equations – in which we ourselves are variables – as solutions we must all first try on for size. And as such we owe a debt to those who went before – in as much as anyone ever goes anywhere...But to the extent they do, we can follow in their footsteps only so far without landing in the same quagmire they did, before finally leapfrogging to enlightenment.

"Inexcusable is he who obfuscates unwittingly," HG was saying to Anja, "as Heidegger does repeatedly."

She only raised her left eyebrow in anticipation. She knew HG too well to walk eyes open into one of his carefully laid traps. Nor was there any point in tackling him head on, as she had once tried to do, accusing him of confrontationalism, to which he'd retorted, "I find that a fairly confrontational thing to say."

"His veneration of the pre-Socratics, for example," HG impugned, knowing full well that Anja's dissertation had been on Heidegger's heterodox view of the Greeks, "is utterly misplaced. He quite benightedly attributes superhuman qualities to Parmenides."

"And how's that?" Anja asked bemused.

"You mean apart from A.J. Ayer's shattering charges of linguistic incompetence?"

Anja was well aware of the British empiricist's criticism of Heidegger's Teutonic predilections and unwarranted philological license, but didn't take these charges seriously.

"Wanton prejudice," she said astringently, offering a light to her husband who nudged his filter cigarette to her burning cigarillo tip. "The British are allergic to the Germans, always have been, always will be," she spoke like a human music box in her wonderfully warm Coppertan tones.

"Granted. But it's utopian to idealize the achievements of the distant past," HG charged, "though given German aversion to Roman vulgarization of Greek classicism, coupled to a deep-seated need of self-aggrandizement, springing from an inferiority complex manifesting as its opposite."

He was banking on the dictum that "diction invites contradiction", one of the cardinal rules of the brand of dialectics to which he knew Anja subscribed.

"Care to be more specific?" came the terse interruption HG had been angling for, taking a bit of a swipe at the over-popular trend of applied historico-psychoanalysis as practiced by every Tom, Dick and Harry with a time-share couch, and which he knew Anja detested more than anything in connection with the man she so loved and admired. How she cringed at the publication of the umpteenth Heidegger biography harping on his shady past! Character assassination pure and simple was what it amounted to, and she, with many pints of German blood coursing through her veins (quite as the Dutch national anthem boasts), would have none of it.

"Take his adoration of Parmenides."

"Adoration, adoration. Heidegger makes a point, an important point. He doesn't adore."

She exhaled violently, and HG sidestepped the bellowing smoke, a first gambit in the tilting contest now in full swing. She was getting riled, the signal HG was waiting for, and he deftly moved into position to thrust to the heart.

"Whatever else it is, it's misguided."

"Elaborate, won't you?" professor de Boer invited, her eyes intently trained on her impromptu jousting opponent, whom she could see was getting into his stride. But she was on her guard, ready to parry his every treacherous move.

"Correct me if I'm wrong, Anja, but Heidegger claims, does he not, that Parmenides made no distinction between Being and Becoming, self and nature, object and knowledge of it; saw these dichotomies as part of the very process the Greeks called *physis*. Takes this as evidence that the pre-Socratics still lived in a utopian world, that pristine paradise, which subsequent western civilization managed somehow to lose sight of, and forget. And having forgotten about Being, and being suddenly confronted with an inexplicable nature, a world of objects, an *ens creatum* that then somehow needed to be accounted for, our forebears were lulled into positing a creator god who had made that world from which they felt they had been freshly ejected, that biblical Garden of Eden. It was an opportunist Christianity that proceeded to usurp this ready-made God for mass consumption, if you'll pardon the pun, yoking mankind for well over a thousand years, and launching us in hot pursuit of our modern metaphysical muddles."

HG paused for effect, knowing that this was all common introductory material in any of Anja's college courses on Heidegger. When he thought she was ready, he sprung the trap she'd suspected all along. "But if you think about it carefully a minute, you'll soon realize that claiming that Parmenides made no distinction between Being and Becoming – citing his famous fragment to that effect, as Heidegger does - is rather a self-contradictory proposition. Parmenides had to have been aware of the distinction Heidegger claims he, Parmenides, wasn't aware of, in order for him to have made it in the first place. It's quite analogous to the dilemma of the naive realist. The minute he knows himself to be a naive realist, he can by definition no longer be one."

Much as she hated to, Anja had to admit that HG had a point, though she'd have to consider it carefully. She knew him to be a first-rate gymnosophist, one who could easily bamboozle one.

She also always felt just a bit queasy in being confronted by HG – and it was no different this time, more so in fact.

"And there's something else," HG continued, backtracking to some extent. "Having 'forgotten' our pristine state – the state Parmenides supposedly still enjoyed, and which we supposedly hanker for, according to Heidegger – implies that all we need to do is 'remember' it in order to rectify the problem. The twofold question could then be put, who is forgetting, and who is remembering? The answer to the former would presumably be the metaphysical muddler. The answer to the latter, however, would also have to be that *same* metaphysical muddler! Why? Because the person aware that he is remembering, would have to constantly remember what it is he'd forgotten. And thus remembering, he's left no choice but to forget in order to get on with life. After all, you can't live life constantly remembering what you've forgotten, just as you can't keep forgetting what it is you're remembering!"

"Rubbish! I'm not buying any of it," Anja said. "I still got a prescription for a bottle of snake oil from the last medicine man that came along, thank you very much!"

"Good, glad to hear it. Ready to play a little hardball then? Ever stop to think what a coincidence it is that Heidegger's view virtually coincides with the old Hindu notion of a play-acting god who purposely forgets himself in order that he may entertain himself through an eternity of time? I don't know what that may say about Heidegger's originality?"

Again, one of those sobering hermeneutical pronouncements of HG's. What was he getting at? Hadn't Richard Rorty also badmouthed Heidegger, calling him an ascetic priest? Maybe they were on to something. She could not rule out the possibility.

"So what are you suggesting?" she said, weary of the roller-coaster conversation that was going nowhere fast.

"That there's no way out of the duality trap by opting for one of an opposite pair, like remembering or forgetting. It just don't get it."

"You and your damn duality! Forget duality! There is no duality! Heidegger's whole point is a subjectless, objectless epistemologicless Being," Anja countered, aghast at her own recalcitrance. She could stand only so much oral porridge being poured into her ear.

"Saying that there's no duality is itself an instance of duality, based as it is on certain undeniable principles of dichotomy. Heidegger does not get out from under by some ad hoc proclamation to the contrary. That's simply not good philosophy, I'm afraid. We can't take the man's word for it, no matter how impressive his authority."

Then more patiently, "You know as well as I, Anja, that distinction is the crux: identity and difference, obverse sides of the same coin, that's the key. A key, a coin Parmenides carried in his pocket no less than you or I, and which moreover he knew he had on him. Without it we would not know of Parmenides, nor Parmenides about himself for that matter. The very fact he did only affirms the man's awareness of the subtle process..."

"The subtle process?"

Anja's husband began looking very tired and bored. His field was import/export, wholesale footwear mostly, leather uppers, that sort of thing – though he had developed a few lucrative sidelines. His family hailed from the Province of North Brabant, once Holland's premier tannery center, which had gone down the tubes before he was even born.

He was proud of his life's achievement in having consolidated what was left of the family's former glory, a glory still reflected in extensive land holdings. He was a competent man, a man of consequence, with several fingers in the economic pie, and the political muscle to keep them there.

But Ir Huibrecht 'Bert' de Boer had no inkling as to the relevance of the present discussion, nor did he much care to make the effort. He had other concerns, of a more practical, mundane nature. In that sense, Anja was his better half, and lent a touch of breeding, of culture, to his life.

He doted on her, had always stimulated and supported her for the sake of her career, but never could get a firm grasp on matters esoteric, and excusing himself, he wandered off towards a familiar face in the crowd beyond, one he knew from a soap he watched on Saturday nights, given half a chance. Often he had to forego the simple domestic pleasures given his position of prominence in Holland's regentesque management circles. Receptions, formal dinners, business meetings till all hours, not to forget his contacts in government, and with the Royal Family! He'd often been on safari with H.R.H. the queen's father (though to his regret they had tended to carry cameras rather than rifles - at least with the viper press present).

To his great satisfaction, however, one of the innumerable progeny of the House of Orange now courted his elder daughter, and as far as that was concerned the future looked bright, bright indeed.

Anja, preoccupied, watched her husband disappear in the crowd. He was a regal, imposing, "outdoorsy" sort of man, with a wide gait; well-kempt always and never at a loss for words, except when it came to her forte.

"My elk versus your ilk, eh darling," as he'd once expressed it in one of the few bedroom spats in over 25 years of marriage that had left her in tears. How hard it was to wring a little happiness from life sometimes; inconsolably she'd sobbed.

Though she knew she should try harder to avoid alienating him the rare moments they spent together, she could not help herself. To her the hallowed line from Schopenhauer to Nietzsche to Heidegger and on to the zenith of postmodernity was gospel, and she – thoroughly hooked – could not pass up an opportunity to further her deepening understanding of the subtleties of the movement she had had a hand in shaping.

She was a respected researcher in her own right, who skillfully guided a bevy of international graduate students through the treacherous post-philosophic landscape pocked with pitfalls. She had learned the trade from some of the founding fathers back in the late '50s and early '60s, at a time when the world at large was mostly heedless to the liberating freshness of postmodernity-proper – not the hyped varieties that cropped up every other week in sundry fields, from art to architecture, literary criticism to lesbian liberation. Originally intended as a powerful antidote to the venom of progress – the sting in the tail of the French Enlightenment – postmodernity had been marketed none too soon, and not inappropriately mainly by the French themselves.

What a thrill to have watched the movement grow and spread, take root (or rhizome, as some preferred) and unfurl in glorious American hybrids, imbued with a characteristic sort of pragmatism that insured survival well into the 21st century. She'd virtually commuted between Paris and New York for a time, back when, holding season tickets for the Concord and Carnegie, and a semi-permanent suite of rooms at the Waldorf – mere perks for the key role she'd played in helping develop aspects of postmodernity in a retrograde world.

She'd personally met many luminaries, including Richard Rorty, and had been on hand when philosophizing was upgraded from a "truth-seeking endeavor" to a "good conversation". Just what distinguished a good conversation from a bad one, however, was still problematical and Anja de Boer wasn't too sure whether or not the present encounter with HG fit into the former or the latter category, though she had her suspicions.

Secretly she worried that she was still partially blind, sensing that a crucial insight eluded her, despite her vast erudition – perhaps because of it. Of late she also worried about her sudden moods of despondency, infrequent, but despondency nonetheless, bordering on ennui, which, she'd noticed, usually followed hard on the heels of a crushing oppressiveness accompanied by visions of being plunged into an all-devouring oblivion. She began to take to heart the old adage that one could tell the tree by its fruit, wondering as to the salubriousness of what her branch of speciality had borne.

To her chagrin she also found that she had begun to cling to an indistinct but palpable hope – that forward-straining intentionality closely akin to ambition, at times indistinguishable from it. To be sure, it was a hope for the present, not the future, precisely because postmodernity deprived one of all such time warps, and thus supplanted one squarely into that mesh of quicksand relations that is our home in the cosmos. To live a life devoid of hope was no longer an easy assignment for Anja de Boer to fulfill and it gave her pause to consider whether hers was a fully-fledged philosophy, or rather less than that – a jejune, truncated vision, perhaps; a rump vision without a heart, or indeed, as one of her most bellicose Spanish criticasters at a recent Madrid conference had it, *sin cojones*.

And in a spectacular reversal that made her head spin, it had suddenly occurred to her one fine Spring day while lecturing to an undergraduate class, though, of course, she never let on – that if postmodernism slackened the reins of progress and afforded each time-frame its own inalienable significance, each context its own relevance without recourse to some arbitrary preferential reference frame, there was no longer any compelling reason to choose postmodernism over modernism, or any other -ism for that matter!

"But if *everything* goes, *all* is lost!!!" that little devil on her shoulder screamed into her ear, freaking her like a high-strung horse.

The circle was unbroken and she came up empty-handed! And that now was intolerable! Utterly intolerable! Had she invested a lifetime of effort to end up "Anja the Apostate"??? The thought alone had caused her many sleepless nights, and when at last she slept she was haunted by a recurrent nightmare of recanting on her deathbed – its cylindrical posts metamorphosing into insect-infested shafts sunk deep into the grave, her grave, where she was sucked dry by millions of fat teeming white maggots. The impact of this spine-chilling nightmare-within-a-nightmare turned her into a blithering religious convert, while a stern and disapproving congregation of her most respected peers witnessed the pitiful scene as she perished ignominiously, deliriously incoherent. She of all people! She, who'd always valued articulate speech above all else!

But if it could happen to Schopenhauer...why *not* to her, this fate truly worse than a fate worse than death?

HG somehow knew about this personality flaw of hers, she realized, this appalling weakness, this wavering stance that could make her lose her footing any second. At moments such as these, moments of extreme defiance in the face of a frontal Herman Gnuticks attack which served as a self-styled litmus test during which she felt he could read off the results of her enfeeblement, she suspected that her rival anticipated a calamitous breakdown – as a matter of fact, did all he could to make her crack. And that's why she always felt so damn uncomfortable around him.

For his part, HG'd noticed the telltale signs of Anja's potentially debilitating infirmity creeping into some of the articles she wrote, some of which for weekly supplements of not only reputable Dutch but also French and German literary magazines. On a few occasions he'd even requested Froukje to respond by sending letters-to-the-editor in an attempt to diagnose the ailment, but these good-Samaritan missives were never even acknowledged, let alone honored with a serious reply. Froukje didn't produce the right credentials; didn't know the right people. In short, didn't count.

It was that sort of detestable "oversight" that confirmed the widely-held suspicion of the arrogance and the unassailability of academe vis-a-vis the man or woman in the street.

But HG, because of his singular position, could no longer be ignored by the establishment and relished his role as iconoclast. He was one of the few to pose a direct, substantive challenge to the postmodern paradigm (rather than mere whimsicality and trendiness) by dint of his formal analysis of the phenomenon. He'd also pointed out early on that to seek to neutralize the nefarious notion of progress was one thing, but to adopt a fatuous fatalism in its stead, quite another. As always, both extremes should be avoided fastidiously.

Some non-western critics were also already accusing postmodernists like Dr Anja de Boer of a repugnant callousness for their tacit endorsement of a business-as-usual attitude to rationalize inaction in the face of so much inequality and injustice rampant in the world. And it was such charges that were helping to undermine Dr. de Boer's erstwhile confidence, to not only prefigure, but hasten the headlong lunge into the morbid pit of nihilism she so dreaded.

"Anja has stumbled upon that Vast Vast Nothingness," one of her colleagues had confided to HG while comparing notes on their common concern for her.

HG was well aware of the appeal Heidegger held out to people like Anja de Boer, and the spin-off his views had generated. But that did not change the fact that his unconscious projections of what he deemed to be laudable mental states upon people of different epochs were jarring anachronisms. And in retrospect, it was easy to see that given that latent strain of German Idealism in his blood, Heidegger's clever interpretations served not only to deceive himself, but whole generations of followers: first the Existentialists, later the Postmodernists, and many in-between – all desperately in search of lifestyles worth living in a bleak and alienating world teetering on the edge of technological disaster, environmental pollution and nuclear war. Such anxiety-ridden states generated frantic flights of fancy that led to sect and cult formation around which, as always, the weak and insecure clustered to the weaker and insecurer.

Anja de Boer had started out a leader. But many decades on the front had shell-shocked her and nowadays she was less certain of the boon of issuing "directionless directions" – she tended to think of her publications as "traveler's advisory bulletins intended to disorient the 'oriented masses'."

And now she'd fallen into her own trap. Her confidence was waning and a nagging feeling pursued her of having taken a wrong turn somewhere along the line; or perhaps of just having gone overboard, who knows? It needed sorting out. What HG might have to say could be helpful and she resolved to give him the benefit of his skeptical doubt, as he advised.

But just as she was preparing herself to rethink basic Heideggerian tenets, HG took a different tack, master as he was at keeping opponents off balance in any debate. "...The subtle process," he reiterated. "Known to Parmenides as *physis* and to you as that cacophony of interrelationships. But knownnnnnnnn!" He stressed the word as though it were raised to the nth power. "And thus an epistemic fact."

"I could say the same of Nonism," Anja retorted, disappointed in herself for reneging on her fledgling resolution so soon, despite herself.

"Now just a femto-second," HG spoke, with typical flourish, "You won't hear me deny it." Then brightening, "But does that mean you've read *Guide for the Apoplexed*?"

"Just the first few pages. I've been asked to review it for a Rotterdam paper. Besides, I caught the Vreeken show."

"Oooops!" Theatrically HG covered his crotch with both hands, crossing his legs and crooking at the waist.

"'Sagacitas' would be better Latin than 'sagaciens'," Anja resumed, ignoring the exhibitionist mock gesture of prudishness. Her cognitive apparatus was still well strung, even though she might be losing the fight against HG on points.

"Better Latin, perhaps. But the association with sapiens would be less overt, if not lost altogether," he replied, straightening back up to his full stature.

His antics were wasted on Anja this particular day. She was plainly not in the mood.

"I must confess your distinction between trivial and non-trivial emptiness is a novel find. I've pondered the problem myself. Even so, it remains a distinction, to quote you, and thus well entrenched in the epistemic realm, if you'll forgive my presumption," Anja said, taking small pleasure in retaliating to some degree for the brazen attack on her, her hero and everything she held dear.

"Ah, but unlike Heidegger, I state so explicitly, as you will see if and when you finish the piece," HG said as graciously as he could, "whereas time and again you tend to try to establish a free-floating monolithic relativism, not to mention that darn Heideggerian empirical bias."

"What empirical bias are you talking about?" Anja asked, feeling flushed and flustered.

In his best German accent that did not elicit as much as a smile from her, HG replied, "Vhy arg dzere Beinks az all, und vhy noz razzer nozzink?" continuing in his normal voice, "Heidegger's overt anti-science stance notwithstanding, the man suffered from a terminal case of materialitis, if you…"

"Anja, dear, you must come and see the exotic aviary! Wood storks and everything…Oh, won't you excuse us, Mr. Gnuticks?" interrupted a stranger.

"Shall we continue this conversation at the university roast on Sunday? I'll have a thing or two to say on the subject," Anja proposed, bowing out.

"That's precisely the trouble, you see, thing…thinginess…"

But it was futile. A tap on the shoulder had killed the conversation. An old friend of Anja's to the rescue. And not a minute too soon.

HG was left to contemplate the state of the reception by now well over its peak. "Thing-i-ness," he muttered under his breath. He spoke the word solemnly, then laughed, repeating himself yet again, "Thing-i-ness."

He looked around. Most of his gang was still occupied entertaining the few guests that remained to the bitter end, polishing off the last of the snacks and colorful drinks. It made him chuckle, thinking of a line from *The Great Gatsby*: "…after two highballs, she became cordial."

Inspired by Fitzgerald's example, HG pulled a pad and pencil from his back pocket and jotted down in no particular order:

-how Mafia gets their own acquitted?: per jury
-skeleton crew at funeral parlor: mortician's strike?
-last ever music craze: apocalypso
-medium in deep trance at seance: "McCluhan is the message..."
-anally fixated psychologist: C.J. Dung?
-Nonadology à la Leibniz?
-Looking out for No. Nil***; (followed by triple asterisks, and a note that read "title for new book?").
-Gidgit goes to Bharat; kids cartoons, with installments on Gidgit goes to Varanasi, Gidgit goes to Khajuraho, Gidgit goes to Bollywood, etc. Discuss with Warren Rabbit of film division;
-the torrid love story of Cannibal Adderley and the Abdominal Snowwoman;
-Medieval period piece exploring the moral and ethical influence of Mother Hood and Father Hood on son Robin?
-first fence went up where first tree went down;
-insanely changeable trouser fashions: panta loony rhei;
-abbot, on being asked by monk: "Buddha is my great expiration";
-two old expressions: "Man does not live by breath alone" & "To curry flavor";
-is time an anachronism, and history hearsay?

He bit the back of his stubby pencil, pondered a minute, changed his mind, and changed it again, deciding not to cross out the snide reference to C.J. Jung after all, and repocketed the note pad. Not a bad harvest considering the many distractions. He had his work cut out for him working out this set of prompts!

HG then meandered into the house to take a leak, followed discreetly as always by one of Sockeye's men. It was standard practice never to let HG out of sight, yet not inconvenience him needlessly, if it could be avoided.

The two downstairs rest rooms were occupied and helpful domestic staff realizing who he was – their guest of honor – directed him to Gerrit & Sjef's private upstairs bathroom by way of exception.

Seconds later, he locked himself in a plush chamber carpeted in deep salmon pile; pink marble sinks; faucets gold-plated; stacks of sumptuous towels; cakes of carved lanolin soap. And to take it all in, flattering indirect lighting created a soothing atmosphere (or was it to accommodate the aging publishing duo's twice face-lifted but thrice-sagging skin?).

No expense had been spared by his vainglorious hosts – down to the twin Duchamp urinals - generously drawing on funds siphoned from a stable of artists who fared considerably less well than did their mentors.

Not that HG had money problems, to the contrary. He hadn't given money a thought for many years. It had become what it ought to be, a convenient medium to transact the business of living. And as he stood there ruminating while answering nature's urgent call in one of the non-functional works of non-art, HG was distracted by a muffled noise coming from the adjacent bedroom – or so he assumed. He was about to leave after washing and drying his hands when he heard it again, and an irrepressible curiosity overtook him, realizing that its source could not be Sjef and Gerrit who were still out in the backyard hovering like humming birds over their honored guests.

Ever so carefully he opened the opposite door from the one leading back into the hallway, only to shut it instantly. Had he seen right? Yes, he'd seen right. Quietly he opened the door again and studied the scene at leisure, because the couple going at it hot and heavy were so preoccupied that they had no inkling they were being observed. Okkels, undressed from the waist down, was humping a plump middle-aged woman from behind, doggy-style, head tilted back in ecstasy. If it was what HG suspected, it could give whole new meaning to the notion that dog owners resembled their pets, certainly after the incident with Janus and Linda that had transpired earlier in the afternoon. Was there a connection? Nah. Nothing that perverse, HG thought, though he wouldn't put it past Okkels. He couldn't vouch for Joke, however, though by the looks of it...it did take two to tango...and Holland was a libertine sort of place, with sodomy never far off.

It was a touching scene but HG'd seen quite enough. He was about to shut the door behind him when he abruptly changed his mind, and entered the bedroom. Within easy reach lay Okkels' crumpled trousers, tossed next to the fax machine sitting on the rosewood credenza, his boxer shorts on the floor beside it. HG conjectured that while Okkels was by no stretch of the imagination a sharp dresser, neither was he a sharp undresser, and he wondered what Sjef and Gerrit would say were they to find out what went on in the sanctity of their bedroom-cum-office?

A pungent hirsute scent prickled his nostrils, triggering a sneeze HG could barely suppress. "Once a sheep farmer, always a sheep farmer," he thought, twitching his nose to ward off another sneeze, and another still.

The reporter's specs, mini-cassette recorder and camera lay on his soiled socks by the wall, while over on the nightstand next to the double bed HG could see Joke's outsized gold-framed glasses, which dominated her pudgy face when she wore them, always precariously perched and threatening to slide off her slim nose. They didn't have a good pair of eyes between them, HG realized, and knew he would not be noticed by the couple who in any case were amorously distracted, moaning and groaning, bare backs and buns towards him, pelvises picking up momentum like a steam locomotive.

Talk about your *tableau vivant,* with the stress on *vivant*!

Mischievous mission accomplished, seconds later HG was merrily on his way down the stairs without the couple any the wiser as to his intrusive presence.

* * * * *

EIGHT

"Let's see you get out of this one, mestkevertje," Ans van As, Ms Dijkstra's feisty secretary, whispered to Okkels on his way into her office. She used the pejorative, making it sound almost sweet, like a pet name, whereas it was meant to sting.

Okkels – trailing a heady odor – hitched up his pants. He chose to ignore the taunt and entered Ms. Dijkstra's office with more than average confidence. He'd had a hugely successful afternoon at the Laren reception. He'd left weighed down with juicy stories – from the Dries & Wilma split-up, to scoops on the fall season's TV programming, a sneak preview of what could be expected at the university roast on the weekend, and much, much more, apart from his liaison with Joke Op 't Land, of course, which he was dying to disclose, but couldn't as yet. Decency forbade it...but then what was decency...ultimately?

"What's the meaning of this?!" Ms. Dijkstra demanded to know, her head in a halo of greyish smoke. She rose from her swivel chair, reached over, and slammed down a stack of black-and-white photographs across the desk separating her from Okkels.

"Those my pictures?" Okkels asked, taken aback by Ms. Dijkstra's vehemence. Inaudibly his bowels discharged a sizable cloud of gas, but the smell of burning tobacco was too powerful for his boss to notice this modest contribution to the unhealthy climate in the room. "Whatta they doin' here? I asked Remco to send them to me pronto as soon as they were developed. I've been waiting to get going on the layout."

"Forget the layout. You're suspended!"

Okkels looked at Dijkstra in bewilderment. "Suspended? What for?" Suspensions and dismissals always seemed uppermost on her mind in connection with him, and he was getting pretty damn fed up, her always yanking his chain that way.

Ms. Dijkstra held her ground, arms folded across her emaciated chest which her loose-fitting printed cotton blouse could not disguise. She just glowered at Okkels, who winced and lowered his gaze to the stack of photos – his mutiny short-lived. He was stunned to see himself caught in the act with Joke Op 't Land in Gerrit & Sjef's bedroom.

"What the hell's this!?" he exclaimed.

"That's what I'm waiting to find out," came the terse reply.

"I don't know, I don't know," Okkels stammered. "I can't figure it? Must be some sorta gag."

"Hilarious gag. You'll have to do better than that, Fokko."

"Really, I don't know anything about this. Must be doctored. One of Remco's tricks. You know how he is."

"I'd send him packing in a minute," Dijkstra promised. "And he knows it. He himself brought the photos over, shocked by the...the filthy porn he found materializing in his developing bath."

"But I really don't now what happened, Rijkje, you gotta believe me."

"Is that you or isn't it? And who's that woman you're...you're with?"

"Yes that's me. And Joke, Joke Op 't Land. You know Joke. She's in the running for the Keetje Tippel series. As a matter of fact..."

"Never mind that now!"

"Sorry, sorry. Yeah, well, we did, ahm...get together. But this...I...I just can't figure it," Okkels stammered foolishly, fidgeting with himself.

There was a knock at the door and the city desk editor brought in an IPA telex.

"You might like to see this," he said to Ms. Dijkstra. "Came in well over an hour ago, but it didn't dawn on me that it might be the same Laren mansion." And to Okkels, "Must've been some hot reception, eh, Fokko-boy?"

Okkels didn't know whether his long-time colleague was referring to the affair being discussed or something else, and wisely kept mum. He trained his eyes on Dijkstra as she read the latest IPA news flash.

"My God, no!" she cried.

"What is it?" Okkels asked meekly.

Dijkstra looked at her watch, nearly 22:00 hours. "Come along to the lounge, we'll just catch the Journaal. The Laren mansion is ablaze. What the hell went on there today?"

Okkels was already more or less in shock, feeling like a zombie, and it was easy to obey Dijkstra. He felt many eyes impinge on him from behind desks as he was force-marched to the other end of the building. And though he liked nothing better than to be the focus of attention, these were not exactly the circumstances he preferred.

There was time for a cup of fresh brew while they waited for the ten o'clock Journaal to come on.

"You're not serious about suspending me, are you?" Okkels braved after a fragrant sip which brought him around.

"I am!" said an adamantine Dijkstra.

"Look, I'm sorry about what happened, but it's my private business. It's got nothing to do with the paper," Okkels said firmly, feeling fortified by the caffeine.

"It does when your film is developed in *our* darkroom and makes its way to *my* desk."

"I already told you I don't know how that happened. You gotta let me finish this project. What about the other photographs, did you see all the celebrities I managed to shoot? It'll be a fabulous spread."

"I'll have Jansen write it up."

"No!" Okkels shouted indignantly, surprised at his own outburst. "Look, I don't care, I want you to call Waterreus on this," he threatened. "It's too important. To me. To the paper."

Dijkstra couldn't help being impressed by Okkels' guts, but called his bluff. "You're on. I've got no qualms clearing this with Waterreus. He'll back me. Don't you doubt it."

Then the news came on and Dijkstra hushed the small crowd of newspapermen and women that had gathered around them. But it took a number of international events before on-the-spot coverage of the Laren fire was aired. The house where Okkels had been only hours ago was burning like a torch, firefighters surrounding the mansion from all sides to try to contain the blaze. But it was obviously a lost cause, something that was readily confirmed by the murmurs of dismay of those watching the tragedy unfolding on the TV screen.

Okkels shuddered to think that he might easily have been incinerated if the conflagration had occurred a bit earlier. He literally would've been caught with his pants down, barbecued to a crisp. How lucky one could get, he reflected. "Here but for the grace of God…," he thought, counting his blessings. And he wondered whether Joke might be watching the news just then, feeling their fates intertwined.

The news reader reeled off the text: "Fire gutted the entire top storey of the Laren mansion belonging to one of Holland's most prominent publishers. Damage is estimated to run in the millions as not only most of the monumental building lay in ruins but an invaluable and unique collection of paintings and sculptures, including genuine Samsons, Cunes, Jansens, Lawsons, a Koons, and several Warhols, apart from a string of Impressionists, Renoir, Monet, Pissarro, and even a minor Van Gogh are feared lost."

Archival slides of some of the works of art appeared on screen.

"Gone up in smoke also is the irreplaceable library of first editions and priceless antiquarian collector's items that had been in the family for generations."

This time the famous facade of the publishers' downtown Amsterdam offices was shown, associated in the public mind with historic publications, second only to Laurens Janszoon Koster's – inventor of the printing press - kept in Haarlem's Saint Bavo Cathedral.

"Fire departments throughout the vicinity cooperated in subduing the blaze, which took many hours. The cause of the inferno is a mystery as yet, but arson is not being ruled out. A thorough-going police investigation is being complicated by the presence of several hundred invited – and uninvited – guests at the reception held in Laren earlier today. But suspect number one, hinging on crucial testimony of some of the household staff, is none other than the guest of honor, WWW's Herman Gnuticks, who apparently was the last one seen to head upstairs, where the fire is thought to have originated."

And on came footage of an interview with one of the shaken staff members who explained that she had personally directed Herman Gnuticks to use the upstairs john because both downstairs rest rooms had been occupied at the time.

"He said his bladder was bursting and that it was in my interest to come up with a solution!" the maid recalled. "Or else he would, a yellow solution! And since I didn't really feel like mopping up after him, I pointed him upstairs. Who'd've guessed such a nice man would do a thing like that? Awful, just awful."

Okkels felt faint, sat down and grabbed the armrest of his chair. HG upstairs? So he was the culprit responsible for the compromising picture of him and Joke! The goddam bastard had gone and done it again! Put one over on him, again. Of course! He might've known!

Okkels was so preoccupied with his own thoughts that he hardly registered the news anchor saying that HG was thought to have had both motive and opportunity: it was too much of a coincidence that such outrageous incidents always seemed to befall the Wiseguy from the West, and that no matter how the nature of the incidents varied, the constant consequence was always unprecedented publicity and commensurate book sales. Now, too, a run on WWW books was anticipated, bookshops all over the country already frantically calling distributors even as the pictures were being aired.

"Of course it is premature for such speculation," the disembodied voice on the TV said, while more footage of fire-fighters tethered to hoses was flashing across the screen, "and a possible electrical fault in appliances, office equipment, lighting or burglar alarm and security systems has not been entirely ruled out as the cause of the fire. But the case is being taken very seriously by local Laren authorities and for the time being at least, Mr. Gnuticks is being detained pending further investigation."

Continued the newsreader: "Top-notch lawyers Mohammed Ali Bi and Otto Man, the two young Turks heading WWW's legal team, have not been successful in getting bail set. Their fearless leader won't be released for at least several days – if at all – which only serves to highlight the severity of the case."

Stills of the two swarthy lawyers resembling mugshots of Middle East terrorists were screened.

"It seems that the Weijers bookshop shooting of only a few days ago is being urgently reviewed, as well as a number of other puzzling incidents in which HG and his group have been implicated worldwide."

Next, jostled footage of a handcuffed HG being taken away by police was shown. Just before disappearing into the back of a patrol car, a white Mercedes with characteristic blue & hot-pink markings, he could be heard to say to reporters outside his Hague hotel, "I guess I can kiss the North Sea Jazz Festival goodbye, eh, whattaya think?"

It was typical of HG that even in times of distress he drew chuckles from the crowd. But it only sent shivers down Okkels' spine.

The TV anchorman droned on, "The fire was first noticed by the owners of the house while waving out their last guest around 18:00 hours..."

Okkels tuned out again, preoccupied in reconstructing the evening's events in accordance with his own agenda. He'd left some 15-20 minutes earlier, eager to get home for a bite, a catnap, then up to the office with a treasure trove of gossip for his two-page spread. He and Joke had left separately in order not to attract any attention to their little tryst. They'd vowed secrecy, though he for one intended to keep his promise only while opportune; after all, he owed disloyalty to a loyal readership.

Once back at the office, Okkels had handed his rolls of film – five in all – to the photography department, impressing upon Remco that he needed the pictures urgently in order to make what he knew would be a fetching collage. Rijkje Dijkstra had promised him the centerfold spread, realizing that the G&S shindig would generate huge interest and sell loose newsstand copies like hotcakes.

It was while Okkels sweated over precise and evocative wording of tentative captions to accompany the anticipated photos that he was summoned to Ms. Dijkstra's office.

News of the world financial markets came on. Rijkje Dijkstra got up and walked back to her office. Okkels automatically followed like an obedient pup. Once back behind her desk Okkels noticed that her face was tense, pensive, erroneously concluding that he was still the object of her tormented preoccupation. As usual he was flattering himself.

Ms. Dijkstra had held HG in great esteem after their interview, and she found it difficult to reconcile what she'd seen on television, of him being implicated not only in arson, for personal gain, but this peeping-Tom business. She couldn't reconcile it with the HG she had come to admire and felt deflated, barrenly empty, and suddenly tired, very, very tired of her life in journalism. She'd become a news junky like everyone else, unable to pass a single day without wallowing in the sordid business of living; of living other people's lives – a secondhand sort of life. Where, she agonized, was real, robust first-hand experience, with sanguine, salutary, mature men and women? She felt like weeping but took heart. She had Okkels to contend with.

"I guess it's pretty obvious that scumbag HG shot the picture of Joke and me, huh? The way I figure it the guy's rotten through and through. Torches the mansion of his own goddamn publishers just so he can benefit from the publicity." Okkels leaned forward in order to simulate a sense of nonexistent camaraderie, but the stench he exuded made Ms. Dijkstra recoil and light up a smoke.

He was not the gossipy type, Okkels ascertained objectively, but his predicament called for drastic action. "You know something, Rijkje," he continued, unaware of the concerted motion he'd triggered, "I'm no rumor-monger but I heard from reliable sources that HG asked Froukje Vrolijk to seduce Odel Wneeg in order to entice him into taking a potshot at him in that bookshop last week? Also for publicity's sake. Can you believe it? The guy's a professional asshole, if you pardon my French. It's not enough that half of Holland was there at his reception. No, he wants it all."

Okkels shook his head, plodding onwards, "Not only does he burn down the Laren mansion, but tries to frame me. Sick I tell ya, sick."

Hearing Okkels jabber on like that brought Rijkje Dijkstra to her senses.

"Bloody unlikely Fokko, use you brains will you, if you got any! HG knew very well that he was seen going upstairs. If he'd intended to commit arson don't you think he'd've made damn sure he went undetected?"

Okkels suddenly realized that Dijkstra was right. She was a better man than he; always a couple of steps ahead. He'd been so preoccupied trying to salve his own conscience, nurse his hurt pride, that he wasn't thinking straight. Of course HG must've known that he'd been seen going upstairs. Not only that but had he intended to burn down the place he could easily have sent one of his henchmen to do the job without sticking out his own neck.

"Look," Dijkstra said to him, "we've got a paper to get out."

Okkels' face instantly lit up, but Ms. Dijkstra purposely averted his gaze, begrudging him even that little satisfaction.

She wasn't doing him any favors. This was purely business.

"I'm having Jansen cover the fire, and its legal ramifications. You do the Society Page as usual, and then take a few days off."

"You're suspending me? But I thought we agreed you were gonna talk to Waterreus first. I'm sure he'll..."

"I know what I said, alright? I'll talk to Waterreus, but not even Waterreus can save your skin, I'm afraid."

"Whattaya mean?"

"I strongly advise you to go to the police before they come to see you," she said bluntly. "They might go easier on you."

"The cops? What for? I haven't done anything."

"Fokko, Fokko! For God's sake, man, use your head! You were there! At the scene of the crime!" Ms. Dijkstra waved the incriminating photograph under his nose. "A picture's worth a thousand words, and the police'll be very interested in hearing every last one of those captivating one thousand words of yours, I'm sure. You better get your story straight, stop by our legal department first thing in the morning."

Okkels was stunned. He'd tacitly assumed Dijkstra would hush up the picture. It was in the interest of the paper not to divulge privileged information. And luckily the paper's interest dovetailed nicely with his own in this case.

"Here's a question for you," Ms. Dijkstra said ominously. She wanted to leave no room for misunderstanding. "Are you sure you didn't start the fire and are trying to pin it on HG?"

She said this with such malice in her voice that it frightened the living daylights out of Okkels.

"What? You think I'd do something like that?"

"No, I don't," she said, weary of her incompetent charge. "But you're missing the point. HG is no longer the prime suspect. It's beyond me why he bothered to take your picture, but he did. What it does mean is that he knows you and Joke were upstairs and he's bound to tell the police. I really can't figure out why he hasn't already and why you haven't been arrested yet, come to think of it."

Okkels suddenly felt cold, icy cold, as though his metabolism had stopped functioning. How could he have been so distracted by irrelevancies that he hadn't realized what trouble he was in. The photo might be hushed up, but the photographer would blab!

"Right, yeah," he stammered. "I gotta go, I gotta go."

"What about the Society Page?" Dijkstra asked.

"It's virtually done. Don't worry. I'll see to it," he said, not at all convinced himself, nor consequently, convincing. "I'll get back to you in a bit. Got a couple o' calls to make."

The second Okkels reached his desk, he rang Joke Op 't Land. She picked up immediately, as though she'd been expecting him. "Have you seen the news?" she asked frantically.

It was a silly question. Fokko was a journalist, she knew, and as such must've had access to diverse sources of information.

"What I mean is," she rephrased, "have we been implicated? I just can't afford any negative publicity right now. Especially something as dreadful as this! It'd sink her career."

"Don't get excited," Okkels said, trying to prepare Joke but achieving the exact opposite. "Promise me. Cause I got some bad news."

"Bad news? What bad news? Don't play games with me, goddamn-you Fokko. Tell me straight, don't keep me dangling!"

Okkels explained about the photo, about HG having seen them, and about the likelihood that they'd both be charged.

It had the expected effect on Joke. She had a near hysterical fit and it took minutes for Okkels to calm her down. Strangely enough her hysteria calmed Okkels, made him feel more self-assured, as he casually analyzed the situation along the lines Dijkstra had laid out, pretending that it was original thinking on his part.

When the severity of the situation had penetrated, a seemingly resigned Joke asked, "Whatta we gonna do, Fokko?"

It sounded almost touching, and it made Okkels feel good, useful, needed.

"Look, get some rest. I got the Society Page to finish," Okkels said as business-like as possible. "Let's take it one step at a time." And in an ultimate gesture to cheer up the depressed actress on the other end of the line, he committed to a generous promise. "Whatever happens, you'll get a wonderful write-up in tomorrow's paper. How's that?"

"Thanks Fokko," Joke said mirthlessly. "But you don't have to bother. It's no use."

Then suddenly she exploded, as though a time-fuze had run its course. "I can kiss the Keetje Tippel series goodbye. That dirty bastard, why did he have to take our picture! We're unnecessarily being dragged into this mess. It's not like you or I started the fire. It's bad enough it happened. But why should it ruin my life? It's so unfair!" She cried, enraged.

Okkels shared her sense of desperation. His own job was at stake. But in addition he felt a sense of abandonment at life mauling him in such a merciless manner. What had he ever done to deserve such ill-treatment? His conscience was clear, and he blamed the injustice on a rotten world.

"We'll go down in flames," he said dramatically, feeling it apropos. "I'm seeing my lawyer first thing in the morning. I advise you to do the same."

* * * * *

Okkels didn't sleep at all well that night. He expected a knock at the door any minute. He stayed up till all hours trying to figure out why HG had not reported Joke and him to the police, or if he had, why the police hadn't come to arrest him. When at last he fell asleep from utter exhaustion, it was with fits and starts, jerking awake, only to doze off again uncomfortably on the leather sofa. So tormented was he, his movements so spasmodic, that Linda, his Rottweiler, gave up her favorite spot on the couch to settle down elsewhere for the duration.

It was a bleary-eyed Okkels who awoke with a jolt at around 8 a.m., pried from unconsciousness by the sounds of traffic in the street below, a distant siren, car horns, a tram squeaking in its rails, jingling at pedestrians.

He washed, shaved and grabbed a bite, fed Linda – asked a neighbor to walk her – and was off.

On his way he stopped at a couple of cigar shops, but *Courandstad Nexus* was already sold out! A bit of good news to compensate for all the misery of the previous night.

Hardly forty-five minutes later he pushed through the turnstile, slipped into the elevator, and shot up to his floor. He grabbed a copy of the morning paper from a big stack at the entrance to his office, and flung himself down in his seat. He felt slightly better in the beehive where he spent most of his life, surrounded by the familiar routine that made him feel an integral part of things; his colleagues behind their terminals, hard at work on stories that formed the patchwork quilt of the nation's shared reality, or at least one modest slice of it.

The front page was mostly devoted to the Laren fire, shots of fire-fighters taming the blaze, an eerie photo of a distraught Gerrit and Sjef taken with a flash in the midnight darkness, making them look quite ghoulish, and of course the mansion being consumed by flames reaching to the sky, a blizzard of cinders descending.

The news was already stale, being from the previous night and before going for the latest IPA telexes, Okkels turned to his two-page spread. It was heartwarming, more than usual, to see the fruits of his labor. A dozen beautiful pictures with provocative captions told the story of the reception held the day before in honor of WWW's Herman Gnuticks. Under normal circumstances everyone involved would have been elated with such a glittering media event. But instead the mansion lay in ruins; the guest of honor himself behind bars.

After perusing his handiwork for a few minutes, checking the text for glitches – some always snuck into any journalist's work – Okkels walked down the hall to collect all IPA messages to do with the Laren fire, in search of the latest news. Would his name crop up? Or Joke's? He skimmed the meters-long bunting with a pounding heart, primed for the least little clue.

Not much had turned up since the night before, other than that the likely site of the origin of the blaze having been traced to the upstairs bedroom. The fire, it appeared, had spread outward in concentric circles from there to engulf the rest of the house.

"How odd,'" Okkels thought, and for a few seconds the incongruity hung in his mind, suspended as it were.

And that's when it hit him like a bolt of lightening. Slapping his forehead with the palm of his hand, he hurried back to his desk to phone Joke.

"Shit! Shit! Shit!" he fumed, and twice fumbled with the phone, mispunching the area code, repunching. He could hardly contain himself. A sleepy Joke answered after a dozen rings.

"Didn't you smoke afterwards?" Okkels unceremoniously launched into his third-degree, without even introducing himself, asking how she was, how she'd slept.

"What?"

"Didn't you smoke afterwards?" Okkels repeated impatiently. "I seem to recall you smoking a cigarette after we...we were done."

"Whattaya talking about? I've got a splitting heading. Hardly slept a wink all night."

"Okay, just take a minute. Think. Did...you...smoke... afterwards?" Okkels repeated as though speaking to a child.

"I don't remember," Joke said. "What the hell's the difference?"

"The difference is that the source of the fire has been traced to the goddamn bedroom! That's what!"

"Really? Oh my god, no."

"I think you did smoke."

"Yes, I think I did."

"So what did you do with it?"

"With what?"

"The cigarette butt, what else?"

"I don't know. Put it out in an astray, I don't remember."

"What astray?" Okkels asked with forced patience.

"Look, I had other things on my mind yesterday than to think about cigarette butts."

"I take that as a compliment," Okkels said, trying to lighten up. "It could've been so wonderful if things had turned out differently." He realized that he was being a bit obnoxious grilling her so early in the morning.

"It wasn't meant to be a compliment," Joke snapped.

"Well, please think. It's important. What about the cigarette? What did you do while I was straightening up the bed?"

"Oh wait, it's coming back to me. Yes, I used that obscene ceramic astray on the nightstand, some Greek dude with a huge erection. I remember now, yes, and while you were straightening the bedspread I cleaned it. I used a couple of tissues to wipe it afterwards."

"Afterwards?"

"You know, after dumping the ashes, the cigarette butt. I didn't want Gerrit and Sjef to find it, now did I?"

"That's not the point! Where? Where did you dump it?"

"In the waste paper basket near that contraption."

"Contraption? What contraption?"

"That contraption on the floor over by the fax machine on the dresser."

"You mean the paper shredder?"

"How would I know? Is that what it was?"

"Good move, Joke."

"I didn't have my glasses on, okay. Anyway, whattaya saying? That I started the fire?" Joke's voice trembled with a volatile mixture of anger and fear.

"You said it, I didn't," Okkels growled contemptuously.

*****

"What took you so long?" was all a droll HG asked when he and Okkels met later that morning on the steps of Police Headquarters.

Joke and Fokko's full confessions had led to HG's immediate, unconditional release, and to yet more publicity. It was item number one on the radio bulletins all day. *Guide for the Apoplexed* and its Dutch translation *Krijg geen beroerte* were sold out all over Holland's urban agglomeration and printers, even as they spoke, were working their fingers to the bone getting a next batch out.

A news-hungry Dutch public had also snapped up the entire lot of 250,000 extra issues of Courandstad Nexus.

Okkels had put only one counter-question to HG: "Why didn't you tell the police about me and Joke? You wouldn't have had to spent the night behind bars."

"What? And miss an opportunity of seeing the Dutch justice system from the inside? I need it for a piece I'm doing on prison reform. Besides, whatever else I am, I ain't no snitch, Fokko."

"Why did you do it then, take the picture, I mean?"

"Oh, I do the unnecessary. But after so many years it comes so much easier," was the lame reply.

"What does that mean? That's no answer," came the irritable retort.

"Okay. Try this on for size. My author's publisher told me that sex sells books. It was either that or a car chase through the streets of downtown the Hague. So you see, you're my love-interest. You should be flattered. Besides. You don't know my author's publisher. He's a bad ass SOB."

"Very funny. Your author's publisher? Don't you pull that postmodern crap on me, man. I've been warned about that. You'd love to reduce me to your frickin' alter ego, wouldn't ya? But I'm real, I tell ya! Real!" Okkels yelled, a hysterical note cracking his voice.

"Relax, will ya? Of course you are," HG pacified his reporter-companion.

"Jesus! You'll go to any extreme to promote you're goddam middle way, won't you?"

"Yep," came the terse reply.

"So?"

"So what?"

"So why did you do it? Why'd you shoot the picture? I'm waiting."

"No reason, really," HG admitted candidly. "Couldn't pass up the opportunity, I guess. Anyone would've done the same in my shoes," he added with a shrug of the shoulders.

"Oh, I don't know about that," Okkels replied, not entirely convinced. The little prank had cost them dearly.

"In retrospect it's a good thing I did."

"What do you mean?"

"Tell me honestly, Fokko, would you have come forward if you and Joke had not been positively linked to the scene of the crime?"

"Of course I would have," Okkels lied. "Though come to think of it, Joke might not have. She said as much."

"Not that I would've blamed you, or her," HG said magnanimously. "I might not have either in your situation."

Okkels looked at him in astonishment. "You serious?"

"Just kidding. Honest."

But Okkels remained unconvinced.

"So what'll happen to Joke?" HG queried.

"The police are satisfied that the fire was an accident. No charges are being pressed. The rest is a formality between her insurance company and Gerrit and Sjef's. Everyone's suitably covered for this sort of liability. But the best news is that the TV series on the life of Keetje Tippel is in the bag. Joke had been sick with grief thinking that the adverse publicity would make the producer decide in favor of one of her younger rivals, Chantal most likely. The opposite turns out to be true. The story of our fiery encounter landed her the job. 'Love hot enough to burn down a house!' as the producer put it. What more could you want? 'Typecasting,' the studios said. Joke did Keetje Tippel proud, I guess."

"Great. And what about yourself?" HG asked.

"No problem. Dijkstra tried to axe me, but Waterreus backed me 100 percent. Sales have never been better. Courandstad Nexus sold all its extra issues. Tomorrow's will do the same, I'm sure, why with your interview and all."

"Interview? What interview?"

Screamed the next morning's banner headlines:

Joke O.'s love confession sets WWW's Herman Gnuticks free
Says Herman: 'North Sea Jazz Festival here I come!'

*****

NINE

A somewhat overexposed color photograph of a startled-looking, sun-drenched HG and Professor Anja de Boer had appeared on the garish *Courandstad Nexus* society page, telling of their reception encounter. It was part of the centerfold collage of close-up shots of a whole constellation of stars (including Joke Op 't Land posing with Janus, her imposing giant mastiff) all of whom had been present at the Laren bash the day before. Brief telegraph-style captions disclosed details as to the faces displayed, and a full column write-up by Okkels sealed their fate.

But events were moving fast and within 36 hours of his latest handiwork, Okkels was out on a story he could only have dreamt of. While most other papers had little more to report on the complications surrounding the visit of the Worldwide Welcome Wagon rolling on through the Lowlands and points beyond, Okkels was on his way to the home of Professor Anja de Boer after having received an frantic call from her distraught husband.

* * * * *

Blazed the next day's headlines:

WWW bags VIP convert
Prominent academic floored by nonism

(by F.Fokko Okkels)

Abcoude, July 18 - In the privacy of her own home, Professor Anja de Boer, shapely occupant of Holland's renowned Heidegger Chair, yesterday revealed that she was zapped by a thunderbolt in the form of a fully revised WWW publication entitled Guide for the Apoplexed, redacted by none other than Chief Scribe Herman Gnuticks himself.

Not quite your naive illiterate, Dr. de Boer testified that in the wee hours of Friday morning, while preparing for the university roast to be held on the weekend and intended to grill the Wiseguy from the West, she suddenly "saw the light".

Said she, "It was quite uncanny, I have no words to describe it. Call it a mystical mindset, an emergent sort of state previously unbeknownst to me. Nothing I ever read prepared me for it, not Plotinus, not St Augustine, not Thomas Aquinas, not Francis of Assisi, not even Meister Eckhart. It was awesome, overwhelming, all-engulfing, I tell you."

Asked to elaborate in terms of Freudian psychoanalysis, Dr. de Boer squealed with laughter, slapping her thighs in uncontrollable mirth. When she recovered from a near-paroxysmal fit so symptomatic of a not uncommon form of hysteria, she was heard to gasp "Freud? Freud? Freud?" thrice in succession.

When finally she composed herself to seriously ponder the quandary, she submitted to this reporter in a more rational manner: "Ever have a nightmare that seemed so real that the possibility of it being a bad dream never occurs to you while you remain asleep? Well, just as the waking state compares to the dream state, enlightenment compares to the ordinary waking state. And just as nothing can convince the sleeper that he or she is caught in a dream – other than being woken from it – the person in the ordinary waking state doesn't have a clue as to what enlightenment could possibly be. Well, now, I guess to be twice-woken is what it takes."

Expulsion?

Only a couple of days before, Dr. de Boer had pleasantly exchanged views with HG at the bash in Laren thrown in his honor by G&S Press, heartily disagreeing on matters of principle which were really "Issues of Insubstantiality", according to the lady scholar with the benefit of hindsight. Asked how the mere reading of a monograph, or rather "nonograph", on Nonism – HG's neologist notion of Nothingness – could possibly have had such a devastating impact on one of Holland's most perspicuous minds, Dr. de Boer remained speechless.

"Perhaps that's just it!" said her worried spouse, former State Secretary of Economic Affairs, Bert de Boer. "There ought to be a law against it! Will she cook again? Will she play tennis, bridge? Will she ever throw another baby shower? I don't know, I just don't know."

Fighting off a nervous twitch, he threatened, "I'm seeing the Justice Minister about it first thing Monday morning! Have that Gnuticks bastard declared *persona non grata* and chucked out of the country forthwith. He'll never set foot on Dutch soil again. Not if I can help it."

Asked whether this meant that the planned university roast was off, the venomous reply was, "Roast? Roast? The electric chair is too good for him."

* * * * *

TEN

In anticipation of tumultuous reaction to his disconcerting article following so hard on the heels of the fire, a glowing Okkels, in the comfort of his own living room, fingered the crisp pages of Herman Gnuticks' – a spare review copy gifted to him by Anja de Boer.

Life could be so sweet sometimes, so right, so rewarding when things were going your way, it occurred to Okkels. And things were going his way. Waterreus, a big, boisterous man, had personally called on him at the office in order to extend his congratulation on the de Boer disclosures. "An ostrich feather in your cap, Fokko m'boy," he'd said for all to see and hear. "A credit to your profession is what you are, my son, and a splendid example to your colleagues," he'd spoken solemnly, and made opaque promises of perks and promotion: closer proximity towards the front page, a generous raise, access to his Swiss chalet...

Waterreus' appreciative slap on the shoulders had rattled Okkels' already poorly anchored teeth – him all the while trying to grin off the compliment without appearing too smug; desperately trying not to break wind like a hippo.

All this had transpired just before leaving the office the previous night. And still basking in the warmth of so much wealth – motivated more than ever to complete his mission with destiny – Okkels contemplated random passages of the thin WWW treatise, wondering just which paragraph, which sentence, which exact word had triggered Dr. Anja de Boer's moment of supreme insight. It was the one question he'd forgotten to ask in his excitement. And with some trepidation, he skimmed pages of text, innocuous recompositions of the 26 letters of the alphabet augmented with a handful of punctuation and diacritical marks.

Inadvertently, he thought of the magic of mathematics and wondered whether there was a parallel between the power of numbers and the power of letters, as HG implied in the introduction to the work on his lap. Okkels being innumerate, having barely passed high school math, wasn't in a position to judge. But he had his sources and he planned to double check, triple check, if that's what it took. Like on Fermat: "Unlike Fermat claimed for his famous Last Theorem," a confident HG had told him, "I got scads of space in the margins to present the proof required for the Theorem of Theorems. Not a single do-or-die lemma anywhere! Now there's food for thought, eh, Fokko?" Adding the always lurking zinger, "Or should I say 'food for thoughtlessness.' Perhaps 'fast-food for thoughtlessness' might even be better."

Double zingers, two-upmanship, why the hell not? Fast food for thoughtlessness indeed! Okkels had blanched in the face of so much incongruity. 'Cause the universe did seem to submit to mathematical formulation, permitting prediction down to the smallest detail and across eons of time, though he – though no one – quite understood how or why. Could it be that WWW researches had revealed comparable features attributable to linguistic formulation? Of course, as a newspaperman, a wordmonger, according to HG, like himself, he was keenly interested in such deep questions. Language was his bread and butter, in a manner of speaking, and he liked to keep abreast of latest developments.

In the comfort of his own living room now, he took a last swig of his Johnny Walker black label, crunching on a mouthful of ice-flakes, took heart and resolved that he was strong enough to embark on the armchair adventure: just he and HG, man-to-man. Shading his eyes against the late afternoon glare with the amber visor he liked to wear on rare poker nights, he scrutinized the pages before him:

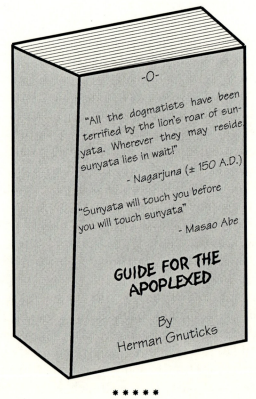

* * * * *

F.Fokko Okkels thoughtfully scratched his head, shut the booklet he had been reading for well over an hour and tossed it aside. The bright red sticker "New & Improved" on the glossy black cover struck him as in poor taste; inappropriate considering the severity of the subject matter. And what about the self-serving blurbs on the back cover?: "The most powerful under-the-counter purgative available" – signed E. Lixer. Or, "Wisdom concentrate; dilute with ample common sense before use" – Newt Rishun. It was all just plain overkill. But that was characteristic of the entire WWW enterprise. They were obviously conmen first and foremost, opportunists secondly, and it was up to him to unmask them; bring them crashing down to earth. Still, he had no wish to throw out the baby with the bath water – they might be on to something. It had made fascinating reading. But the message was beyond him as yet and he groped for a handle on the thing.

"Guess I'm one of them poor Homo sapiens sons o' bitches," he muttered under his breath.

Linda, thinking that her boss was talking to her, sleepily wagged her stubby tail.

Okkels rose from the white leather couch, his shirt sticking to him from the extreme humidity in the air, sweat on his back, boils, paunch – excrescences great and small. He freshened his Black Label and took a big swig of the iced elixir, swishing it around in his mouth and gulping it down with decided pleasure. Up came a loud burp that made Linda prick up her ears once more, only to sink back in slumber, recognizing it as a familiar noise in the Okkels repertoire of aerostatics.

It was sweltering out, tolerably hot inside. Such days were rare in Holland and didn't warrant procuring an expensive air conditioner, certainly not till he'd paid off some bills. A battered fan that had been with him for as long he could remember swiveled monotonously in the corner of the room, straining to churn the moisture-laden air, but managing merely to redistribute the mugginess more evenly. Whenever the swiveling fan reached a critical juncture in its trajectory, the blades emitted an irritating series of clicks, which drove him mad, but insufficiently so to undertake any action. Another week or two and it would be sentenced to solitary confinement in the allotted "storage box" in the basement of the apartment building for another turn of the seasons.

On the spur of the moment Okkels dialed the University of Amsterdam and asked for the Mathematics Department. "When in doubt consult an expert," was one of the cardinal rules of journalism that had stood him in good stead, though he applied it too infrequently, since expert opinion needlessly tended to torpedo potential controversy – and controversy was Okkels' middle name. But the case at hand stymied him, and he could use a little help.

After a couple of internal transfers, curt referrals, and being put on hold for several minutes, he came up empty-handed. The university as bureaucratic institution. It was almost closing time, no one qualified to answer his questions was available, and would he mind calling back next morning. He was about to let it slide, when he tried again, this time the University of Utrecht. He was luckier. He actually got the home number of one of Holland's foremost professors of mathematics.

Okkels rang, introduced himself, took a few minutes to explain the background, and posed the question as to the origin of the zero digit, and its "preverbal" significance.

"No idea. Of no possible consequence."

But lo and behold, after some insistence on his part, Okkels got the moderately cooperative, "Zero is only special because it's the first number in a set, that's all," whereupon the conversation ended abruptly.

He mulled this over, fanning himself with the TV guide. The lack of interest of a supposed specialist in the field only piqued his own, and thoughtfully he nursed his drink. Questions galore. Soon HG would arrive. He'd agreed to meet Okkels to discuss the De Boer apostasy and had a lot of explaining to do. Not only about the zero, but also the "smell of satori" – reference invoked to rationalize the professor's (debilitating?) indisposition caused by reading a screwball work of "philosofiction".

The poor woman had been reduced to virtual zombie status, her husband had claimed, unable to perform even the most rudimentary household chores. She hadn't slept more than 48 winks in 48 hours, refusing to dress, shower, or go to church with him. She even turned down a gala luncheon for a visiting envoy at Soestdijk Palace hosted by his Royal Contact.

"Kings and queens? In this day and age?? For Pete's sake!!!" she'd scoffed. It was more of the same antiseptic skepticism of the hermeneutical type that stripped life naked of any and all illusion, and thus – to Ir. de Boer at least – made that life unlivable, as he complained to anyone who cared to listen.

And what of Anja? One minute she floated around the house, light as a feather, only to wander out into their spacious garden in her chiffon nightgown the next, rooting in the chocolate-rich organic humus of their compost heap, scooping up arms of dirt, and working it into the flower beds with her bare hands. At midnight Ir. de Boer, thinking his wife was at last sound asleep next to him, turned over to find her missing. Alarmed by her absence, he finally discovered her fluttering around their fruit-laden cherry tree bathing in the bluish-green floodlights like some Isadora Duncan gypsy moth, singing "Hi-Ho-Holland-Hypland! Hi-Ho-Holland-Hypland! Hollow be thy name!"

Though to a neutral bystander it might've appeared quite an adorable fairy-tale scene, Ir de Boer could stand it no more, and dragged his spouse into the house by her silken sash lest the neighbors hear. He was even beginning to think in terms of having her committed, he'd confided to the *Courandstad Nexus* reporter summoned to the house for – as it turned out – ulterior motives of publicity to prepare public opinion for some fast manipulative footwork needed to deliver the political KO to the man he held responsible for his domestic woes.

*****

"Not to worry," HG had said when confronted by Okkels on telephone with the news, lightly dismissing the seemingly deviant behavior being displayed by Dr. de Boer as "par for the course." And when challenged by Okkels to account in more comprehensible terms, had said, "Anja is just climbing down from her Heidegger Highchair. Relax will ya," adding with a mischievous chuckle, "Except for a nose-bleed maybe, descending from those rarified heights, she'll be fine."

It all sounded rather bizarre to Okkels and he was glad that he was a humble, god-fearing soul who steered clear of such obscurantism as the WWW group dispensed.

And so, in advance of the session with HG, Okkels had dutifully read *Guide for the Apoplexed* only to familiarize himself with its contents sufficiently to cross-examine its author. But he couldn't make more out of it than a meaty treatise, marbled with lots of interesting quotations. Though heavy, high-calorie fare, it was too rich for even his blood. Whereas he happily downed deep-fried foods that invited instant cardiac arrest in most, he found this particular dish wholly indigestible. Yet, Okkels couldn't entirely exclude the possibility that it contained certain nutrients a well-balanced diet required. HG was definitely driving at something, or perhaps, in view of its crux, Nothing. But a Nothingness that stubbornly kept eluding Okkels' grasp.

The whiskey and the heat in conjunction with the exertion of concentrated reading had made him feel languidly lazy and his thoughts drifted off to his liaison with Joke Op 't Land, possibly also because he was trying to avert the lingering discomfort at the potent pages that still haunted him.

Luckily the book lay obediently where he'd tossed it, dead as a doornail, Okkels was glad to see. For the disconcerting notion persisted that perhaps HG had supernatural powers that could leap off the pages of any of his influential publications – *Guide for the Apoplexed* being the most potent, sustained effort he'd come across so far. Okkels smiled nervously, unconvinced by his own feeble reassurances, trying unsuccessfully to belittle his atavistic sense of superstitions.

But that in itself fueled an irksome anxiety that would not leave him be. And in order to assuage his sense of apprehension, he tried to tell himself that he was strong, mentally and physically, and that he felt good about himself, better than he'd felt for some time. He was pretty damn confident as a matter of fact. Things were going well for him of late, turning out better than could be hoped for, even when he erred. He couldn't do anything wrong of late, it seemed, and he was especially pleased that once he turned on the charm, he could still score.

Soon he might even retire his inflatable Miss Piggy doll, which was becoming a bit raunchy anyway, with the paint rubbing off where he kneaded it most.

Of course it had done no harm that Joke was one hard-up lady perennially starved for sex and publicity despite the satisfaction she got on both counts wherever she ventured. And in that regard, the Keetje Tippel role suited her well. The mere thought of appearing in *Courandstad Nexus'* Society Page had been enough for her to make love to Okkels' camera outdoors, and to the man-behind-the-camera indoors, once they'd snuck up unnoticed to Gerrit and Sjef's bedroom-cum-office.

That she'd managed to put the joint on fire Okkels interpreted as quite symbolic in retrospect, and the highest personal compliment anyone could possibly have paid him, or indeed ever had. Of course he nurtured no illusions about her come-on, he told himself; didn't much mind the implications festering just below the surface – his motto being that there were many ways to skin a feline and one did what one had to.

His own ploy had worked well enough. His momentary cold-shoulder treatment, his hard-to-get-act informing Joke that his Society Page would be devoted in its entirety to HG and his gang and not to the usual Dutch celebrities, had only made her redouble her efforts, ostensibly enticing Okkels into the house to divulge some juicy tidbit of news about that fiendish nemesis of hers who stooped at nothing.

"Wait till I tell you what I've heard from very reliable sources," Joke had said, luring a more-than-willing Okkels to follow her into the relative seclusion of the house. "Chantal does it in the sauna with her Polish driver," she'd whispered in his overly receptive ear, "*and* her Philippine cook, *and* her French chamberlain, *and* both her Italian bodyguards, not to forget."

"You don't say!"

"All at the same time!"

"Wow!"

Okkels had responded by getting her alone upstairs to discuss "this incendiary material", making sure no one saw them steel away up the spiral staircase with its thick mauve runner.

The rest was history. Joke had caught his drift and did the needful to insure her face would not be left out of the exclusive *Nexus* photographic coverage, certainly in view of the likelihood that Chantal's wouldn't. Should the Keetje Tippel series elude Joke's grasp, it would augur ill for her future, and drastic measures were called for; drastic indeed, for what could be more drastic than being Fokko-ed by Okkels, even for a sexual glutton like Ms. Op 't Land, who, it was rumored, liked to be hectored and rogered by every Roger and Hector, morning, noon and night?

With thoughts of Joke and promiscuity fresh on his mind, Okkels lovingly petted his Rottweiler bitch Linda who lay peacefully asleep on the white leather couch next to him, caught in heat-induced reverie as he was.

Linda had softened his grief over Harry's death. The kick in the ribs that had done in the little terrier had been unintentional to be sure, a regrettable incident, he told himself – knowing better deep down, for he had a mean streak that could be fatal in conjunction with an explosive temper that irrupted unpredictably. And so, in order to prevent a recurrence, he'd made sure he got himself a sturdy replacement for Harry, one that could take lots of abuse. Because Okkels knew himself, knew his attacks of blind rage at the myriad frustration that disgraced the banal life he tended to lead. And lord knew a Rottweiler could stand a little manhandling, having served well the soldiers of the Unholy Roman Empire, as guard dog, companion, camp follower, and god knows what else.

Besides, lavishing his love on Linda was a way of making it up to Harry, he rationalized. And he'd nearly forgiven himself for the incident, with only faint tremors of remorse about having pushed the quivering little canine with the punctured lung from the fifth floor balcony to make its death look accidental. This mainly for the benefit of his nosy downstairs neighbors from whom he'd gotten Harry as a pup. They knew the dog to be youthfully vigorous and would never have accepted its death passively. There would've been no end to probing questions. Besides they were notorious gossips and life-time subscribers to *Courandstad Nexus*. They wouldn't think twice about squealing on him were they to find out the truth. And the one thing he didn't need just then – after barely getting in the clear with Rijkje Dijkstra – was bad press in his own paper in the form of a poison pen letter-to-the-editor!

So he'd made sure no one saw him dispose of the dying dog, hunkering down behind the balcony door and using his telescoping deep-sea fiberglass fishing rod to push Harry through the space under the railing. Afterwards he'd run down all five flights of stairs screaming like a banshee, "Harry! Harry! Oh my God! Harry! Harry!" to make sure his alibi registered, and stuck.

The whole building had shared in Okkels' grief, mystified as to why such an appalling thing should have happened. "Is there no justice in the world?" one neighbor had bemoaned the terrier's lot, and several others nodded in dumbfounded silence. But once the scenes of public mourning were over, and he'd carried the tiny corpse back upstairs cradled in his arms, an inconsolable Okkels had unceremoniously stuffed the limp body into the plastic container meant for recyclable kitchen waste, which was promptly dumped the next day.

Okkels assured everyone who inquired that Harry lay pretty as you please in a private plot in a nearby pet cemetery where he could visit him whenever he was overcome by grief.

It's what he preferred to have seen done for Harry, but of course it had been out of the question considering the exorbitant rates charged these days – he knew, cause he'd once done a piece on pet funerals of Hilversum stars.

This morbid lark notwithstanding, he graciously accepted the high approval ratings bestowed on him by friends and acquaintances for that presumed act of kindness shown a dumb animal.

Absentmindedly, Okkels petted Linda as his thoughts seamlessly turned back to Joke, the two inextricably entwined in his mind somehow – Linda and Joke, Joke and Linda. Though preoccupied, daydreaming, he winced at the rancid odor he exuded. Momentarily it had the effect on him of smelling-salts and cleared his head. He really oughta bring forward his weekly shower, he thought, feeling hot and icky.

Meanwhile, there was still a time until HG arrived for the interview, and he reached over to his old-fashioned table model telephone in contemplation of calling the woman who'd managed to get under his skin - the woman he now so desperately needed, wanted, desired, lusted after. How would she respond after the Laren debacle, the compromising photograph, the fire, the compulsory confessions, the negative publicity?

That negative publicity had in the final analysis turned out rather well for her. 'Cause, he'd been given to understand, Joke had bagged the Keetje Tippel series precisely due to the debacle that had cost the Laren publishers their mansion. The producer of the show had thought to capitalize on the stereotypecasting in the minds of the Dutch viewing public and called her to talk turkey the minute word had leaked out, telling her that she was perfect for the part and that she could not have done a better audition had she tried. Not that she'd needed to, 'cause she was a natural. The additional idle flattery that Chantal had never even been a distant second was grist to her mill, and she ate it up.

Okkels downplayed the mercenary nature of Joke's initially feigned affections for him, generated by her zeal for publicity in what was to her a crucial juncture in her career. He couldn't help but feel that now that the "connection" had been made, other, more noble forces would take hold, giving them a realistic shot at a genuine relationship; a relationship he hankered for but that had painfully eluded him each time he'd made an overt attempt at reaching out to a desirable female.

His heart throbbed as he punched Joke's unlisted number with his stubby index finger.

A male voice answered. "Joke? Ja, moment, asjeblieft,' he heard, not recalling having spoken, the alien voice blotting out all trace of memory.

In the time it took for her to come on the line, Okkels barely managed to marshal his thoughts. Foolishly, he had not expected this complication, though he might've. Joke was no wallflower, and time was a-wastin'.

"Joke? Hi, it's me, Fokko."

"Oh, hello Fokko, how are you?"

"Fine, fine. I was just thinking about you," he said, and it sounded like a confession. It sounded weak, while he had intended to sound strong.

"Well, that's nice, Fokko."

"Look, is this a bad time? I mean, you've got...company."

"No, it's not a bad time. What's up?"

"Yes it is. I'll call back when you're alone."

"What for? I've got no secrets from Hans. Go ahead, what's on your mind."

"No, well, I was just thinking about you," Okkels repeated, almost inanely, nervously petting Linda as he spoke, desperately trying to muster some sort of comportment that might pull him through. He felt intimidated by the presence on the other side of what he took to be a rival, though it might've been her brother for all he knew. But knowing Joke, he knew better.

"Well? What can I do for you, Fokko? Wait, let me guess. Of course. How foolish of me. You wanna do an interview about my role in the new series, right? Shooting starts next month, Hans tells me. It'll be great. You get an exclusive if you want. You deserve it. It's the least I can do." She was obviously in a buoyant mood, which only made Okkels more depressed. "It'll be my way of reciprocating for your generous inclusion of Janus and me in the *Nexus* spread. My agent is convinced it helped clinch the deal, you know," Joke said, adding generously, "And so do I, frankly."

"Thanks. But that's not why I called. Actually I was thinking that I'd like to...see you. You know, sort of on a regular basis? After all we went through together?" And before he could stop himself, he blurted out, "Besides, Linda misses Janus something terrible, too."

After an embarrassed silence, which nearly blighted Okkels, Joke said, "Oh, I see. You mean...Now, just a minute, Fokko. I don't want you to get the wrong idea, but that was...well, that was different." She obviously did not wish to be reminded of certain events.

"Whattaya mean, 'different'?" Okkels asked, with a fairly uncontrollable quiver in his voice, of distress, indignation, burgeoning rage. He really did not need to ask. He already knew what Joke was going to say. It was a mere formality, finishing the conversation in a civil manner. Certain sentences needed uttering, that was all. Joke had used him, got the publicity she'd sought, and now she was off to greener pastures, had no more need of what he could do for her. No doubt half the Dutch press would be falling all over her from here on in.

"Look, you're sweet, Fokko. But frankly, I make a point of never seeing the same man, not on a regular basis, I mean. Life is too short. And I got a lot of balling to do."

She said this with such malicious pleasure in her voice, her all too sexy voice, that Okkels nearly lost it.

"Like Hans?!" he demanded to know.

"Yes, like Hans, if you must know, though frankly it's none of your business as far as I can see."

Okkels was fuming. He felt an uncontrollable rage surge through his body but could not turn it into any sort of coherent thought, let alone an audible statement. Joke's sharp rebuke was calculated to hurt, and hurt it did. Okkels slammed the receiver onto the cradle which he held in his other hand, smashing his thumb. He screamed out in pain, hit tilt, his mind awhirl with a sado-masochistic mix of imagery: Joke with a smirk on her face, ridiculing him to her à-la-carte lover-for-a-day. Him shooting them both from point-blank range; watching them squirm in agony until they bled to death, slowly, ever so slowly.

He rose to his feet and kicked the couch as hard as he could, scaring the crap out of Linda who tried to make a safe getaway. Okkels grabbed the agate ashtray off the coffee table and threw it after his Rottweiler, who submissively turned, doubling back to her boss, wondering what in the world she'd done to displease him so. Okkels punted her a good one in the hindquarters but unlike Harry, Linda hardly budged. Instead she emitted an ominous growl, a preliminary warning Okkels took as insolent effrontery. Determined to punish the dog – and

Joke by proxy – Okkels tried another kick, but this time his shoe was instantly seized in a fierce maw that snapped shut around his instep like a vise.

"Why, you goddamn bitch!" Okkels screamed at the top of his lungs, trying to free himself from Linda's iron grip.

Unable to keep his balance, however, he painfully dropped with his shins against the hard edge of the wrought-iron coffee table, making him see fire-engine red. Awkwardly, he twisted around as best he could in the cramped space, grabbed Linda by the throat with both hands, and began violently shaking and choking the animal. In this hysterical state, Okkels was imagining his hands around Joke's throat, squeezing with all his might.

"You goddamn bitch! You goddamn bitch!!" he hissed between his teeth.

Momentarily, Linda seemed resigned to this second, manual assault. But then being slowly throttled, she suddenly twisted her powerful neck out of Okkels' stranglehold and lashed out at the murderous hands, catching a wayward finger, and snapping the digit off like a brittle twig.

Okkels roared with pain more imaginary than real as he withdrew his mutilated hand that began bleeding furiously within fractions of a second. His hand felt anaesthetized though he knew he should hurt badly. In shock, he gazed helplessly at the place where once an index finger grew, trembling and feeling faint.

Linda, having tasted blood, continued growling menacingly at her assailant, not only holding her ground, but inching towards Okkels across the polished parquet baring her teeth. Her terrified quarry tried to back off when the incensed Rottweiler ferociously snapped in his direction, again, and again, and yet again.

Seeing no other sanctuary, a terror-struck Okkels instinctively spelunked under the white couch for protection, Linda lunging for his thrashing trouser leg. A lucky kick to the snout signaled the dog's retreat, and the doorbell diverted her attention altogether, dispatching her towards the door, barking up a storm at the intruders on the other side, leaving a whimpering Okkels stuck beneath the sepulcher couch where once a mortally-wounded Harry had sought refuge.

* * * * *

"Don't worry," HG joked the following morning, trying to cheer up Okkels as they emerged from the hospital where his finger had been skillfully sewn back on. "You'll be able to wag it at the world like a true Dutchman in no time."

"Very funny." Okkels was clearly not amused. "It's my goddamn typing finger! I may never be able to bend it properly again!"

"C'mon, Fokko, count your blessings. Look on the bright side. If Sockeye and I hadn't come along, you'd be an index-fingerless amputee right now."

"Isn't it amazing what modern medicine can do?" Sockeye marveled aloud, trying to draw Okkels' ire. "Neatly grafting and splinting it to your middle finger so that it'll be nourished back to health. The surgeon told me that they splice the two together, so that the good one feeds the injured one; increases the chances of success manifold."

"What you'd call 'splint-and-splice', I suppose," HG ad-libbed. "Isn't that just super?"

The two Americans were so preoccupied that they hardly paid any heed – as they otherwise might've done – to the colorful Jan Snoek ceramic sculptures placed smack-dab in the fountain in front of the entrance to Westeinde Ziekenhuis they were exiting. It was a ward-scene of bulky, contorted shapes in hospital beds, each figure assembled out of brick-like segments and done up in characteristically festive, glossy glazes.

Sockeye shook his head in wonderment. "Apparently Linda's digestive juices kept your finger in pristine antiseptic condition so that the danger of infection was kept to a minimum, Fokko. Especially in this hot weather. It's what did the trick," HG's broad-shouldered sidekick explained, but Okkels was clearly not interested in the medical bulletin update.

"I hope Fokko appreciates that you had the presence of mind to make the dog regurgitate the finger she'd swallowed," HG said to Sockeye by way of hint to Okkels. "Wash it and pack it in ice-flakes."

"Oh shucks, 't weren't nuttin'," Sockeye said in mock modesty. "A little gentle persuasion's all it took. She's rather a sweet mutt, when you treat 'er right."

"What ya do to her anyway, Fokko, to make her mad like that?" HG taunted.

"I already told you! I accidentally stepped on her paw! Now can we please change the subject," Okkels pleaded, obviously in a foul mood, adding, "You're lucky I'm letting you keep that killer bitch. I ought to have her destroyed!"

"We're truly grateful," HG acknowledged. "On Linda's behalf, too."

And a sarcastic Sockeye chimed in, "You're a real gentleman, Mr. Okkels, sir, no denyin' that."

Looking for a stick to beat his companions with, Okkels mentioned the news he'd heard while calling in sick from the hospital earlier that morning. He wouldn't be reporting in to the paper for a while, quite a while, which for some reason didn't seem to upset his editor-in-chief, Ms. Dijkstra, a great deal – though she was diplomatic about it, interpreting the injury as having been sustained in the line of duty.

"Yes, well, I guess you'll be able to use a good watchdog on the road. Which is where you'll be sooner than you might think. I heard Anja de Boer's husband's been talking to his pal the Justice Minister. Word has it you're being chucked out of the country," Okkels said with some glee, which, however, was rather short-lived.

"The shit of state. Yep, I heard," HG replied.

"You have? Who from?"

"Good new travels fast, don't ya know? My publisher called to tell me they're immediately having another batch of *Guide for the Apoplexed* printed up. We're going mass market, banking on the expected 'Rushdie-effect', which should spark a real run on my books, don't you think? Government ban, suppression of freedom of speech. That's what it amounts to after all, despite the thinly veiled charges. Go ahead, tell 'm, Sockeye."

"Our people are organizing a book-burning bonfire outside Nijmegen before our border-crossing tonight. You're more than welcome to attend, Fokko, needless to say. I'm sure there's a story in it," Sockeye obliged.

"Just a gag, you understand. We're against that sort of thing normally. We draw the line at arson, like yourself," HG complemented Sockeye.

"But this is different and we've decided to make an exception, haven't we HG?"

"Sure have. Cause it's for a good cause. You see, Fokko, Anja de Boer will be solemnizing the event and announcing her decision to join the Worldwide Welcome Wagon. As *persona grata,* of course."

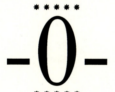

HG
12/'98
Outhouse Inn
Miramar, CA
USA

P.L.
12/'00
Vista Hotel
Scilly Isles
UK

Herman Gnuticks

Adds the helpful bodhisattva poet, lest we forget:

Buddhas, disconnecting as they prove to be,
Are not so at first;
They start out slowly, disconnecting
At the heart;
There they'll survive a while,
But sink still lower;
Thru the mire of flotsam and family ties,
To rock bottom.
ROCK BOTTOM.
Finally, they'll disappear altogether,
Scurrying into dictionaries
And tales of the East.

GUIDE FOR THE APOPLEXED

Greek and most western science is based on objectification and has thereby cut itself off (italics added) from an adequate understanding of the mind.

Margenau then quotes Schrödinger himself: "But I do believe that this is precisely the point where our present way of thinking does need to be amended, perhaps by a bit of blood-transfusion from Eastern thought."

Such a blood transfusion recommended by pre-eminent men like Margenau and Schrödinger as well as many others, including Aldous Huxley (*Perennial Philosophy*), is hopefully herewith provided.

CAUTIONARY NOTE

The above (mutagenic) argument may readily be self-administered as a shot in the arm by any Homo sapiens aspiring to Homo sagaciens status. However, incongruous as it may sound, it must be strenuously borne in mind that this argument can only be deemed successful if it fails to persuade!

Verses 22 and 23 of the *Lokatitastava* (*Master of Wisdom*) state:

The ambrosial teachings of sunyata aims at abolishing all conceptions. But if someone believes in sunyata You [have declared that] he is lost!'

Similarly, verses 36 and 41 of the *Acintyastava*:

Therefore You have declared that all phenomena are merely abstractions. Even the abstraction through which sunyata is conceived You have declared nonexistent.

...Whoever awakens to this is called Buddha.

s/he can shed laboratory smock, as well as separate observer status, to slip agilely back into non-duality or "nonality" from whence s/he came, if and when required (hark, you theoreticians especially). Playing the science game may be fun and remunerative, but dangerously restrictive and the known cause of Pandora's boxes full of neuroses/psychoses.

A case in point is Sir Isaac Newton, who had a history of mental illness, and of whom Roger M. Cooke writes in his sober book with the ambiguous title Geloof in Wetenschap (Faith in Science), Van Gorcum, Assen, 1983, pages 4/5, loosely translated here:

> The strange case of Isaac Newton (1642-1727) deserves special attention, because in his person are united an exceptional scientific genius and an exceptional preoccupation with the occult...Newton believed that long ago God once revealed all the secrets of natural philosophy to a number of privileged persons. That knowledge was partially lost, partially confounded. What remained was hidden in coded language in myths and fables. With the aid of experimental philosophy and clever sleuthing that knowledge could once more be brought to light.' Asks Cooke rhetorically, "Was Newton the last sorcerer? Will our psychoanalysis and our theories regarding the origin of the universe seem less ridiculous in 2283 than Boyle's potions and Newton's faith in alchemy?

WHO AM I?

It is only our long dualistic conditioning which reinforces the impression of separate-being status. On closer inspection — under the strictest scrutiny of the sciences, physical or psychological — there is no evidence of any sort supporting such separate-being status. All is relative, radically relative, and residuelessly so. Yet the relative implies the non-relative, and the radically relative, the radically non-relative. The Indian sage assures us: Tat tvam asi – thou art that. The more we investigate the world, the not-I, the more we find it to be a fleeting, evanescent mirage. In chasing the Other, we chase ourselves, a will-o'-the-wisp.

Margenau quoting one of the pioneers of qm theory and fellow Nobel Prize winner, E. Schrödinger, writes that he, Schrödinger:

> ...admits that this doctrine (of the Upanishads) has little appeal in the West, and he traces our tendency to belittle it to a seduction by Greek science, which is the model of our own scientific enterprise.

GUIDE FOR THE APOPLEXED

infinite number of possible truth values. These demonstrations showed, in the words of one of their creators, that 'the law of the excluded middle is not writ in the heavens.' In 1932, the American logician Alonzo Church drew out the significance of the creation of these new logics and the parallels with the creation of the new geometries; it encapsulated the new attitude of mathematicians to the *relativism of logics* (italics added).

Even though astronomical observations spectacularly confirmed Einstein's assumption that the geometry of space and time was a non-Euclidian one, it was still the case that as one surveyed smaller and smaller dimensions, the geometry of the world approximated that of Euclid to greater and greater accuracy. The situation with logics was not quite so transparent. *Rather, it is positively incestuous* (italics added). For while we do not need to assume any particular geometry applies to the real world in order to discuss the issue, *we do need logic to talk about logic. All our discussions about logic one might employ...take place using the two-valued logic of ordinary parlance, which assumes it to be either true or false.*

Concludes Dr. Barrow: "The psychological effects of the realization that one could invent all manner of different, self-consistent forms of logical reasoning were deep and wide. They had a liberating effect upon thinkers struggling with problems that seemed to defy traditional forms of argument for their solution."

And not surprisingly the names which are mentioned in this connection are Heisenberg, Gödel and Penrose. Equally unsurprising is the quotation by Christopher Morley with which the next section of this illuminating books begins: "A great truth is a truth whose opposite is also a great truth."

In this connection it would be remiss not to mention an important reference made in a footnote to the previous section. It reads: "In a non-Western culture like that of the Jains in ancient India one finds *a more sophisticated attitude* (stress added) towards the truth status of statements...Jainian logic admits seven categories for a statement which reflects both its intrinsic uncertainty and the incompleteness of our knowledge of it."

It should be added that the ancient Jain logicians were contemporaries of the ancient Buddhist logicians, whose work culminated in Nagarjuna's.

By way of remedy, then, when we find ourselves in hot metaphysical waters, it may be good to recall the Ultimate Escape Clause: "Everything implies its opposite," and its close corollary, "Affirming is denying." This can become the temporary refuge of the skeptic who can upset any dogmatist's apple cart with ease. Both these partial doctrines — Aristotle's and the skeptic's — are subsumed, however, in the more versatile non-skeptical Nonist view, as has been amply reiterated. In case of the qm scientist,

GUIDE FOR THE APOPLEXED

By

Herman Gnuticks

"All the dogmatists have been terrified by the lion's roar of sunyata. Wherever they may reside, sunyata lies in wait!"

- Nagarjuna (± 150 A.D.)

"Sunyata will touch you before you will touch sunyata."

- Masao Abe

PROLOGUE

The uncanny convergence of the way modern physics views "reality" and the way the ancient Buddhists did has frequently been noted in recent years (Capra, Zukav, Bohm etc.). But never have the astounding similarities in outlook been explained in anything but anecdotal terms. Now a more rigorous argument is proposed based on the 'interface' between the distinct disciplines of philosophy and physics, namely that mysterious and unique digit which was last to join our numeral system: zero. We ask where the zero came from and what it signifies.

We note that in skeleton simplicity, the customary ontologies available to philosophy in the West range upward from 1: monism, dualism, pluralism. Whereas in India, for example, these same ontologies exist, we also find an ontology which could be said to be zero-based. When we scrutinize this divergent philosophical system, we discover that the philosophy of Sunyavada, unlike others East and West, asserts that the world is not made of three or more substances or principles, nor two, nor one. Sunyavada, issuing from the Mahayana tradition, and whose main exponent Nagarjuna fully worked it out based on the concept of Sunyata, or emptiness, can be said to be based on zero (sunya in Sanskrit). Its claim about the world would be that it is not made of any substance or principle. In fact it is not made at all – a blatant Creationist bias.

The first of two contentions to be made here is that though the West functionally adopted the zero as part of the Hindu digital system (via the Arabs), its true significance has never been fully grasped. The striking thing to be noted in this regard, however, is that after ten centuries of exposure to the numeral system in which the zero was embedded, modern physics is led to similar insights as regards the nature of matter. This, it is claimed here, is no mere coincidence but a virtual inevitability.

The second contention to be made is that the significance of the preverbal concept of zero, or non-trivial nothingness, is that it marks the point in history when mankind became an enlightened species. In this connection, an anthropological novelty of the first degree is documented, namely the emergence of a subspecies of Homo sapiens, coined here as Homo sagaciens. Its distinctive feature is free passage between dual and non-dual realms.

In order to explore these far-reaching issues, an analysis of philosophy East and West is offered, a historic overview of developments in mathematics, a bird's eye view of anthropology, and a close correlation of all the above disciplines in an attempt to distil (wo)man's accumulated wisdom.

INTRODUCTION

As we stand poised on the threshold of the 21st century, a true coming of age, humanity is in dire need of a worthy philosophy for the brand-new epoch ahead; one supplying us with acceptable answers to the perennial "Hows, Whats & Whys" — again. Again, because as will be shown, such a philosophy is already around today; has been around for centuries, though little understood, if not largely misunderstood. The accomplishment of this coveted feat of successfully unraveling the conundrum of conundrums is also precisely the claim to fame of Homo sagaciens — in evolutionary terms a relatively young subspecies branching off sapiens main trunk. Its characteristic feature — free passage between the dual and non-dual realms — is also documented below.

This treatise therefore serves not only to announce an anthropological novelty of the first degree, but also presents a farther-reaching philosophical analysis putting into proper perspective (wo)man's accumulated wisdom in this regard, hard-fought and painstakingly won over the millennia. For how many individual lives have not passed and how much energy has not been expended historically in attempting to solve the seemingly eternal riddle of existence? And to what avail? Humanity, by the looks of it, still is ceaselessly in search of answers to the age-old preoccupations and this alone would justify an unequivocal undertaking to put into proper perspective our struggle to acquire the inextinguishable light by which to read the script of life — metaphorically speaking. It is especially wry, therefore, that what we are after was essentially already attained long ago, though few realize it, even in these days of international telecommunications and global villagedom. Much trivia is brought to our attention daily, both in print and electronic media, but news of truly momentous import is overlooked or ignored. Still, throughout the ages, a select and diligent few have homed in on a viable solution to the problem, tantalizingly skirting around its edges, coming breathtakingly close, yet remaining agonizingly far away. Fewer still have ever caught on.

Traditionally, it was the task of the metaphysician to deal with this tricky subject matter, but needless to say, in the final analysis such questions and their answers encompassed all disciplines. Over the centuries scientists have hurled themselves into the fray, and seemingly quite successfully, offering us a choice of challenging cosmological options that touch on our sanguine and salient concerns for First Things. We shall therefore attempt to forge a synthesis between the fields of philosophy, mathematics, physics and anthropology on the most fundamental level, that is, their logical, ontological and epistemological bases in order to penetrate and gauge their relative merit in helping to realize our aim. What we will endeavor to show is that considered together in this way, these disciplines can, and do, provide a deeper understanding, which will self-destruct, whereupon the questions originally posed

3

will also themselves vanish — somewhat akin to Wittgenstein's ladder, used then discarded. If done successfully, no nagging doubts should remain to haunt the questioner, to whose final judgment the validity and credibility of this admittedly proleptical piece will, indeed must be left — with full right of veto.

Herman Gnuticks

A BRIEF HISTORY OF PHILOSOPHY

Writes A.C. Grayling in Wittgenstein (Oxford University Press, 1988, p.12):

> One can describe philosophy as an attempt to make clear, and if possible to answer, a range of fundamental and puzzling questions which arise when, in a general and inclusive way, we try to understand ourselves and the universe we inhabit. Among many other things these questions concern existence and reality, knowledge and belief, reason and reasoning, truth, meaning, and value both ethical and aesthetic. The questions themselves are of the form: what is reality? What kinds of things ultimately exist? What is knowledge, and how do we come by it? How can we be sure that our claims to knowledge are not in some systematic way mistaken?

Grayling is quoted at length here because not only does he provide us with a concise explanation of philosophy, but he also gives us a good sense of its place in western tradition when he says:

> Over the millennia a great investment of genius has been brought to the task of clarifying and answering the questions of philosophy. Some philosophers have attempted to construct explanatory theories, occasionally very elaborate in scope; others have tried to clarify and resolve particular questions by painstaking analysis and criticism. Almost all those who have contributed to philosophy throughout its history have agreed that the matters mentioned above, existence, knowledge, truth, value, are deeply important; and it is upon this consensus that the philosophical debate, which has gone on at least since classical antiquity, has been based.

The investment of all this creative energy Grayling alludes to has led to some pretty wild goose-chases and not surprisingly a magnificent amount of confusion and obfuscation to boot. Apprising oneself of the achievements of the cream of human civilization in this notoriously inaccessible field, we are struck by the myriad claims and counterclaims. Indeed the history of philosophy reads like one long tug-of-war between intellectual titans and dwarfs alike, each contradicting the other and often themselves. Nor are we any better off today, as Alan Watts points out:

> Modern academic philosophy, the discipline of logic, epistemology, ontology, and the like, is about as far as it could be from providing

5

GUIDE FOR THE APOPLEXED

modern society with any principle of unity. Sincere and brilliant as its disciples may be, it would be difficult to find a group more uncertain and confused in its collective mind. (*The Supreme Identity*, Vintage Books, New York, 1972, p.21.)

"This is the voice of Wisdom herself," Will Durant contends in *The Story of Philosophy* (p.462) after he has cited Henri Bergson: "I believe that the time given to refutation in philosophy is usually time lost. Of the many attacks directed by the many thinkers against each other, what now remains? Nothing, or assuredly very little." Ironically Bergson must have jinxed himself because his philosophy proved a passing fad of the Parisian *beau monde*.

We shall assiduously keep all this in mind as we take a slightly different approach to the problem and not try to construct fresh answers to ancient questions but concentrate instead on weeding the overgrown philosophical garden so long neglected. We shall find that most of the tools we need to tackle the job have already been provided, and what's more, the bulk of our work already done for us. All that really remains is to snip and prune, to lay bare first lineaments and later contours of the philosophical landscape offering the widest possible vista, whereupon the viewer and the view may be neatly telescoped and pocketed.

To accomplish this singular feat we shall first look closely at the ontological roots nurturing the fruits philosophers throughout the ages have provided us with. In this way we shall hopefully gain a handy overview of the most fundamental assumptions about the world which thinkers have generally entertained. Apparently disparate systems will thus be seen to agree or disagree in their bare-bone essentials, leaving aside the frills. Once we reach a degree of clarity in this regard, we shall proceed to compare the state of western philosophy with that attained in modern science; and then to contrast in this respect the East and the West, to see whether there is anything to be learnt from our Asian brethren, and if so, what. That done, we shall draw on insights in mathematics and anthropology to correlate these and other disciplines in order to arrive at *the big picture*. Finally, returning to our starting point, we shall find the cosmic code cracked once and for all.

And indeed, the best-kept secret is the open one...

Herman Gnuticks

A TRIO OF ONTOLOGIES

We begin with a bird's eye view of western philosophy, to conclude that all systems of thought conceived in the West from pre-Socratic times onward may be categorized as forms of pluralism, dualism or monism – that is, three (3) or more substances or principles to account for the world; two (2); or only one (1). Natural, pagan, or heathen (wo)mankind with a proclivity towards superstition, zoolatry, idolatry, or what have you, may be lumped together as pluralist for convenience sake. While some of the ancient Greeks from Socrates onwards also tended towards such pluralism, dualism was on the rise, although a complete cocktail of ontologies prevailed in exhilarating (ad)mixture.

Sextus Empiricus (A.D. 160-210), notorious skeptic and man about town, puts it thusly:

> Seeing, then, that those who, in the department of Physics, seem to have classified most precisely the principles of the Universe declare that some of these are efficient, others material,...'All things were together, and Mind came and set them in order,' assuming that Mind, which according to him (Homer) is God is the efficient principle and the multi-mixture of homoeomeries (things of like parts) the material principle. And Aristotle says that Hermotimus of Clazomenae and Parmenides of Elea and, much earlier, Hesiod held this view. Moreover, the Stoics also, when they declared that there are two principles, God and unqualified matter, suppose that God acts and that matter is passive and altered: – seeing then that some such classification is made by the best of Physicists. (The Loeb Classical Library, *Sextus Empiricus*, 1987).

Dualism, in other words.

Subsequently, after a mad transitional phase ranging from polytheism and pantheism through henotheism to monotheism (all major "revealed" religions) and other intermediate states, the western tradition in natural philosophy, too, continued to vacillate strongly between pluralism, dualism and monism for many centuries. A revival of pure dualism during the 17th century found its main exponent in Descartes, whom we could refer to as the "stepfather of science" – after Aristotle, two millennia earlier, considered its patriarch. In a Europe emerging from an era of religiosity, this fresh and versatile form of dualism permitted god-fearing men to salve their consciences while satisfying their curiosity about the world they lived in. There seemed nothing contradictory in their worshipping God and analyzing His Creation at the same time.

GUIDE FOR THE APOPLEXED
WESTERN PHILOSOPHY & SCIENCE

Sir Isaac Newton who took Descartes' philosophy to heart vastly expanded the frontiers of the new science, which formed the basis of the "classical" worldview. In general terms, this era which lasted some 300 years, saw matter as continuous, its motion as predictable, and the universe it comprised as utterly predetermined and thus determinable, as well as predestined, and thus predictable – given sufficient data. Moreover, the individual was a passive player in the ongoing cosmic show presumably staged by a beneficent God guiding human destiny. There seemed to be no room for free will, and at best giants like Newton were able to comprehend the laws which governed His universe.

Towards the end of the 19th century, however, Albert Einstein burst on the scene. This humble little man threw a monkey wrench in Newton's cold, mechanical universe, which caused the entire works to grind to a halt in a manner of speaking. Einstein reintroduced the observer as variable into the calculable and calculated universe, and (re)endowed each individual with his/her inalienable birthright, that is, unique personal experience and concomitant interpretation of "events" by calling into question absolute time. Absolute space had already been dealt a death-blow by Newton, though he was loath to accept his own conclusion. Einstein's theories of special and general relativity, which further pulled the rug out from under Sir Isaac, opened (wo)men's eyes to an astounding new world where the observer turned out to be intimately connected to unfolding events. And, more importantly to us here, matter and energy were equated, which fit well into the trend away from dualism towards scientific monism. In fact so confident was Einstein of the underlying unity of the four fundamental forces at work in the universe – including the gravitational – that his avowed aim was to formulate a Unified Field Theory. In other words, monism.

No sooner had this fresh world view been introduced or Planck, Heisenberg, Schrödinger and others, in an attempt to explain puzzling laboratory observations having to do with the behavior of both light and subatomic particles, formulated the theory of quantum mechanics (qm) – in its original form seen by them as a mere simulacrum; a mathematical trick or makeshift – with which they had to make do until a more principled solution to the baffling problem was found. (This is a highly telling hint, as will be made abundantly clear as we proceed!) Diffracted light, for example – the famous two-slit experiment – exhibited 'dual' characteristics, acting sometimes as particle, sometimes as wave. In order to overcome this regression to distasteful dualism, the Principle of Complementarity was postulated, which permitted a monistic interpretation of one of the most basic of natural phenomenon light (electromagnetic radiation), and thus by implication the universe at large.

As stated, Einstein had already equated matter and energy, which reinforced the movement away from Cartesian dualism to monism within the domain of science.

8

Matter – such as the early Greek's earth, air, water and fire – was reduced to complex molecules, simple atoms and finally subatomic particles. With some justifiable confidence, it was fully expected that the discovery of one single such elementary particle would wind up man's search of thousands of years. All there was to know about the material world would then be known. The only thing remaining once that had been achieved would be to account for Descartes' irksome cogito, that is, the "knowing-I", or "mind". But that, few doubted, would be found to reduce to an epiphenomenon of the newly homogenized matter – and most likely grafted somehow onto the organic brain. We could then sit back and relax, thoroughly in control, and manipulate nature at will through our certain knowledge of the laws that govern the universe. We would be capable of guiding our own destinies, aspiring to attain paradise on earth. The tables could then be turned on God, if He existed at all, and He could be relegated to a passive role formerly reserved for His creatures. Such was the trend in science – while a brazen philosopher like Nietzsche went further and announced God's demise altogether in an arrogant obituary.

CLASSICAL REALISM VERSUS QM ANTI-REALISM

But in the sciences at least, things turned out quite differently than expected. State-of-the-art qm physics indeed proved capable of accounting for most subatomic phenomena, and was even able to make accurate predictions of thitherto undiscovered elementary particles, including antimatter – later amazingly verified in the lab. But this same qm theory also incidentally unveiled a world which was chaotic, discontinuous and indeterminate! An element of chance was (re)introduced into the world, and with it, potentially at least, the ancient philosophical bone of contention: free will (as opposed to determinism or strict necessity). Einstein, for one, did not buy it, protesting that God did not play dice, and this controversial issue seriously split the allegiance of men inhabiting ivory towers of science all over the globe, pushing them into rival camps.

To their chagrin hard-nosed "realists" had to seek recourse to a world of matter which was constituted of the abstractest probability waves instead of the reliable terra firma of former days. Matter virtually vanished into thin air, or rather the quantum vacuum. Not only were physicists unable to pinpoint any subatomic particle with classical certainty (that is, position and velocity), but moreover such particles only seemed to materialize at all when measured or observed! Unmeasured or unobserved – physicists were forced to conclude – the material world existed only in a statistical array of potentialities!

9

GUIDE FOR THE APOPLEXED

Quantum theory, in the words of Stanford physicist Nick Herbert, "is the most far-ranging and successful attempt to understand the physical world ever devised by human beings." Just how far-ranging is hinted at by Paul Davies, professor of theoretical physics (University of Newcastle upon Thyne) in his challenging book *Other Worlds* (Penguin Books, 1980, p.13) when he writes:

> ...for unlike all previous revolutions, which have successively demoted mankind from the centre of creation to the role of a mere spectator of the cosmic drama, quantum theory reinstates the observer at the centre of the stage. Indeed some prominent scientists have even gone so far as to claim that quantum theory has solved the riddle of the mind and its relation to the material world, asserting that the entry of information into the consciousness of the observer is the fundamental step in the establishment of reality. Taken to its extreme, this idea implies that the universe only achieves a concrete existence as a result of this perception — it is created by its own inhabitants!

This postulated "co-authorship" may seem an unwarranted extrapolation; an instance of intoxicated science overconfidently outreaching itself, overstepping certain sacrosanct boundaries of common sense — if not committing a downright unforgivable sin born of hubris.

ONTOLOGICAL QUANDARY

One of a number of attendant theoretical problems accompanying the introduction of revolutionary quantum mechanics was the necessity to postulate "immaterial fields" which insofar as these were mutually irreconcilable compelled Nobel Prize-winning physicists like Henry Margenau — Emeritus Professor of Physics and Natural Philosophy at Yale University — to adopt once more a sophisticated form of detestable pluralism as ontological base. This erudite gentleman-scholar writes in *The Miracle of Existence* (New Science Library, 1987, p.36/39) that: "Most philosophers and many scientists dealing with the mind-body problem classify their views as either monistic or dualistic. I wish to show that this is an anachronism that can no longer be tolerated (stress added) in the science in which it arose: physics."

After careful re-examination of the (limited) options available to him, Professor Margenau concludes that if we wish to preserve the old-style language, we "must confess our allegiance to pluralism." The reason he gives is as follows: "Perhaps much to the reader's surprise, I do not find the 'body', generally conceived as matter, tending

toward a merger with the mind; I find it splitting into an increasing variety of essences that are nonmaterial, highly elusive, incomprehensible to 'common sense', often incapable of visualization and localization, illustrating Whitehead's 'fallacy of simple location.'"

He adds, "No one is sure at this time whether these essences include the mind, although this hypothesis has been voiced." And, in a leap of perspicuity, he states, "My own conclusion is that the old distinction has become superannuated and meaningless."

To our extreme disappointment, the elderly professor then goes on to build a case for a Universal Mind (capitalization is his)! Margenau, too, turns out to be a crypto-Idealist, or monist, after all. One who a few chapters earlier had confessed to pluralism. We can only put such fickleness down to lack of choice — as will be shown. Nor is he the only one cornered into an indefensible ontological stance, for in a dust jacket blurb, we are urged by another Nobel Laureate, Sir John C. Eccles, to consider his friend's views carefully since in his opinion *The Miracle of Existence* is "one of the great books of our age." Eccles himself, as it turns out, subscribes to "transcendental dualism"!

It seems that with each new generation, the same mistakes are repeated without anyone ever catching on. In the lucid introduction to a useful little book awkwardly titled *Structuralism and Since* on Levi-Strauss, Barthes, Foucault, Lacan and Derrida, edited by John Sturrock of *The Times Literary Supplement*, it is written of this notorious French fivesome who represent views on anthropology, psychology, linguistics, literary criticism and philosophy: "They are against the singular and for the plural, preferring whole galaxies of meanings to emerge from a limited set of phenomena to the notion that it must hold one, unifying dominant meaning." Pluralism rather then monism.

To the list of illustrious luminaries giving it a shot and shooting wide of the mark may equally be added Gilbert Ryle (*The Concept of Mind*), Thomas Nagel (*What is it like to be a Bat?*), John Searle (*The Rediscovery of the Mind*), Douglas R. Hofstadter (*The Mind's I*), no less than his co-author Daniel C. Dennett (*Gödel, Escher, Bach*), to mention but an arbitrary few. All claim their right to be wrong, and all amply exercise that right to the hilt.

ONTOLOGICAL AMBIVALENCE IN SCIENCE

Pluralism, dualism, monism...and dualism or pluralism once again — in all their rainbow flavors. Back and forth, to and fro, it goes over the centuries. Nor are philosophers, like scientific theoreticians, spared the embarrassment of having to dress up

GUIDE FOR THE APOPLEXED

in the restricted fashions of the day. Arguably, each system has its advantages and disadvantages, but each remains ultimately problematical. As Julian Huxley, former Director General of UNESCO, and renowned scientist, scholar and author puts it (*Evolution in Action*, The New American Library, 1953, p.77): "For a biologist, much the easiest way is to think of mind and matter as aspects of a single, underlying reality – shall we call it world substance, the stuff out of which the world is made. At any rate, this fits more of the facts and leads to fewer contradictions than any other view."

In other words, Huxley, too, acknowledges inherent difficulties men of science face, and opts for monism albeit under duress. Margenau-the-physicist would not agree with him, while Margenau-the-philosopher might. And Eccles would be compelled to disagree with both.

It is not surprising, therefore, that to date no consensus exists among philosophers or scientists on how best to answer the fundamental questions which continue to linger. Questions like, "Why is there something rather than nothing?" "How can anything be?" and, "What do our scientific theories mean?" Or more generally, "What is it all about?"

ONTOLOGY IN EASTERN PHILOSOPHY

Let us now make an earnest effort to shed our blinkers and correct our strong Euro-astigmatism, that is, our general western bias. We shall look elsewhere in the world as to how other people who have also thought long and hard about these perennial questions tried to resolve these thorny philosophical dilemmas. In India, for example, the same trio of admittedly problematical ontologies exists. For example, the philosophic mother lode of India, Vedantism, breaks down as follows, according to V.M. Apte (*Brahma-Sutra Shankara-Bhashya*, Popular Book Depot, Bombay, 1960, p.xiii): "These several sub-systems are the 'Advaita' (Absolute Monism) of Shankara, the 'Vishishtadvaita' (Qualified Monism) of Ramanuja, the 'Dvaitadvaita' (Dualism with Monism) of Nimbarka, the 'Shuddhadvaita' (Pure Monism) of Vallabha, the 'Dvaita' (Dualism) of Madhva."

There are also frequent references to "rigorous monism", "extreme monism", apart from a host of pluralistic systems as well.

Not surprisingly perhaps, we even find an Indian equivalent of the famous Cartesian cogito or svatmanam darsanam surfacing more than 20 centuries before Descartes saw the light of day, and which it is claimed:

>...led to the belief in a permanent and eternal self during the period
>of the Upanishads and continued to flourish in the speculations of

12

the later Indian philosophical schools. It is the definition that produced the most metaphysical ideas, such as the conception of the 'inner controller' that turns out to be the permanent and eternal self or soul. Any form of perception, for them, involved self-awareness as a necessary pre-condition, after which every other form of activity follows. (Nagarjuna, The Philosophy of the Middle Way, David J. Kalupahana, SUNY Press, 1986, p.37)

UNIQUE ONTOLOGY

Amidst this teeming diversity, however, a unique ontology is also found, Nagarjuna's, which deviates from the limited range available in both the West as well as the East. That is, in addition to the entire spectrum mentioned, ranging from 3 or more, 2 and/or 1, there also exists an ontology based on 0 (zero). The philosophy so constructed is known as Sunyavada (Shyoon'-ya-vaad') — derived from the Sanskrit word sunya, meaning empty or void. Its answer to the perennial questions phrased at the outset of this piece are not restricted to the traditional either/or, something/nothing, real/unreal, or any other stark dualistic choice of opposites. Sunyavada states simply that the world is not real or unreal, nor both, nor neither, nor different from neither or both.

Master of Wisdom (Chr. Lindtner, Dharma, 1986, p.95), Nagarjuna himself, devoted seventy verses to the doctrine in his Sunyatasaptati (circa 100-200 A.D.), the first three of which run:

> Though the Buddhas have spoken of duration, origination, destruction, being, non-being, low, moderate, and excellent by force of worldly convention, [they] have not done [so] in an absolute sense.
>
> Designations are without significance, for self, non-self, and self-non-self do not exist.
> [For] like Nirvana, all expressible things are empty (sunya) of own-being.
>
> Since all things altogether lack substance — either in causes or conditions, [in their] totality,
> or separately — they are empty."

GUIDE FOR THE APOPLEXED

PHILOSOPHY OF EMPTINESS

This philosophical formulation differs radically from the usual options available in the Occident, and for that matter in the Orient — since birth east of some arbitrary geographical line does not automatically confer this deeper insight. It must be painfully acquired through earnest agonizing and concentrated effort — which in itself should offer a measure of hope to the unacquainted but dedicated investigator: layman, philosopher and scientist alike!

D.T. Suzuki in *Essays in Zen Buddhism* (Grove Press, Inc., 1961, p.58) recommends the notion of sunya to the reader as follows:

> The Mahayana doctrine of Sunyata was a natural conclusion. But I need not make any remark here to the effect that the Sunyata theory is not nihilism or acosmism, but that it has its positive background which sustains it and gives life to it...They finally found out that Enlightenment was not a thing exclusively belonging to the Buddha, but that each one of us could attain it if he got rid of ignorance by *abandoning the dualistic conception of life and of the world.* (italics added).

And indeed the outlook between the dualist and the non-dualist which we shall explore throughout can justifiably be said to be radical, because literally poles apart, according to the eminent S. Radhakrishnan. This King George V Professor of Philosophy, University of Calcutta — and later India's second President — under the heading "Sunyavada and Its Implications" writes (*Indian Philosophy*, Vol. I, George Allen & Unwin Ltd., 1948, p.662/3):

> Nagarjuna admits the existence of a higher reality, though with the Upanishads he considers it to be not an object of experience. "The eye does not see and the mind does not think; this is the highest truth, wherein men do not enter. The land wherein the full vision of all objects is obtained at once has by the Buddha been called the paramartha, or absolute truth, which cannot be preached in words...It cannot be called void or not void, or both or neither, but in order to indicate it, it is called the void...There is fundamental reality, without which things would not be what they are. Sunyata is a positive principle."

Radhakrishnan ascertains:

As applied to the world of experience, sunyata means the ever-changing state of the phenomenal world. In the dread waste of endlessness man loses all hope, but the moment he recognises its unreality he transcends it and reaches after the abiding principle. He knows that the whole is a passing dream, where he might sit unconcerned at the issues, certain of victory.

But, he continues, in a note of caution:

About the ultimate reality we cannot say anything...The absolute is neither existent nor non-existent, nor both existent and non-existent, nor different from both non-existence and existence...From our point of view the absolute is nothing. We call it sunyam, since no category used in relation to the conditions of the world is adequate to it...Thought is dualistic in its functions, and what is, is non-dual or advaita (a-dvaita = not-two, HG). Buddha is reported to have said: "What description can be given and what knowledge devised of an object which cannot be represented by the letters of the alphabet? Even this much of description that it does not admit of representation by the letters of the alphabet is made by means of attributing letters to the transcendent, absolute, signified by the term sunyata."

Observes the erudite Radhakrishnan, "It is in this sense of transcending all relations that Duns Scotus says: 'God is not improperly called nothing. For thought, what is not relative, is nothing.'"

To place this pivotal concept firmly within Buddhist tradition, John Snelling attests under the heading "New Bearings in Philosophy" (*The Buddhist Handbook*, Rider, London, 1989, p.101):

At the core of Mahayana philosophy lies the notion of Emptiness: Shunyata. This is very much in the spirit of anatta...at first taught by the Buddha. It is often used to imply, not mere or sheer nothingness (that would be the nihilistic view), but 'emptiness of inherent existence'; that is the absence of any kind of enduring or self-sustaining essence. There is also a sense in which it has connotations of 'conceptual emptiness': absence of thoughts. It could be regarded too as a non-term signifying the ineffable understanding arising within the practice of meditation. Although seemingly negative, it also has its positive uses – and of course ultimately points beyond the positive/negative dichotomy.

GUIDE FOR THE APOPLEXED
NON-TRIVIAL NOTHINGNESS AND MATHEMATICS

Just precisely what the significance of non-trivial emptiness is, when and where it surfaced as the concept of zero in mathematics, and how it can satisfactorily help us remedy our chronic ontological ailment in philosophy may be better appreciated after two brief sorties into history. But before embarking on these, we may do well to consider a sampling of quotations paying tribute to the triumph of the human intellect which the innovation of the concept of nothing as numeral constitutes: *The Encyclopaedia Britannica* (1980, Vol. 1, p.1174) writes:

> The devising of a scheme whereby an infinitude of things can be represented by means of but a small number of symbols must be ranked among the most important achievements of the human intellect, for without it an advanced development of either language or arithmetic is unimaginable (italics added). The key ideas are two: the positional principle and the symbol zero...Similarly, the invention, probably by the Hindus, of the digit zero has been described as one of the greatest importance in the history of mathematics.

In his *Vedic Mathematics* (Motilal Banarsidass, Delhi, p.xviii), Jagadguru Sri Bharati Krishna quotes Professor G.P. Halstead as having written: "The importance of the creation of the zero mark can never be exaggerated. This giving of airy nothingness...is the characteristic of the Hindu race whence it sprang."

In a timely article titled "Indian Science's Place in History", appearing in the publication *India Abroad* (Jan. 11, 1991), co-authors A.B. Krishna and A. Jayakrishna echo the same sentiment. "India's most important contribution to science is nothing: the concept of nothing, or zero, is central to the understanding of all else."

Emeritus Professor John McLeish of the University of Victoria, British Colombia, in his book Number (Fawcett Columbine, New York, 1991, p.115) puts it thus:

> From the time of their earliest civilisations, the inhabitants of the Indian subcontinent had a highly sophisticated awareness of numbers. For example, the people of Mohenjo Daro, an Indus Valley civilisation of some 5000 years ago (2550-1550 BC) used a simple decimal system and had methods of counting, weighing and measuring far in advance of their contemporaries in Egypt, Babylon or Mycenaean Greece...From the mathematical point of view, the most significant Hindu contribution to world knowledge was the decimal system, which they developed from the counting methods of Mohenjo

16

Daro and perfected by three inventions. These were first, the use of special number-symbols unconnected with any 'outside' influence, such as letters of the alphabet or pictures of fingers and toes; second, the use of a place system (in which the value of a number depends on its position in the units, tens, hundreds, thousands place, and so on); and third, but most important of all – and a milestone as vital in the history of civilisation as the invention of the wheel – the use of a symbol for zero, to show that the place in question adds nothing to the number. These discoveries were the foundation of centuries of Hindu superiority in arithmetic, algebra and trigonometry.

And this "at a time when most of Europe was culturally in limbo," according to Professor McLeish.

Or take Professor A.L. Basham, who assesses the contribution of the person who single-handedly changed the course of history as follows, in *The Wonder That Was India* (Sedgewick & Jackson, London, 1985, p.496):

The debt of the Western world to India in this respect cannot be overestimated. Most of the great discoveries and inventions of which Europe is so proud would have been impossible without a developed system of mathematics, and this in turn would have been impossible if Europe had been shackled by the unwieldy system of Roman numerals. The unknown man who devised the new system was from the world's point of view, after the Buddha, the most important son of India (italics added). His achievement, though easily taken for granted, was the work of an analytical mind of the first order, and he deserves much more honour than he has so far received.

As regards the merit of the legendary Buddha himself, a suggestive passage may here be quoted from the *Lalithavistara*, as translated in *The Voice of the Buddha* (Dharma Publishing, Vol.I, 1983, p.221-2):

The Sakyas said: 'Let the young man reveal his knowledge of mathematics; let him show the extent of his abilities.'

And the great mathematician Arjuna (ibid.), filled with admiration, recited these two verses:

So quick is his mind,
that even five hundred young Sakyas,

GUIDE FOR THE APOPLEXED

all together, cannot match his
knowledge of numbers.

According to the *Lalithavistara* the Buddha had an aptitude for juggling huge numbers. Whether or not he — or for that matter his examiner Arjuna — were conversant with the zero digit unfortunately remains unknown. But to establish a plausible link between (Buddhist) philosophy and mathematics will suffice at this stage of the argument.

For now let's not lose sight of how different zero is from the "concrete" digits. On the one hand, addition and subtraction by zero leaves all digits unchanged, while on the other multiplication by zero reduces any digit to zero. Division by zero mysteriously points to infinity — the link between finitude and infinity!

Psychologically speaking, non-trivial nothingness is incalculably more important still. Suffice it to say here that language (and thus philosophy), mathematics, geometry and physics all separate at One and (re)join at Zero. For these and other disciplines are all complementary facets of the fully integrated faculties of the human mind, and must therefore not only be rooted in the intellect but somehow be firmly anchored and accurately gauged there in order to function harmoniously in healthy men and women.

In his *Discourse on Method* Descartes himself wrote: "If we could see how the sciences are linked together, we would find them no harder to retain in our minds than the series of numbers."

Tom Sorell, in the *Past Masters* series (Oxford University Press, p.10/14) on Descartes says that:

> ...he actually asserts the existence of a 'universal mathematics': I came to see that the exclusive concern of mathematics is with the questions of order or measure and that it is irrelevant whether the measure in question involves numbers, shapes, stars, sounds, or any other object whatever...and that this science should be termed *mathesis universalis* [universal mathematics]...for it covers everything that entitles...other sciences to be called branches of mathematics...He (Descartes) goes on to say that this science surpasses the subordinate ones of geometry, astronomy, music, optics, mechanics and others in 'unity and simplicity', and he adds that on account of its extremely high level of generality it lacks some of the difficulties that impede the special sciences.

Not that the interpretation of the significance of mathematics is an uncontested matter. As Dr John D. Barrow, professor of astronomy in the Astronomy Centre,

Herman Gnuticks

University of Sussex, writes in his thoroughly entertaining and informative book *Pi In The Sky* (Clarendon Press, Oxford, 1992, pages 21/22):

> This state of affairs leads us to the overwhelming question: Is mathematics just an analogy or is it the real stuff of which the physical realities are but a particular reflection? This leads us to our first glimpse of the mysterious foundations of modern science. It uses and trusts the language of mathematics as an infallible guide to the way the world works without a satisfactory understanding of what mathematics actually is and why the world dances to the mathematical tune. If you question a variety of scientists about their trust in mathematics, you probably won't get a very convincing answer. They will not have given it a moment's thought. But in general they work as though they discover mathematical truths about the world rather than invent them or simply organize them into a pattern that fits the available catalogue of mathematical notions. Mathematicians, likewise, will typically have ignored this awkward question unless they happen to work on those areas of pure mathematics that wander perilously close to the subjects of logic and philosophy. If you pressed the mathematician harder, you would get a more considered response than you did from the physicist. You would find him working from Monday to Friday as if mathematical ideas really existed independently of himself waiting to be discovered. But, questioned at the weekend, reclining more thoughtfully in his armchair he would find this view very difficult to defend and most likely plump for regarding mathematics as a sort of logical game which you explore using the stated rules. The fact that it works as a description of the world he would regard as a side issue that doesn't affect what he does. Nonetheless he would stress that he works as if he is discovering new truths. He acts as if mathematical objects exist in the absence of any mathematicians at all.

Dr. Barrow once more illustrates the fundamental theme of this piece, namely that scholars in all fields finding themselves strapped for ontological choice, and thus handicapped, are time and again goaded into the Aristotelian either/or option. Either mathematical truths are *discovered*, or else they are *invented*; either the world is Real, or the world is a copy of some Ideal, Platonic world; subjective or objective. Once again: monism versus dualism.

GUIDE FOR THE APOPLEXED

BRIEF HISTORY OF HINDU NUMERALS

Time to hit the road. Our first sojourn, then, takes us to the Indian subcontinent prior to the Year O. This is the approximate venue of the historical introduction of the very symbol of zero (or sunya), and its inclusion in the already existing Hindu numeral system of the digits 1 through 9. Research reveals that one of the earliest recorded instances of the inclusion of the zero symbol (small circle) as fully-fledged numeral dates back to Pingala's *Chandah-sutra* of about 200 B.C. (B. Datta and A.N. Singh, *History of Hindu Mathematics*, Asia Publishing House, 1962, p.75/81). Prior to this date the zero also had existed but probably was represented by a simple point or sunya bindu (zero dot). Taking into account a reasonable time-frame for its natural evolution to have reached even this stage, it is estimated that the zero dot may have come into use several hundred years earlier, that is, around 300 or 400 B.C., perhaps earlier. Where and how the dot arose, and prior to it the concept itself, will be discussed later.

Next our excursion takes us to Syria of the 7th century A.D. Newly discovered evidence, writes Prof. J. Ginsburg of Columbia University in the *Bulletin of the American Mathematical Society* (Vol. XXIII, 1916-17, p.367/69), shows that, "the Hindu numerals were known to and justly appreciated by the writer Severius Sebokht who lived in the second half of the seventh century..."

Ginsburg is here himself quoting from the French Orientalist M.F. Nau's contribution to *Journal Asiatique*, series 10, Vol. 16 (1910), in which it is said, "that not only did Severius Sebokht know something of the numerals, but he understood their full significance, and may even have known the zero as Rabbi ben Esra did..."

A number of references can also be found to a Hindu scholar named Kanka, who was invited from Ujjain (India) to the famous Court of Baghdad by Khalif Al-Mansur around 770 A.D. to lecture there on astronomy. To the delight of his keen host, Kanka carried with him calculations involving the zero, as well as the Hindu decimal system in which it was already firmly embedded. His lectures proved a watershed to the progress of Arab and later, western mathematics.

B.B. Dutta in the *Indian Historical Quarterly* (Vol. 3, p.530), following the trail of the slow migration of the zero, wrote:

> From Arabia, the numerals marched towards the West through Egypt and Northern Arabia; and they finally entered Europe in the 11th century. The Europeans called them the Arabic notation, because they received them from the Arabs. But the Arabs themselves, the Eastern as well as the Western, have unanimously called them the Hindu figures (Al-Arqan-Al-Hindu).

Herman Gnuticks

Dr. John D. Barrow, quoted above, also wrote (pages 89/90) in this connection:

> Whereas the place-value system can be found in use on Chinese coins in the sixth to fifth century BC, the zero symbol, again denoted by a circle, was only added very late in the development of the system, in the eighth century AD, and was imported from India.
> The Indian development of these ideas is unusual in many ways. It was a flowering of the great Indus culture that arose near Mohenjo-daro and Harappa at about the same period (3000 BC) as the early Egyptian and Sumerian civilizations. These Hindu cultures developed a true place-value system that has been much studied because by the sixth century A.D. it evolved into a system of numerals that we employ in the West today. But whereas the mathematicians and astronomers of Sumer and Babylon laboured for nearly 1500 years before they introduced the notion of a 'zero' symbol, *in India it was introduced much earlier* (italics added). Moreover, unlike in other examples, the notion of 'zero' or the 'null number', as it was known, was originally associated with the notion of 'nothing' in the abstract sense. The literal meaning of the number word was 'void' and it represented both an empty slot in a counting system and the answer to a sum like 'ten minus ten'. Its subsequent evolution as a symbol was not dissimilar to that in Mesopotamia, but the development of the terminology during the gradual synthesis of Indian and Arab cultures is interesting. In Sanskrit, the Hindu name for zero is *sunya*, whilst the Arabic is *as-sifr*; both mean 'the empty one'. When it was written in medieval Latin, the Arab word transcribed as *zefirum* or *cefirum*. In Italian it gradually evolved from *zefiro* to *zefro* and *zevero*. When the latter was expressed in the Venetian dialect, it became our 'zero'.

Dr. Barrow falls prey here to the very distinction he tries to highlight as the signal attribute of the zero notion, namely its abstractness, its representation of emptiness or void. That he opts for the trivial meaning of emptiness — "nothing" as the mere absence of "something" — rather than its non-trivial profundity, should be abundantly clear. But more about this later. For the present it is worth noting that conservatively speaking, and taking the earlier of the two dates, the Arabs can be said to have first *functionally* adopted the zero (as well as the rest of the decimal system) some 800 to 900 or perhaps even 1000 years after its birth in India. It was to be another 400 years or so before it reached Europe proper! It is striking, to say the least, that no other civilization had previously come up with the concept of zero as numeral — save perhaps the Mayas, but they were well isolated from the Eurasian

GUIDE FOR THE APOPLEXED

landmass until the 16th century. All extant "counting systems" employed by cultural-ly and/or racially diverse peoples across the surface of the earth in those early days began at 1 and ran upwards — a fact requiring our close attention. For if we are to suc-ceed in our stated aim, we must eventually also be able to account for this striking global convergence, which makes the Indian divergence the more remarkable. While mulling this over let's keep on the zero's trail.

ZERO AND OTHER DISCIPLINES

As indicated above it was generally acknowledged that the concept of zero con-stitutes a truly high-water mark in the development of human thought. But just how tremendous this innovation was has never really been fully spelled out, not even by those who laud its invention in superlatives. A faint echo is audible in a book written by David Wells, Cambridge scholar in mathematics, who authored *The Penguin Dictionary of Curious and Interesting Numbers*. He devotes a full two pages (p.23/25) to the zero and discloses that, "The twelfth-century Salem Monastery manuscript (a translation by Robert of Chester of Arab texts) had sounded a Platonic note: 'Every number arises from One, and this in turn from the Zero. In this lies a great and sacred mystery,'" Wells adding somewhat nonplussed, "though Plato started with One and knew nothing of any zero." This should come as no surprise, considering the fact that Plato was a self-confessed dualist, who, moreover, exercised a disproportionate influ-ence down the centuries, with a majority of mathematicians and physicist in our day and age propounding patent Platonist views.

Nor have the wider implications of the advent of the concept of zero in fields other than mathematics, such as philosophy and anthropology ever been inventoried. This raises the serious question as to whether the profundity of the concept of zero has really ever truly been grasped in the West at all. David Wells again: "We so easily take zero for granted, that it is surprising to consider that the Greeks had no conception of nothing, or emptiness, as a number, and doubly curious that this did not stop them, or many other cultures, from creating mathematics."

Famous mathematician Pierre-Simon Laplace, speaking of the zero, concurs: "...and we shall appreciate the grandeur of this achievement the more when we remem-ber that it escaped the genius of Archimedes and Apollonius, two of the greatest men produced by antiquity." (A.B. Krishna and A. Jayakrishna, *India Abroad*)

Penetrating to the heart of the matter, "Samurai of Sunyata", Professor Masao Abe, in his August 1993 address to the Parliament of World Religions no less, noted that:

Since the 'zero' is free from any form of duality and plurality true oneness can be realized through the realization of 'zero'. My usage of 'zero' in this regard, however, may be misleading, because the term 'zero' is [generally] used to indicate something negative. But here in this context I use 'zero' to indicate the principle which is positive and creative as the source from which one, two, many and the whole emerge.

And so, as to leave no possible room for misunderstanding, the Emeritus Professor of Nara University went on to stress: "Since I use the term 'zero' not in a negative but positive and creative sense I may call it 'great zero'."

NOTHINGNESS IN WESTERN PHILOSOPHY

It is the first of two contentions to be made in this treatise that indeed the profundity of the concept of zero (i.e. non-trivial nothingness) has never truly been fathomed in the West.

The reason is quite simple, namely that the zero was only functionally adopted – first in South Asia, much later in the Middle East, and finally in the West. Its proven utility alone – as that of the entire revolutionary digital system of the Hindus – demonstrated it to be superior to all extant counting systems, as a result of which it was ubiquitously accepted over time. Astronomers and merchants alike used it to great practical benefit without wanting or needing to know the underlying theoretical and philosophical significance of the concept of zero.

Philosophers in the West, hamstrung by their flawed ontologies, at best construed the zero as mere lack, or absence, and at worst, in terms of a nefarious nihilism (see Snelling above). Consider a notable example from among the Existentialists, of whom it may be said – of all the myriad schools of philosophy in the West – made the most valiant effort at coming to terms with the preverbal experience of emptiness. Phenomenologists like Husserl, Heidegger and Sartre stood on the very threshold to the gateway leading to the Void, and espied its awesomeness. But they shrank from the challenge, poised on the brink, kept safe by virtue of being due-paying members of the Club of Latent Monists. In pursuit of the Zero, they remained in the Land of the One. Or as the inimitable Masao Abe put it: "Monistic oneness is a kind of oneness which lacks the realization of 'great zero', whereas nondualistic oneness is a kind of oneness which is based on the realization of 'great zero'."

Consider, and recognize, the inherent confusion diagnosed above in Margenau, as Sartre struggles in vain with the unseen ontological foe. The quote is from the very first paragraph of the Introduction to his famous Being and Nothingness

GUIDE FOR THE APOPLEXED

(Washington Square Press, 1966, translation by Hazel E. Barnes): "Modern thought has realized considerable progress by reducing the existent to the series of appearances which manifest it. Its aim was to overcome a certain number of dualisms which have embarrassed (italics added) philosophy and to replace them by the monism of the phenomenon. Has the attempt been successful?"

Clearly our contention is that it has not (been successful). We remain caught in the equally drab as suffocating one-dimensional world of monism with its severe lack of freedom. Sartre's (read: Kant's) cumbersome "In-itself" and "For-itself" continue to amount to One (the monism of phenomenon) instead of Zero (the emptiness of existence). Sartre's assessment that we "thus get rid of that dualism which in the existent opposes interior to exterior," insightful as it may seem, is the flimsiest figment of a fiction.

For in the final analysis pluralism, dualism as well as monism, were, are and always will be dualisms themselves by virtue of being conceptions, and thus founded on juxtaposition of opposite-pairs or antipodes.

Alan Watts (*The Supreme Identity*, p.64):

> Language and thought, being finite faculties, are necessarily dualistic, and thus simply cannot escape setting up an opposition between the passive and the active, the ground and the objects, the knower and the known. It is then impossible to derive the one from the other, and the only way to get out of the dualism is to abolish one side of it - to say that only the ground is real, or that only the forms are real. This is the solution proposed by monism, whether spiritual (only the subjective is real) or material (only the objective is real). But monism does not actually escape from dualism.

Monism, then, denied a rational contrast-gaining capacity, because it signifies a single substance or principle, faces the additional, insurmountable difficulty, namely that of not being able to account for the bewildering diversity of phenomena. Monism is thus the most insidious of all philosophical attempts to wriggle out of the stranglehold of one's own thought processes. This is also the reason why Heidegger's device of evolving a "subtler language" to surmount the difficulty he envisaged was doomed to failure in advance. For language, no matter how subtle, is by definition caught in the inextricable web of dualism. It is precisely with this realization in mind that the concept of sunya — itself the subtlest of all dualisms — aims to raise this very issue, whereupon the tenacious problem can be resolved once and for all.

Sartre's claim therefore that, "The obvious conclusion is that the dualism of being and appearance is no longer entitled to any legal status within philosophy," is misplaced. Dualism of being — including its variants of pluralism and monism — remains as firmly entrenched in our thinking as ever. As it must. For in fact it is its very raison

d'être (dans le neant). No wonder therefore that the Existentialists were such a bleak bunch of characters. Anyone who held that "Nothingness lies coiled in the heart of being – like a worm," naturally would be. The deep-seated aversion that leads a person of Sartre's stature to retch at having to countenance the underlying profundity of the concept of zero, is an adequate barometer-reading of the state of the western mind. It may be concluded without too much exaggeration therefore that as yet we are far removed from making the concept our own. For who would be willing to yield up a warm heart to a cold worm?

Nagarjuna himself playfully frightens the faint-at-heart as follows, but then confidently looking out from within the void and not fearfully peering in from without like Sartre: "All the dogmatists have been terrified by the lion's roar of sunyata. Wherever they may reside, sunyata lies in wait!" (on p.51 of Lindtner's magnificent edition mentioned above)

Truly, in the words of psychiatrist R.D. Laing, there is *nothing* to be afraid of.

NON-DUALITY IN THE EAST

Consider also in this connection the words of Sri Aurobindo (in his Life Divine, Arya Publishing House, Calcutta, p.3), pre-dating Sartre's seminal work by a dozen years or so, and acknowledging the latter's apprehensions, as also mirroring Kant's antinomic concerns:

> It is possible indeed to question the need of positing an Infinite which contains our formed universe, although this conception is imperatively demanded by our minds as a necessary basis to its conceptions – for it is unable to fix or assign a limit whether in Space or Time or essential existence beyond which there is nothing or before or after which there is nothing – although too the alternative is a Void or Nihil which can be only an abyss of the Infinite into which we refuse to look; an infinite mystic zero (italics added) of Non-Existence would replace an infinite x as a necessary postulate, a basis for our seeing of all that is to us existence.

Though in most instances as rational yet at the same time much more subtle than its counterpart in the West, the Eastern sage displays an equally disconcerting lack of insight as to the crux of the problem we face in contrasting the dual with the non-dual realm which subsumes it. Such instances are even found in the renowned Upanishads themselves, repositories of ancient wisdom, as Sri Aurobindo amply illustrates in his own book. A few samples should suffice to underscore this point:

GUIDE FOR THE APOPLEXED

From the *Mandukya Upanishad* (7): "The Unseen with whom there can be no pragmatic relations, unseizable, featureless, unthinkable, undesignable by name, whose substance is the certitude of One Self, in whom world-existence is stilled, who is all peace and bliss — that is the Self, that is what must be known."

From the *Gita* (12): "When men seek after the Immutable, the Indeterminable, the Unmanifest, the All Pervading, the Unthinkable, the Summit Self, the Immobile, the Permanent — equal in mind to all, intent on the good of all beings - it is to Me that they come."

Though noble in its striving, the blatant contradictions must be apparent to any freshman student of logic. On the one hand, the non-dual is described as featureless, unseen etc., on the other hand a whole host of features is recited as its attributes. But then this is precisely the difficulty and accounts for the benighted multitudes throughout the millennia.

NONISM

Zero, then, and all that it implies, has remained a virtual enigma to this very day — in the West as well as in much of the East. And while zero-based mathematics — and thus quantum mechanics in which it found its present culmination — made progress by leaps and bounds, western philosophy lacking the concept of zero, has floundered, muddling on with the archaic ontologies of pluralism, dualism and monism.

The Indian variant of Sunyavada, or *nonism* (a neologism coined especially to represent the *missing* "-ism" in the West) is herewith introduced to supplement that restricted ontological choice historically available to us. If for no other reason, it would seem a prudent import product from the mysterious Orient in view of the supply-and-demand world of globalization we inhabit. No other justification for its introduction would seem required, though naturally a deeper appreciation of the underlying concept of zero is the ostensible purpose of this monograph, or rather "nonograph", if you will.

To start with a proper definition of this versatile concept of nonism, we can say that it is the philosophical theory which states that the world is not made of any substance or principle. In fact, nonism holds that the world is not *made* at all — which in any case is a blatant Creationist anachronism, as well as the source of confusion historically in philosophy and science alike. Nonism, like Sunyavada, would answer any fundamental question about the ultimate reality of the world by stating that it is not real or unreal, nor both, nor neither, nor different from neither or both. This affords us all the room we need to extricate ourselves from our conventional ontological straitjackets. We can hang them on the willows for posterity to see and rejoice. The prize awarded is that viewer and view neatly telescope into the *non-dual realm*, from whence we can emerge only at the expense of paying a (re)admission charge, namely: the view-

er regaining a view. Withdrawal of the charge once again suspends our (auto)incarceration in the realm of duality. We get time off for good behavior, are mercifully paroled, and granted lifetime passage in and out of the non-dual realm on our own recognizance.

"This is what we call the Advaitic vision in India," says Swami Ranganathananda in *The Human Condition Today* (Clarion Books, 1988, p.88), "the vision of non-duality, non-separateness." But then he, too, proceeds to mislead the earnest seeker by telling us (p.120/21) that: "It is unknown, but it is not unknowable...It has been known by people...You can also test, you can also verify...The inner dimension is a big field for exploration...It is an experiential rather than objective intellectual formulation."

Though well-meaning, his urgings are misplaced, for the good swami is too eager to please. But then this is a fundamental handicap facing anyone attempting to express the inexpressible - asserting the self-effacing, or, effacing the self-asserting. All one can hope to do is hint. An old Chinese proverb says, "We stand on a whale and catch minnows." Or consider Lao-tzu when he intones: "The spoken Tao is not the true Tao." The earnest poet submits: "Between my brothers crippled tongues my orphan finger points."

Wittgenstein in his famous *Tractatus* claims that, "What can be said at all can be said clearly, and what we cannot talk about we must consign to silence." Elsewhere (p.14 of Grayling's book mentioned in the Introduction) he asserts, "There are, indeed, things that cannot be put into words. They make themselves manifest. They are what is mystical." Adds Grayling, who is lecturer in philosophy at St. Anne's College, Oxford: "Here 'showing' rather than 'saying' is all that is possible."

Misinterprets David Kalupahana, on page 93 of his *Nagarjuna, The Philosophy of the Middle Way:*

> ...what Wittgenstein was *not willing* to explain is 'what is hidden,' and this 'something' is, indeed, comparable to what Nagarjuna was referring to...that is the hidden substance in phenomenon. Neither 'the empty' (sunya) nor 'emptiness' (sunyata)...represent a hidden something which Nagarjuna was *reluctant* to explain. On the contrary, if it can be shown that Wittgenstein did not provide any *explanation* of experience, or did not attempt to *formulate* in linguistic terms what a true experience is, as opposed to a confused one, then he could certainly be enlightened by the language of 'emptiness' or of 'dependence' adopted by the Buddha and Nagarjuna. (italics added)

We say that Kalupahana misreads Nagarjuna/Buddha on this crucial score because his interpretation of the crux of the former's philosophical system amounts to a kind of averaged result, midway between "the two absolutistic theories prevalent in Indian philosophy, namely, permanent existence propounded in the early Upanishads

GUIDE FOR THE APOPLEXED

and nihilistic non-existence suggested by the Materialists" (p.1). Such a reading is hyper-nominal and does the gravest injustice to the profound, not to say earth-shattering, significance of the original realization of the early Buddhists.

We dwell here on this point not to browbeat Kalupahana but precisely because it is central to our thesis. Buddha was a pragmatist interested only in leading people in the most direct way possible to what he saw as the desired goal, release from suffering (a psychological preference, by the way, which though noble in intent, must in the end remain quite arbitrary or idiosyncratic). Nagarjuna on the other hand sought to capture the essence of the Buddha's teachings in a formal philosophical system. But due to the sheer elusiveness of the message, he was not "reluctant to explain", as Kalupahana asserts, but unable to explain (as Wittgenstein was not unwilling, but also unable to explain). For explanation itself is one of the snares further entangling the hapless seeker in duality.

What is the "Middle Way" other than a metaphor? But a metaphor for what? What does it mean for someone to embark on a path midway between "the extremes of eternalism and annihilationism, of strict determinism and chaotic indeterminism, of absolute reality and nihilistic unreality, of permanent identity and absolute difference," as Kalupahana maintains? Can one simply average these categories to find one's true bearings? And what of cultural relativity and personal fancy or whim?

On enlightenment, the Buddha – after long experimental stints of self-denial, perhaps even self-mortification, following on the life of indulgence of a prince – must have realized that moderation was a boon and that extreme self-denial as well as self-indulgence were to be shunned. In this narrow sense a Middle Way can roughly be traveled. But we may assume that in those days a sober citizenry – of necessity leading a Spartan life – would not have needed a Buddha to show them that trivial insight. The secret that lay behind the Buddha's enigmatic smile as he sat under the bodhi tree, looking up at the morning star, was not something as mundane as what Kalupahana suggests therefore. But if not that, then what? We may turn to Alan Watts for a tentative answer: "The solution lies in the realm of metaphysical realization, not at all in the realm of theory."

NON-TRIVIAL EMPTINESS

Admittedly, our present ontological analysis, in conjunction with the pregnant implications of the underlying, non-trivial significance of the concept of zero, is intended here to act as sledge hammer delivering triple blows between the eyes to call attention to the elusive nature of the non-dual realm, and to make it a plausible subject of contemplation – though by definition a "fruitless" endeavor. In this connection, Sri Ramakrishna (1834-86) likened his quest to that of a doll made of salt diving into

the ocean to fathom its depth. Instead of an answer to its question, it finds itself dissolving into the ocean, whereupon there is no doll and no ocean! By analogy, the dualist can be said to be taking a carefree swim on the surface of a fathomless sea. As long as s/he does not look down, there is no panic, indeed no inkling of the depth of the thing, and life can be superficial and gay. But sooner or later s/he does look down, and then, watch out!

Snorkler Wittgenstein's own dip in the cosmic sea explains the difficulty he found in expressing his intuitions despite formidable skill as a logician — or perhaps because of it? "He speaks of the 'more important unwritten second half' of the *Tractatus*, meaning by this that the truly significant issues are identified by what the *Tractatus* does not say, for the *Tractatus* shows from within the limits of language what is important" — (Grayling).

Put differently, we could set ourselves the task of rereading the world's literature afresh, this time *between the lines* — that is, concentrate on all the blank spaces, or the silence between the words. But there is an easier, less time-consuming way, as will be demonstrated once the two mutually exclusive realms referred to are clearly delineated.

SCIENCE REVISITED

First, though, in the light of our new zero-based ontology of nonism, we return to the controversy raging in modern physics between the realists and anti-realists, and see it as being a bogus one. Einstein was a confirmed realist, Niels Bohr an equally convinced anti-realist. The latter claimed that it was not quantum mechanics which behaved funny, but that matter itself did. Both men being (in Margenau's word) "superannuated" monists, by dint of their preferred ontological style being cramped, may be forgiven the misconceptions they labored under. Their life-long row could have been settled amicably through the good offices of the local practicing Nonist — had there been one on hand. The advice would have been: not real or unreal, nor both, nor neither, nor different from both or neither. And they could've gotten on with their important work without needless metaphysical fussing. (The Nonist's disclaimer of being anti-science needs no more than perfunctory mention at this juncture.)

Another futile attempt worth mentioning here contriving to escape the dilemma posed by either Einstein's realism, or Bohr's anti-realism ("Copenhagen interpretation"), namely the "many-universes" theory propounded by Everett/DeWitt, is also an unfortunate regression, this time again to pluralism — and thus accepted by few in the prevailing Age of Monism. Nor does the Anthropic Principle get us very far, as Paul Davies enlightens us (p.145):

GUIDE FOR THE APOPLEXED

According to the conventional Copenhagen interpretation...only our world 'really' exists, the other regions of superspace being 'failed' worlds — potential alternatives to nature, with random caprice, rejected. In which case we cannot say that our own existence explains the structure and organization of the universe (at least inasmuch as it affects the survival of intelligent life) because that would involve circular reasoning: we are here because we are here. All that the anthropic principle can provide is a comment on how lucky it is that we are here. If a vastly greater number of alternative worlds cannot support intelligent life, then they would pass unwitnessed, with no cosmologists to wonder about how improbable they are.

It is never "the facts" (repeatable, verifiable and standardized sense data) themselves which produce the difficulties but "the facts" in conjunction with the "interpreter of the facts". It is not qm that is behaving funny, we might concur with Niels Bohr. But neither is it "reality" alone which is behaving funny. The interpreter of the funny qm data is also behaving quite funnily, as it turns out.

To wit: Sir Arthur Stanley Eddington, astronomer, physicist, mathematician and writer on science and the philosophy of science says in his book *Space, Time and Gravitation*:

> All through the physical world runs that unknown content which must surely be the stuff of consciousness. Here is a hint of aspects deep within the world of physics, and yet unattainable by the methods of physics. And, moreover, we have found that where science has progressed the farthest, the mind has but regained from nature that which the mind has put into nature. We have found a strange footprint on the shores of the unknown. We have devised profound theories, one after the other, to account for its origin. At last, we have succeeded in reconstructing the creature that made the footprint. And lo! it is our own.

Without delving into tedious detail here it may be stated that Bell's Theorem, based on an experiment (EPR) conducted only in the 1960s but (co-)devised by Albert Einstein himself long ago to test once and for all whether the outcome would support "reality" as he saw it, or else the funny (anti)reality of qm of people like Bohr, turned out to confirm the latter! The new and baffling phenomenon of "non-locality", or "action-at-a-distance" was shown to be operative throughout the universe. The old Newtonian worldview, requiring interaction based on physical proximity, was now definitely defunct. And so by circuitous, ever-so compelling means, science was forced to augment its original (tacit) assumption of locality, with its Siamese twin of non-local-

Herman Gnuticks

ity – as per Heraclitean prescription – only to be instantly rejected or simply forgotten by and by, as David Bohm contends.

Professor David Bohm, in *Unfolding Meaning* (Ark Paperbacks, 1987, p.7) issues a
stern warning which should be taken seriously by all:

> The people who founded quantum mechanics...all understood this;
> but since that time this understanding has gradually faded out as
> people have more and more concentrated on using quantum mechan-
> ics as a system of calculation for experimental results, and each
> time a new text book is written, some of the philosophical meaning
> gets lost. So now we have a situation where I don't think the major-
> ity of physicists realizes how radical the implications of quantum
> mechanics are.

It may be added – somewhat irreverently – that Bohm's is an understatement
because physicists, being the heirs of a mysterious legacy bequeathed to them in the
form of an as yet incompletely deciphered qm theory (i.e. Zero), have never truly
caught on in the first place – though they are on the brink. Attention continues to be
focused on something, or the substantial One, rather than *nothing*, i.e. the insubstantial Zero (or what is referred to throughout as non-trivial emptiness). And so, in
pursuit of the "unknown", science leads back to the scientist (Eddington), as it must.
The experimenter interferes in his/her own experiment (Heisenberg). The dog is chasing its own tail (anon.). And, without exception, all our modern scientific theoreticians
as well as philosophers, still can be seen to be merrily barking up the wrong ontological tree (HG).

The conclusion would seem warranted, therefore, that the real insight into the
true significance of the concept of zero (and its concomitant philosophy of nonism)
is yet to take place on a large scale. And since nothing is as powerful as an idea whose
time has come, one is inclined to predict a revolution of major proportions to sweep
the earth if and when the notion of nonism fully dawns.

PARADISE REVISITED

In order to prepare the ground for such a revolution, we can now set off on our
second excursion into history. This time we must go back not 40 but 40 million centuries. The daring soul courageous enough to take the trip can be guaranteed ample
reward as well as safe passage home. Admittedly, this is the most speculative part
of our exploration and must not be seen as factually correct in every detail, either in

GUIDE FOR THE APOPLEXED

terms of time frame or anthropologia. We are embarking on a purely heuristic sojourn - nothing more, but nothing less either.

With these qualifications in mind, let us briefly review the ascent of man over millions of years in the concise words of none other than the H.G. Wells (*The Science of Life*, Garden City Publishing Co., Inc., New York, 1939, p.805):

It was necessary for man's ancestral stock to acquire size, so union of cells to form a many-celled organism was essential, and all single-celled animals are ruled out. The mouth and nerves of Coelenterates and the crawling of Flatworms were essential steps towards a head and bilateral symmetry; blood and body-cavity had to be evolved to give further size and efficiency; segmentation, internal skeleton, and swimming tail were required for speed and activity in the water; jaws and teeth for efficient feeding. On land, however, insects and other arthropods developed along quite another line, were extremely efficient; but we have seen how their external skeleton and especially their method of breathing prevented them from growing big, and tied them to a mainly instinctive type of behaviour. Thus the vertebrate path remains, it appears, as the only one which could lead to an intelligent reasoning creature. The Sponges, the Echonoderms, the Molluscs, and all the horde of Arthropods were, from this point of view, all essentially doomed to come to a barrier to progress at one level or another. Within the Vertebrates, land life was necessary for further advance; the more specialized fish are a blind alley. The evolution of leg, lung and shelled egg were the next essentials. Then came warm blood: without this, the equability of internal process needed as a basis for true thinking, could hardly have arisen. This cuts off Reptiles. The Birds, though warm-blooded, set themselves a barrier to unlimited advance in turning their fore-limbs into a specialized flying organ: so we are left with mammals. Among mammals, only arboreal life could have led to the subordination of smell to sight, the development of binocular vision, the formation of a true hand, the tendency to intelligent manipulation. Thus all other mammalian branches save the tree-shrew-monkey-ape line were excluded. Further, only the subsequent return to the ground could have liberated the hand from over-specialization and imposed the necessity of winning through by intelligence, and only a gregarious species could have acquired speech. Thus only a mammal, gregarious and of ground habits, with a long arboreal phase in its ancestry, could have evolved to the level of speech and conscious reason. All other groups and lines were excluded.

We next go to the infancy of our species, a period when a split was already being forced in the evolutionary pathways taken by anthropoids and hominids – or, man apes and man. It may be speculated that at this juncture, the apes who had descended from an arboreal life to a terrestrial life had a particularly great potential to develop into creatures capable of (dualistic) associative thinking. Interestingly, this may be deduced from the fact that associative thinking is the mental counterpart of the physical brachiation which they had engaged in for millions of years prior to the appearance of even Aegyptopithecus. They were pre-programmed as it were to "leap" from thought to thought (our forte to this day), as they had from branch to branch in earlier, arboreal times.

Their eyes were well developed, stereoscopic, color-detecting, facilitating hand-eye coordination; hands having the crucial feature of thumb juxtaposed to fingers, made them particularly adept at "grasping". This, in turn would allow for later tool-making, while a number of other characteristics made these primates best suited of all competitors not only to learn to think, communicate and socialize, but also in time of putting thoughts and ideas that occurred to them into practice.

Writes H.G. Wells together with co-author Julian Huxley, quoted above in *The Science of Life* on p.799:

> The brain and hand and eye progressed and pushed the early Primate on from tree-shrew condition, through early lemur type with dog-like head, and Tarsioid monkey-faced lemur, up to a new state, a new condition of animal life, in the shape of monkey. Here the handling of objects and the brain's interest in them has progressed so far that the creatures are possessed of a new biological feature in the shape of a veritable overflow of curiosity and inquisitive manipulation; and they have retained and improved the stereoscopic and concentrated vision of Tarsius.

And, what after all, is (wo)man's later empirical science but the concentrated and concerted application of this "veritable overflow of curiosity and inquisitive manipulation" to all facets of his/her natural surroundings? Is it any wonder that a motivated and well-paid army of professional researchers would make rapid progress within the natural sciences once its methodology and procedure became well established?

The two elements then, physical and mental development in our early ancestors, kept tread nicely. One without the other would have severely handicapped the species' evolution. As it is, we are around today to talk, type and print about it. (A variation of the Anthropic Principle, this time in Darwinian guise: what is, is, because it is best suited to be.)

GUIDE FOR THE APOPLEXED

THE DAWNING OF CONSCIOUSNESS

Having said this, we can arbitrarily take a fictitious proto-Proconsul africanus as our earliest forebear, and attribute to it the germinating faculty of language, à la Noam Chomsky — the same Chomsky who asserts that our propensity for mathematics is an offshoot from the language faculty! Thus, the link between the concept of emptiness (sunya) in language and its symbolic presence in our arithmetical system as zero, has been established, provisionally at least; as was earlier done in the *Encyclopaedia Britannica* article. This is an important building block in our argument, and must be borne in mind carefully as we proceed.

So a creature living a basically instinctive life existed, which, for the first time, becomes dimly aware of its natural environmental backdrop, and obversely of itself (the dawning of self-reflective consciousness as we know it, a unique and valued feature which, moreover, constitutes the source of our logical/ontological/epistemological confusion). Over time, natural selection first nudged and later urged on our primate ancestors to not only vocalize but vocabularize. We can think of this as having occurred as a result of a particularly favorable change (Chomsky refers to it as "discrete infinity" and ascribes it to mutation) conferring a considerable degree of survival value on its possessor. The creature who could already distinguish certain features in nature could also begin to manipulate these, tag them with a sound/name, and later, much later, a number. For instance: pebble, one pebble; stick, two sticks; apple, three apples; etc. After a rather slow start in stolid proto-Proconsul, this process favoring articulate speech probably really speeded up only some two million years ago and accounts for significant brain development during the latter epochs only, as Carl Sagan explains in *Broca's Brain* (Ballantine Books, New York, 1979, p.9/10). Most likely Homo habilis was that charmed, if not charming, hominid.

H.G. Wells, again:

> Not only the teeth, but the muscles for biting could be reduced, and so the muzzle shrank into a face. This release of the jaws and neighbouring regions from the savage activities of offence and defence meant that they could be used for more delicate activities, and as violent biting spasms of the jaws were less needed, the delicate rippling contractions of the speech-muscles could be developed. All these changes again reinforced each other and stimulated the main central change, the growth of brain.

Herman Gnuticks

CREATURES OF DUALISM

Central to our argument is that this process of identifying objects and its obverse of dawning awareness is uni-directional and concrete. The original "leap" from the environmental backdrop (of instinctive life) was and remained beyond the creatures' ken for millions of years.

Alan Watts (ibid. p. 148):

> It has ceased to identify itself with the *totality* of experience. It is now identified only with the more proximate objects in the field of consciousness...At first undifferentiated and vague, the field of consciousness next includes distinct objects, and then becomes polarized into subject and object...But because the true centre is still unconscious of itself and is identified with things which, because they are finite objects, are essentially impermanent, the Self experiences anxiety and dread. To protect its vehicle, the ego, from dissolution there must be a struggle for security, for property, for power...

Such a process required, and thus insured, the development, eventually, of not only a language of concretes but also a "counting system" of concretes having as its starting point, one (whole), and proceeding upwards by wholes – something which nicely tallies with the facts. Aboriginals to this day still count in ones and twos, as paleo/neolithic (wo)men everywhere had once been compelled to do. It thus accounts for the peculiar fact that all early arithmetical systems started at one and proceeded upwards, though the method by which, varied from people to people and place to place – in true cultural-relativist fashion.

It may be conjectured here that to primitive beings, the absence or disappearance of objects (*trivial emptiness*) – such as perhaps the depletion of food stocks, or the death of clan members – simply could not be "grasped". To the extent that such loss was noticed or intuited at all it must have remained on the level of a nagging sense of discomfort, unarticulated, because inexpressible – yet at the same time serving to further cultivate an inchoate propensity for the "spiritual" (abstract). This "humanizing" tendency of wrestling with such very elusive aspects of being is probably what eventually lifted (wo)man to a higher evolutionary plane. In evolutionary terms, it could be seen as a vigorous exercising of a rapidly expanding consciousness or mind (grey matter), and signaling as it does the linguistic/arithmetical sophistication of the species. Such a scenario is intimately related to our central theme, as may be obvious, and points the way ahead – after a brief detour.

GUIDE FOR THE APOPLEXED
TIME AND THE SENSE OF SELF

Time is an extremely elusive concept. To illustrate this we may dwell on the uni-directional evolutionary mechanism of reciprocity (the emergence of self-reflective consciousness as a unique historical development in the animal kingdom) suggested above, leading to the concretization of an "object" and the obverse "consciousness" thereof in the subject. This would appear to explain why time flows, as follows. For each fleeting instance of identification of an object by a subject, an obverse fleeting instance of consciousness confers not only a sense of "substantiality" upon the object, but also a sense of self upon the subject. The conscious observer has the impression of events unfolding before his eyes, quite like the passing frames of a movie would induce a sense of motion, and thus time-flow.

In fact, our sense of time and our sense of self-awareness are intimately interre-lated, as this process suggests, and the two cannot be neatly disentangled. One could, for example, formulate time-flow as "the incremental growth of self-awareness through other-awareness." But there is a hitch in as much as 'incremental growth' presupposes the concept of time, just as self-awareness presupposes a self. This must remain the intractable dilemma of the dualist, since the very consciousness of the conscious observer attempting to define time depends on the passage of time.

The *Random House Dictionary of the English Language*, for example, is left no choice but to define time *in terms of time* by referring to "sequential relations", and "continuous duration". In fact, time and self seem to be such basic quantities that no definition in terms of other variables can be given that does not presuppose what we are trying to define in the first place – a notion which ties in closely with Kant's insight that time (as well as space, or better yet, updated Einsteinian spacetime) is an innate Form of Sensibility. This should indicate to us that we have reached ontologi-cal bedrock and can recede no further.

In this connection we may appreciate the catchy title of Stephen Hawking's best seller, *A Brief History of Time* – it being a circular tautology, if you will pardon the redundancy – in as much as "brief" and "history" are both functions of 'time', and thus rendering the phrase quite vacuous as a result. It appears that Hawking enjoys pulling our leg.

We are here giving him the benefit of the doubt because there are cogent reasons to second-guess not only Hawking but many others on this crucial point, including Paul Davies – see his chapter on Supertime (p.188): "Are they just complete illusions, or do our perceptions probe a structure of time – supertime – that is as yet unre-vealed in the laboratory? Does true reality depend upon the existence of a present moment?" Apart from wrestling with the highly contentious issue of "true reality", is Davies here trying to externalize time by submitting it to laboratory testing? If so,

36

pray tell what conceivable test could any scientist conduct that does not necessarily presuppose time?

We can see here, once more, the paradox arise of having to choose between a subjective and objective world; the same problem that has dogged (wo)mankind for millennia. In ontological terms, we are back to being forced to opt for either monism, or dualism, and should kindly but firmly decline the honor.

BUDDHIST EPISTEMOLOGY

Not surprisingly, perhaps, we find early Buddhist thinking on the concept of time, or what is referred to as "momentariness", making valuable contributions to our gropings. In his *Epistemology and Spiritual Authority* (published by Ernst Steinkellner, Vienna, 1989, p.56), the author, Dr V.A. van Bijlert of Leiden University, the Netherlands, writes:

> If this is taken in a purely ontological sense, we could say that everything is ephemeral, impermanent; that is to say that everything has its own unique being which lasts only for a moment...The general characteristics of all things are their impermanence...emptiness and insubstantiality...The real thing lasts only for one moment...therefore everything is said to be momentary...

Van Bijlert, below, himself quotes from old Nyaya and Buddhist School texts — including Vasubandhu, Dignaga and Dharmakirti — some of which he has provided in original annotated translation. The portions in brackets have been added by him to smooth over the fragmentary nature of the verses:

> [Bodily activity] is not a [flowing] movement because [whatever is] produced is momentary [i.e. lasts for one moment]...What is this moment? [It is] the coming into being which ends immediately; momentary [means:] for this [particular thing] there is this [one moment of existence only;] therefore [the particular thing is called] momentary, as having a moment, existing for one moment, in brief 'momentary']. For everything that is produced does not exist anymore after its coming into being, [that is to say] where [something] is born, there it decays...

Van Bijlert also points out that the early Buddhists drew no distinction between perception and cognition. They are two ways of viewing the same thing (p.62/63):

GUIDE FOR THE APOPLEXED

[We say that] a means of valid cognition is identical with the resultant [cognition and not different from it] because [the resultant cognition] is cognized together with the activity [of cognizing a thing through a means of valid cognition]...Dignaga does not distinguish between the act of correctly cognizing an object and the state of having correctly cognized, the state of possessing valid cognition of an object.

The central theme that Van Bijlert painstakingly develops throughout is that early Buddhists epistemology is thoroughly rational and well founded. Valid cognition can only be gained through direct perception and proper inference, and as such corresponds closely to western science's own methodology of accumulating knowledge. The striking difference with western science, however, is noteworthy, inasmuch as the purpose and justification for the entire body of Buddhist epistemology is only to establish what sound knowledge is with the aim of conferring credence upon the Buddha(s) as provider(s) of the same reliable knowledge in realms where such strict epistemological criteria are not applicable, i.e. in the metaphysical realm.

Van Bijlert (p.158/160), like Watts, provides us with a bit more ammunition against Kalupahana's hypernominal interpretation that all is utter simplicity, open and above board:

Dharmakirti implies here that the teachings of the Buddha constitute trustworthy knowledge and reveal to the hearer facts that were not known to him before...The Buddha's trustworthiness about *invisible things* (italics added) must be inferred from his trustworthiness about visible things...As for the invisible object that is indicated in the teachings of the Buddha, it seems that this sort of object will, in the course of time, have to become visible to the hearer.

It must be stated emphatically again here, that "visibility" by definition lands us in the dual realm, whereas the Buddha in his own inimitable way is directing our attention towards the non-dual. And since no object, by definition, survives the journey across the frontiers of nonism, none (that is, no objects) can be expected there and thus none need be looked for. In fact, the very attempt is counterproductive and the password for the obsessive (westerner) might be, "*Stop seeking and ye shall find.*" We must never forget that the historical Buddha has now himself become an object of consciousness, and thus according to his own urging, dependently arisen, and empty of own-being. But even when living, one without own-being, and awakened to this highest realization, would scarcely have preached anything either "permanent" or "substantial".

Herman Gnuticks

BECOMING AND BEING

In view of the aforesaid, one may appreciate the interrelatedness of the two fundamental aspects of dynamic "becoming" and the more static sense of "being" (our steady sense of self). Equally, the *illusory* nature of such fleeting, incremental "becoming" and the more static, permanent sense of "being" may be appreciated — something which we have already alluded to as regards the rival philosophy of nonism (Sunyavada). It is in this that early Buddhist theory differed from the materialist, eternalist schools — of which there was such a hodgepodge around in the days of the ancient Vedic tradition. In fact the Buddha's constituted an overt rebellion against these tendencies — a view which is widely shared these days.

We may here dwell on a surviving "gatha", attributed to the first Buddha. In his History of Zen essay D.T. Suzuki writes (p.171): "…for, according to tradition prevalent already among primitive Buddhists, there were at least six Buddhas prior to the Buddha of the present kalpa (age)…" This first Buddha preceding Siddhartha, is known as Vipasyi. He is alleged to have said:

> This body from within the Formless is born,
> It is like through magic that all forms and images appear:
> Phantom beings with mentality and consciousness have no reality
> from the very beginning;
> Both evil and happiness are void, have no abodes.

ORIGIN OF VISUAL CONSCIOUSNESS

Seven hundred years later, Nagarjuna himself dwelt on this subject/object interaction as being central to the origin of consciousness, and the illusory sense of self it creates, as we find in Kalupahana's book mentioned earlier (p.132/139):

> Just as the birth of a son is said to be dependent upon the mother
> and the father the arising of [visual] consciousness is said to be
> dependent upon eye and material form.

> …What has been explained as hearing, smelling, tasting, touching,
> and mind, as well as the hearer, the sound, etc. should be known in
> the same way as seeing.

GUIDE FOR THE APOPLEXED

Explains Kalupahana:

> Being a competent and insightful philosopher, Nagarjuna immediate-
> ly perceives the difference between the Buddha's analysis and those
> of his 'substantialist' protagonists. Abandoning the misleading ter-
> minology of the substantialists, Nagarjuna adopts the Buddha's
> own terminology to explain the process of perception: "Depending
> upon the eye and visible form arises visual consciousness."

We could compare this to the modern conception (re)introduced by Franz Brentano, that "consciousness" or "awareness" more accurately refer to "conscious-ness of something" or "awareness of something". "Seeing" (something) then is synonymous with being conscious of something — ditto for the other senses.

This explanation of the reciprocal relationship between "eye and material form" accords closely with the view held by modern qm theorists that observer and observed create the universe in intimate co-authorship, as Paul Davies and others have point-ed out. As indeed Fritjof Capra does in an essay entitled *The New Vision of Reality: Towards a Synthesis of Eastern Wisdom and Western Science*, included in the anthol-ogy *Ancient Wisdom and Modern Science* (State University of New York Press, Albany, p.138):

> According to contemporary physics, the material world is not a
> mechanical system made of separate objects, but rather appears
> as a complex web of relationships. Subatomic particles cannot be
> understood as isolated, separate entities but must be seen as
> interconnections, or correlations, in a network of events. The notion
> of separate objects is an idealization that can be useful but has no
> fundamental validity.

Capra himself quotes Nagarjuna in this connection: "Things derive their being and nature by mutual dependence and are nothing in themselves." Capra, who fails to grasp the quintessence of Sunyata or nonism, urges us to, "go beyond physics, to a framework that seems to be a natural extension of the concepts of modern physics. This framework is known as systems theory...It is rather a particular approach, a lan-guage, and a particular perspective." (We need hardly point out here that, like Heidegger's attempt, the answer to the problem does not lie in enhanced subtlety of representation, but in radical departure from any and all dualistic pursuits.)

Herman Gnuticks

UNCANNY CONVERGENCE

We have here a wonderfully graphic illustration of the pivotal importance of the profundity of non-trivial nothingness at work. Modern physics – which functionally adopted the concept of zero via a third party (the Arabs) from the very tradition (the Vedic) which gave rise to the preverbal concept of emptiness – arrives at uncannily similar insights by a detour of over 2000 years and many more miles. Could this be mere coincidence? One would hardly think so.

The fruits of this functional adoption, for instance, finally permits Stephen Hawking (p.136) to assert that, "In the case of a universe that is approximately uniform in space, one can show that this negative gravitational energy exactly cancels the positive energy represented by the matter. So the total energy of the universe is zero (stress added)." Substituting "sunyata" or emptiness for zero, we reach the pinnacle of Indian wisdom. If only the scientific insight matched the philosophical!

But alas this is not yet quite the case, and modern science has a thing or two to learn from the ancient savants. Claims Kalupahana, "While the Buddha was willing to recognize consciousness or 'self-consciousness' as an important constituent of the human personality as well as its experiences, he was not willing to assume a metaphysical substratum such as the 'self' or 'I' as being the object of such awareness. He was clearly aware that this latter epistemological method was the source of most obsessive conceptions." This "latter epistemological method" referred to is of course the very one adopted by the empirical sciences, which inexorably leads to our stubborn ontological paradox (see Margenau, above). Nor is its origin hard to trace.

As Davies explains (p.183): "Dealing with matters of consciousness and perception is alien to the whole tradition of physical science, which usually attempts to abstract away from the individual observer and treat only objective reality...However, we have seen...that 'objective reality' is an illusion."

Nagarjuna, following the Buddha's lead, time and again stresses the illusory nature of both "subject" as well as "object" – or self and other. Subjects have no separate-being status, it is reiterated *ad nauseam* in extant texts, and objects are "dependently arisen", or "co-originated". Referring to the latter, Kalupahana informs us (p.15): "That terminology is indeed conspicuous by its absence in the pre-Buddhist Indian literature." We can take this as an important piece of evidence supporting our argument that something momentous was afoot in those early days, when the philosophy of emptiness arose amidst its harder-core substantialist or materialist counterparts.

This, then, is the mainstay of zero-based philosophy, and though qm theory (mathematics) has adopted the same ontological base unwittingly, it has never recognized the paramount philosophical implications – as we advocate should be done without fail. In this connection one would think that the Herculean effort of a man like

41

GUIDE FOR THE APOPLEXED

Wittgenstein to stake a claim to the non-dual realm, by delimiting the dual, would be applauded. But no. Instead, we find that he is ridiculed in this connection by a pre-eminent scientific pioneer like Hawking when — while cursorily evaluating Wittgenstein's work — the Cambridge scholar occupying the Chair Newton did 300 years earlier, laments that philosophy has sunk low indeed since its earlier halcyon days.

Hawking (p.185):

> ...the people whose business it is to ask why, the philosophers, have not been able to keep up with the advance of scientific theories. In the eighteenth century, philosophers considered the whole of human knowledge, including science, to be their field and discussed questions such as: Did the universe have a beginning? However, in the nineteenth and twentieth centuries, science became too technical and mathematical for the philosophers, or anyone else except a few specialists. Philosophers reduced the scope of their inquiries so much that Wittgenstein, the most famous philosopher of this century, said 'The sole remaining task for philosophy is the analysis of language.' What a comedown from the great tradition of philosophy from Aristotle to Kant!

And this from a man who seriously contemplates unadulterated metaphysical notions:

- a big bang theory we shall never be able to verify/falsify; and by doing so, postulates de facto "objective reality" in contravention of qm implications against any such thing;
- a Grand Unified Theory (GUT) to provide a rational explanation for Everything; failing to realize that the irrational half of Everything can never be explained by the rational half (or that any theory, no matter how comprehensive, can never account for the theoretician, nor logic for the logician - hence his frequent head-on encounters with the Anthropic Principle, among other things);
- all this quite apart from Gödelian objections of consistency and completion;

Solomonian judgment in this uncivil — because unfair — dispute in which Wittgenstein is unable to defend himself may be to dock points from Hawking as well as from poor Wittgenstein; but surely the former stood to have gained a great deal from the latter. For particle physicists, including Hawking, continue to perpetuate much obfuscation — at their own peril needless to say — in their singular struggle to conquer/control nature, thereby enslaving themselves and their followers. Nowhere is this more apparent than in the physicist's view of space, time and reality. The following quotation from Hawking may serve to illustrate this more clearly (p.147/148), as too much juggling makes his own head spin:

42

> This might suggest that the so-called imaginary time is really the real time, and that what we call real time is just a figment of our imagination...So maybe what we call imaginary time is really more basic, and what we call real is just an idea that we invent to help us describe what we think the universe is like. But...a scientific theory is just a mathematical model we make to describe our observations: it exists only in our minds. So it is meaningless to ask: Which is real, 'real' or 'imaginary' time? It is simply a matter of which is the more useful description.

Actually this mumbo jumbo is not unexpected since he had already (p.10) casually hinted at his light-hearted, not to say frivolous, approach when in connection with scientific model-building he wrote: "I shall take the simpleminded view that a theory is just a model of the universe...It exists only in our minds and does not have any other reality (whatever that might mean)."

Indeed "(whatever that might mean)" — and not just parenthetically! It is precisely to sort out these and similar fundamental questions that philosophers like Wittgenstein were/are sometimes driven to analyze language. What do we mean by reality? It would seem of paramount importance to say the least.

Interestingly enough, the Later Wittgenstein — a prototypical Homo ludens — sought to amend the Early Wittgenstein because he had come to realize that language as picturing device, as copy theory, may have been inadequate, and that meaning emerges in the richer relational context of communication — "language games" — of which science is a particular example. Wittgenstein, one might say, experienced an "Einsteinian relativity revolution" within his own thinking, paving the way for all manner of (post)modernity.

Unquestionably, Hawking is a master physicist. But philosophically, it is a different matter — and Wittgenstein, as Kant, would have winced at his folly. His nimble mind permits him to juggle concepts, even antinomic ones, and select only those useful to him in explaining what he feels needs explaining. This he does in a quite mercenary manner, proposing ideas and just as easily discarding them again when it suits — meanwhile losing himself (and no doubt many of his readers) in a fog of "reality" and "unreality", while also fudging materialism and idealism in the bargain. Both of course are quite predictable consequences of the western ontological quandary he finds himself in.

Writes Hawking (p.144):

> ...the quantum theory of gravity has opened up a new possibility, in which there would be no boundary to space-time and so there would be no need to specify the behavior at the boundary. There would be no singularity at which the laws of science broke down and no edge

GUIDE FOR THE APOPLEXED

of space-time at which one would have to appeal to God or some new law to set the boundary conditions for space-time...The universe would be completely self-contained and not affected by anything outside itself. It would neither be created nor destroyed. It would just BE.

This is Hawking-the-idealist contradicting Hawking-the-materialist. The nonist would have to judge him only partly right at best — though fundamentally wrong. A better answer being: "It would not BE, or NOT-BE, nor both nor neither, nor different from both or neither." This, it must be stressed, is no mere casuistry, but the crux of the matter — *the crucial difference in outlook to be grasped*. Nonism vs. monism.

And as Watts reminds us (p.64):

> To materialistic monism belong such current notions as behaviourism and mechanism, which attempt to reduce the experience of consciousness to the terms of the objects of which the observer is conscious." Ascertains he in a bull's-eye footnote on the same page: "They have as much difficulty in explaining consciousness as an epiphenomenon of matter as the spiritualists in explaining matter as an epiphenomenon of consciousness.

The above should serve to alert us once again to the unsure footing of science benefiting from the functional adoption of zero, yet being compelled to theorize without the benefit of a zero-based philosophy. In his intrepid, but circuitous manner, Hawking compounds his crime when he concludes the chapter from which the previous quotation was taken, by reiterating for good measure: "But if the universe is really completely self-contained, having no boundary or edge, it would have neither beginning nor end: it would simply be. What place, then, for a creator?" By clinging to his substantialist principles, Hawking is in double jeopardy here not taking to heart the urgings of Kant whom he says to admire so much. Kant quite clearly set out the proper domain for science, and fate respectively. So apart from other considerations, Hawking does not need to bring God into this by straying into paralogisms.

Why then does he do so over and over, as Carl Sagan notes in the Introduction: "The word God fills these pages. Hawking embarks on a quest to answer Einstein's famous question about whether God had any choice in creating the universe. Hawking is attempting, as he explicitly states, to understand the mind of God." Again, the Nonist would remind Hawking (as Einstein, were he alive) that the universe is not created at all, this being a superstitious anachronism and quite unworthy of consideration for men of science.

Arguably, it is quite unfair to judge (wo)men unaware of nonism by Nonist standards. Yet unless and until nonism is adopted by science, as the zero had been before,

44

trouble will continue to brew. For example, since our sense of time is intimately entwined with our concomitant sense of self (and both are empty, according to the Nonist), the scientist's punishment could ultimately well be commensurate with the crime committed. And the sentencing may just come to pass as follows: The benighted scientist industriously whittles down the span of "existence" of subatomic particles to K-meson dimensions (both in time and space) and clutches such ephemerality to glean what meaning it may hold for his/her own "existence". Subject and object, as has been shown, being intimately interrelated, as are sense of time and sense of self, it is a patent inevitability that this slimmest of threads linking the scientist to the dual realm is bound to snap, sooner rather than later. And this is guaranteed to precipitate the severest crisis of identity: Hegelian megalomania (*vide infra*). An estimation of the scale of such a crisis may be appreciated if we consider Hawking's concluding paragraph (p.185):

> However, if we discover a complete theory, it should in time be understandable in broad principle by everyone, not just a few scientists. Then we shall all, philosophers, scientists, and just ordinary people, be able to take part in the discussion of the question of why it is that we and the universe exist. If we find the answer to that, it would be the ultimate triumph of human reason — for then we would know the mind of God.

We have here all the telltale symptoms of the monist's syndrome rolled into one and compounded by an aggravated case of Kantitis — an ailment whose nonistic cure has already been suggested.

CONSCIOUS CREATURES

Fritjof Capra writes (p.144):

> This brings me to my last topic, the nature of consciousness — a fundamental existential question that has fascinated men and women throughout the ages. To facilitate discussion of this important subject, let me first clarify my terms. I use the term 'consciousness' to mean self-awareness. Awareness is a property of mentation at any level, from single cells to human beings, but self-awareness emerges only at high levels of complexity and unfolds fully in human beings. We are not only aware of our sensations, but also of ourselves as think-

GUIDE FOR THE APOPLEXED

ing and experiencing individuals. It is this property of mind, which emerges together with the 'inner world,' that I call consciousness.

In connection with the ascent of this (self-reflective) human consciousness, an interesting suggestion may be mentioned here which was once made by physicist/philosopher Danah Zohar in her fascinating book *The Quantum Self* (Flamingo, 1990). She proposes a physical basis for consciousness in an attempt to surmount the mind-body problem from within the domain of science, as it were. She does so — on the tacit urging of men like David Bohm and Roger Penrose who discern quantum mechanical characteristics in the phenomenon known as consciousness — by attributing to the mind these same quantum mechanical qualities. The model she employs is the prosaic "pumped Frölich-type Bose-Einstein condensate". It allows the quantum mechanical brain to engage in intimate relationship both with other quantum mechanical (animate) selves, as well as (inanimate) quantum mechanical matter. As a qm model, such a mind has both wave and particle features, accounting for genuine relationships, instead of mere classical "billiard ball" encounters. She rejects alternative computer and holographic models as "classical" in the above-mentioned sense. As classical models they disqualify themselves for not being able to account for a "knowing I". A qm brain itself induces the sense of a "knowing I", she contends, as a result of a higher-level integration (qm ground and excited states).

It may be said that of all the "maverick models of mind" (Stanford University physicist Nick Herbert's phrase) being put forward these days, Ms. Zohar's ideas are perhaps the most consistent and convincing and should be taken seriously by anyone investigating the elusive nature of consciousness in the laboratory. Equally, though, we are obliged to caution against the map/territory trap ahead, namely that of taking the proposed qm features to be the consciousness to be account for, as Ms. Zohar argues — for then we would simply be assuming what we are trying to prove, since anything that can be said about consciousness presupposes consciousness, as it must. In other words, one might ask what it means for a qm brain to investigate qm brain features.

CONSCIOUSNESS VS SELF-REFLECTIVE CONSCIOUSNESS

What we are seeking to establish in connection with hominid development, however, is the following: to force a distinction (as Capra, above, indicates) between a more widespread *consciousness*, qm-based or otherwise (what may be referred to here as the "primordial dualism" possessed by even the most primitive creatures interacting with their environment no matter on how rudimentary a level), and a *self-reflective*

consciousness (probably significantly enhanced with the arrival of "Broca's Area", though already emergent over 10 million years previous). This distinction would mark a departure between "hominid intellect" and that of "lesser developed" creatures such as anthropoid apes – as Chomsky requires. Though chimpanzees are known to be able to focus the attention of their fellows on specific "objects" by articulate calls, Chomsky considers the mechanism to be fundamentally different from that of the human language faculty. Be that as it may.

PARADIGM SHIFT

If now we mark this emergent faculty of hominid brain development, i.e. articulate speech, taking place millions of years ago, as the first of two crucial bifurcation points (Alpha, say) in the evolution of humans, we find the second bifurcation point (Omega) – the paradigm of paradigm shifts – occurring only some 5000 years. This coincides precisely with the time of rapid development of the (pre-)Vedic tradition in North India, whence arises the concept of zero!

Our second contention therefore is that the preverbal experience which underlies the advent of the concept of zero marks the moment in history when individual Homo sapiens become enlightened.

It is at this point – Omega, say – that "creatures of primordial duality" born billions of years ago are able for the first time ever to reverse the uni-directional process that originally wrested them from non-conscious nature/existence. That long and winding road described above by H.G. Wells ends in us rejoining the non-dual realm whence we sprang. The way is discovered at last and the moment of discovery elevates Homo sapiens to Homo sagaciens status. Or put differently, Homo sapiens dualis evolved (through mutational change?) into Homo sapiens non-dualis; or Homo sapiens-d turn into Homo sapiens-n (that is, Homo sagaciens). Ever since, a small but steady population of this subspecies has been present on earth. Though he might have, Teilhard de Chardin did not in fact know that select individuals had, already passed the Omega Point projected by him into the (distant) future, long ago!

It is with some fanfare, then, that the (im)patient reader is herewith invited to engage in an instance of the purest empiricism to look up from the text to discover to which of the subspecies s/he belongs. Is s/he the proud possessor of the revolutionary nonistic TURBOSE-EINSTEINER (in adapted Zoharesque terminology), or the old-fashioned dualistic pumped Frölich-type Bose-Einstein brain? The former is capable of grasping the profundity behind the concept of zero (sunya), the latter, alas, is not. To (micro)biologists is left the task of finding that needle in the DNA haystack, that much-vaunted "gene of enlightenment".

GUIDE FOR THE APOPLEXED

GENE OF ENLIGHTENMENT?

The perspicuous reader might inquire as to the strict necessity of making as far-reaching a commitment as postulating a new subspecies of (wo)mankind in this connection. Though a selfish Richard Dawkins, congenitally impelled, would no doubt heartily concur, the point is nevertheless granted. There is no strict necessity, and one could as easily interpret the paradigm shift as smooth continuity of conceptual(izing) sophistication within the same the species. In defense of the more dogmatic assertion involving mutation it may be said that had a significant "physical" feature suddenly appeared in one of the many races of (wo)man, one would not have hesitated to assume that it must have been the result of a mutation in the genetic material of the individual displaying the change in question. Positing a full-fledged mutation to account for the sudden surfacing of the concept of zero in man would seem justifiable on the same grounds.

And remember, the zero came out of the blue, just as an eleventh "physical digit" (finger or toe) might have done, and sometimes does. The latter did not prove of inestimable survival value, and natural selection militated against it. And so today we (still) have ten fingers and toes, and hence also tend to favor in advance a "digital" system of ten – early (wo)man is thought to have begun his/her math career by counting fingers and/or toes. In the case of the former, that is, the sudden appearance after hundreds of thousands of years of an extra "mental digit", i.e. zero, it apparently did have great survival value, and the zero has been with us ever since - spreading slowly but steadily across the globe.

Noam Chomsky, who has been mentioned several times in connection with his pioneering work, found that all naturally evolved human languages display an uncanny similarity in "deep" grammar and syntax, leading him to suggest that the language faculty is a genetically programmed feature of the human brain. The languages which we find in use today are those that were most "natural" for (wo)men, and especially children, to learn early on. Now, were any distinct new language feature to emerge, it would point to mutational change. And since the link between the faculties of language and mathematics had already been established by him, the sudden emergence after hundreds of thousands of years of something as airy (abstract) as the "zero" concept where the solid (concrete) "one" had prevailed all along, it would surely signal a fundamental change of some sort in our genetic material.

ACHILLES HEEL

But whatever the case may be, the above point regarding mutation vs. gradual sophistication of conceptual capacities is irrelevant to the central argument of this

piece, the real Achilles heel of which, in all honesty, is acknowledged to be the unproved (unprovable?) transition from the preverbal experience itself to the concept of zero, and later to its inclusion as mathematical numeral. Research shows that it would have to have occurred somewhere on the Indian subcontinent between 1000 to 400 B.C. To date there is no physical evidence to document this transition. Nor is such evidence likely to materialize in view of the perishable nature of recording materials like palm leaves used back then. That it did occur in philosophy (Sunyavada) is beyond doubt. It would have been ideal of course had there been a "primus inter pares polymath yogi" who not only managed to get himself enlightened, but also dabbled in arithmetic. But as it is unrealistic to expect one such as that to turn up at this late stage, we must settle for circumstantial evidence. And such circumstantial evidence abounds.

To indicate that there was indeed a strong historical link between the "spiritually" and "practically" inclined in India, we may quote from John Snelling's *The Buddhist Handbook* (A Rider Book, London, 1987, p16/17):

> These noble teachings, which really touched the spiritual heights, were recorded, though not in a systematic form, in the 200 or so Upanishads, which were composed between about 800 and 400 B.C... Like the Vedas, the Upanishads are the work of great poets but ones whose lyrical inspiration was fully informed by profound insight. Some of the ascetics who had gained direct knowledge...must have left their mountain caves and forest hermitages to return to the world to share their wisdom with their fellow men. They must have impressed the ordinary people very much...
> Unfortunately, even the highest teachings seem invariably to undergo a fall when they are packaged for popular consumption by a professional priestly class," Snelling cautions. "Thus it was with the Upanishads...It was part of the Buddha's project to point out these debasements of the once noble teachings of the Upanishads, which in their original and highest forms were quite consistent with his own teachings. (Snelling was General Secretary of the Buddhist Society from 1980 to 1984, and subsequently, editor of its quarterly journal.)

The continuity of this link between wisdom and pragmatism is also confirmed by the authors of the *India Abroad* article when they write: "India's work in science is both adolescent and ancient: young as a secular pursuit, old as an auxiliary interest of her priests. Science started with the priests, originating in astronomy and mathematics governing religious festivals, and was preserved in the temples and transmitted through the generations."

GUIDE FOR THE APOPLEXED

The authors even go on to mention an Indian atomic theory predating that of Democritus (Pakudha Kayayana, 580 B.C., a contemporary of the Buddha), who postulated tanmatra. This undifferentiated potential matter is the universal energy of the cosmos that forms atoms. A contemporary qm theorist would be amazed to learn of this, one may assume, since it correlates closely with the prevailing view held in the field of modern physics. The non-trivial qm vacuum may easily be compared with tanmatra and/or Nagarjuna's later non-trivial emptiness (sunyata):

> The quantum vacuum is very inappropriately named because it is not empty. Rather, it is the basic fundamental and underlying reality of everything in this universe — including ourselves. As British physicist Tony Hey and his colleague Patrick Walters express it, "Instead of a place where nothing happens, the 'empty' box should now be regarded as a bubbling 'soup' of virtual particle/anti-particle pairs." Or, in the words of American physicist David Finkelstein, "A general theory of the vacuum is thus a theory of everything." (From Danah Zohar's book mentioned above, p.207)

SOCIO-CULTURAL FACTORS

That emptiness was in air then, so to speak, can also be gleaned from a poetic account in Subandhu's novel *Vasavadatta* (c 600 A.D., edited by F. Hall, Calcutta 1859, p.182, and translated into English by Louis H. Gray, New York, 1913):

> And at the time of the rising moon with its blackness of night, bowing low, as it were, with folded hands under the guise of closing blue lotuses, immediately the stars shone forth,..........like zero dots (sunya-bindu), because of the nullity of metempsychosis, scattered in the sky as if on the ink-blue rug of the Creator who reckoneth the sum total with a bit of the moon for chalk.

(Note the ease of poetic association between stars, zero dots, nullity of the transmigration of souls, and the shape of a round/circular moon — all highly suggestive of a facile process of the playful evolution of conceptions in the human mind, accounting for the possible transition leading to the introduction of the symbol of zero from the preverbal experience of sunya, or void.)

A tentative scenario, which could account for the putative transition from the preverbal experience of emptiness to the zero symbol is also conceivable on souci-cultural grounds. It seems reasonable to assume that the earliest yogis of the Vedic tra-

dition due to their temperament or "spiritual bent", found that on prolonged meditation release was obtained from the world of duality; a release at first subconscious-
ly sought, later consciously pursued, and ultimately realized. This process, oft enough
repeated, later ritualized and institutionalized, enlightened them and their kindred
spirits as to the true nature of being. They discovered the long-kept secret of an operative principle of duality, or attachment of mind to matter, which had all along made
captives out of them. On realization of the true nature of (dualistic) being vouchsafed
to the yogi, separate-being status was revoked forthwith, and forever after.
Admission to the non-dual realm was obtained, and with it (wo)man's historic mission
fulfilled.

Close analysis of the newly discovered secret, would readily lead to such formula-
tions as abound everywhere in the Upanishads cited earlier (from approximately 800
B.C. onwards). These lend themselves to interpretation by practical-minded people
exposed to the rich cultural heritage of the Vedic tradition. It was quite common in
the India of that time for the elite (even, or especially, royalty) to send their offspring
to revered sages nearby for instruction in spiritual development so highly prized in
that society. One such devotee need only have made the connection that before the
one, the concrete, there is emptiness or sunya in its deep and abiding sense. First
there is nothing, then there is something. "First zero, then one" (to paraphrase
Robert of Chester who first translated Arab texts on Hindu numerals in the 12th century, ushering the enigmatic new digit into Europe). Carrying this knowledge back to
the mundane world with them, the zero is born. And in the thriving cradle of civilization which North India was, such a concept was functionally adopted and readily put
to good use by merchants, bureaucrats (i.e. administrators, tax collectors) and
astronomers alike.

Even at the time of the Buddhist monk Nagarjuna (c. 100 to 200 A.D.), who fully
fleshed out his versatile philosophy of Sunyavada based on the Mahayana tradition,
acceptance of his formidable insights remained a matter of faith for the newly emergent subspecies of Homo sagaciens. Either someone had the deep and abiding experience of sunya (marked by personal enlightenment), or not. Only when faith was supplanted by actually experiencing preverbal sunya – marking a rebirth of sorts, or passage beyond the Omega Point – could the individual be said to have discovered his/her
membership to the new subspecies. Even to the present day this remains the case.

DUALITY VS NON-DUALITY

Apart from all the arguments presented above, there are plenty of hints pointing
in the direction of a non-dual realm, that is, the realm subsuming the dual. Of course
it must always be borne in mind that nothing can ever be said in a positive sense

GUIDE FOR THE APOPLEXED

about the non-dual, since any verbalization is by definition dual in nature, and thus counterproductive to underpinning our case. Conversely, it is easy to see why it is that one's overwhelming impressions are of the dual world, since every "experience" is self-reinforcing, literally and figuratively. Kalupahana quoting Nagarjuna:

> Someone is made known by something. Something is made known by someone. How could there be someone without something and something without someone?

> When grasping exists, becoming on the part of the grasper proceeds. If he were to be a non-grasper, he would be released, and there would be no further becoming. (p.373)

> When it is assumed that there is no self separated from grasping, grasping itself would be the self. Yet, this is tantamount to saying that there is no self. (p.379)

These injunctions urged upon us by Nagarjuna are reminiscent of the analysis offered in our anthropological jaunt in connection with subject/object interaction, and the concomitant sense of self and time-flow. A brief tragicomic anecdote may be mentioned here to illustrate our primate proclivity towards grasping, first physical, later mental — a skill highly developed in our immediate evolutionary past. It pertains to a particular hunting technique to catch monkeys employed by forest dwellers in the South American jungles. Some delicacies are placed inside an empty coconut, with the only access to it being a small hole in the hard outer shell. One end of the coconut is tied by a string to a tree trunk. When a monkey comes along and sticks its hand inside the coconut to "grasp" the food, it finds that because of its clenched fist holding the morsel it cannot be withdrawn. Even at the peril of impending capture the monkey, screaming bloody murder, will not release the bait. So strong is its tendency to "grasp", and hold on. In this context, (wo)man's acquisitiveness is a mere euphemism and reflects the tenacity of our attachments, both physical and mental.

COGITO, ERGO SUM

Truly, in the Cartesian sense, one thinks (or grasps) therefore one is. This leaves open the tantalizing possibility, however, that to not think (or grasp), infers that one is not. This makes it plausible at least to consider why it is that precisely the yogic tradition of sitting quietly, relaxing, and letting go, could induce that vanishing feeling of non-being leading to an ultimate plunge into the void or sunya beyond (the earliest

recorded form of bungee-jumping, tied only by a nonistic gossamer thread). Re-emergence from the non-dual into the dual realm of the tug-and-pull on the senses (and the gathering of sense data, the very foundation of the empirical sciences) re-enmeshes us in our safe and secure world of convention. Our culturally transmitted languages and systems of thought (complex relativistic, dual structures) permit us to carry on conversations and exchange views on everything under the sun — and beyond. Except for the non-dual world, which must forever remains beyond the reach of the senses, and of language.

ANTICLIMAX

In *The Story of Philosophy* (Washington Square Press, 1962), Will Durant praises Immanuel Kant as follows:

> ...the strong and steady current of the Kantian movement flowed on, always wider and deeper; until today its essential theorems are the axioms of all mature philosophy. Nietzsche takes Kant for granted, and passes on, Schopenhauer calls the *Critique* 'the most important work in German literature,' and considers any man a child until he has understood Kant; Spencer could not understand Kant, and for precisely that reason, perhaps, fell a little short of the fullest philosophic stature. To adapt Hegel's phrase about Spinoza: to be a philosopher, one must first have been a Kantian.

Adds Durant enthusiastically, "Therefore let us become Kantians at once."

The relevance of this quotation bears on the anticlimactic paragraphs to follow, for we are now obliged to deconstruct our whole line of argument, Derrida-like. We begin by provisionally concluding with Kant (and indeed Nagarjuna in his *Madhyamika Karika*) that time and space (or spacetime), cause and effect (or causeffect), et cetera, are the grammar of our various ingeniously conceived and constructed, manifold formal and informal languages (including the sciences and mathematics). We are then compelled to acknowledge the limitation inherent in our whole scientific endeavor, based as it is on the gathering of sense data, standardizing of same, hypothesizing, and constructing of theories. In other words, a highly dual enterprise. This being so also is the reason why we run into the basic ontological/epistemological trap we warned against at the outset, inasmuch as our empirical bias confines us (condemns us, some would say) to the dual realm, and consequently excludes us from the non-dual.

GUIDE FOR THE APOPLEXED

In addition, we find that the construction of much of the anthropological argument presented above is also undermined therefore. Kant and with him Chomsky assert that the human brain organizes "afferent stimuli", perception, into conceptions for consumption and manipulation by our Faculty of Understanding, and expression through our Faculty of Language/Mathematics. This reasoning, however, is subject to some pure and devastating critique, if one asks how it is possible to make any such assertion since that assertion itself presumably entails the application of the very conceptualizing apparatus present in the brain doing the conceiving (of such elaborate assertions as Kant's and Chomsky's)!

The dualist, any dualist, will inevitably come face to face with the ultimate paradox as a necessary consequence of his/her original sin, namely that of splitting subject from object, viewer from view, dreamer from dream, conceiver from conceived, et cetera. Our very strength is thus also our weakness.

Historically, of course, it is easy to see how and why a man like Kant, made an immense impact on contemporaries lost in the philosophical jungle with its quicksand ontologies. If one considers Kant's quest to have been basically reactionary – having been woken from his "dogmatic slumbers" – and wanting to set right the "heretical" speculations of Locke, Berkeley and Hume, Kant, too, can be forgiven his folly of postulating his Categories.

Note that the very conception of Categories is spatial in nature, for it implies something that can contain something else. It illustrates the awkwardness of his innovation of postulating such qualities of mind, which must then be applied to itself – an in/convolutional enterprise at best. We often assume what we want to prove, or else prove what we assume - in fact a dualist can scarcely do otherwise! For even logic presupposes the logician! Though this device of Kant's saved both science and religion for a time, it also permitted the world to turn over on its other (dualistic) shoulder and slumber on in its king-size dual bed.

"Kant's greatest merit," wrote Schopenhauer, "is the distinction of the phenomenon from the thing-in-itself (*The World As Will And Idea*) Kant in other words remained a convinced dualist, happily chopping the world (and himself) in twos. Ditto Chomsky, that linguistic axe-wielding lumberjack, following suit. The very language he analyzes to gather clues as to the internal structure of his postulated language faculty, issues from...the very language faculty under scrutiny, and is expressed in terms of that very same language issuing from that very same language faculty! Whatever else the merit of such an enterprise may be said to be, philosophically speaking, that is logically and ontologically it is exceedingly weak. And it only goes to show how dangerous it is to construct an entire theoretical edifice on such a defective foundation.

F. Hegel engages in a hazardous game of one-upmanship by taking Kant's dualism (noumena/phenomena) and turning it into extreme monism by an ad hoc deletion of the Kantian substrata. Thus Hegel is left with pure mind, a dubious asset at best, but certainly in the light of our previous ontological analyses. We can clearly see Hegel

54

derailing full tilt — and given his stature and mental might, he is headed for grave trouble. The following quotation will amply illustrate this. It also characterizes the vast dispositional difference between the dualist and the monist on the one hand, and either in comparison with the nonist. A strict dualist keeps his hubris under control through the contingent man-god dichotomy he is compelled to make, whereas the (extreme) monist in principle is capable of aspiring to divine status. The nonist on the contrary, sees through both fallacies, smiles wanly, and gets on with the business at hand.

Says Peter Singer, Professor of Philosophy at Monash University, in discussion with Bryan Magee (*The Great Philosophers*, Oxford University Press, 1987):

> The end point of the dialectical process is Mind coming to know itself as the ultimate reality, and thus as seeing everything that it took to be foreign and hostile to itself as in fact part of itself. Hegel calls this Absolute Knowledge. It is also a state of absolute freedom, because now Mind, instead of being controlled by external forces, is able to order the world in a rational way. This can be done only when Mind sees that the world is in fact itself. Then Mind has only to implement its own principle of rationality in the world in order to organise the world rationally.
>
> One remarkable feature of this process arises from the fact that the culmination occurs when for the first time Mind understands that it is the only ultimate reality. Ask yourself: when does this actually happen? The answer must be that it happens when Hegel's own mind, in his philosophical thinking, grasps the idea that Mind is everything that is real. So it's not just that Hegel *describes* the goal, the state of Absolute Knowledge and Absolute Freedom towards which all previous human history had been unconsciously struggling: Hegel's philosophy actually *is* the very culmination of the whole process.

Asks interlocutor Magee in awe: "I wonder if that penny ever dropped with Hegel himself — whether he actually realised that what he was doing was putting himself-as-philosopher forward as the culmination of world history?"

This painful *faux pas* is the inevitable consequence of Homo dualis (of monist suasion in this case) grasping the One, and not the Zero. Seek Mind and ye shall find Mind, might be the motto (just as Marx, turning Hegel upside-down, sought and found Materialism; just as Locke posited the same, consequently condemning himself to being a mindless body; while Berkeley turning Locke upside-down became an Idealist, or disembodied mind; only Hume, though a strict dualist, displayed a healthy sense of skepticism, which is all to his credit (and as such his case may be "exhumed", if you

GUIDE FOR THE APOPLEXED

will pardon the pun). Most of western history can be treated in a similar manner, as can much in the East, until, that is, the ascent of Homo sagaciens. The baptismal plunge into the void cleared the cobwebs, and with it, the last traces of the Long Dream — some would say Nightmare.

It was precisely to torpedo such perceived metaphysical/ontological problems as we have been discussing to the point of nausea, that Wittgenstein advised climbing to safety via his ladder-like *Tractatus*. It would seem prudent for us to take the hint seriously and do the same, lest we are tempted to aspire to Hegelian megalomania and assorted mental illness. The ladder — or more appropriately, the gateway — presented here in the shape of the transitional concept of nonism links the dual and non-dual realms. It tells us that all concepts — including nonism itself — are anthropocentric at heart, and thus what we "see" depends on the way we "look" — inferring also facile movement in principle from sticky pluralism, to dualism, to monism, and potentially at least, to no-stick, non-fixional nonism. This interpretation furthermore flexibly accommodates all living organisms, no matter how "lowly", having their own unique, species-dependent (non-)experience of the non-dual realm. The operative principle of primordial dualism breaking through the windows of their respective senses is instrumental in achieving this. Thus to a snail the non-dual takes on dual "snail reality" or gastropodomorphism; to the lion, dual "lion reality" or felinomorphism, etc. But this aside.

The one cardinal sin which accounts for millennia of utter pre/post-Socratic Homo dualis confusion, is the great temptation to jump to the Holistic conclusion (Bohm, Capra, Pribram and many, many others). It signifies that taken together the dual and non-dual realms comprise the One Whole, the Absolute, God, or whatever one cares to call it. This is the last fatal error standing in the way of full comprehension of the concept of sunya, or void. Jumping to such an apparently obvious conclusion which moreover "feels right", is still latent monism come to haunt us. It is that deeply ingrained tendency of Homo dualis — sheer atavistic bent or ontogenetical reflex, if you will — to reach for the One (1) rather than the Zero (O). This is precisely what our forebears did. And still, most of us today blunder into this pitfall. But we are in good company considering that the greatest minds in the western tradition and most in the eastern as well, have never caught on to the Silent Secret of the Soul: the Zero. It is hither that nonism beckons the diehard dualist...but the diehard dualist shall not be rushed. And if it turns out to be the lack of mutational change which aborts any attempted leap from the dual to the non-dual realm, s/he is indeed doomed "to dual to the death!"

56

Herman Gnuticks

MONOTHEISM VS NONOTHEISM

As the "creature of dualism" that Homo sapiens-d is, emerged from the mists of history and evolved from a primitive, superstitious being, mythologizing and later demythologizing the world of which s/he became aware, a strong teleological pull was exerted on him/her, manifesting eventually as religious devotion. The present stage of development reached is, by and large, monotheistic. Again, this makes apparent the irresistible magnetism of the One, rather than the Zero (mono vs. nono). What is awaited therefore is the conversion from monotheism, to "nonotheism" – or Zero worship (ill-advisedly). This can only occur once the concept of zero is fully grasped (only to be ungrasped, needless to say). Monotheism enforces an absolute dichotomy between man and god. Nonotheism would assert - in tandem with the epitome of Eastern sagacity! – that man and god are...no, not one...but zero: utter and total emptiness or void.

ANTIDOTE

Just as Darwin's Dogma asserts survival of the fittest, Buddha's Bromide holds to extinction of the fittest. Only thus can all of Darwin's species not only spring forth out of Buddha's Void, but evolve to its realization (the Misanthropic Principle?). A steady population of the Homo sagaciens subspecies has borne silent witness to the miracle for several millennia now. Quantum theory has found contemporary terminology to state the same thing and in effect says that Everything springs from Nothing, i.e. the cosmic vacuum. Etymological analysis of qm's arithmetical language-base shows how/why this was possible.

CONCLUSION

Someone had to be first, and evolutionarily speaking – which history nicely bears out – we find that the (pre-)Vedic tradition for whatever reason (see: S. Radhakrishnan's *Indian Philosophy* for helpful hints) was first past the post. It is to them we owe the concept of zero, and its clandestine effect on western culture through the functional adoption of the zero symbol unwittingly imported via the "Trojan horse" decimal system. Today, zero-based quantum mechanics, fired by zero-power, is knocking hard on the gates of the non-dual realm. The cross-cultural, intercontinental detour of several millennia taken – from the innovation of the zero, to its

GUIDE FOR THE APOPLEXED

culmination in qm theory — is a truly breath-taking one. "The circle is unbroken!", a 21st-century vox might well proclaim with a sigh of relief.

The questions that have all along plagued us will be found to evaporate, in Wittgensteinian fashion. Why is there something rather than nothing, as Heidegger poses? We have seen that this and similar questions put equally in philosophy as science (qm) are based on misconceptions, revealing our deeply ingrained empirical bias. If we think of ourselves as separate beings, something which is reinforced by the very process of thinking itself — I think/see/feel/ hear/smell/taste therefore I am — we are laboring literally under a self-generating illusion. Yet it is precisely the point of departure of the scientist as well as of the philosopher. The ultimate paradox was sure to arise, and might even have been anticipated. This is precisely what is now occurring in quantum theory. Observer and observed, experimenter and experiment are inextricably linked and in fact are each other's obverse. We do indeed co-author the universe, in a manner of speaking — for this itself is a metaphorical representation of the unrepresentable.

Philosophy generally lags behind even further — barring that single clear strain of post-Vedic tradition which teaches us that we do not exist, or not-exist, nor both, nor neither, nor different from both or neither. The extremely deceptive "sleight-of-mind" involved here is as difficult for the unsuspecting dualist to detect as would catching a glimpse of the back of his/her own head in a mirror; or trying to ditch one's own shadow. Compare it to an act of uncommon prestidigitation. The eye is faster than the eye! This understood, we can at first experimentally correct wrong ontologies in order to derive the de facto philosophical benefits, just as arithmetic did on adoption of the practical zero symbol. Switching from dual-based (3, 2 or 1) ontologies to the non-dual-based (0) ontology sweeps away metaphysical obfuscation! The newly-gained degree of freedom will soon prove its own merit, whereupon the deep and abiding insight is sure to follow, i.e. Nagarjuna's non-trivial emptiness.

The rationale for instigating such a major ontological shift can be easily justified on the grounds that our liberty is enhanced, and permits easy reversal from non-duality back to duality; whereas commitment to one of the non-zero-based ontologies only handicaps, not to say truncates, us. The Nonist, in other words, can engage perfectly well in any dualistic pursuit — including the sciences — whereas the dualist is forcibly excluded from the non-dual realm. Now this wouldn't be so bad if exclusion from the non-dual realm didn't imply susceptibility to myriad dualistic ailments of body and mind which can only be remedied by a booster shot of nonism. In the sciences alone, it would instantly eradicate the needless theoretical clutter, no less than in ordinary life. The perennial questions of philosophy are also instantly resolved.

Herman Gnuticks

HISTORY OF DUALISM IS DUALISM OF HISTORY

Like stepfather of science Descartes, father Aristotle played a not insignificant role in charting the dualistic course traveled in the West by propounding his Principle of Non-Contradiction (*Metaphysics IV*), later instituted as one of the axioms of logic. His was a sharp "mental" tool permitting delicate operation on the "material body". A dualist's delight, it strengthened our grip on the world of objects by severing us from them through the assertion that contradictory properties could not simultaneously apply to the same subject/object. This seemingly obvious conclusion merrily propelled us on our uni-directional dualistic way, suffering from the self-inflicted delusion of separateness. It is zero-based qm theory that brought us face to face with the limitations of two-valued either/or logic but only after long agonizing over the particle-wave "duality" of the subatomic world: a photon acts both as wave and as particle, and no amount of Aristotelian coercion will change that ever again.

"Logic is invincible," wrote Pierre Boutroux, quoted in Dr. Barrow's aforementioned book, "because in order to combat logic it is necessary to use logic." This tantalizing aphorism is prelude to an enthralling chapter from which the following is culled:

> If Euclid's geometry was a cornerstone of the Universe, it was built upon that foundation stone of rationality which is logic itself. From Aristotle's first systematization of logical argument two thousand years ago, the laws of logic had been equated with the 'laws of thought'. This was never questioned, because the traditional laws governing the machinery of logical deduction, which had been laid down by Aristotle, are seemingly uncontentious.

After elaborating on the three so-called laws of thought (the law of identity; the law of non-contradiction; and the principle of the excluded middle), Dr. Barrow surmizes:

> All of the three 'laws of thought' were challenged by logicians exploring new systems. But it was the so called 'principle of the excluded middle', that came under the closest scrutiny. This assumption made simple logic a two-valued logic because every statement has two possible truth values: it is either true or false.
> In the early 1920s logicians...showed that there could exist perfectly consistent logics which are not two-valued...And indeed, one could even invent logics in which every proposition may take on any one of an

59